OVER
5,000,0
COPIES OF
A. MERRITT'S
BOOKS SOLD
IN AVON EDITIONS

OUT OF THE FANTASTIC
WORLDS OF A. MERRITT come
the heroic exploits of Nicholas
Graydon, whose search for Incan
gold leads him to the lost civilization of Yu-Atlanchi, a paradoxical
world of exotic women and grotesque monsters, of immortality
and brutal death. The lovely maid-
en Suarra waits to claim his love,
but first he must help the Snake
Mother fight and destroy THE
FACE IN THE ABYSS.

Other Avon books by
A. Merritt

The Face in the Abyss

A. Merritt

AVON
PUBLISHERS OF BARD, CAMELOT AND DISCUS BOOKS

Cover painting by Rodney Matthews.

AVON BOOKS
A division of
The Hearst Corporation
959 Eighth Avenue
New York, New York 10019

First Avon Printing, April, 1978

Printed in the U.S.A.

Contents

CHAPTER I

Suarra

NICHOLAS GRAYDON ran into Starrett in Quito. Rather, Starrett sought him out there. Graydon had often heard of the big West Coast adventurer, but their trails had never crossed. It was with lively curiosity that he opened his door to his visitor.

Starrett came to the point at once. Graydon had heard the legend of the treasure train bringing to Pizarro the ransom of the Inca Atahualpa? And that its leaders, learning of the murder of their monarch by the butcher-boy Conquistador, had turned aside and hidden the treasure somewhere in the Andean wilderness?

Graydon had heard it, hundreds of times; had even considered hunting for it. He said so. Starrett nodded.

"I know where it is," he said.

Graydon laughed.

In the end Starrett convinced him; convinced him, at least, that he had something worth looking into.

Graydon rather liked the big man. There was a bluff directness that made him overlook the hint of cruelty in eyes and jaw. There were two others with him, Starrett said, both old companions. Graydon asked why they had picked him out. Starrett bluntly told him—because they knew he could afford to pay the expenses of the expedition. They would all share equally in the treasure. If they didn't find it, Graydon was a first-class mining engineer, and the region they were going into was rich in minerals. He was practically sure of making some valuable discovery on which they could cash in.

Graydon considered. There were no calls upon him. He had just passed his thirty-fourth birthday, and since he had

1

been graduated from the Harvard School of Mines eleven years ago he had never had a real holiday. He could well afford the cost. There would be some excitement, if nothing else.

After he had looked over Starrett's two comrades—Soames, a lanky, saturnine, hard-bitten Yankee, and Dancret, a cynical, amusing little Frenchman—they had drawn up an agreement and he had signed it.

They went down by rail to Cerro de Pasco for their outfit, that being the town of any size closest to where their trek into the wilderness would begin. A week later with eight burros and six *arrieros,* or packmen, they were within the welter of peaks through which, Starrett's map indicated, lay their road.

It had been the map which had persuaded Graydon. It was no parchment, but a sheet of thin gold quite as flexible. Starrett drew it out of a small golden tube of ancient workmanship, and unrolled it. Graydon examined it and was unable to see any map upon it—or anything else. Starrett held it at a peculiar angle—and the markings upon it became plain.

It was a beautiful piece of cartography. It was, in fact, less a map than a picture. Here and there were curious symbols which Starrett said were signs cut upon the rocks along the way; guiding marks for those of the old race who would set forth to recover the treasure when the Spaniards had been swept from the land.

Whether it was clew to Atahualpa's ransom hoard or to something else—Graydon did not know. Starrett said it was. But Graydon did not believe his story of how the golden sheet had come into his possession. Nevertheless, there had been purpose in the making of the map, and stranger purpose in the cunning with which the markings had been concealed. Something interesting lay at the end of that trail.

They found the signs cut in the rocks exactly as the sheet of gold had indicated. Gay, spirits high with anticipation, three of them spending in advance their share of the booty, they followed the symbols. Steadily they were led into the uncharted wilderness.

At last the *arrieros* began to murmur. They were approaching, they said, a region that was accursed, the Cordillera de Carabaya, where only demons dwelt. Promises of more money, threats, pleadings, took them along a little further. One morning the four awakened to find the *arrieros* gone, and with them half the burros and the major portion of their supplies.

They pressed on. Then the signs failed them. Either they had lost the trail, or the map which had led them truthfully so far had lied at the last.

The country into which they had penetrated was a curiously lonely one. There had been no sign of Indians since more than a fortnight before, when they had stopped at a Quicha village and Starrett had gotten mad drunk on the fiery spirit the Quichas distill. Food was hard to find. There were few animals and fewer birds.

Worst of all was the change which had come over Graydon's companions. As high as they had been lifted by their certitude of success, just so deep were they in depression. Starrett kept himself at steady level of drunkenness, alternately quarrelsome and noisy, or brooding in sullen rage.

Dancret was silent and irritable. Soames seemed to have come to the conclusion that Starrett, Graydon and Dancret had combined against him; that they had either deliberately missed the trail or had erased the signs. Only when the pair of them joined Starrett and drank with him the Quicha brew with which they had laden one of the burros did the three relax. At such times Graydon had the uneasy feeling that all were holding the failure against him, and that his life might be hanging on a thin thread.

The day that Graydon's great adventure really began, he was on his way back to the camp. He had been hunting since morning. Dancret and Soames had gone off together on another desperate search for the missing marks.

Cut off in mid-flight, the girl's cry came to him as the answer to all his apprehensions; materialization of the menace toward which his vague fears had been groping since he had left Starrett alone at the camp, hours ago. He had sensed some culminating misfortune close—and here it was! He broke into a run, stumbling up the slope to the group of gray-green *algarrobas,* where the tent was pitched.

He crashed through the thick undergrowth to the clearing.

Why didn't the girl cry out again, he wondered. A chuckle reached him, thick, satyr-toned.

Half crouching, Starrett was holding the girl bow fashion over one knee. A thick arm was clenched about her neck, the fingers clutching her mouth brutally, silencing her; his right hand fettered her wrists; her knees were caught in the vise of his bent right leg.

Graydon caught him by the hair, and locked his arm under his chin. He drew his head sharply back.

"Drop her!" he ordered.

Half paralyzed, Starrett relaxed—he writhed, then twisted to his feet.

"What the hell are you butting in for?"

His hand struck down toward his pistol. Graydon's fist caught him on the point of the jaw. The half-drawn gun slipped to the ground and Starrett toppled over.

The girl leaped up, and away.

Graydon did not look after her. She had gone, no doubt, to bring down upon them her people, some tribe of the fierce Aymara whom even the Incas of old had never quite conquered. And who would avenge her in ways that Graydon did not like to visualize.

He bent over Starrett. Between the blow and the drink he would probably be out for some time. Graydon picked up the pistol. He wished that Dancret and Soames would get back soon to camp. The three of them could put up a good fight at any rate ... might even have a chance to escape ... but they would have to get back quickly ... the girl would soon return with her avengers ... was probably at that moment telling them of her wrongs. He turned—

She stood there, looking at him.

Drinking in her loveliness, Graydon forgot the man at his feet—forgot all else.

Her skin was palest ivory. It gleamed through the rents of the soft amber fabric, like thickest silk, which swathed her. Her eyes were oval, a little tilted, Egyptian in the wide midnight of her pupils. Her nose was small and straight; her brows level and black, almost meeting. Her hair was cloudy, jet, misty and shadowed. A narrow fillet of gold bound her low broad forehead. In it was entwined a sable and silver feather of the *caraquenque*—that bird whose plumage in lost centuries was sacred to the princesses of the Incas alone.

Above her elbows were golden bracelets, reaching almost to the slender shoulders. Her little high-arched feet were shod with high buskins of deerskin. She was lithe and slender as the Willow Maid who waits on Kwannon when she passes through the World of Trees pouring into them new fire of green life.

She was no Indian ... nor daughter of ancient Incas ... nor was she Spanish ... she was of no race that he knew.

There were bruises on her cheeks—the marks of Starrett's fingers. Her long, slim hands touched them. She spoke—in the Aymara tongue.

"Is he dead?"

"No," Graydon answered.

In the depths of her eyes a small, hot flame flared; he could have sworn it was of gladness.

"That is well! I would not have him die—" her voice became meditative—"at least—not this way."

Starrett groaned. The girl again touched the bruises on her cheek.

"He is very strong," she murmured.

Graydon thought there was admiration in her whisper; wondered whether all her beauty was, after all, only a mask for primitive woman worshiping brute strength.

"Who are you?" he asked.

She looked at him for a long, long moment.

"I am—Suarra," she answered, at last.

"But where do you come from? What are you?" he asked again. She did not choose to answer these questions.

"Is he your enemy?"

"No," he said. "We travel together."

"Then why—" she pointed again to the outstretched

5

figure—"why did you do this to him? Why did you not let him have his way with me?"

Graydon flushed. The question, with all its subtle implications, cut.

"What do you think I am?" he answered, hotly. "No man lets a thing like that go on!"

She looked at him, curiously. Her face softened. She took a step closer to him. She touched once more the bruises on her cheek.

"Do you not wonder," she said, "now do you *not* wonder why I do not call my people to deal him the punishment he has earned?"

"I do wonder," Graydon's perplexity was frank. "I wonder indeed. Why do you not call them—if they are close enough to hear?"

"And what would you do were they to come?"

"I would not let them have him—alive," he answered. "Nor me."

"Perhaps," she said, slowly—"perhaps that is why I do not call."

Suddenly she smiled upon him. He took a swift step toward her. She thrust out a warning hand.

"I am—Suarra," she said. "And I am—Death!"

A chill passed through Graydon. Again he realized the alien beauty of her. Could there be truth in these legends of the haunted Cordillera? He had never doubted that there was something real behind the terror of the Indians, the desertion of the *arrieros*. Was she one of its spirits, one of its—demons? For an instant the fantasy seemed no fantasy. Then reason returned. This girl a demon! He laughed.

"Do not laugh," she said. "The death I mean is not such as you who live beyond the high rim of our hidden land know. Your body may live on—yet it is death and more than death, since it is changed in—dreadful—ways. And that which tenants your body, that which speaks through your lips, is changed—in ways more dreadful still! . . . I would not have that death come to you."

Strange as were her words, Graydon hardly heard them;

certainly did not then realize their meaning, lost as he was in wonder at her beauty.

"How you came by the Messengers, I do not know. How you could have passed unseen by them, I cannot understand. Nor how you came so far into this forbidden land. Tell me—why came you here at all?"

"We came from afar," he told her, "on the track of a great treasure of gold and gems; the treasure of Atahualpa, the Inca. There were certain signs that led us. We lost them. We found that we, too, were lost. And we wandered here."

"Of Atahualpa or of Incas," the girl said, "I know nothing. Whoever they were, they could not have come to this place. And their treasure, no matter how great, would have meant nothing to us—to us of Yu-Atlanchi, where treasures are as rocks in the bed of a stream. A grain of sand it would have been, among many—" she paused, then went on, perplexedly, as though voicing her thoughts to herself—"But it is why the Messengers did not see them that I cannot understand . . . the Mother must know of this. . . . I must go quickly to the Mother. . . ."

"The Mother?" asked Graydon.

"The Snake Mother!" her gaze returned to him; she touched a bracelet on her right wrist. Graydon, drawing close, saw that this bracelet held a disk on which was carved in bas-relief a serpent with a woman's head and woman's breast and arms. It lay coiled upon what appeared to be a great bowl held high on the paws of four beasts. The shapes of these creatures did not at once register upon his consciousness, so absorbed was he in his study of that coiled figure. He stared close—and closer. And now he realized that the head reared upon the coils was not really that of a woman. No! It was reptilian.

Snake-like—yet so strongly had the artist feminized it, so great was the suggestion of womanhood modeled into every line of it, that constantly one saw it as woman, forgetting all that was of the serpent.

The eyes were of some intensely glittering purple stone. Graydon felt that those eyes were alive—that far, far away some living thing was looking at him through them. That they were, in fact, prolongations of some one's—some *thing's*—vision.

The girl touched one of the beasts that held up the bowl.

"The Xinli," she said.

Graydon's bewilderment increased. He knew what those animals were. Knowing, he also knew that he looked upon the incredible.

They were dinosaurs! The monstrous saurians that ruled earth millions upon millions of years ago, and, but for whose extinction, so he had been taught, man could never have developed.

Who in this Andean wilderness could know or could have known the dinosaurs? Who here could have carved the monsters with such life-like detail as these possessed? Why, it was only yesterday that science had learned what really were their huge bones, buried so long that the rocks had molded themselves around them in adamantine matrix. And laboriously, with every modern resource, haltingly and laboriously, science had set those bones together as a perplexed child would a picture puzzle, and put forth what it believed to be reconstructions of these long-vanished *chimeræ* of earth's nightmare youth.

Yet here, far from all science it must surely be, some one had modeled those same monsters for a woman's bracelet. Why then—it followed that whoever had done this must have had before him the living forms from which to work. Or, if not, had copies of those forms set down by ancient men who had seen them.

And either or both these things were incredible.

Who were the people to whom she belonged? There had been a name—Yu-Atlanchi.

"Suarra," he said, "where is Yu-Atlanchi? Is it this place?"

"This?" She laughed. "No! Yu-Atlanchi is the Ancient Land. The Hidden Land where the six Lords and the Lords of Lords once ruled. And where now rules only the Snake Mother and—another. This place Yu-Atlanchi!" Again she laughed. "Now and then I hunt here with—the—" she hesitated, looking at him oddly—"So it was that he who lies there caught me. I was hurting. I had slipped away from my followers, for sometimes it pleases me to hunt alone. I came through these trees and saw your *tetuane,* your lodge. I came face to face with—him. And I was amazed—too amazed to strike with one of these." She pointed to a low knoll a few feet away. "Before I could conquer that amaze he had caught me. Then you came."

Graydon looked where she had pointed. Upon the ground lay three slender, shining spears. Their slim shafts were of gold; the arrow-shaped heads of two of them were of fine opal. The third—the third was a single emerald, translucent and flawless, all of six inches long and three at its widest, ground to keenest point and cutting edge.

There it lay, a priceless jewel tipping a spear of gold— and a swift panic shook Graydon. He had forgotten Soames and Dancret. Suppose they should return while this girl was there. This girl with her ornaments of gold, her gem-tipped spears—and her beauty!

"Suarra," he said, "you must go, and go quickly. This man and I are not all. There are two more, and even now they may be close. Take your spears, and go quickly. Else I may not be able to save you."

"You think I am—"

"I tell you to go," he interrupted. "Whoever you are, whatever you are, go now and keep away from this place. To-morrow I will try to lead them away. If you have people to fight for you—well, let them come and fight if you so desire. But take your spears and go."

She crossed to the little knoll and picked-up the spears. She held one out to him, the one that bore the emerald point.

"This," she said, "to remember—Suarra."

"No," he thrust it back. "Go!"

If the others saw that jewel, never, he knew, would he be able to start them on the back trail—if they could find it. Starrett had seen it, of course, but he might be able to convince them that Starrett's story was only a drunken dream.

The girl studied him—a quickened interest in her eyes.

She slipped the bracelets from her arms, held them out to him with the three spears.

"Will you take these—and leave your comrades?" she asked. "Here are gold and gems. They are treasure. They are what you have been seeking. Take them. Take them and go, leaving that man here. Consent—and I will show you a way out of this forbidden land."

Graydon hesitated. The emerald alone was worth a fortune. What loyalty did he owe the three, after all? And Starrett had brought this thing upon himself. Nevertheless—they were his comrades. Open-eyed he had gone into this venture with them. He had a vision of himself skulking away with the glittering booty, creeping off to safety while he left the three unwarned, unprepared, to meet—what?

He did not like that picture.

"No," he said. "These men are of my race, my comrades. Whatever is to come—I will meet it with them and help them fight it."

"Yet you would have fought them for my sake—indeed, did fight," she said. "Why then do you cling to them when you can save yourself, and go free, with treasure? And why, if you will not do this, do you let me go, knowing that if you kept me prisoner, or—killed me, I could not bring my people down upon you?"

Graydon laughed.

"I couldn't let them hurt you, of course," he said. "And I'm afraid to make you prisoner, because I might not be able to keep you free from hurt. And I won't run away. So talk no more, but go—go!"

She thrust the gleaming spears into the ground, slipped the golden bracelets back on her arms, held white hands out to him.

"Now," she whispered, "now, by the Wisdom of the Mother, I will save you—if I can."

There was the sound of a horn, far away and high in air it seemed. It was answered by others closer by; mellow, questing notes—with weirdly alien beat in them.

"They come," the girl said. "My followers. Light your

10

fire to-night. Sleep without fear. But do not wander beyond these trees."

"Suarra—" he began.

"Quiet now," she warned. "Quiet—until I am gone."

The mellow horns sounded closer. She sprang from his side and darted away through the trees. From the ridge above the camp he heard her voice raised in one clear shout. There was a tumult of the horns about her—elfin and troubling. Then silence.

Graydon stood listening. The sun touched the high snowfields of the majestic peaks toward which he faced, touched them and turned them into robes of molten gold. The amethyst shadows that draped their sides thickened, wavered and marched swiftly forward.

Still he listened, hardly breathing.

Far, far away the horns sounded again; faint echoings of the tumult that had swept about the girl—faint, faint and fairy sweet.

The sun dropped behind the peaks; the edges of their frozen mantels glittered as though sewn with diamonds; darkened into a fringe of gleaming rubies. The golden fields dulled, grew amber and then blushed forth a glowing rose. They changed to pearl and faded into a ghostly silver, shining like cloud wraiths in the highest heavens. Down upon the *algarroba* clump the quick Andean dusk fell.

Not till then did Graydon, shivering with sudden, inexplicable dread, realize that beyond the calling horns and the girl's clear shouting he had heard no other sound—no noise either of man or beast, no sweeping through of brush or grass, no fall of running feet.

Nothing but that mellow chorus of the horns.

CHAPTER II

The Unseen Watchers

STARRETT HAD DRIFTED out of the paralysis of the blow into a drunken stupor. Graydon dragged him over to the tent, thrust a knapsack under his head, and threw a blanket over him. Then he went out and built up the fire. There was a trampling through the underbrush. Soames and Dancret came up through the trees.

"Find any signs?" he asked.

"Signs? Hell—no!" snarled the New Englander. "Say, Graydon, did you hear somethin' like a lot of horns? Damned queer horns, too. They seemed to be over here."

Graydon nodded, he realized that he must tell these men what had happened so that they could prepare some defense. But how much could he tell?

Tell them of Suarra's beauty, of her golden ornaments and her gem-tipped spears of gold? Tell them what she had said of Atahualpa's treasure?

If he did, there would be no further reasoning with them. They would go berserk with greed. Yet something of it he must tell them if they were to be ready for the attack which he was certain would come with the dawn.

And of the girl they would learn soon enough from Starrett.

He heard an exclamation from Dancret who had passed on into the tent; heard him come out; stood up and faced the wiry little Frenchman.

"What's the matter wit' Starrett, eh?" Dancret snapped. "First I t'ought he's drunk. Then I see he's scratched like wild cat and wit' a lump on his jaw as big as one orange. What you do to Starrett, eh?"

Graydon had made up his mind, and was ready to answer.

"Dancret," he said, "Soames—we're in a bad box. I came in from hunting less than an hour ago, and found Starrett wrestling with a girl. That's bad medicine down here—the worst, and you two know it. I had to knock Starrett out before I could get the girl away from him. Her people will probably be after us in the morning. There's no use trying to get away. We don't know a thing about this wilderness. Here is as good as any other place to meet them. We'd better spend the night getting it ready so we can put up a good scrap, if we have to."

"A girl, eh?" said Dancret. "What she look like? Where she come from? How she get away?"

Graydon chose the last question to answer.

"I let her go," he said.

"You let her go!" snarled Soames. "What the hell did you do that for? Why didn't you tie her up? We could have held her as a hostage, Graydon—had somethin' to do some tradin' with when her damned bunch of Indians came."

"She wasn't an Indian, Soames," said Graydon, then hesitated.

"You mean she was white—Spanish?" broke in Dancret, incredulously.

"No, not Spanish either. She was white. Yes, white as any of us. I don't know what she was."

The pair stared at him, then at each other.

"There's somethin' damned funny about this," growled Soames, at last. "But what I want to know is why you let her go—whatever the hell she was?"

"Because I thought we'd have a better chance if I did than if I didn't." Graydon's own wrath was rising. "I tell you that we're up against something none of us knows anything about. And we've got just one chance of getting out of the mess. If I'd kept her there, we wouldn't have even that chance."

Dancret stooped, and picked up something from the ground, something that gleamed yellow in the firelight.

"Somet'ing funny is right, Soames," he said. "Look at this!"

He handed the gleaming object over. It was a golden

bracelet, and as Soames turned it over in his hand there was the green glitter of emeralds. It had been torn from Suarra's arm, undoubtedly, in her struggle with Starrett.

"What that girl give you to let her go, Graydon, eh?" Dancret spat. "What she tell you, eh?"

Soames's hand dropped to his automatic.

"She gave me nothing. I took nothing," answered Graydon.

"I t'ink you damned liar," said Dancret, viciously. "We get Starrett awake," he turned to Soames. "We get him awake quick. I t'ink he tell us more about this, *oui*. A girl who wears stuff like this—and he lets her go! Lets her go when he knows there must be more where this come from—eh, Soames! Damned funny is right, eh? Come now, we see what Starrett tell us."

Graydon watched them go into the tent. Soon Soames came out, went to a spring that bubbled up from among the trees; returned, with water.

Well, let them waken Starrett; let him tell them whatever he would. They would not kill him that night, of that he was sure. They believed that he knew too much. And in the morning—

What was hidden in the morning for them all?

That even now they were prisoners, Graydon was sure. Suarra's warning not to leave the camp had been explicit. Since that tumult of the elfin horns, her swift vanishing and the silence that had followed, he no longer doubted that they had strayed, as she had said, within the grasp of some power as formidable as it was mysterious.

The silence? Suddenly it came to him that the night had become strangely still. There was no sound either of insect or bird, nor any stirring of the familiar after-twilight life of the wilderness.

The camp was besieged by silence!

He walked away through the *algarrobas*. There was a scant score of the trees. They stood like a little leafy island peak within the brush-covered *savanna*. They were great trees, every one of them, and set with a curious regularity; as though they had not sprung up by chance; as though indeed they had been carefully planted.

Graydon reached the last of them, rested a hand against a bole that was like myriads of tiny grubs turned to soft brown wood. He peered out. The slope that lay before him was flooded with moonlight; the yellow blooms of the *chilca* shrubs that pressed to the very feet of the trees shone wanly in the silver flood. The faintly aromatic fragrance of the *quenuar* stole around him. Movement or sign of life there was none.

And yet—

The spaces seemed filled with watchers. He felt their gaze upon him. He knew that some hidden host girdled the camp. He scanned every bush and shadow—and saw nothing. The certainty of a hidden, unseen multitude persisted. A wave of nervous irritation passed through him. He would force them, whatever they were, to show themselves.

He stepped out boldly into the full moonlight.

On the instant the silence intensified. It seemed to draw taut, to lift itself up whole octaves of stillnesses. It became alert, expectant—as though poised to spring upon him should he take one step further.

A coldness wrapped him, and he shuddered. He drew swiftly back to the shadow of the trees; stood there, his heart beating furiously. The silence lost its poignancy, drooped back upon its haunches—watchful.

What had frightened him? What was there in that tightening of the stillness that had touched him with the finger of nightmare terror? He groped back, foot by foot, afraid to turn his face from the silence. Behind him the fire flared. His fear dropped from him.

His reaction from his panic was a heady recklessness. He threw a log upon the fire and laughed as the sparks shot up among the leaves. Soames, coming out of the tent for more water, stopped as he heard that laughter and scowled at him malevolently.

"Laugh," he said. "Laugh while you can. Maybe you'll laugh on the other side of your mouth when we get Starrett up and he tells us what he knows."

"That was a sound sleep I gave him, anyway," jeered Graydon.

"There are sounder sleeps. Don't forget it," Dancret's voice, cold and menacing came from the tent.

Graydon turned his back to the tent, and deliberately faced that silence from which he had just fled. He seated himself, and after a while he dozed.

He awakened with a jump. Halfway between him and the tent Starrett was charging on him like a madman, bellowing.

Graydon leaped to his feet, but before he could defend himself the giant was upon him. The next moment he was down, overborne by sheer weight. The big adventurer crunched a knee into his arm and gripped his throat.

"Let her go, did you!" he roared. "Knocked me out and then let her go! Here's where you go, too, damn you!"

Graydon tried to break the grip on his throat. His lungs labored; there was a deafening roaring in his ears, and flecks of crimson began to dance across his vision. Starrett was strangling him. Through fast dimming sight he saw two black shadows leap through the firelight and clutch the strangling hands.

The fingers relaxed. Graydon staggered up. A dozen paces away stood Starrett. Dancret, arms around his knees, was hanging to him like a little terrier. Beside him was Soames, the barrel of his automatic pressed against his stomach.

"Why don't you let me kill him!" raved Starrett. "Didn't I tell you the girl had enough green ice on her to set us up the rest of our lives? There's more where it came from! And let her go! Let her go, the—"

Again his curses flowed.

"Now look here, Starrett," Soames's voice was deliberate. "You be quiet, or I'll do for you. We ain't goin' to let this thing get by us, me and Dancret. We ain't goin' to let this double-crossin' louse do us, and we ain't goin' to let you spill the beans by killin' him. We've struck somethin' big. All right, we're goin' to cash in on it. We're goin' to sit down peaceable, and Mister Graydon is goin' to tell us what happened after he put you out, what dicker he made with the girl and all of that. If he won't do it peaceable, then Mister Graydon is goin' to have things done to him that'll make him give up. That's all. Danc', let go his legs. Starrett, if you kick up any more trouble until I give the word I'm goin' to shoot you. From now on I boss this crowd—me and Danc. You get me, Starrett?"

Graydon, head once more clear, slid a cautious hand down toward the pistol holster. It was empty. Soames grinned, sardonically.

"We got it, Graydon," he said. "Yours, too, Starrett. Fair enough. Sit down everybody."

He squatted by the fire, still keeping Starrett covered. And after a moment the latter, grumbling, followed suit. Dancret dropped beside him.

"Come over here, Graydon," said Soames. "Come over here and cough up. What're you holdin' out on us? Did you make a date with her to meet you after you got rid of us? If so, where is it—because we'll all go together."

"Where'd you hide those gold spears?" growled Starrett. "You never let her get away with them, that's sure."

"Shut up, Starrett," ordered Soames. "I'm holdin' this inquest. Still—there's something in that. Was that it, Graydon? Did she give you the spears and her jewelry to let her go?"

"I've told you," answered Graydon. "I asked for nothing, and took nothing. Starrett's drunken folly had put us all in jeopardy. Letting the girl go free was the first vital step toward our own safety. I thought it was the best thing to do. I still think so."

"Yeah?" sneered the lank New Englander, "is that so? Well, I'll tell you, Graydon, if she'd been an Indian maybe I'd agree with you. But not when she was the kind of lady Starrett says she was. No, sir, it ain't natural. You know damned well that if you'd been straight you'd have kept her here till Danc' and me got back. Then we could all have got together and figured what was the best thing to do. Hold her until her folks came along and paid up to get her back undamaged. Or give her the third degree until she gave up where all that gold and stuff she was carrying came from. That's what you would have done, Graydon—if you weren't a dirty, lyin', double-crossin' hound."

Graydon's anger flared up.

"All right, Soames," he said. "I'll tell you. What I've said about freeing her for our own safety is true. But outside of that I would as soon have thought of trusting a child to a bunch of hyenas as I would of trusting that girl to you three. I let her go a damned sight more for her sake than I did for our own. Does that satisfy you?"

"Aha!" jeered Dancret. "Now I see! Here is this strange lady of so much wealth and beauty. She is too pure and good for us to behold. He tell her so and bid her fly. 'My hero!' she say, 'take all I have and give up this bad company.' 'No, no,' he tell her, t'inking all the time if he play his cards right he get much more, and us out of the way so he need not divide, 'no, no,' he tell her. 'But long as these bad men stay here you will not be safe.' 'My hero,' she say. 'I will go and bring back my family and they shall dispose of your bad company. But you they shall reward, my hero, *oui!*' Aha, so that is what it was!"

Graydon flushed; the little Frenchman's malicious travesty had shot uncomfortably close. After all, Suarra's unasked promise to save him could be construed as Dancret had suggested. Suppose he told them he had warned her that whatever the fate in store for them he was determined to share it, and would stand by them to the last? They would not believe him.

Soames had been watching him, closely.

"By God, Danc'," he said, "I guess you hit it. He changed color. He's sold us out."

He raised his automatic, held it on Graydon—then lowered it.

"No," he said, deliberately. "This is too big a thing to let slip by bein' too quick on the trigger. If your dope is right, Danc', and I guess it is, the lady was mighty grateful. All right—we ain't got her, but we have got him. As I figure it, bein' grateful, she won't want him to get killed. She'll be back. Well, we'll trade him for what they got that we want. Tie him up."

He pointed the pistol at Graydon. Unresisting, Graydon let Starrett and Dancret bind his wrists. They pushed him over to one of the trees and sat him on the ground with back against its bole. They passed a rope under his arms and hitched it securely around the trunk; they tied his feet.

"Now," said Soames, "if her gang show up in the morning, we'll let 'em see you, and find out how much you're worth. They won't rush us. There's bound to be a palaver. And if they don't come to terms—well, Graydon, the first bullet out of this gun goes through your guts. That'll give you time to see what we do to her before you die."

Graydon did not answer him. He knew that nothing he might say would change them from their purpose. He made himself as comfortable as possible, and closed his eyes. Once or twice he opened them, and looked at the others. They sat beside the fire, heads close together, talking in whispers, their faces tense, and eyes feverish with the treasure lust.

After a while Graydon's head dropped forward. He slept.

CHAPTER III

The White Llama

IT WAS DAWN when Graydon awakened.

Some one had thrown a blanket over him during the night, but he was, nevertheless, cold and stiff. He drew his legs up and down painfully, trying to start the sluggish blood. He heard the others stirring in the tent. He wondered which of them had thought of the blanket, and why he had been moved to that kindness.

Starrett lifted the tent flap, passed by him without a word and went on to the spring. He returned and busied himself, furtively, about the fire. Now and then he looked at the prisoner, but seemingly with neither anger nor resentment. He slipped at last to the tent, listened, then trod softly over to Graydon.

"Sorry about this," he muttered. "But I can't do anything with Soames and Dancret. Had a hard time persuading 'em even to let you have that blanket. Take a drink of this."

He pressed a flask to Graydon's lips. He took a liberal swallow; it warmed him.

"Sh-h," warned Starrett. "Don't bear any grudge. Drunk last night. I'll help you, if—" He broke off, abruptly; busied himself with the burning logs. Out of the tent came Soames.

"I'm goin' to give you one last chance, Graydon," he began, without preliminary. "Come through clean with us on your dicker with the girl, and we'll take you back with us, and all work together and all share together. You had the edge on us yesterday, and I don't know that I blame

20

you. But it's three to one now and the plain truth is you can't get away with it. So why not be reasonable?"

"What's the use of going over all that again, Soames?" Graydon asked, wearily. "I've told you everything. If you're wise, you'll let me loose, give me my guns and I'll fight for you when the trouble comes. For trouble is coming, man, sure—big trouble."

"Yeah!" snarled the New Englander. "Tryin' to scare us, are you? All right—there's a nice little trick of drivin' a wedge under each of your finger nails and a-keepin' drivin' 'em in. It makes 'most anybody talk after awhile. And if it don't, there's the good old fire dodge. Rollin' your feet up to it, closer and closer and closer. Yeah, anybody'll talk when their toes begin to crisp up and toast."

Suddenly he bent over and sniffed at Graydon's lips.

"So that's it!" he faced Starrett, tense, gun leveled from his hip pocket. "Been feedin' him liquor, have you? Been talkin' to him, have you? After we'd settled it last night that I was to do all the talkin'. All right, that settles you, Starrett. Dancret! Danc'! Come here, quick!" he roared.

The Frenchman came running out of the tent.

"Tie him up," Soames nodded toward Starrett. "Another damned double-crosser in the camp. Gave him liquor. Got their heads together while we were inside. Tie him."

"But, Soames," the Frenchman hesitated, "if we have to fight, it is not well to have half of us helpless, *non*. Perhaps Starrett he did nothing—"

"If we have to fight, two men will do as well as three," said Soames. "I ain't goin' to let this thing slip through my fingers, Danc'. I don't think we'll have to do any fightin'. If they come, I think it's goin' to be a tradin' job. Starrett's turnin' traitor, too. Tie him, I say."

"Well, I don't like it—" began Dancret; Soames made an impatient motion with his automatic; the little Frenchman went to the tent, returned with a coil of rope, and sidled up to Starrett.

"Put up your hands," ordered Soames. Starrett swung them up. But in midswing they closed on Dancret, lifted him like a doll and held him between himself and the gaunt New Englander.

"Now shoot, damn you!" he cried, and bore down on Soames, meeting every move of his pistol arm with Dancret's wriggling body. His own right hand swept down to the Frenchman's belt, drew from the holster his automatic, leveled it over the twisting shoulder at Soames.

"Drop your gun, Yank," grinned Starrett, triumphantly. "Or shoot if you want. But before your bullet's half through Dancret here, by Christ, I'll have you drilled clean."

There was a momentary, sinister silence—it was broken by a sudden pealing of tiny golden bells.

Their chiming cleft through the murk of murder that had fallen on the camp; lightened it; dissolved it as the sunshine does a cloud. Soames' pistol dropped; Starrett's iron grip upon Dancret relaxed.

Through the trees, not a hundred yards away, came Suarra.

A cloak of green covered the girl from neck almost to slender feet. In her hair gleamed a twisted string of emeralds. Bandlets of gold studded with the same gems circled her wrists and ankles. Behind her a snow-white llama paced, sedately. There was a broad golden collar around its neck from which dropped strands of little golden bells. At each of its silvery sides a pannier hung, woven it seemed from shining yellow rushes.

And there was no warrior host around her. She had brought neither avengers nor executioners. At the llama's side was a single attendant, swathed in a voluminous robe of red and yellow, the hood of which covered his face. His only weapon was a long staff, vermilion. He was bent, and he fluttered and danced as he came on, taking little steps backward and forward—movements that carried the suggestion that his robes clothed less a human being than some huge bird. They drew closer, and Graydon saw that the hand that clutched the staff was thin and white with the transparent pallor of old, old age.

He strained at his bonds, a sick horror at his heart. Why had she come back—like this? Without strong men to guard her? With none but this one ancient? And decked in jewels and gold? He had warned her; she could not be ignorant of what threatened her. It was as though she had come thus deliberately—to fan the lusts from which she had most to fear.

"*Diable!*" whispered Dancret—"the emeralds!"

"God—what a girl!" muttered Starrett, thick nostrils distended, a red flicker in his eyes.

Soames said nothing, perplexity and suspicion replacing the astonishment with which he had watched the approach. Nor did he speak as the girl and her attendants halted close beside him. But the doubt in his eyes grew, and he scanned the path along which they had come, searching every tree, every bush. There was no sign of movement, no sound.

"Suarra!" cried Graydon, despairingly, "Suarra, why did you return?"

She stepped over to him, and drew a dagger from beneath her cloak. She cut the thongs binding him to the tree. She slipped the blade beneath the cords that fettered his wrists and ankles; freed him. He staggered to his feet.

"Was it not well for you that I did come?" she asked, sweetly.

Before he could answer, Soames strode forward. And Graydon saw that he had come to some decision, had resolved upon some course of action. He made a low, awkward, mocking bow to the girl; then spoke to Graydon.

"All right," he said, "you can stay loose—as long as you do what I want you to. The girl's back and that's the main thing. She seems to favor you a lot, Graydon. I reckon that gives us a way to persuade her to answer our questions. Yes, sir, and you favor her. That's useful, too. I reckon you won't want to be tied up an' watch certain things happen to her, eh—" he leered at Graydon. "But there's just one thing you've got to do if you want things to go along peaceable. Don't do any talkin' to her when

I ain't close by. Remember, I know the Aymara as well as you do. And I want to be right alongside listenin' in all the time, do you see? That's all."

He turned to Suarra.

"Your visit has brought great happiness, maiden," he spoke in the Aymara. "It will not be a short one, if we have our way—and I think we *will* have our way—" There was covert menace in the phrase, yet if she noted it she gave no heed. "You are strange to us, as we must be to you. There is much for us each to learn, one of the other."

"That is true," she answered, tranquilly. "I think though that your desire to learn of me is much greater than mine to learn of you—since, as you surely know, I have had one not too pleasant lesson." She glanced at Starrett.

"The lessons," he said, "shall be pleasant—or not pleasant, as you choose."

This time there was no mistaking the menace in the words, nor did Suarra again let it pass. Her eyes blazed sudden wrath.

"Better not to threaten!" she warned. "I, Suarra, am not used to threats—and if you will take my counsel you will keep them to yourself hereafter!"

"Yeah, is that so?" Soames took a step toward her, face grown grim and ugly. There came a dry chuckling from the hooded figure in red and yellow. Suarra started; her wrath vanished, she became friendly once more.

"I was hasty," she said to Soames. "Nevertheless, it is never wise to threaten unless you know the strength of what it is you menace. And remember—of me you know nothing. Yet I know all that you wish to learn. You wish to know how I came by this—and this—and this—" she touched her coronal, her bracelet, her anklets. "You wish to know where they came from, and if there are more of them there, and if so, how you may possess yourself of as much as you can carry away. Well, you shall know all that. I have come to tell you."

At this announcement, so frank and open, all the doubt

and suspicion returned to Soames. Again his eyes narrowed and he searched the trail up which Suarra had come.

"Soames," Dancret gripped his arm, and his voice and hand were both shaking, "the baskets on the llama. They're not rushes—they're gold, pure gold, pure soft gold, woven like straw! *Diable!* Soames, what have we struck!"

Soames's eyes glittered.

"Better go over and watch where they came up, Danc'," he answered. "I don't quite get this. It looks too cursed easy to be right. Take your rifle and squint out from the edge of the trees while I try to get down to what's what."

"There is nothing to fear," said the girl, as though she had understood the words, "no harm will come to you from me. If there is any evil in store for you, you yourselves will summon it—not we. I have come to show you the way to treasure. Only that. Come with me and you shall see where jewels like these"—she touched the gems meshed in her hair—"grow like flowers in a garden. You shall see the gold come streaming forth, living, from—" she hesitated; then went on as though reciting some lesson—"come streaming forth like water. You may bathe in that stream, drink from it if you will, carry away all that you can bear. Or if it causes you too much sorrow to leave it, why—you may stay with it forever; nay, become a part of it, even. Men of gold."

She turned from them, and walked toward the llama.

They stared at her and at each other; on the faces of three, greed and suspicion; bewilderment on Graydon's.

"It is a long journey," she faced them, one hand on the llama's head. "You are my guests—in a sense. Therefore, I have brought something for your entertainment before we start."

She began to unbuckle the panniers. Graydon was aware that this attendant of hers was a strange servant—if servant he was. He made no move to help her. Silent he stood, and motionless, face-covered.

Graydon stepped forward to help the girl. She smiled

up at him, half shyly. In the depths of her eyes was a glow warmer than friendliness; his hands leaped to touch hers.

Instantly Soames stepped between them.

"Better remember what I told you," he snapped.

"Help me," said Suarra. Graydon lifted the basket and set it down beside her. She slipped a hasp, bent back the soft metal withes, and drew out a shimmering packet. She shook it and it floated out on the dawn wind, a cloth of silver. It lay upon the ground like a web of gossamer spun by silver spiders.

Then from the hamper she brought forth cups of gold, and deep, boat-shaped golden dishes, two tall ewers whose handles were winged serpents, their scales made, it seemed, from molten rubies. After them small golden-withed baskets. She set the silver cloth with the dishes and the cups. She opened the little baskets. In them were unfamiliar, fragrant fruits and loaves and oddly colored cakes. All these Suarra placed upon the plates. She dropped to her knees at the head of the cloth, took up one of the ewers, snapped open its lid and from it poured into the cups clear amber wine.

She raised her eyes to them; waved a white hand, graciously.

"Sit," she said. "Eat and drink."

She beckoned to Graydon; pointed to the place beside her. Silently, gaze fixed upon the glittering hoard, Starrett and Dancret and Soames squatted before the other plates. Soames thrust out a hand, took up one and weighed it, scattering what it held upon the cloth.

"Gold!" he breathed.

Starrett laughed, crazily, and raised his wine-filled goblet to his lips.

"Wait!" Dancret caught his wrist. " 'Eat and drink,' she said, eh? Eat, drink and be merry—for to-morrow we die, eh—is that it?"

Soames started, his face once more dark with suspicion.

"You think it's poisoned?" he snarled.

"Maybe no—maybe so," the little Frenchman shrugged. "Anyway I t'ink it better we say 'After you' to her."

The girl looked at them, then at Graydon, inquiringly.

"They are afraid. They think it is—that you have—" Graydon stumbled.

"That I have put sleep—or death in it? And you?" she asked.

For answer, Graydon raised his cup and drank.

"Yet it is natural," she turned to Soames. "Yes, it is natural that you three should fear this, since—is it not so—it is what you would do if you were we, and we were you? But you are wrong. I tell you again that what there may be to fear is only that which is in yourselves."

She poured wine into her own cup and drank it; broke off a bit of Starrett's bread and ate it; took a cake from Dancret's plate and ate that; set white teeth in one of the fruits.

"Are you satisfied?" she asked them. "Oh, be very sure that if it is in my wish to bring death to you, it is in no such shape as this."

For a moment Soames glared at her. He jumped to his feet, strode over to the hooded figure and snatched aside the cowl. The uncovered face was like old ivory. It was seamed with scores of fine lines. It was a face stamped with an incredible ancientness—but the eyes were as bright and as youthful as their setting was ancient.

It stared at Soames, inscrutably. For a dozen heartbeats the gaunt New Englander stared back. Then, slowly, he let the hood drop. He returned to the silver cloth. As he passed, Graydon saw that all color had drained from his cheeks. He threw himself down at his place, and drank deep of the wine, the hand that raised the goblet shaking.

He drank, and drank again from the flagon. And soon, whatever the terror he had felt, the wine drowned it. The first ewer and a second, drawn by Suarra from the llama's panniers, were emptied by the three before Soames lurched to his feet.

"You're all right, sister," he said, half-drunkenly. "Just keep on treatin' us like this, and we'll end by all bein' little pals together."

"What does he say?" asked Suarra of Graydon.

"He approves of your—entertainment," answered Graydon, dryly.

"Good," Suarra, too, arose. "Then let us be going."

"We're going, sister, never fear," grinned Soames. "Danc', you stay right here and watch things. Come on, Bill—" he slapped Starrett on the back. "Everything's just fine. Come on, Graydon—bygones is bygones."

Starrett scrambled up. He linked his arm in the New Englander's. They staggered over to the tent. Dancret, upon whom the wine seemed to have had little effect, settled down on a bowlder just beyond the fire and began his watch, rifle at readiness.

Graydon lingered. Soames had forgotten him, for a time at least. He meant to make the best of that time with this strange maid whose beauty and sweetness had touched him as no other woman's ever had. He drew so close that the fragrance of her cloudy hair rocked him; so close that her touching shoulder sent a flame through him.

"Suarra—" he began. She turned, and silenced him with slender fingers on his lips.

"Not now—" she whispered. "Not now—tell me nothing now of what is in your heart—Not now—nor, it may be, ever! I promised that I would save you—if I could. Of that promise was born another—" her glance turned to the silent figure, meaningly. "So speak to me not again," she went on hurriedly, "or if you must speak—let it be of—commonplace things."

She began packing the golden cups and dishes. He set about helping her. He thought, ruefully, that this was a commonplace thing enough to satisfy her. She accepted his aid without comment, looked at him no more.

When the last shining cup was in the pannier, he turned and went toward the tent to get together his duffle, pack his burro. The voices of Starrett and Soames came to him.

"But she's not Indian, Soames," Starrett was speaking. "She's whiter than you and me. What are they? And the girl—Christ!"

"What they are we'll find out, never fear," and Soames.

"To hell with the girl—take her if you want her. But I'd go through a dozen hells to get to the place where that stuff they're carryin' samples of comes from. Man—with what we could carry out on the burros and the llama and come back for—man, we could buy the world."

"Yes—unless there's a trap somewhere," said Starrett, dubiously.

"We've got the cards in our hands," the wine was wearing off Soames. "What's against us? An old dummy and a girl. Now, I'll tell you what I think. I don't know who or what they are, but whoever or whatever, you can bet there ain't many of 'em. If there was, they'd be landing on us hard. No—they're damned anxious to get us away and they're willin' to let us get out with what we can to get us away. They want to get rid of us, quick and cheap as possible. Yeah—that's what they want. Why—because they damn well know the three of us could wipe 'em all out."

"Three of us?" echoed Starrett. "Four, you mean. There's Graydon."

"Graydon don't count—the louse! Thought he'd sold us out, didn't he? All right—we'll fix Mister Graydon when the time comes. Just now he's useful to us on account of the girl. She's stuck on him. But when the time comes to divide—there'll be only three of us. And there'll only be two of us—if you do anything like you did this morning."

"Cut it out, Soames," growled Starrett. "I told you it was the hooch. I'm through with that, now that we've seen this stuff. I'm with you to the limit. Do what you want with Graydon. But—I want the girl. I'd be willing to make a bargain with you—give up a part of my share."

"Oh, hell," drawled Soames. "We've been together a good many years, Bill. There's enough and plenty for the three of us. You can have the girl for nothing."

Little flecks of red danced before Graydon's eyes. Hand stretched to tear open the tent flap, he checked himself.

That was no way to help Suarra. Unarmed, what could he do? In some way, he must get his guns. And the danger

29

was not imminent—they would do nothing before they reached that place of treasure to which Suarra had promised to lead them.

He stole back a dozen paces, waited for a moment or two; then went noisily to the tent. He thrust aside the flap and entered.

"Been a long time comin'," snarled Soames. "Been talkin'—after what I told you?"

"Not a word, " lied Graydon, cheerfully—he busied himself with his belongings. "By the way, Soames, don't you think it's time to stop this nonsense and give me back my guns?"

Soames made no answer.

"Oh, all right then," said Graydon. "I only thought that they would come in handy when the pinch comes. But if you only want me to look on while you do the scrapping— well, I don't mind."

"You'd better mind," said Soames. "You'd better mind, Graydon! If the pinch comes—we're takin' no chances of a bullet in our backs. *That's* why you've got no guns. And if the pinch does come—well, we'll take no chances on you, anyway. Do you get me?"

Graydon shrugged. In silence the packing was completed; the tent struck; the burros loaded.

Suarra stood awaiting them at the side of the white llama. Soames walked up to her, drew from its holster his automatic, balanced it in outstretched hand.

"You know what this is?" he asked her.

"Why, yes," she answered. "It is the death weapon of your kind."

"Right," said Soames. "And it deals death quickly, quicker than spears or arrows—" He raised his voice so there could be no doubt that her silent attendant must also hear—"Now, I and these two men here carry these and others still more deadly. This man's we have taken from him. Your words may be clearest truth. I hope they are— for your sake and this man's and his who came with you. You understand me?" he asked, and grinned like a hungry wolf.

"I understand." Suarra's eyes and face were calm. "You need fear nothing from us."

"We don't," said Soames. "But you have much to fear—from us."

Another moment he regarded her, menacingly; then shoved his pistol back into his holster.

"You go first," he ordered. "Your man behind you. And then him—" he pointed to Graydon. "We three march in the rear—death-weapons ready."

In that order they passed through the giant *algarrobas*, and out into the oddly park-like spaces beyond.

CHAPTER IV

The Thing That Fled

THEY HAD TRAVELED over the *savanna* for perhaps an hour when Suarra turned to the left, entering the forest that covered the flanks of a great mountain. The trees closed on them. Graydon could see no trail, yet she went on without pause. Another hour went by and the way began to climb, the shade to deepen. Deeper it became and deeper, until the girl was but a flitting shadow.

Once or twice Graydon had glanced at the three men behind him. The darkness was making them more and more uneasy. They walked close together, eyes and ears strained to catch the first faint stirrings of ambush. And now, as the green gloom grew denser still, Soames ordered him to join Dancret and Starrett. He hesitated, read murder in the New Englander's eyes, realized the futility of resistance and dropped back. Soames pressed forward until he was close behind the cowled figure. Dancret drew Graydon between himself and Starrett, grinning.

"Soames has changed his plan," he whispered. "If there is trouble, he shoot the old devil—quick. He keep the girl to make trade wit' her people. He keep you to make trade wit' the girl. How you like—eh?"

Graydon did not answer. When the Frenchman had pressed close to him, he had felt an automatic in his side pocket. If an attack did come, he could leap upon Dancret, snatch the pistol and gain for himself a fighting chance. He would shoot Soames down as remorselessly as he knew Soames would shoot him.

Darker grew the woods until the figures in front were only a moving blur. Then the gloom began to lighten. They had been passing through some ravine, some gorge whose unseen walls had been pressing in upon them, and had now begun to retreat.

A few minutes longer, and ahead of them loomed a prodigious doorway, a cleft whose sides reached up for thousands of feet. Beyond was a flood of sunshine. Suarra stopped at the rocky threshold with a gesture of warning, peered through, and beckoned them on.

Blinking, Graydon walked through the portal. He looked out over a grass-covered plain strewn with huge, isolated rocks rising from the green like menhirs of the Druids. There were no trees. The plain was dish-shaped; an enormous oval as symmetrical as though it had been molded by the thumb of some Cyclopean potter. Straight across it, three miles or more away, the forests began again. They clothed the base of another gigantic mountain whose walls arose, perpendicularly, a mile at least in air. The smooth scarps described an arc of a tremendous circle—round as Fujiyama's sacred cone, but many times its girth.

They were on a wide ledge that bordered this vast bowl. This shelf was a full hundred feet higher than the bottom of the valley whose side sloped up to it like the side of a saucer. And, again carrying out that suggestion of a huge dish, the ledge jutted out like a rim. Graydon guessed that there was a concavity under his feet, and that if one should fall over the side it would be well-nigh impossible to climb back because of the overhang. The surface was about twelve feet wide, and more like a road carefully leveled by human hands than work of nature. On one side was the curving bowl of the valley with its weird monoliths and the circular scarp of the mysterious mountain; on the other the wooded cliffs, unscalable.

They set forth along the rimlike way. Noon came, and in another ravine that opened upon the strange road they had snatched from saddle bags a hasty lunch. They did not waste time in unpacking the burros. There was a little brook singing in the pass, and from it they refilled their canteens, then watered the animals. This time Suarra did not join them.

By mid-afternoon they were nearing the northern end of the bowl. All through the day the circular mountain

33

across the plain had unrolled its vast arc of cliff. A wind had arisen, sweeping from the distant forest and bending the tall heads of the grass far below them.

Suddenly, deep within the wind, Graydon heard a faint, far-off clamor, a shrill hissing, as of some onrushing army of serpents. The girl halted, face turned toward the sound. It came again—and louder. Her face whitened, but when she spoke her voice was steady.

"There is danger," she said. "Deadly danger for you. It may pass and—it may not. Until we know what to expect you must hide. Take your animals and tether them in the underbrush there—" she pointed to the mountainside which here was broken enough for cover—"the four of you take trees and hide behind them. Tie the mouths of your animals so that they can make no noise."

"So!" snarled Soames. "So here's the trap, is it! All right, sister, you know what I told you. We'll go into the trees, but—you go with us where we can keep our hands on you."

"I will go with you," she answered, gravely.

Soames glared at her, then turned abruptly.

"Danc'," he ordered, "Starrett—get the burros in. And Graydon—you'll stay with the burros and see they make no noise. We'll be right close—with the guns. And we'll have the girl—don't forget that."

Again the hissing shrilled down the wind.

"Be quick," the girl commanded.

When the trees and underbrush had closed in upon them it flashed on Graydon, crouching behind the burros, that he had not seen the cloaked famulus of Suarra join the retreat and seek the shelter of the woods. He parted the bushes, and peered cautiously through them. There was no one upon the path.

A sudden gust of wind tore at the trees. It brought with it a burst of the hissing, closer and more strident, and in it an undertone that thrilled him with unfamiliar terror.

A thing of vivid scarlet streaked out from the trees which here were not more than a half a mile away. It scuttled over the plain until it reached the base of one of the monoliths. It swarmed up its side to the top. There it paused, apparently scanning the forest from which it had come. He caught the impression of some immense insect, but touched with a monstrous, an incredible suggestion of humanness.

The scarlet thing slipped down the monolith, and raced through the grasses toward him. Out of the forest burst what at first glance he took for a pack of huge hunting dogs—then realized that whatever they might be, dogs they certainly were not. They came forward leaping like kangaroos, and as they leaped they glittered green and blue in the sunlight, as though armored in mail of emeralds and sapphires. Nor did ever dogs give tongue as they did. From them came the hellish hissing.

The scarlet thing darted to right, to left, frantically; then crouched at the base of another monolith, motionless.

From the trees emerged another monstrous shape. Like the questing creatures, it glittered—but as though its body were cased in polished jet. Its bulk was that of a giant draft-horse. Its neck was long and reptilian. At the base of its neck, astride it, was a man.

Graydon cautiously raised his field glasses and focused them on the pack. Directly in his line of vision was one of the creatures which had come to gaze. It stood rigid, its side toward him, pointing like a hunting dog.

It was a dinosaur!

Dwarfed to the size of a Great Dane, still there was no mistaking it. He could see its blunt and spade-shaped tail which with its powerful, pillarlike hind legs made a tripod upon which it squatted. Its body was nearly erect. Its short forelegs were muscled as powerfully as its others. It held these forelegs half curved at its breast, as though ready to clutch. They ended in four long talons, chisel shaped, one of which thrust outward like a huge thumb.

And what he had taken for mail of sapphire and emerald were scales. They overlapped like those of the armadillo. From their burnished surfaces and edges the sun struck out the jewel glints.

The creature turned its head upon its short, bull neck. It seemed to stare straight at Graydon. He saw fiery red eyes set in a sloping, bony arch of broad forehead. Its muzzle was that of a crocodile, but smaller and blunted. The jaws were studded with yellow, pointed fangs.

The rider drew up beside it. Like the others, the creature he rode was a true dinosaur. It was black scaled and longer tailed, with serpentine neck thicker than the central coil of the giant python.

The rider was a man of Suarra's own race. There was the same ivory whiteness of skin, the more than classic regularity of feature. But his face was stamped with arrogance, indifferent cruelty. He wore a close-fitting suit of green that clung to him like a glove, and his hair was a shining golden. He sat upon a light saddle fastened at the base of the long neck of his steed. Heavy reins ran up to the jaws of the jetty dinosaur's small, snakelike head.

Graydon's glasses dropped from his shaking hand. What manner of man was this who hunted with dinosaurs for dogs and a dinosaur for steed!

He looked toward the base of the monolith where the scarlet thing had crouched. It was no longer there. He caught a gleam of scarlet in the high grass not a thousand feet away. The thing was scuttering toward the rim—

There was a shrieking clamor like a thousand hissing fumaroles. The pack had found the scent, were leaping forward like a glittering green and blue comber.

The scarlet thing jumped up out of the grasses. It swayed upon four long and stiltlike legs, its head a full twelve feet above the ground. High on these stilts of legs was its body, almost round and no bigger than a half-grown boy's. From the sides of the body stretched two sinewy arms—like human arms pulled out to twice their normal length. Body, arms and legs were covered with fine scarlet hair. Its face, turned toward its pursuers, Graydon could not see.

The pack rushed upon it. The thing hurled itself like a thunderbolt straight toward the rim.

Graydon heard beneath him a frantic scrambling and scratching. Gray hands came over the edge of the road, gripping the rock with foot-long fingers like blunt needles of bone. They clutched and drew forward. Behind them appeared spindling, scarlet-haired arms.

Over the edge peered a face, gray as the hands. Within it were two great unwinking round and golden eyes.

A man's face—and not a man's!

A face such as he had never seen upon any living creature ... yet there could be no mistaking the humanness of it ... the humanness which lay over the incredible visage like a veil.

He thought he saw a red rod dart out of air and touch the face—the red rod of Suarra's motley-garbed attendant. Whether he saw it or not, the clutching claws opened and slid away. The gray face vanished.

Up from the hidden slope arose a wailing, agonized shriek, and a triumphant hissing. Then out into the range of his vision bounded the black dinosaur, its golden-haired rider shouting. Behind it leaped the pack. They crossed the plain like a thunder cloud pursued by emerald and sapphire lightnings. They passed into the forest, and were gone.

Suarra stepped out of the tree shadows, the three adventurers close behind her, white-faced and shaking. She stood looking where the dinosaurs had disappeared, and her face was set, and her eyes filled with loathing.

"Suarra!" gasped Graydon. "That thing—the thing that ran—what was it? God—it had the face of a man!"

"It was no man," she shook her head. "It was a— Weaver. Perhaps he had tried to escape. Or perhaps Lantlu opened a way for him that he might be tempted to escape. For Lantlu delights in hunting with the Xinli—" her voice shook with hatred—"and a Weaver will do when there is nothing better!"

"A Weaver? It had a man's face!" It was Soames, echoing Graydon.

"No," she repeated. "It was no—man. At least no man as you are. Long, long ago his ancestors were men like you—that is true. But now—he is—only a Weaver."

She turned to Graydon.

"Yu-Atlanchi by its arts fashioned him and his kind. Remember him, Graydon—when you come to our journey's end!"

She stepped out upon the path. There stood the cowled

figure, waiting as tranquilly as though it had never stirred. She called to the white llama, and again took her place at the head of the little caravan. Soames touched Graydon, arousing him from the troubled thought into which her enigmatic warning had thrown him.

"Take your place, Graydon," he muttered. "We'll follow. Later I want to talk to you. Maybe you can get your guns back—if you're reasonable."

"Hurry," said Suarra, "the sun sinks, and we must go quickly. Before to-morrow's noon you shall see your garden of jewels, and the living gold streaming for you to do with it as you will—or the gold to do as it wills with you."

She looked the three over, swiftly, a shadow of mockery in her eyes. Soames' lips tightened.

"Get right along, sister," he said, sardonically. "All *you* have to do is show us. Then your work is done. We'll take care of the rest."

She shrugged, carelessly. They set forth once more along the rimmed path.

The plain was silent, deserted. From the far forests came no sound. Graydon strove for sane comprehension of what he had just beheld. A Weaver, Suarra had named the scarlet thing—and had said that once its ancestors had been men like themselves. He remembered what, at their first meeting, she had told him of the powers of this mysterious Yu-Atlanchi. Did she mean that her people had mastered the secrets of evolution so thoroughly that they had learned how to reverse its processes as well? Could control—devolution!

Well, why not? In man's long ascent from the primeval jelly on the shallow shores of the warm first seas, he had worn myriad shapes. And as he moved higher from one form to another, changing to vertebrate, discarding cold blood for warm, still was he kin to the fish he caught to-day, to the furred creatures whose pelts clothed his women, to the apes he brought from the jungles to study or to amuse him. Even the spiders that spun in his gardens, the scorpion that scuttled from the tread of his feet, were abysmally distant blood-brothers.

When St. Francis of Assisi had spoke of Brother Fly,

Brother Wolf, Brother Snake, he had voiced scientific truth.

All life on earth had a common origin. Divergent now and Protean shaped, still man and beast, fish and serpent, lizard and bird, ant and bee and spider, all had come from those once similar specks of jelly, adrift millions upon millions of years ago in the shallow littorals of the first seas. Protæbion, Gregory of Edinburgh had named it— the first stuff of life from which all life was to develop.

Were the germs of all those shapes man had worn in his slow upward climb still dormant in him?

Roux, the great French scientist, had taken the eggs of frogs and, by manipulating them, had produced giant frogs and dwarfs, frogs with two heads and one body, frogs with one head and eight legs, three-headed frogs with legs numerous as centipedes'. And he had produced from these eggs, also, creatures which in no way resembled frogs at all.

Vornikoff, the Russian, and Schwartz, the German, had experimented with still higher forms of life, producing *chimeræ*, nightmare things they had been forced to slay— and quickly.

If Roux and the others had done all this—and they had done it, Graydon knew—then was it not possible for greater scientists to awaken those dormant germs in man, and similarly create—such creatures as the scarlet thing? A spider-man!

Nature, herself, had given them the hint. Nature from time to time produced such abnormalities—human monsters marked outwardly if not inwardly with the stigmata of the beast, the fish, even the crustacean. Babies with gill slits in their throats babies with tails; babies furred. The human embryo passed through all these stages, from the protoplasmic unicell up—compressing the age-long drama of evolution into less than a year.

Might it not well be, then, that in Yu-Atlanchi dwelt those to whom the crucible of birth held no secrets; who could dip within it and mold from its contents what they would?

A loom is a dead machine upon which fingers work

more or less clumsily. The spider is both machine and artisan, spinning and weaving more surely, more exquisitely than can any lifeless mechanism worked by man. What man-made machine had ever approached the delicacy, the beauty of the spider's web?

Suddenly Graydon seemed to behold a whole new world of appalling *grotesquerie*—spider-men and spider-women spread upon huge webs and weaving with needled fingers wondrous fabrics, mole-men and mole-women burrowing, opening mazes of subterranean passages, *cloaca*, for those who had wrought them into being; amphibian folk busy about the waters—a phantasmagoria of humanity, monstrously twinned with Nature's perfect machine, while still plastic in the womb!

Shuddering, he thrust away that nightmare vision.

CHAPTER V

The Elfin Horns

THE SUN was halfway down the west when they came to the end of the oval plain. Here the mountain thrust out a bastion which almost touched the cliff at the right. Into the narrow cleft between the two they filed, and through the semi-gloom of this ravine they marched over a smooth rock floor, their way running always up, although at an easy grade. The sun was behind the westward peaks and dusk was falling when they emerged.

They stood at the edge of a little moor. Upon the left, the arc of the circular mountain resumed its march. The place was, indeed, less a moor than a barren. Its floor was clean white sand. It was dotted with hillocks, mounds flat-topped as though constantly swept by brooms of wind. Upon the slopes of these mounds a tall grass grew sparsely. The hillocks arose about a hundred feet apart, with a singular regularity, like tumuli, graves in a cemetery of giants. The little barren covered about five acres. Around it clustered the forest. He heard the gurgling of a brook.

Suarra led them across the sands until she reached a mound close to the center of the place.

"You will camp here," she said. "Water is close by. You may light a fire, and you can sleep without fear. By dawn we must be away."

She left them, and walked with red-and-yellow robe toward one of the neighboring knolls. The white llama followed her. Graydon had expected Soames to halt her, but he did not. Instead, his eyes flashed some message to Dancret and Starrett. It seemed to Graydon they were pleased that the girl was not to share their camp, that they welcomed the distance she had put between them.

And their manner toward him had changed. They were comradely once more.

"Mind takin' the burros over to water?" asked Soames. "We'll get the fire goin', and chow ready."

Graydon nodded and led the animals over to the brook. Taking them back after they had drunk their fill, he looked over at the mound to which Suarra had gone. At its base stood a small square tent, glimmering in the twilight like silk. Tethered close to it was the white llama, placidly munching grass and grain. Its hampers of woven golden withes were still at its sides. Neither Suarra nor the hooded man was visible. They were, he supposed, within the tent.

At his own hillock a fire was crackling and supper being prepared. As he came up, Starrett jerked a thumb at the little tent.

"Took it out of the saddle-bags," he said. "Looked like a folded umbrella and went up like one. Who'd ever think to find anything like that in this wilderness!"

"Lots of things I t'ink in those saddle-bags we have not yet seen maybe," whispered Dancret.

"You bet," said Soames. "An' the loot we've already seen 's enough to set us all up for life. Eh, Graydon?"

"She has promised you much more," answered Graydon, troubled by the undercurrent in the New Englander's voice.

"Yeah," said Soames, "yeah—I guess so. But—well, let's eat."

The four sat around the burning sticks, as they had for so many nights before his fight with Starrett. And, to Graydon's astonishment, they ignored the weird tragedy of the plain; avoided it, swiftly changed the subject when twice, to test them, he brought it up. Their talk was all of the treasure so close to them, and of what could be done with it when back in their own world. Piece by piece they went over the golden hoard in the white llama's packs; discussed Suarra's jewels and their worth. It was as though they were bent upon infecting him with their own avarice.

"Hell! Why, with only her emeralds none of us'd have to worry!" Starrett repeated, with variations, over and over.

Graydon listened with increasing disquiet. There was

something behind this studied avoidance of the destruction of the scarlet thing by the dinosaurs, this constant reference to the rich loot at hand, the reiterated emphasis upon what ease and luxuries it would bring them all.

Suddenly he realized that they were afraid, that terror of the unknown struggled with treasure lust. And that therefore they were doubly dangerous. Something was hidden in the minds of the three to whose uncovering all this talk was only the preamble.

At last Soames looked at his watch.

"Nearly eight," he said, abruptly. "Dawn breaks about five. Time to talk turkey. Graydon, come up close."

The four drew into a huddle in the shelter of the knoll. From where they crouched, Suarra's tent was hidden—as they were hidden to any watchers in that little silken pavilion looking now like a great silver moth at rest under the moonlight.

"Graydon," began the New Englander, "we've made up our minds on this thing. We're goin' to do it a little different. We're glad and willin' to let bygones be bygones. Here we are, four white men among a bunch of God knows what. White men ought to stick together. Ain't that so?"

Graydon nodded, waiting.

"All right, then," said Soames. "Now here's the situation. I don't deny that what we seen to-day gave us all a hell of a jolt. We ain't equipped to go up against anything like that pack of hissin' devils. But, an' here's the point, we can beat it out an' come back equipped. You get me?"

Again Graydon nodded, alert to meet what he sensed was coming.

"There's enough stuff on that llama and the girl to make all comfortable," went on Soames. "But also it's enough to finance the greatest little expedition that ever hit the trail for treasure. An' that's just what we plan doin', Graydon. Get the hampers an' all that's in 'em. Get the stuff on the girl. Beat it, an' come back. We'll get together a little crowd of hard-boiled guys. The four of us'll take half we find an' the others'll divide the other half. We'll pack along a couple of planes, an' damn soon find out where the girl comes from. I bet those hissin' devils wouldn't stand up long under machine guns an' some bombs dropped from the flyin' crates. An' when the smoke clears away we'll lift the loot an' go back an' sit on the top of the world. What you say to that?"

Graydon fenced for time.

"How will you get the stuff now?" he asked. "And if you get it, how will you get away with it?"

"Easy," Soames bent his head closer. "We got it all planned. There's only the girl an' that old devil in that tent, They ain't watchin', they're too sure of us. All right, if you're with us, we'll just slip over there. Starrett and Danc', they'll take care of the dummy. No shootin'. Just slip a knife between his ribs. Me an' you'll attend to the girl. We won't hurt her. Just tie her up an' gag her. Then we'll stow the stuff on a couple of burros, an' beat it."

"Beat it where?" asked Graydon. He edged a bit closer to Dancret, ready to jerk the automatic from his pocket.

"Beat it out, damn it!" growled Soames. "Me an' Starrett seen a peak to the west both of us recognized when we come in here. Once we hit it I know where we are. An' travelin' light an' all night we can be well on our way to it by this time to-morrow. These woods ain't so thick an' it's full moon."

Graydon moved his hand cautiously and touched Dancret's pocket. The automatic was still there. Before he made that desperate move he would try one last appeal—to fear.

"But you've forgotten one thing, Soames," he said. "There would be pursuit. What could we do with those hell-beasts on our track? Why, man, they'd be after us in no time. You couldn't get away with anything like that."

Instantly he realized the weakness in the argument.

"Not a bit of it," Soames grinned evilly. "That's just the point. Nobody's worryin' about that girl. Nobody knows where she is an' she don't want 'em to. She was damned anxious not to be seen this afternoon. No, Graydon—I figure she slipped away from her folks to help you out. I take my hat off to you—you're a quick worker an' you sure got her hooked. The only one that might raise trouble is the old devil. He'll get the knife before he knows it. Then there's only the girl. She'll be damned glad to show us the way out, happen we get lost again. But me an' Starrett know that peak, I tell you. We'll carry her along so she can't start anybody after us, an' when we get where we know the country we'll turn her loose for a walk back home. An' none the worse off either—eh, boys?"

Starrett and Dancret nodded.

Graydon feigned to consider. He knew exactly what was in Soames' mind—to use him in the cold-blooded murder the three had planned and, once beyond the reach of pursuit, to murder him, too. Nor would they ever allow Suarra to return to tell what they had done. She would be slain—after they had thrown her to Starrett.

"Come on, Graydon," whispered Soames, impatiently. "It's a good scheme, an' we can work it. Are you with us? If you ain't—"

His knife glittered in his hand. Simultaneously Starrett and Dancret pressed close. Their movement gave him the one advantage he needed. He thrust his hand into the Frenchman's pocket, plucked out the gun and as he did so landed a side kick that caught Starrett in the groin. The big man rolled over, groaning. Graydon leaped to his feet. But before he could cover Soames, Dancret's hands were around his ankles, his legs jerked from under him.

"Suarra!" shouted Graydon as he fell. At least, his cry might awaken and warn her. A second shout was choked in mid-utterance. Soames' bony hands were around his neck.

He reached up, and tried to break the strangling clutch. It gave a little, enough to let him grasp one breath. Instantly he dropped his hold on Soames' wrists, hooked the fingers of one hand in the corner of the New Englander's mouth, pulling with all his strength. There was a sputtering curse from Soames, and his hands let go. Graydon tried to spring up, but an arm of the gaunt man slipped over the back of his head and held his neck in the vise of bent elbow against shoulder.

"Knife him, Danc'," snarled Soames.

Graydon suddenly twisted, bringing the New Englander

on top of him. He was barely in time for, as he did so, Dancret struck, his blade just missing Soames. Soames locked his legs around his, trying to jerk him over in range of the little Frenchman. Graydon sank his teeth in the shoulder pressing him. Soames roared with pain and rage; threshed and rolled trying to shake off the grip of Graydon's jaws. Around them danced Dancret, awaiting a chance to thrust.

There came a bellow from Starrett.

"The llama! It's running away! The llama!"

Involuntarily, Graydon loosed his teeth. Soames leaped up. Graydon followed on the instant, shoulder lifted to meet the blow he expected from Dancret.

"Look, Soames, look!" the little Frenchman was pointing. "He's loose! Christ! There he goes—wit' the gold— wit' the jewels—"

The moon had gathered strength, and under its flood the white sands were a silver lake in which the hillocks stood like tiny islands. Golden hampers gleaming on its sides, the white llama was flitting across that lake of silver, a hundred paces away and headed for the cleft through which they had come.

"Stop it!" shouted Soames, forgetting all else. "After it, Starrett! That way, Danc'! I'll head it off!"

They ran out over the shining barren. The llama changed its pace, trotted leisurely to one of the mounds, and bounded to its top.

"Close in! We've got it," cried Soames. The three ran to the hillock, on which the white beast stood looking calmly around. They swarmed up the mound from three sides.

As their feet touched the sparse grass a mellow note rang out, one of those elfin horns Graydon had heard chorusing so gayly about Suarra that first day. It was answered by others, close and all about. Again the single note. And then the answering chorus swirled toward the hillock of the llama, hovered over it, and dropped like a shower of winged sounds upon it.

Graydon saw Starrett stagger as though under some blow, then whirl knotted arms as though warding off invisible attack. A moment the big man stood thus, flailing with frantic arms. He cast himself to the ground and rolled down to the sands. The notes of the elfin horns swarmed away from him, to concentrate upon Soames. He had thrown himself face downward on the slope of the mound and was doggedly crawling to the top. He held one arm stiffly, shielding his face.

Shielding his face against what?

All that Graydon could see was the hillock and on it the llama bathed in the moonlight, Starrett at the foot of the mound and Soames now nearly at its crest. Dancret, upon the opposite side, he could not see at all.

The horn notes were ringing in greater volume, scores of them, like the bugles of a fairy hunt. What it was that made those sounds was not visible to him, nor did they cast any shadow in the brilliant moonlight. But he heard a whirring as of hundreds of wings.

Soames had reached the edge of the mound's flat summit. The llama bent its head, contemplating him. As he scrambled over that edge and thrust out a hand to grasp its bridle, it flicked about, sprang to the opposite side and leaped to the sands.

The clamor of the elfin horns about Soames had never stilled. Graydon watched him wince, strike out, bend his head and guard his eyes as though from a shower of blows. And whatever was that attack of the invisible, it did not daunt him. He leaped across the mound and slid down its side, close behind the llama. As he reached the base, Starrett arose, swaying drunkenly.

The horn notes ceased abruptly, like candles blown out by a sudden blast. Dancret came running around the slope. The three stood arguing, gesticulating. Their clothes were ripped to rags, and as Soames shifted and the moonlight fell full upon him, his face showed streaked with blood.

The llama was walking across the sands, as slowly as though it were tempting them to further pursuit. It was strange how its shape now stood out sharply, and now faded almost to a ghostly tenuity. When it reappeared, it was as if the moonbeams thickened, swirled, wove swiftly, and spun it from themselves. The llama faded—and then grew again upon the warp and woof of the rays like a pattern on an enchanted loom.

Starrett's hand swept down to his belt. Before he could cover the white beast with his automatic, Soames caught his wrist. He spoke wrathfully, peremptorily. Graydon knew he was warning Starrett of the danger of the pistol crack, urging silence.

The three scattered, Dancret and Starrett to the left and right to flank the llama, Soames approaching it cautiously to keep from frightening it into a run. But as he neared it, the animal broke into a gentle lope and headed for another hillock.

For an instant Graydon thought he saw upon the crest of that mound the figure in motley, red staff raised and pointing at the llama. He looked more intently and decided his eyes had played a trick upon him, for the crest was empty. The llama leaped lightly up to it. As before, Soames and the two others closed in. They swarmed up the mound.

Instantly the elfin horns rang out—menacingly. The three hesitated, stopped their climbing. Then Starrett slid down, ran back a few paces, raised his pistol and fired. The white llama fell.

"The fool! The damned fool!" groaned Graydon.

The silence that followed the shot was broken by a tempest of the elfin horns. It swept down up the three. Dancret shrieked, and ran toward the camp, beating the air as he came. Halfway, he dropped and lay still. And Soames and Starrett they, too, were buffeting the air with great blows, ducking and dodging. The elfin horns were now a raging tumult—death creeping into their notes.

Starrett fell to his knees, arose and lurched away. He fell again, not far from Dancret and lay as still as he. And now Soames went down, fighting to the last. The three lay upon the sands, motionless.

Graydon shook himself into action, and leaped forward. He felt a touch upon his shoulder. A tingling numbness ran through his body. With difficulty he turned his head. Behind him was the figure in motley. His red staff it was that had taken from him all power to move, even as it had paralyzed the spider-man and sent him into the jaws of the dinosaurs.

The red staff pointed to the three bodies. Instantly, as at some command, the clamor of the horns lifted from around them, swirled high in air—and stilled. At the top of the hillock the white llama was struggling to its feet. A band of crimson ran across one silvery flank, the mark of Starrett's bullet. The llama limped down the mound.

As it passed Soames it nosed him. The New Englander's head lifted. He tried to arise, and fell back. The llama nosed him again. Soames squirmed up on hands and knees; eyes fixed upon the golden panniers, he began to crawl after the beast.

The white llama walked slowly, stiffly. It came to Starrett's body and touched him as it had Soames. And Starrett's massive head lifted and he tried to rise, and failing even as had Soames, began like him to crawl behind the animal.

The white llama paused beside Dancret. He stirred, and lurched, and followed it on knees and hands.

Over the moon-soaked sands, back to the camp they trailed—the limping beast with the blood dripping from its wounded side. Behind it the three crawling men, their eyes fixed upon the golden-withed panniers, their mouths gasping, like fish being drawn up to shore.

The llama reached the camp fire and passed on. The crawling men reached the fire and were passing in the llama's wake. The figure in motley lowered his rod.

The three men ceased their crawling. They collapsed beside the embers as though all life had abruptly been withdrawn.

The strange paralysis lifted from Graydon as swiftly as it had come upon him; his muscles relaxed, and power of movement returned. Suarra ran by him to the llama's side, caressed it, strove to stanch its blood.

He bent over the three. They were breathing stertorously, eyes half closed and turned upward so that only the whites were visible. Their shirts had been ripped to ribbons. And on their faces, their breasts and their backs were dozens of small punctures, the edges clean cut as though by sharp steel punches. Some were bleeding, but on most of them the blood had already dried.

He studied them, puzzled. The wounds were bad enough, of course, yet it did not seem to him that they accounted for the condition of the three. Certainly they had not lost enough blood to cause unconsciousness; no arteries had been touched, nor any of the large veins.

He took a bucket and drew water from the brook. Returning, he saw that Suarra had gotten the llama upon its feet again, and over to her tent. He stopped, loosed the golden panniers, and probed the wound. The bullet had plowed almost through the upper left flank, but without touching the bone. He extracted the lead and bathed and dressed the injury with strips of silken stuff the girl handed him. He did it all silently, nor did she speak.

He drew more water from the brook, and went back to his own camp. He saw that the hooded figure had joined the girl. He felt its hidden eyes upon him as he passed. He spread blankets, and pulled Soames, Dancret and Starrett up on them. They had passed out of the stupor, and seemed to be sleeping naturally. He washed the blood from their faces and bodies, and dabbed iodine into the deepest of the peck-like punctures. They showed no sign of awakening under his handling.

Graydon covered them with blankets, walked away from the fire, and threw himself down on the white sands, Foreboding rested heavily on him, a sense of doom. And as he sat there, fighting against the depression sapping his courage, he heard light footsteps, and Suarra sank beside him. His hand dropped upon hers, covering it. She leaned toward him, her shoulder touched him, her cloudy hair caressed his cheek.

"It is the last night, Graydon," she whispered, tremulously. "The last night! And so—I may talk with you for awhile."

He answered nothing to that, only looked at her and smiled. Correctly she interpreted that smile.

"Ah, but it is, Graydon," she said. "I have promised. I told you that I would save you if I could. I went to the Mother, and asked her to help you. She laughed—at first.

But when she saw how serious it was with me, she was gentle. And at last she promised me, as woman to woman—for after all the Mother *is* woman—she promised me if there was that within you which would respond to her, she would help you when you stood before the Face and—"

"The Face, Suarra?" he interrupted her.

"The Face in the Abyss!" she said, and shivered. "I can tell you nothing more of it. You—must stand before it. You—and those three. And, oh Graydon—you must not let it conquer you . . . you must not. . . ."

Her hand drew from beneath his, clenched it tight. He drew her close to him. For a moment she rested against his breast.

"The Mother promised," she said, "and then I knew hope. But she made this condition, Graydon—if by her help you escape the Face, then you must straightway go from this Forbidden Land, nor speak of it to any beyond its borders—to no one, no matter how near or dear. I made that promise for you, Graydon. And so"—she faltered—"and so—it is the last night."

In his heart was stubborn denial of that. But he did not speak, and after a little silence she said, wistfully—

"Is there any maid who loves you—or whom you love—in your own land, Graydon?"

"There is none, Suarra," he answered.

"I believe you," she said, simply, "and I would go away with you—if I could. But I cannot. The Mother loves and trusts me. And I love her—greatly. I could not leave her even for—"

Suddenly she wrenched her hand from his, clenched it and struck it against her breast.

"I am weary of Yu-Atlanchi! Yes, weary of its ancient wisdom and its deathless people! I would go into the new world where there are babes, and many of them, and the laughter of children, and life streams swiftly, passionately—even though it is through the opened Door of Death that it flows at last. For in Yu-Atlanchi not only the Door of Death but the Door of Life is closed. And there are few babes, and of the laughter of children—none."

51

He caught the beating hand and soothed her.

"Suarra," he said, "I walk in darkness, and your words give me little light. Tell me—who are your people?"

"The ancient people," she told him. "The most ancient. Ages upon ages ago they came here from the south where they had dwelt for other ages still. One day the earth rocked and swung. It was then that the great cold fell, and the darkness and the icy tempests. And many of my people died. Then those who remained journeyed north in their ships, bearing with them the remnant of the Serpent-people who had taught them the most of their wisdom. And the Mother is the last of that people.

"They came to rest here. At that time the sea was close and the mountains had not yet been born. They found hordes of the Xinli occupying this land. They were larger, far larger, than now. My people destroyed most of them, and bred down and tamed those they spared, to their own uses. And here for another age they dwelt as they had in the south, where their cities were now beneath mountains of ice.

"Then there were earth shakings, and the mountains began to lift. Their wisdom was not strong enough to keep the mountains from being born, but they could control their growth around their city. Slowly, steadily, through another age the mountains uprose. Until at last they girdled Yu-Atlanchi like a vast wall—a wall which could not be scaled. Nor did my people care; indeed, it gladdened them. Because by then the Lords and the Mother had closed the Gate of Death. And my people cared no more to go into the outer world. And so they have dwelt—for other ages more."

Again she was silent, musing. Graydon looked at her, struggling to hide his incredulity. A people who had conquered death! A people so old that their ancient cities were covered by the Antarctic ice! The latter—well, that was possible. Certainly, the South Polar continent had once basked beneath a warm sun. Its fossils of palms and other vegetation that could only have lived at tropical temperatures were proof of that. And quite as certainly what are now the poles at one time were not. Whether the change had come about a sudden tipping of earth's axis, or a gradual readjustment, science was not agreed. But whatever it was that had happened, it must have taken place at least a million years ago. If Suarra's story were true, if she were not merely reciting myth, it placed the origin of man back into an inconceivable antiquity.

And yet . . . it might be . . . there were many mysteries . . . legends of lost lands and lost civilizations that must have some basis in fact . . . the Mother Land of Mu, Atlantis, the unknown race that ruled Asia from the Gobi when that dread desert was a green Paradise . . . yes, it might be. But that they had conquered Death? No! That he did not believe.

He spoke with an irritation born of his doubts.

"If your people were so wise why did they not come forth and rule this world?"

"Why should they have?" she asked in turn. "If they had come forth what could they have done but build the rest of earth into likeness of this Yu-Atlanchi—as it was built in likeness of that older Yu-Atlanchi? There were none too many of them. Did I not say that when the Door of Death was closed so also was the Door of Life? It is true that always there have been some who elect to throw open these doors—my father and my mother were of these, Graydon. But they are few—so few! No, there was no reason why they should go beyond the barrier. All that they needed, all that they wanted, was here.

"And there was another reason. They had conquered dream. Through dream they create their own worlds; do therein as they will; live life upon life as they will it. In their dreams they shape world upon world—and each of these worlds is as real to them as this is to you. And so—many let the years stream by while they live in dream. Why should they have gone or why should they go out into this one world when they can create myriads of their own at will?"

"Suarra," he said, abruptly. "Just why do you want to save me?"

"Because," she murmured, slowly, "because you make me feel as I have never felt before. Because you make me

53

happy—because you make me sorrowful! I want to be close to you. When you go—the world will be darkened—"

"Suarra!" he cried, and drew her, unresisting now, to him. His lips sought hers and her lips clung.

"I will come back," he whispered. "I will come back, Suarra."

"Come back!" her soft arms tightened round his neck. "Come back to me—Graydon!"

She thrust him from her, leaped to her feet.

"No! No!" she sobbed. "No—Graydon! I am wicked. No—it would be death for you."

"As God lives," he told her, "I will come back to you."

She trembled; leaned forward, pressed her lips again to his, slipped from his arms and ran to the silken tent. For a moment she paused there—stretched wistful hands toward him; and was hidden in its folds. There seemed to come to him, faintly, heard only by his heart, her voice—

"Come back! Come back—to me!"

CHAPTER VI

The Face in the Abyss

THE WHITE SANDS of the barren were wan in the first gleam of the dawn. A chill wind was blowing down from the heights. Graydon walked over to the three men, and drew their blankets aside. They were breathing normally, seemed to be deep in sleep, and the strange punctured wounds had closed. And yet—they looked like dead men, livid and wan as the pallid sands beneath the spreading dawn. He shivered again, but this time not from the touch of the chill wind.

He drew his automatic from Soames' belt, satisfied himself that it was properly loaded and thrust it into his pocket. Then he emptied all their weapons. Whatever the peril they were to meet, he was convinced that it was one against which firearms would be useless. And he had no desire to be again at their mercy.

He went back to the fire, made coffee, threw together a breakfast and returned to the sleeping men. As he stood watching them, Soames groaned and sat up. He stared at Graydon blankly, then stumbled to his feet. His gaze roved round restlessly. He saw the golden panniers beside Suarra's tent. His dull eyes glittered, and something of crafty exultance passed over his face.

"Come, Soames, and get some hot coffee in you," Graydon touched his arm.

Soames turned with a snarl, his hand falling upon the butt of his automatic. Graydon stepped back, his fingers closing upon the gun in his pocket. But Soames made no further move toward him. He was looking again at the panniers, glinting in the rising sun. He stirred Starrett with his foot, and the big man staggered up, mumbling. The movement aroused Dancret.

Soames pointed to the golden hampers, then strode stiffly to the silken tent, useless pistol in hand, Starrett and Dancret at his heels. Graydon began to follow. He felt a light touch on his shoulder. Suarra stood beside him.

"Let them do as they will, Graydon," she said. "They can harm no one—now. And none can help them."

They watched silently as Soames ripped open the flap of the silken tent and passed within. He came out a moment later, and the three set to work pulling out the golden pegs. Soames rolled tent and pegs together and thrust them into one of the hampers. They plodded back to camp, Starrett and Dancret dragging the hampers behind them.

As they passed Graydon, he felt a wonder filled with vague terror. Something of humanness had been withdrawn from them, something inhuman had taken its place. They walked less like men than like automatons. They paid no heed to him or the girl. Their eyes were vacant except when they turned their heads to look at the golden burden. They reached the burros and fastened the hampers upon two of them.

"It is time to start, Graydon," urged Suarra. "The Lord of Folly grows impatient."

He stared at her, then laughed, thinking her jesting. She glanced toward the figure in motley.

"Why do you laugh?" she asked. "He stands there waiting for us—the Lord Tyddo, the Lord of Folly, of all the Lords the only one who has not abandoned Yu-Atlanchi. The Mother would not have let me take this journey without him."

He looked at her more closely—this, surely, was mockery. But her eyes met his steadily, gravely.

"I bow to the wisdom of the Mother," he said, grimly. "She could have chosen no fitter attendant. For all of us."

She flushed; touched his hand.

"You are angry, Graydon. Why?"

He did not answer; she sighed, and moved slowly away. He walked over to the three. They stood beside the embers of the fire, silent and motionless. He shivered—they were so much like dead men, listening for some dread command. He felt pity for them.

He filled a cup with coffee and put it in Soames' hand. He did the same for Starrett and Dancret. Hesitantly, jerkily, they lifted the tins to their mouths, and gulped the hot liquid. He handed them food, and they wolfed it. But always their faces kept turning to the burros with their golden loads. Graydon could stand it no longer.

"Start!" he called to Suarra. "For God's sake, start!"

He picked up the rifles of the others and put them in their hands. They took them, as mechanically as they had the coffee and the food.

Now Suarra's enigmatic attendant took the lead, while between him and the girl plodded the burros.

"Come on, Soames," he said. "Come, Starrett. It's time to go, Dancret."

Obediently, eyes fixed upon the yellow hampers, they swung upon the trail, marching side by side—gaunt man at left, giant in the center, little man at right. Like marionettes they marched. Graydon swung in behind them.

They crossed the white sands, and entered a trail winding through close growing, enormous trees. For an hour they passed along this trail. They emerged from it, abruptly, upon a broad platform of bare rock. Before them were the walls of a split mountain. Its precipices towered thousands of feet. Between them, was a narrow rift which widened as it reached upward. The platform was the threshold of this rift.

He whom Suarra had called the Lord of Folly crossed the threshold, behind him Suarra; and after her the stiffly marching three. Then over it went Graydon.

The way led downward. No trees, no vegetation of any kind, could he see—unless the ancient, gray and dry lichen that covered the path and whispered under their feet could be called vegetation. But it gave resistance, that lichen; made the descent easier. It covered the straight rock walls that arose on each side. The light that fell through the rim of the gorge, hundreds of feet overhead, was faint. But the gray lichen seemed to take it up and diffuse it. It was no darker than an early northern twilight; every object was plainly visible. Down they went and ever down; for half an hour; an hour. Always straight ahead the road stretched, never varying in the width and growing no darker.

The road angled. A breast of rock jutted abruptly out of the cliff, stretching from side to side like a barrier. The new path was darker than the old. He had an uneasy feeling that the rocks were closing high over his head; that what they were entering was a tunnel. The gray lichen dwindled rapidly on the walls and underfoot. And as they dwindled, so faded the light.

At last the gray lichen ceased to be. He moved through a half darkness in which barely could he see, save as shadows, those who went before. And now he was sure that the rocks had closed overhead, burying them. He fought against a choking oppression that came with the knowledge.

And yet—it was not so dark, after all. Strange, he thought, strange that there should be light at all in this covered way—and stranger still was that light. It seemed to be in the air—to be of the air. It came neither from walls nor roof. It seemed to filter in, creeping, along the tunnel from some source far ahead. A light that was as though it came from radiant atoms that shed their rays as they floated slowly by.

Thicker grew these luminous atoms whose radiance only, and not their bodies, could be perceived by the eye. Lighter and lighter grew the way.

Again, and as abruptly as before, it turned.

They stood within a cavern that was like a great square auditorium to some gigantic stage. Perhaps it was the smooth wall of rock a hundred yards ahead that gave Graydon that suggestion. It was like a curtain, raised an inch above the floor. Out of that crack flowed the radiant atoms whose slow drift down the tunnel filled it with the ever-growing luminosity. Here they streamed swiftly, like countless swarms of fireflies each carrying a tiny lamp of diamond light.

As he searched for some outlet to the place, the rocky curtain moved. It slid soundlessly aside for a yard or more. He turned—beside him gaunt man, little man, giant man, stood with blank, incurious eyes—

He thought he saw the red staff of the Lord of Folly pass over their heads ... how could that be? ... there stood the silent figure in motley, rod in hand, far off at the entrance of the cavern.

He heard the nasal cursing of Soames, a bellow from Starrett, the piping of Dancret. He swung round to them. Gone, all gone, was that unnatural deadness which had so perplexed him, gone all vagueness of action and of purpose. They were alive, alert—again their old selves.

"What the hell's this place, Graydon? How the hell did I get here?" Soames caught his wrist in iron grip. Suarra answered for him.

"This is the treasure house I promised you—"

"Yeah?" the savage snarl silenced her. "I'm talkin' to you, Graydon. How did I get here? You know, Danc'? You, Bill?"

Their own amazed faces gave him his answer. He swung the rifle against Graydon's side.

"Come clean!"

Again Suarra answered, tranquilly.

"What matter how you came, since you are here—the four of you. There, where the light streams out, is the cavern where the jewels grow from the walls like fruit, and the gold streams like water. They are yours for the taking. Go take them."

He lowered the rifle; studied her, wickedly.

"And what else is there, sister?"

"There is nothing else there," she said. "Except a great face carved of stone."

Slow seconds passed as he weighed her.

"Only a face carved of stone, eh?" he said at last. "Well, then—we will all go to look at it together. Call your man over here."

"No," she said, steadily. "We go no farther with you. You must go alone. I have told you and I tell you again— you have nothing to fear except what may be in yourselves. You fools!" She stamped her foot in sudden wrath—"If we had wished to kill you, could we not have abandoned you to the Xinli? Have you forgotten last night when you pursued the llama? I have fulfilled my promise to you. Argue no more. And beware of me—beware how you anger me further!"

Now Graydon saw Soames' face whiten as she spoke of the llama, and saw him glance furtively at Dancret and Starrett who, too, had paled. The New Englander stood for a minute in thought. When he spoke it was quietly, and not to her.

"All right. As long as we've come this far we won't go without takin' a look at the place. Danc', take your gun an' go over there where we came in. Cover the old dummy, an' keep watch. Bill an' me'll hold on to the girl. An' you, Mister Graydon, you go an' take a peep at the joint, an' tell us what you see. You can take your gun. If we hear you shootin', we'll know there's somethin' there except gold and jewels an'—what was it—yeah, a stone face. March, Mister Graydon—on your way."

He gave him a push toward the radiant opening, and he and Starrett closed in on each side of the girl. Graydon noticed that they were careful not to touch her. He caught a glimpse of Dancret at the cavern's opening. Suarra lifted her face to him. In her eyes were sorrow, agony—and love!

"Remember!" he said. "I am coming back to you!"

Soames could not know the hidden meaning of that farewell; he took its obvious one.

"If you don't," he sneered, "it's goin' to be damned hard on her! I'm tellin' you, fellow."

Graydon did not answer. He walked over to the curtain's edge, swinging his automatic free as he went. He went past the edge, and full into the rush of the radiance. The opened passage was little more than ten feet long. He reached its end, and stood there, motionless. The pistol dropped from his nerveless hand, and clattered upon the rock.

He looked into a vast cavern filled with the diamonded atoms. It was like an immense hollow globe that had been cut in two, and one-half cast away. The luminosity streamed from its curving walls, and these walls were jetty black and polished like mirrors. The rays that issued from them seemed to come from infinite depths within them, darting up and out with prodigious speed—like rays shot up through inconceivable depths of black water beneath which blazed a sun of diamond incandescence.

Out of these curving walls, hanging to them like the grapes of precious jewels in the enchanted vineyards of the Paradise of El-Shiraz, like flowers in a garden of the King of the Jinns, grew clustered gems!

Great crystals, *cabochon* and edged, globular and angled, alive under that jubilant light with the very soul of fire that is the lure of jewels. Rubies that glowed with every rubrous tint from that clear scarlet that is sunlight streaming through the finger tips of delicate maids to deepest sullen red of bruised hearts; sapphires that shone with blues as rare as that beneath the bluebird's wings and blue as deep as those which darken beneath the creamy crest of the Gulf Stream's crisping waves; huge emeralds that gleamed now with the peacock verdancies of tropic shallows, and now were green as the depths of a jungle glade; diamonds that glittered with irised fires or shot forth showers of rainbowed rays; great burning opals; gems burning with amethystine flames; unknown jewels whose unfamiliar beauty checked the heart with wonder.

But it was not the clustered jewels within this chamber of radiance that had released the grip of his hand upon the automatic and had turned him into stone.

It was—the Face!

From where he stood a flight of Cyclopean steps ran down into the heart of the cavern. At their left was the semi-globe of gemmed and glittering rock. At their right was—space. An abyss, whose other side he could not see, but which fell sheer away from the stairway in bottomless depth upon depth.

The Face looked at him from the far side of the cavern. Bodiless, its chin rested upon the floor. Colossal, its eyes of pale blue crystals were level with his. It was carved out of the same black stone as the walls, but within it was no faintest sparkle of the darting luminescences.

It was man's face and the face of a fallen angel's in one;

Luciferean; imperious; ruthless—and beautiful. Upon its broad brows power was enthroned—power which could have been godlike in beneficence, had it so willed, but which had chosen instead the lot of Satan.

Whoever the master sculptor, he had made of it the ultimate symbol of man's age-old, remorseless lust for power. In the Face this lust was concentrate, given body and form, made tangible. And within himself, answering it, Graydon felt this lust stir and awaken, grow swiftly stronger, rise steadily like a wave, lapping and threatening to submerge the normal barriers that had restrained it.

Something deep within him fought against this evil rising tide; fought to hold him back from the summoning Face; fought to drag his eyes from the pallid blue ones.

And now he saw that all the darting rays, all the flashing atoms, were focused full upon the Face, and that over its brow was a wide circlet of gold. From the circlet globules of gold dripped, like golden sweat. They crept sluggishly down its cheeks. From its eyes crept other golden drops, like tears. And out of each corner of the merciless mouth the golden globules dribbled like spittle. Golden sweat, golden tears and golden slaver crawled and joined a rivulet of gold that oozed from behind the Face, thence to the verge of the abyss, and over its lip into the depths.

"Look into my eyes! Look into my eyes!"

It seemed to him that the Face had spoken—that it could not be disobeyed. He did obey. Up leaped the wave, breaking all bonds.

Earth and the dominion of earth, that was what the eyes of the Face were promising him! And from them and into him streamed a flaming ecstasy, a shouting recklessness, a jubilant sense of freedom from every law.

He tensed himself to leap down the steps, straight to that gigantic mask of black rock that sweated, wept and slavered gold; to take from it what it offered; to pay it whatever it should demand of him in return—

A hand gripped his shoulder, a voice was in his ears—Soames' voice:

"Takin' a hell of a long while, ain't you—"

Then a high-pitched, hysterical shouting:

"Bill—Danc'—come quick! Look at this! Christ—"

He was hurled down to the stone; sent rolling. Rushing feet trampled him, kicked him, knocked the breath from him. Gasping, he raised himself on hands and knees, struggled to rise.

Abruptly, the shouts and babble of the three were silenced. Ah . . . he knew why that was . . . they were looking into the eyes of the Face . . . it was promising them what it had promised him . . .

He made a heart-straining effort. He was up! Swaying, sick, he glared into the cavern. Racing down the steps, halfway down them, were gaunt Soames, giant Starrett, little Dancret.

By God—they couldn't get away with that! Earth and the dominion of earth . . . they were his own for the taking . . . the Face had promised them to him first . . .

He leaped after the three—

Something like the wing of an immense bird struck him across the breast. The blow threw him back, and down again upon hands and knees. Sobbing, he regained his feet, stood swaying, then staggered to the steps . . . the eyes of the Face . . . the eyes . . . they would give him strength . . . they would—

Stretched out upon the radiant air between him and the Face, her misty length half-coiled, was the phantom shape of that being, part woman and part serpent, whose image Suarra bore upon her bracelet—that being she had named the Snake Mother.

At one and the same time real and unreal, she floated there. The diamonded atoms swirled round and through her. He saw her—and still plainly through her he could see the Face. Her purple eyes were intent upon his.

The Snake Mother . . . who had promised Suarra as woman to woman that she would help him . . . if he had that within him which could avail itself of her help.

Suarra!

With that memory, his rage and the poison that had poured into him from the eyes of the Face vanished. In their place flowed shame, contrition, a vast thankfulness.

He looked fearlessly into the eyes of the Face. They were but pale blue crystals. The face itself was nothing but carved rock. Its spell upon him was broken!

He looked down the stairway. Soames, Starrett and Dancret were at its end. They were still running—running straight toward the Face. In the crystalline luminosity they stood out like moving figures cut from black cardboard. They were flattened by it—three outlines, sharp as silhouettes cut from black paper. Lank and gaunt silhouette, giant silhouette and little one, they ran side by side. And now they were at the point of the huge chin. He watched them pause there for an instant, striking at each other, each trying to push the others away. Then as one, and as though answering some summons irresistible, they began to climb up the cliffed chin—climbing up to the cold blue eyes and to what those eyes promised.

And now they were in the full focus of the driving rays, the storm center of the luminous atoms. For an instant they stood out, still like three men cut from cardboard, a little darker than the black stone.

They grayed, their outlines grew misty. They ceased their climbing. They writhed—

They faded out!

Where they had been hovered three wisps of stained cloud. The wisps dissolved.

In their place were three great drops of gold.

Sluggishly the three globules began to roll down the Face. They drew together. They became one. This dribbled slowly down to the crawling golden stream; was merged with it; was carried to the lip of the abyss—

Over into the gulf.

From high over that gulf came a burst of the elfin horns, a rush of unseen wings. And now, in the strange light of that cavern, Graydon saw them. Their bodies were serpents, silver scaled. They were winged. They dipped and drifted and eddied before the Face on snowy pinions, like those of ghostly birds of paradise.

Large and small, some the size of the great python, some no longer than the asp, they whirled and coiled and spun through the sparkling air, trumpeting triumphantly, calling to each other with their voices like elfin horns, fencing joyously with each other with bills that were like thin, straight swords.

Winged serpents, paradise-plumed, whose bills were sharp rapiers. Winged serpents sending forth their pæans of fairy trumpets while that crawling stream of which Soames—Dancret—Starrett—were now a part dripped, dripped, slowly, so slowly, down into the abyss.

Graydon dropped upon the step, sick in every nerve and fiber of his being. He crept past the edge of the rock curtain, out of the brilliancy of the diamonded light, out of the sight of the Face and out of hearing of the trumpet-clamor of the flying serpents.

He saw Suarra, running to him.

And consciousness left him.

CHAPTER VII

The Guarded Frontier

THE DIM GREENNESS of a forest glade shadowed Graydon when he opened his eyes. He was lying upon his blanket, and close beside him was his burro, placidly nibbling the grass.

Some one stirred in the shadow and came toward him. It was an Indian, but Graydon had never seen an Indian quite like him. His features were clean cut and delicate, his skin was more olive than brown. He wore a corselet and kilt of quilted blue silk. There was a thin circlet of gold around his forehead, upon his back a long bow and quiver of arrows, and in his hand a spear of black metal. He held out a silken-wrapped packet.

Graydon opened the packet. Within was Suarra's bracelet of the Snake Mother and a *caraquenque* feather, its shaft cunningly inlaid with gold.

"Where is she who sent me these?" he asked. The Indian smiled, shook his head, and laid two fingers over his lips. Graydon understood—upon the messenger had been laid the command of silence. He restored the feather to its covering, and thrust it into the pocket over his heart. The bracelet he slipped with some difficulty over his own wrist.

The Indian pointed to the sky, then to the trees at his left. Graydon knew that he was telling him they must be going. He nodded and took the lead-strap of the burro.

For an hour they threaded the forest—trailless so far as he could see. They passed out of it into a narrow valley between high hills. These cut off all view of the circular mountain, even had he known in what direction to look for it. The sun was half down the western sky. They reached, at dusk, a level stretch of rock through which a little stream cut a wandering channel. Here, the Indian indicated by signs that they would pass the night.

Graydon hobbled the burro where it could graze, made a fire and began to prepare a sketchy meal from his dwindling stores. The Indian had disappeared. Shortly he returned with a couple of trout. Graydon cooked them.

Night fell and with it the Andean cold. Graydon rolled himself up in his blanket, closed his eyes, and began to reconstruct, as far as possible, every step of the afternoon's journey; impressing upon his memory each landmark he had carefully noted after they had emerged from the trees. Soon these blended into a phantasmagoria of jeweled caverns, great faces of stone, dancing old men, in motley—then Suarra floated among these phantoms, banishing them. And then she, too, vanished.

It was long after noon when, having passed through another belt of trees, the Indian halted at the edge of a plateau stretching for unknown distances west and east. He pushed aside some bushes and pointed down. Graydon, following the pointing finger, saw a faint trail a hundred feet beneath him—some animal's runway, he thought, not marked out by human feet. He looked at the Indian, who nodded, pointed to the burro and to Graydon, then down to the trail and eastward. Pointed next to himself, and back the way they had come.

"Plain enough!" said Graydon. "Frontier of Yu-Atlanchi. And here is where I'm deported."

The Indian broke his silence. He could not have understood what Graydon had said, but he recognized the name of Yu-Atlanchi.

"Yu-Atlanchi," he repeated gravely, and swung his hand behind him in a wide gesture. "Yu-Atlanchi! Death! Death!"

He stood aside, and waited for Graydon and the burro to pass him. When man and beast had reached the bottom, he waved his hand in farewell. He slipped back into the forest.

Graydon plodded on for perhaps a mile, eastward as he had been directed. He sank in the underbrush and waited for an hour. Then he turned back, retraced his way, and

driving the burro before him reclimbed the ascent. He had
but one thought, one desire—to return to Suarra. No matter what the peril—to go back to her. He drew over the
edge of the plateau, and stood listening. He heard nothing. He pushed ahead of the burro—walked forward.

Instantly, close above his head, a horn note rang out—
menacingly, angrily. There was a whirring of great wings.

Instinctively, he threw up his arm. It was the one upon
whose wrist he had fastened the bracelet of Suarra. The
purple gems flashed in the sun. He heard the horn note
sound again, protestingly. There was a whistling flurry in
the air close beside him, as of some unseen winged creature striving frantically to check its flight.

Something struck the bracelet a glancing blow. Something like a rapier-point thrust through his shoulder just
where it joined the base of his neck. He felt the blood
gush forth. Something struck his breast. He toppled over
the verge of the plateau, and rolled over and over down to
the trail.

When he came to his senses, he was lying at the foot
of the slope with the burro standing beside him. He must
have lain there unconscious for a considerable time, for
shoulder and arm were stiff, and the stained ground testi-
fied he had lost much blood. There was a gash above his
temple where he had struck a stone during his fall.

He got up, groaning. The shoulder wound was in an
awkward place for examination, but so far as he could
tell, it was a clean puncture. Whatever had made the
wound had passed through the muscles of the shoulder
and neck. It must have missed the artery by a hair, he
thought, painfully dressing the stab.

Whatever had done it? Well, he knew what had
wounded him. One of those feathered serpents he had
seen above the abyss of the Face! One of those Messengers, as Suarra had called them, which had so inexplicably let the four of them pass the frontiers of the
Forbidden Land.

It could have killed him . . . it had meant to kill him . . .
what had checked its slaying thrust . . . diverted it? He
strove to think . . . God, how his head hurt! What had

stopped it.... Why, the bracelet, of course... the glint of the purple gems.

But that must mean the Messengers would not attack the wearer of the bracelet. That it was a passport to the Forbidden Land. Was that why Suarra had sent it to him? So that he could return?

Well, he couldn't determine that now... he must heal his wounds first... must find help... somewhere... before he could go back to Suarra...

Graydon staggered along the trail, the burro at his heels. It stood patiently that night while he tossed and moaned beside the ashes of a dead fire, and fever crept slowly through every vein. Patiently it followed him the next day as he stumbled along the trail, and fell and rose, and fell and rose, sobbing, gesticulating, laughing, cursing—in the scorching grip of that fever. And patiently it trotted after the Indian hunters who ran across Graydon when death was squatting at his feet, and, who being Aymara and not Quicha, carried him to the isolated little hamlet of Chupan, nearest spot in all that wilderness where there were men of his own color who could look after him; and doctored him with their own unorthodox but highly efficient medicines as they went.

Two months passed before Graydon, wounds healed and his strength back, could leave Chupan. How much of his recovery was due to the nursing of the old *padre* and his household, and how much to the doses the Indians had forced into him, he did not know. Nor did he know how much he had revealed in his ravings. But, he reflected, these had probably been in English, and none in Chupan, nor the Indian hunters had a word of that language. Yet it was true that the old *padre* had been strangely disturbed about his leaving, had talked long about demons, their lures and devices, and of the wisdom of giving them wide berth.

During his convalescence there had been plenty of time for him to analyze what he had beheld; rationalize it; dissolve its mystery. Had the three actually turned into globules of gold? There was another explanation—and a far more probable one. The cavern of the Face might be a laboratory of Nature, a crucible wherein, under unknown rays, transmutation of one element into another took place. Within the rock out of which the Face was carved might be some substance which by these rays was transformed into gold. Fulfillment of that old dream ... or inspiration ... of the ancient alchemists which modern science is turning into reality. Had not Rutherford, the Englishman, succeeded in turning an entirely different element into pure copper by depriving it of an electron or two? Was not the final product of uranium, the vibrant mother of radium—dull, inert lead?

The concentration of the rays upon the Face was terrific. Beneath the bombardment of those radiant particles of energy the bodies of the three might have been swiftly disintegrated. The three droplets of gold might have been oozing from the rock behind them ... the three had vanished ... he had seen the drops ... thought the three changed into them ... an illusion.

And the Face did not really sweat and weep and slaver gold. That was the action of the rays upon it. The genius who had cut it from the stone had manipulated that ... Of course!

The lure of the Face? Its power? A simple matter of psychology—once one understood it. That same genius had taken the stone, worked upon it, and reproduced so accurately man's hunger for power that inevitably he who looked upon it responded. The subconsciousness, the consciousness as well, leaped up in response to what the Face portrayed with such tremendous fidelity. In proportion to the strength of that desire within him was the strength of the response. Like calls to like. The stronger draws the weaker. A simple matter of psychology. Again—of course!

The winged serpents—the Messengers? There, indeed, one's feet were solidly on scientific fact. Ambrose Bierce had deduced in his story "The Damned Thing" that there might be such things: H. G. Wells, the Englishman, had played with the same idea in his "Invisible Man"; and de Maupassant had worked it out, just before he went insane, in his haunting tale of the Horla. Science knew the thing was possible, and scientists the world over were trying to find the secret to use in the next war.

Yes, the invisible Messengers were easily explained. Conceive something that neither absorbs light nor throws it back. In such case the light rays stream over that something as water in a swift brook streams over a submerged bowlder. The bowlder is not visible. Nor would be the thing over which the light rays streamed. The light rays would curve over it, bringing to the eyes of the observer whatever image they carried from behind. The intervening object would be invisible. Because it neither absorbed nor threw back light, it could be nothing else.

There is a traveler in the desert. Suddenly he sees before him a rivulet and green palms. They are not there. They are far behind the mountain at whose base they seem to be. The rays of light carrying their images have struck upward, angled over the mountain, struck down, and have been reflected in denser hot air. It is a mirage. The example was not entirely analogous, but the basic principle was the same.

Ah, yes, thought Graydon—the winged Messengers were not hard to understand. And as for their shape—is not the bird but a feathered serpent, or feathered lizard? The plumes of the bird of paradise are only developments of the snake's scales. Science says so. The bird is a feathered serpent. The first bird, the Archeopterix, still had the jaws and teeth and tail of its reptilian ancestors.

But—these creatures understanding and obeying human command? Well, why not? The dog could be trained to do the same thing. There was nothing to puzzle about in that. The dog is intelligent. There was no reason why the flying serpents should have less intelligence than the dog. And that explained the recognition of Suarra's bracelet by the unseen creature that had attacked him.

The Snake Mother?—well, he'd have to see her before he believed in anything half-snake and half-woman. Let that be.

Having explained everything except the Serpent-woman to his own satisfaction, Graydon ceased to think, and in consequence grew rapidly better.

When he had fully recovered, he tried to pay some of his debt of life to whomsoever it was he owed that life. He sent messengers to Cerro de Pasco for funds, and other things. The *padre* could have the altar trappings he had long wished for, and what he gave the Indians made them thank their patron saints or secret gods that they had found him.

He had been lucky, too. He had lost his rifle in his wanderings, and his messengers had been able to pick up a superior, high-power gun in Cerro.

And now, with plenty of ammunition, four automatics, and all the equipment he needed, Graydon was on his way back to the hidden haunted trail. With him was that same patient burro which had shared his adventures in the Hidden Land.

Since leaving Chupan he had borne steadily toward the Cordillera. For the past few days he had seen no trace of Indians. Something whispered to him to be cautious.

Cautious? He smiled at the thought. It was hardly the word for this journey—one man headed deliberately into the range of the power Suarra had named Yu-Atlanchi! Cautious! Graydon laughed outright. Yet, he reflected, one probably could exercise caution even in invading Hell. And Suarra's land, from what he had seen of its phenomena, seemed rather close to some such place of the damned, if not well over its borders. Lingering upon this interesting idea, he took stock of his assets for its invasion.

A first class rifle and plenty of ammunition; four serviceable automatics, two in one of the packs, one at his belt and one tucked in a holster under his armpit. Good enough—but Yu-Atlanchi might have, and probably did have, weapons that could make these look like a bushman's bow and arrow. And what use would automatics and rifles be against the scaly armor of the dinosaurs?

What else had he? A flicker of purple light from his wrist answered him—the gleam of the jewels in Suarra's bracelet. That would be worth a hundred guns and pistols—if it were passport to the Forbidden Land.

When dusk fell on the fourteenth day of his journeying, he was in a little valley between sparsely wooded,

72

close lying ranges. A friendly stream gurgled and chuckled close to him. He made camp beside the brook, stripped the burro, hobbled it, and turned it loose to graze. He built his fire, boiled his tea, and prepared his supper. He measured with his eyes the southern range of hills. Till now he had been lucky in being able to follow the valleys, with few climbs and none of them a stiff one. Here, a mountain lay directly in his path. About two thousand feet high, he reckoned it; not difficult to get over. The trees marched all the way up to its summit, singly and in platoons, and always with the curious suggestion of careful planting.

He lay for awhile, thinking. His right arm was stretched outside his blanket. In the light of the dying fire the purple gems in the bracelet gleamed and waned—gleamed and waned. Larger they seemed to grow—and larger still. Sleep swept over Graydon.

He slept, and he knew that he slept. Still, even in his sleep he saw the gleaming purple jewels. He dreamed— and they guided his dream. He passed swiftly over a moonlit waste. Ahead of him frowned a black barrier. It shrouded him and was gone. He had a glimpse of an immense circular valley rimmed by sky-piercing peaks. He caught the glint of a lake, the liquid silver of a mighty torrent streaming out of the heart of a cliff. He had wheeling visions of colossi, gigantic shapes of stone bathed in the milky flood of the moon, each guarding the black mouth of a cavern.

A city rushed up to meet him; a city ruby-roofed and opal-turreted and fantastic as though built by Djinns from the stuff of dreams.

He came to rest within a vast and columned hall from whose high roof fell beams of dimly azure light. High arose those columns, unfolding far above into wide petalings of opal and emerald and turquoise flecked with gold.

He saw—the Snake Mother!

She lay coiled in a nest of cushions just beyond the lip of a wide alcove set high above the pillared pave. Between her and him the azure beams fell, curtaining the immense niche with a misty radiance that half-revealed, half-shadowed, her.

Her face was ageless—neither young nor old; free from time, free from the etching acid of the years. She might have been born yesterday—or a million years ago.

Her eyes, set wide apart, were round and luminous; they were living jewels filled with purple fires. Her forehead was wide and low; her nose delicate and long, the nostrils a little dilated. Her chin was small and pointed. Her mouth was small, and heart-shaped; her lips were a vivid scarlet.

Down her narrow, childish shoulders flowed hair that gleamed like spun silver. It arrow-headed into a point on her forehead. It gave her face that same heart shape in which her lips were formed—a heart of which the pointed chin was the basal point.

She had little high breasts, uptilted.

Her face, neck, shoulders and breasts were the hue of pearls suffused faintly with rose.

Her coils began just below her tilted breasts.

They were half buried in a nest of silken cushions; thick coils and many; circle upon circle of them, covered with gleaming heart-shaped scales; each scale as exquisitely wrought as though by an elfin carver-of-gems; opaline; mother-of-pearl.

Her pointed chin was cupped in hands as small as a child's. Like a child's were her slender arms, their dimpled elbows resting on her topmost coil.

On her face which was both face of woman and face of serpent—and in some strange fashion neither serpent nor woman—there dwelt side by side an awesome wisdom and a weariness beyond belief—

The Serpent-woman—memory of whom or of her sisters may be the source of those legends of the Naga Princesses whose wisdom reared the cities of the vanished Khmers in the Cambodian jungles; yes, and may be the source of those persistent stories of serpent-women in the folklore of every land.

May even be the germ of truth in the legend of Lilith, first wife of Adam, whom Eve ousted.

It was thus that Graydon saw her—or thus he thought

he saw her. For again and again that question of whether she was as she seemed to him to be, or whether he saw her as she willed him to see her, was to rise to torment him.

He thrilled to the beauty of that little heart-shaped face, the glistening argent glory of her hair, the childish exquisiteness of her.

He gave no heed to her coils, her—monstrousness. It was as though she reached down into his heart and plucked some deep hidden string, silent there since birth.

And in that dream—if dream it was—he knew that she was aware of all this and was well pleased. Her eyes softened, and brooded upon him; the rose-pearl coil upon which was her body raised until her head swayed twice the height of a tall man above the alcove's pave. She nodded toward him. She raised her little hands to her forehead and cupped them; then with oddly hieratic gesture lowered them, tipping the palms as though she poured from them.

Beyond her was a throne that seemed cut from the heart of a colossal sapphire. It was oval, ten feet or more in height, and hollowed like a shrine. It rested upon, or was set within, the cupped end of a pillar of milky rock-crystal. It was empty, although around it clung, he thought, a faint radiance. At its foot were six lesser thrones. One was red as though carved from ruby; one was black as though cut from jet; the four thrones between the two were yellow gold.

The crimson lips of the Snake Mother opened; a slender, pointed, scarlet tongue flicked out and touched them. Whether she spoke or did not speak, Graydon heard her thought.

"I will hold up the hands of this man. Suarra loves him. He pleases me. Except for Suarra, I have no interest in those who dwell in Yu-Atlanchi. The desire of the child flies to him. So let it be! I grow weary of Lantlu and his crew. For one thing, Lantlu draws closer than I like to that Shadow of Nimir they call the Dark Master. Also, he would take Suarra. He shall not."

"By the ancient compact," the Lord of Folly spoke—

"by that compact, Adana, you may not use your wisdom against any of the Old Race. Your ancestors swore it. It was sworn to long and long and long ago, before the ice drove us north from the Homeland. The oath has never been broken. Even you, Adana, cannot break that oath."

"S-s-s-s!" the Snake Mother's scarlet tongue flickered wrathfully—"Say you so! There was another side to that compact. Did not the Old Race swear never to plot against any of us, the Serpent-people? Yet Lantlu and his followers plot with the Shadow. They plot to free Nimir from the fetters which long ago we forged for him. Free, he will seek to destroy us... and why should he not... and perhaps he may!

"Heed that, Tyddo! I say perhaps he may! Lantlu plots with Nimir, who is our enemy; therefore he plots against me—the last of the Serpent-people. The ancient compact is broken. By Lantlu—not by me."

She swayed forward.

"Suppose we abandon Yu-Atlanchi? Pass from it as did my ancestors, and the Lords who were your peers? Leave it to its rot?"

The Lord of Folly did not answer.

"Ah, well, where there is little left but folly, you of course must stay," she nodded her childish head toward him. "But what is there to keep me? By the wisdom of my people! Here was a race of hairless gray apes that we took from their trees. Took them and taught them, and turned them into men. And what have they become? Dwellers in dream, paramours of phantoms, slaves of illusion. The others—swinging ever toward the darkness, lovers of cruelty; retainers of beauty, outwardly—and under their masks, hideous. I sicken of them. Yu-Atlanchi rots—nay, it is rotten. Let it die!"

"There is Suarra," said the Lord of Folly, softly. "And there are others who are still sound. Will you abandon them?"

The Serpent-woman's face softened.

"There is Suarra," she whispered, "and there are—others. But so few! By my ancestors, so few!"

"If it were their fault alone!" said the Lord of Folly.

"But it is not, Adana. Better for them had we razed the barrier that has protected them. Better for them had we let them make their own way against the wilderness, and what of enemies it held. Better for them had we never closed the Door of Death."

"Peace!" answered the Serpent-woman, sadly. "It was my woman's tongue speaking. Yet there is a deeper reason why we may not abandon them. This Shadow of Nimir seeks a body. What this Shadow is, how strong Nimir still may be, what he has forgotten of his old arts, or what new arts he has learned through the ages—I do not know. But this I do know—if this Shadow seeks a body, it is to free Nimir from the stone. We must prepare for battle, Old One. Nimir freed, and victorious—*we* must go! Nor would our going be orderly and as we may desire. And in time he would spread his dominion over all the world, as other ages ago he planned to do. And that must not be!"

The Lord of Folly stirred upon the red throne, flapping about like a great red and yellow bird, uneasily.

"Well," said the Serpent-woman, practically, "I am glad I cannot read the future. If it is to be war, I have no desire to be weakened by knowing I am going to lose. Nor to be bored by knowing I am going to win. If one must exert oneself to such a degree as such war promises, one is surely entitled to the interest of uncertainty."

Graydon, for all the incredible weirdness of what he seemed to be seeing and hearing, chuckled involuntarily at this, it was so amazingly feminine. The Serpent-woman glanced at him, as though she had heard him. There was a half-malicious twinkle in her glowing eyes.

"As for this man who seeks Suarra," she said, "let him come and find me! There is much in what you have said of our error in making life too easy for Yu-Atlanchi, Tyddo. Let us not repeat it. When this man, by his own wit and courage, has found the way to me, and stands before me in body as now he stands in thought, I will arm him with power. If we win, Suarra shall be his reward. In the meantime, for sign, I shall send my winged Messengers to him, that they may know him—and also that he may know he need fear them no more."

The temple faded, and disappeared. Graydon seemed to hear around and above him a storm of elfin buglings. He thought that he opened his eyes, threw off the blanket and arose—

And that all around him, glimmering with pale silver fires, were circles upon circles of the silver-feathered serpents! Whirling and wheeling in countless spirals; hundreds upon hundreds of them, great and small, their plumes gleaming, fencing gayly with long rapier beaks, horn notes ringing—

And were gone.

At dawn he threw together a hasty breakfast, caught the burro and adjusted the packs upon it. Whistling, he set forth, up the mountain. The ascent was not difficult. In an hour he had reached the summit.

At his feet the ground sloped down to a level plain, dotted with huge standing stones. Up from this plain and not three miles from where he stood arose the scarps of a great mountain. Its precipices marched in the arc of an immense circle, on and on beyond sight—

The ramparts of Yu-Atlanchi!

CHAPTER VIII

The Lizard Men

THERE COULD BE no doubt of it. Behind the barrier upon which he looked lay Yu-Atlanchi—and Suarra! The plain studded with the giant menhirs was that over which the spider-man had scuttled. The path along which Graydon had trodden on his way to the Face must be just below him.

He heard high overhead a mellow bugle-call. Three times the notes sounded, then thrice again—from the base of the slope whose top he trod; from far out on the plain; and, last, close to the mountain wall.

He began to descend.

It was early afternoon when he reached the mountain. The rock was basaltic, black and adamantine. Its scarps thrust almost perpendicularly from the plain. They were unscalable; at least, those before him were. Which way should he go? As though answering his question he heard once more the mellow horn note high in air, and southward.

"South it is," said Graydon, cheerfully, and resumed his march.

His eye caught a verdancy, a green banner streaming down the face of the escarpment a hundred feet or more above its base. As he drew near, he saw that there had been a shattering of the rock at this point. Rubble studded with immense bowlders lay piled against the cliff. Bushes and small trees had found foothold and climbed to the top of the breast.

Studying the breast to determine its cause, Graydon saw a narrow crack in the rock wall above the mound. Curiosity drove him to examine it. The burro watched him until he was halfway up the hill, and then with a protesting bray scrambled after him.

He pressed on. He pushed through the last of the bushes. Here he found that the end of the fissure was about four feet wide. It was dark within it. He knelt and shot around the rays of his searchlight. Rocks littered the floor, but the place was dry. He came out, and began to collect his firewood.

When he had thrown down the last armload of faggots, he walked back along the fissure. A hundred paces and his light fell upon a rock wall—the end of it, he supposed. But he found when he reached it that the cleft made an abrupt turn. He heard water dripping, at his left, drops were exuding from the stone, were caught in a small natural basin, then trickled away in a thin stream. He turned his flash upward. He could see no roof, but neither could he see the sky.

Well, he would do some exploring next morning. He drove the burro into the shelter, and tethered it to a spur of rock. After he had eaten, he rolled himself up in his blanket and went to sleep.

He awakened early, the desire hot within him to see where the fissure led. Without bothering to breakfast, he swung down it. When he had gone about three hundred paces past the tiny spring, the passage turned sharply, this time resuming its original direction. Not far ahead was a gray, palely luminous curtain. He snapped off his flash, and crept forward—

It was daylight.

He looked down a rift in the mountain, a hundred feet wide, with smoothly precipitous walls. It ran due east, facing the rising sun. There was no other way to account for the volume of light that filtered down into the narrow canyon. Its floor was level and smooth. Along one side it ran the trickle of the spring. There was no vegetation—not even the hardy, rock-loving lichens.

Graydon went back, watered the burro and tethered it among the bushes.

"Eat hearty, Sancho Panza," he said. "God alone knows when you get your next meal."

He made a fire and broke his own fast. He waited until the burro had filled itself, fastened on the packs, and finally, with considerable difficulty, got the little brute to the canyon door. After that, it ambled along ahead of him contentedly enough.

For a mile the canyon ran as straight as though laid out by a surveyor's level. Then it began to turn and twist, widen and narrow, dip and climb. Small rocks and bowlders appeared in ever-growing numbers on its floor. The trickle, augmented by other seepages from the cliffs, had grown into a small brook. The rocky walls had changed from black to a reddish-yellow. A stunted, pallid vegetation grew sparsely beside the flowing water and among the broken stones.

From time to time he caught glimpses of roughly rounded holes high up the cliffs at his right, apertures that seemed to be the mouths of tunnels or caves. They stared at him from the ocherous rock like huge pupilless eyes. With that sharpening of the faculties the wilderness effects, Graydon sensed that something deadly lurked there. He watched them warily, rifle ready. There was a taint in the air, a faintly acrid, musky odor, vaguely familiar. It was like—now what was it like? It was like the reek of alligators in some infested, sluggish, jungle creek.

The taint in the air grew stronger. The number of the cave mouths increased. The burro began to show nervousness, halting and sniffing.

The canyon made another of its abrupt turns. From beyond the angle that hid the way from Graydon there came an appalling outburst of hissings and gruntings. At the same time gusts of the musky stench smote his nostrils, nauseating him. The burro stood stock-still.

He heard the cries of men. He sprang forward; turned the corner. Just ahead of him were three Indians like the one who had led him to the frontier of the Forbidden Land, but in yellow instead of blue. Circling them, tearing at them with fangs and claws, were a score or more of creatures which at first glance he took for giant lizards. And at second, realized that they were, if not men, at least semi-human.

The things stood a little over four feet high. Their leathery skins were a dirty yellow. They balanced themselves upon squat, stocky legs whose feet were like paws, flat and taloned. Their arms were short and muscular. Their hands were pads, duplicates almost of their feet, but with longer claws.

It was their faces that chilled Graydon's blood. There was no mistaking the human element in them. They were man and lizard inextricably, inexplicably, mingled—as man and spider had been mingled in the scarlet thing Suarra had named the Weaver.

Beyond their narrow, pointed foreheads their heads were covered with scarlet scales which stood upright like multiple cockscombs. Their eyes were red, round and unwinking. Their noses were flat, but under them their jaws extended in a broad six-inch snout armed with yellow fangs, strong and cruel as a crocodile's. They had no chins, and only rudiments of ears.

What sickened him most was that around their loins were filthy strips of cloth.

The three Indians stood back to back in a triangle, battering at the lizard-men with maul-headed clubs of some shining metal. That they had given good account of themselves a half dozen of the creatures, heads crushed in, gave proof. But now in rapid succession first one Indian and then a second was pulled to the ground and hidden by the loathsome bodies.

Graydon threw off his paralysis and shouted to the remaining Indian.

He raised his rifle, took rapid aim, and fired. The lizard-man he had picked out staggered under the impact of the bullet, then dropped. At the report, echoing like a miniature peal of thunder from the rocky walls, the pack turned as one toward him, fanged mouths open and staring, bodies crouched, glaring at him with the unwinking red eyes.

The Indian stooped, lifted the body of one of his comrades, and sprang clear. Freed from fear of hitting him, Graydon emptied his rifle into the creatures. He rapidly reloaded his magazine. Then, as he began dropping them, they broke from their stupor, leaped for the walls, and like true lizards swarmed up the sheer faces of the cliffs. Hissing and screeching, they darted into the black mouths of the caves. They vanished into their dark depths.

The Indian stood with his wounded comrade in his arms. There was amazement and awe on his finely featured brown face. Graydon threw the rifle thong around his neck, and held out both hands in the universal gesture of peace. The Indian gently lowered the other to the ground, and bowed low, the backs of his hands to his forehead.

Graydon walked toward the Indian. He stopped for a moment to look more closely at the creatures his bullets had dropped. He saw that only those whose skulls had been pierced by the high power bullets lay there. And the limbs of these drew up and down spasmodically as though they still lived. One of them had been shot straight through the heart. But still that heart beat on. He could see the leathery yellow chest throb with its pulsations. Only those whose skulls had been crushed by the clubs seemed quite dead.

And again the perverted humanness of these things shook him.

One of them lay face down. The stained breech-clout had slipped off. At the base of its spine was a blunt, scaled tail.

He was aware of the first Indian beside him. He saluted again, and methodically began to crush with his club the heads of those Graydon had shot.

"This," he said in the Aymara, "so they cannot live again. It is the only way."

Graydon walked over to the second Indian. He was unconscious and badly mauled, but not necessarily fatally, so he thought, going carefully over the wounds. He took his emergency kit out of the saddle-bag, treated and bandaged the worst of them. He looked up to see the other Indian standing over him, watching with eyes in which the awe was stronger.

"If we can get him to some place where those brutes can't interrupt, I can do more for him," said Graydon, also in the Aymara tongue, rising.

"A little way," answered the Indian, "and we shall be safe from them, Mighty Lord!"

"Let's go," said Graydon, in English, grinning at the title.

He bent down and lifted the wounded man's shoulders. The Indian took his feet. Burro once more in the lead, they made their way down the canyon.

The openings of the caves watched them. Within them nothing stirred, but Graydon felt upon him the gaze of malignant eyes—the devil eyes of the lizard-men hidden in the shadow of their dens.

CHAPTER IX

In the Lair of Huon

THE CLIFF BURROWS of the lizard-men became fewer; at last the precipices were clean of them. The Indians gave them no attention whatever, satisfied apparently of Graydon's ability to handle any fresh assault by the monsters.

The man they were carrying groaned, opened his eyes, and spoke. His comrade nodded, and set his feet on the ground. He stood upright, looking at Graydon with the same amazement his fellow had shown, and then, as he saw the bracelet of the Snake Mother, with the same awe. The first Indian spoke rapidly, too rapidly, for Graydon to understand. When he had finished, the second took his hand, laid it first upon his heart and then upon his forehead.

"Lord," he said, "my life is yours."

"Where is it that you go?" Graydon asked.

They looked at each other, uneasily.

"Lord, we go to our own place," answered one at last, evasively.

"I suppose you do," said Graydon. "Is that place—Yu-Atlanchi?"

Again they hesitated before replying.

"We do not go into the City, Lord," said the first Indian, finally.

Graydon weighed their evasiveness, their reluctance to give him straight answer, wondering how far he might trust their gratitude. They had asked him no questions whence he had come, nor why, nor who nor what he was. But that reticence had been due to courtesy or some other potent reason; not to any lack of curiosity, for clearly that

85

burned in each. He felt he could expect no such consideration from others he might meet, once he was inside the Hidden Land. He could look for no help, at least not yet, from the Snake Mother. He was convinced that his vision of the Temple had been no illusion. The guiding buglings of the flying serpents, and his immunity from them was proof to him of that. And the Serpent-woman had said that he must win to her by his own wit and courage before she would aid him.

He could not win to her by blundering into Yu-Atlanchi like any reckless fool. But where could he hide until he had been able to reconnoiter, to make some plan. . . .

"You," he turned to the wounded man, decision made for good or bad, "have said your life is mine?"

The Indian again took his hand, and touched it to heart and forehead.

"I would enter Yu-Atlanchi," said Graydon, "but for a time I would not be seen by others there. Can you guide me, give me shelter, none but you knowing of my presence, until such time as I choose to go my own way?"

"Do you jest with us, Mighty Lord?" asked the first Indian. "What does one who wears the symbol of the Mother, and who wields this," he pointed to the rifle, "need of our guidance? Are you not a messenger of . . . her? Did not those who are her servants let you pass? Lord, why jest with us?"

"I do not jest," said Graydon, and, watching them narrowly, added, "Know you the Lord Lantlu?"

Their faces hardened, their eyes became suspicious; he knew that the two hated the master of the dinosaur pack. Good, he would tell them something more.

"I seek the Mother," he said. "If I am not her messenger, I at least am her servant. The Lord Lantlu stands between her and me. There are reasons why I must cope with him without her help. Therefore I must have time to plan, and he must know nothing of me until I have made my plan."

There was relief in their faces, and a curious elation. They whispered.

"Lord," said the first, "will you swear by the Mother,"

again they made reverence to the bracelet, "raise her to your lips and swear by her that what you have said is truth; that you are no friend nor—spy—of the Lord Lantlu?"

Graydon raised the bracelet.

"I do swear it," he said. "May the Mother destroy me utterly, body and spirit, if what I have told you is not truth."

He kissed the tiny coiled figure.

Once more the Indians whispered.

"Come with us, Lord," said the one who had vowed himself to Graydon. "We will take you to the Lord Huon. Until we come to him, ask us no more questions. You have asked us for shelter against the Lord Lantlu. We guide you to the only shelter against him. And you shall have it —if the Lord Huon wills it. If he does not will it—we will go with you or die with you. Can we do more?"

"By God!" said Graydon, touched to the heart, "neither you nor any man could do more for another. But I do not think that your Lord Huon, whoever he may be, will hold grudge against you for bringing me to him."

Rapidly he went again over the wounded man; the tears and gashes were bad enough, but no arteries had been cut and no vital organs touched.

"You have lost much blood," Graydon told him. "I think we should carry you."

But he would not have it so.

"It is but a little way now," he said. "There is poison in the fangs and claws of the Urd, the lizard-men. The water of flame which you poured into my wounds burned most of it away, but not all. I feel it, and it is better that I walk if I can."

"The Urd poison carries sleep," explained the first Indian. "The sleep ends in death. The Mighty Lord's water of flame conquered that sleep and made him awaken. Now he fears if he is carried he may sleep again, since, he says, the flame-water has ceased to burn."

Graydon smiled at the description of the iodine that he had used on the wounds. Nevertheless, the reasoning was sound enough. If the venom of the lizard-men had a narcotic action, then in the absence of any neutralizing agent the exercise of walking would help throw off the poison. He lifted the bandages from the deepest gashes and poured more iodine into them. By the tightening of the muscles, he knew that the stuff bit.

"It is good," said the Indian, "the water of flame burns."

"It burns the poison," said Graydon cheerfully. "If you have any other medicine, it will be well to use it."

"There is such where we go," said the first Indian. "But had it not been for yours, Lord, he would now be well advanced in the Urd sleep—and that is no peaceful one. Now let us go as quickly as we can."

They resumed their way along the canyon. They had traveled probably a mile when, abruptly, the two walls of the cliffs swung toward each other. Separating them was a fissure some twenty feet wide, clean cut as though chiseled out of the rocks, and black as a starless night.

"Wait here," said the first Indian, and walked to the fissure's mouth. He drew from his pouch something that seemed to be a globe of rock crystal about as big as a tennis ball, its back cased in a cone of metal. He raised the globe above his head. A light sprayed from it into the tunnel. It was not a ray; it was like a swiftly moving, luminous ball of cloud. He dropped the globe back into his pouch, and beckoned.

They entered the fissure. It was no longer dark. It was filled with a pale luminosity, as though the cloud from the globe had dispersed a phosphorescent mist. They walked on a thousand feet or more. The Indian did not use the globe again, yet the light persisted.

He halted. Graydon saw that the fissure had ended. Outside was blackness. Far below was the sound of rushing water. The Indian raised the cone. Again the luminous cloud sprayed out.

Graydon gasped. The luminous vapor was speeding over an abyss. Suddenly the face of a cliff sprang out, a hundred yards away. The cloud of light had impinged upon it. Instantly a part of the cliff lifted like an immense curtain. Out of the revealed portal shot a metal tongue, flat, ten feet wide. It licked over the abyss, following the path of light. It halted at their feet.

The Indians smiled at Graydon, reassuringly.

"Follow me, Lord," one said. "There is no danger."

Graydon stepped upon the span, the burro at his heels. The roar of the torrent, hundreds of feet below, came up to him.

They reached the end of that strange bridge. The Indians drew up beside him. They marched on for fifty paces. Looking back, he saw the entrance to the passage like a great gate of twilight. He heard a soft sighing, and the rectangle of twilight was blotted out. The curtain of rock had fallen.

Now light was all around him, soft and suffused as though it were a quality of the air itself. He stood in a chamber that was a hollow cube perhaps a hundred feet square. Walls and roof were of polished black stone, and in the stone were tiny, swiftly moving luminous corpuscles like those he had watched stream out of the ebon walls of the cavern of the Face. They were the source of the light.

The place was empty, no sign of the passage through which they had come, nor of openers of the rock, nor machinery that controlled its opening; nor was there sign of door; nor was there trace of openings within the other walls. Yet Graydon heard a murmuring as of many people whispering within the chamber, and then a curt sentence, too rapidly spoken for him to understand.

The unwounded Indian saluted, and walked forward a few paces. He answered the challenger in the same rapid speech. But Graydon had no difficulty in getting his meaning. He was telling of the battle with the lizard-men. He finished; there was a brief silence, and then from the unseen speaker came another quick command. The Indian beckoned.

"Lord, hold up the bracelet," he said.

By now, of course, Graydon had realized that the unseen speaker was not really in the rock chamber, but behind the wall. His voice was carried by some tube device no doubt, and there were probably peepholes. Still, he could see no sign of either, the shining black surface seemed unpierced, smooth as unbroken glass. He lifted the wrist on which was the golden image of the Snake Mother. The purple eyes gleamed. There was a louder burst of the murmurings, exclamations; another command.

"Lay down your weapon, Lord," said the Indian, "and go forward to the wall."

And then as Graydon hesitated:

"Do not fear. We will stand beside you—"

The voice of the unseen speaker interrupted, sternly. The Indian shook his head, and took his stand beside Graydon, his comrade at the other hand. Graydon, knowing they had been ordered to remain behind while he went on alone, laid his rifle upon the floor, and whispered to them to obey. He walked forward, loosening the pistol in his armpit holster. And as he halted, the light blinked out.

Only for a moment did the darkness hold. When the radiance returned a third of the wall had vanished. Where it had been there stretched a corridor, wide and well lighted. On each side of it was a file of the Indians. Another file stood between him and the pair with the burro. They carried spears tipped with some shining black metal; they bore small round shields of the same substance. Their straight black hair was held by narrow fillets of gold. They were naked except for short kilts of quilted yellow silk. All this Graydon saw in one swift glance before his gaze came to rest upon the man beside him.

He was a giant of a man, his face that of a pure-blood of Suarra's and Lantlu's race; or had been, before catastrophic fight had marred it. He stood a good eight inches over Graydon's six-foot height. His hair was silver white, cut to the nape of his neck and held by a fillet of amber lacquer. From right temple to chin ran four parallel lines of livid scars. His nose had been broken and flattened. From his shoulders fell a coat-of-mail of the black metal, linked like those the Crusaders wore. It was gathered in at his waist by a belt. Chain mail breeches covered his thighs and legs to the knees, baggily. The lower legs were protected by grieves from knees to the ankles of the sandaled feet. His right arm had been cut off at the elbow, and attached to that elbow by a band of gold and held by a shoulder harness was a murderous three-foot metal bar. In his belt was a short double ax, twin to those which were the symbols of ancient Crete.

Formidable enough he was, but Graydon, looking into his eyes, drew from them reassurance. There were wrinkles of laughter at their corners, and humor and toleration that even his present suspicion and puzzlement could not entirely efface. Nor, despite his silver hair, was he old; forty at most, Graydon judged.

He spoke in the Aymara, and with a gusty, huskily roaring bass.

"And so you want to see Huon! Well, so you shall. And do not think us lacking in gratitude that I kept you waiting so long, and took from you your weapon. But the Dark One is subtle, and Lantlu, may his Xinli shred him, is like him. Nor would this be the first time that he has tried to foist spies upon us in the guise of those who would do us service. Regor is my name, Black Regor some call me. My blackness is not that of the Dark One, yet I, too, am subtle. But it may be that you know nothing of this Dark One—eh, lad?"

He paused, eyes shrewd.

"Some little I have heard of him," answered Graydon, cautiously.

"Eh, some little you have heard of him! Well, and what did that little make you think of him?"

"Nothing!" answered Graydon, quoting an Aymara proverb that holds certain obscurely improper implications, "nothing that would make me want to sit cheek by jowl and break eggs with him."

"Ho! ho!" roared the giant, and swung his bar dangerously close. "But that is good! I must tell Huon that—"

"And besides," said Graydon, "is he not the enemy of—her?" He lifted the bracelet.

Black Regor checked his laughter; gave an order to the guard.

"Walk beside me," he told Graydon. Looking back before obeying, he saw one of the two Indians pick up his rifle gingerly, and both of them take up the march on each side of the burro. He wondered uneasily, as he tried to match Regor's strides, whether he had locked the gun before dropping it; then decided that he had.

A graver doubt began to grow. He had been building up a fabric of hope based on the idea that Huon, whoever he might be, was bitter enemy of Lantlu, would welcome his aid and help him in return for it. And he had intended to tell him the whole story of his encounter with Suarra, and what had followed. Now this seemed too naïve of him. The situation was not so simple as all that. After all, what did he know of these people with their sinister arts—their spider-folk and their lizard-folk and God alone knew what other monstrosities?

And what after all did he really know of that utterly weird, incredible creature—the Snake Mother?

Graydon felt a momentary despair. He resolutely put it aside. He would have to recast his ideas, that was all. And he had few enough minutes in which to do it. Better make no plans at all until he met this Huon, and had a chance to gauge him.

A sharp challenge brought him back to alertness. Before him the corridor was barred by immense doors of the black metal. Guarding them was a double file of the yellow-kilted soldiers, the first rank made up of spears, and the second of archers bearing long metal bows. They were captained by a thick-set, dwarfish Indian whose double ax almost dropped from his hand as he caught sight of Graydon.

To him Regor whispered. The captain nodded, and stamped upon the floor. The valves of the great door separated, folds of filmy curtains like a waterfall of cobwebs through which an amber sun was shining billowing out between them.

"I go to tell Huon of you," rumbled Regor. "Wait patiently." He melted within the webs. The door closed silently behind him.

And silently Graydon waited; silently the yellow-kilted guards stared at him, and long minutes passed by. A bell sounded; the great doors parted. He heard a murmur from beyond the webs. The captain beckoned to the two Indians. Driving the burro before him they passed into the hidden room. A still longer time, and then once more the bell and the opened door. The captain signaled, and Graydon walked forward and through the webs.

His eyes were dazzled by what seemed sunlight flooding through amber glass. Details sharpened. He had a vague impression of walls covered with tapestries of shifting hues. He blinked up, and saw that the roof of the chamber was of the same polished stone as the corridors, amber colored instead of black, and that the intenser light came from denser spirals of the radiant swirling corpuscles.

A woman laughed. He looked toward the laughter—and leaped forward, the name of Suarra on his lips. Some one caught him by the arm and held him back—

And suddenly he knew that this laughing woman was not Suarra.

She lay stretched upon a low couch, head raised and resting upon one long white hand. Her face was older, but still it was the exquisite twin of Suarra's, and like Suarra's was her cloudy midnight hair. There the resemblance ended. Upon that lovely face was a mockery alien to the sweetness of the girl. There was a touch of cruelty upon the perfect lips, and something of inhuman withdrawal in the clear dark eyes—nothing of the tenderness within Suarra's; something, rather, of what he had seen on the face of Lantlu when the dinosaur pack had sighted the Scarlet Weaver. A slender white foot swung over the edge of the couch, negligently balancing upon a toe a silken sandal.

"Our unbidden guest seems impetuous, Dorina," came a man's voice, speaking the Aymara. "If simple tribute to your beauty, I applaud. Yet to me it seemed to savor something of—recognition."

The speaker had risen from a chair at the head of the couch. His face was of that extraordinary beauty which seemed the heritage of all this strange race. The eyes were the deep blue that usually promises friendliness, but there was none of it in them now. Like Regor, his ruddy hair was filleted with amber. Under the white, toga-like robe that covered him, Graydon sensed the body of an athlete.

"You know I am no Dream-maker, Huon," drawled

the woman. "*I* am a realist. Where but in dreams could I have met him? Still, although no Dreamer—perhaps—had I known—"

Her voice was faintly languishing, but there was malicious mockery in the glance she gave Graydon. Huon flushed, his eyes grew bleak; he spoke one sharp word. Immediately, Graydon's chest was encircled as though by a vise, crushing his ribs, stifling him. His hands flew up to break that grip, and closed on a thin, stringy arm that seemed less flesh than leather. He twisted his head. Two feet above him was a chinless, half-human face. Long, red elf locks fell over its sharply sloping forehead. Its eyes were round and golden, filled with melancholy; filled, too, with intelligence.

A spider-man!

Another stringy arm covered with scarlet hair circled his throat. A third caught him under the knees and lifted him on high.

He heard a roar of protest from Regor. Blindly, he struck out at the chinless face close to his, and as he struck, the purple stones in the golden bracelet flashed like a tiny streak of fire. He heard a grunt from the spider-man, a sharp cry from Huon.

He felt himself falling, falling ever faster through blackness—then felt and heard no more.

CHAPTER X

Outlaws of Yu-Atlanchi

HIS SENSES were struggling back; a gusty voice was shouting wrathfully.

"He wears the ancient symbol of the Mother. He passes her Watchers. He routs the stinking Urd who serve the Dark One, spittle on his name! Each alone enough to win a hearing! I tell you again, Huon, here was a man to be received with courtesy; one who had a tale to tell and that tale a matter of concern not only to you but all the Fellowship. And you toss him to Kon, unheard! What of Adana when she learns of it? By every jeweled scale of her coils, we have yearned lustily enough for her aid, and never broken through her indifference! This man might have won her to us!"

"Enough, Regor, enough!" It was Huon's voice, depression in it.

"It is not enough," stormed the giant. "Was it the Dark One bade you do this? By the Lord of Lords, the Fellowship must deal with you!"

"You are right, of course, Regor. It is your duty to summon the Fellowship, if you think best. I am sorry and I am ashamed. When the stranger awakens from his swoon, and indeed I am sure it is no worse, I will make amends to him. And the Fellowship, not I, shall decide what is to be done with him."

"All of which does not seem to flatter me," thus Dorina, sweetly suave, and too sweetly. "Do you hint, Regor, that I am an agent of the Dark One, for clearly it was I who gave the impulse to Huon's rage?"

"I hint nothing—" began the giant, and was interrupted by Huon.

"Dorina, I will answer that. And I say to you that it is no unfamiliar doubt to me. Be careful that some time you do not change that doubt to certainty. For then I will kill you, Dorina, and there is no power in Yu-Atlanchi, nor above it nor below it, that may save you."

It was said calmly enough, but with a cold implacability.

"You dare say that, Huon—"

Graydon knew that more of truth often enters ears thought closed than those believed open. Therefore he had kept quiet, listening, and mustering his strength. A quarrel among these three could not help him. He groaned, and opened his eyes, and thereby silenced whatever had been on the woman's tongue to say. He looked up into Huon's face, in which was nothing but concern; at Dorina, her black eyes blazing, long white hands clenched to her breast in effort to control her rage.

His eyes fell upon a scarlet figure beyond them both. It was Kon, the spider-man, and Graydon forgot his danger and all else, contemplating him.

He was something that might have stepped out of one of Dürer's nightmare fantasies of the Witches' Sabbath, stealing from the picture into reality through a scarlet bath. And yet there was nothing demonic, nothing of the Black Evil, about him. Indeed, he was touched with a grotesque charm, as though created by a master in whom the spirit of beauty was so vital that even in shaping a monster it could not be wholly lost.

The spider-man's head hung three feet above Huon's. The torso, the body, was globular, and little bigger than a lad's. The round body was supported on four slender stilt-like legs; from the center of it stretched out two more, longer by half than the others and terminating in hands or claws whose fingers, delicately slender and needle pointed, were a foot in length.

He had no neck. Where head joined body there was a pair of small arms whose terminations were like the hands of a child. And over these hands was the face, chinless and earless, framed in matted red locks. The mouth was human, the nose a slender beak. Except for face and hands and feet, which were slate gray, he was covered with a vivid scarlet down.

But the eyes, the great lidless lashless eyes of phosphorescent gold, were wholly human in expression, sorrowful, wondering, and apologetic, too—as though Huon's present mood were reflected in them. Such was Kon, highest of all his kind in Yu-Atlanchi, whom Graydon was destined to know much more intimately.

He staggered up, Regor's arm supporting him. He looked straight at the woman.

"I thought," he muttered, "I thought—you were—Suarra!"

The anger flew from Dorina's face; it sharpened, as though with fear; Huon's grew intent; Regor grunted.

"Suarra!" breathed the woman, and loosed her clenched hands.

If Suarra's name brought fear to her, and Graydon felt a fleeting wonder at that, it carried no such burden to Regor.

"I told you, Huon, that this was no ordinary matter," he cried jubilantly, "and here is still another proof. Suarra whom the Mother loves—and he is friend of Suarra! Ha—there is purpose here, a path begins to open—"

"You go a little too fast along it," broke in Huon warningly, yet with a certain eagerness, a repressed excitement. He spoke to Graydon.

"For what has occurred, I am sorry. Even if you are an enemy—still I am sorry. Our welcome to strangers is never too cordial, but this ought not to have happened. I can say no more."

"No need," answered Graydon, a bit grimly. "If not too cordial, at least the welcome was warm enough. It is forgotten."

"Good!" There was a flash of approval in Huon's eyes.

"Whatever *you* may be," he went on, "*we* are hunted men. Those who would destroy us are strong and cunning, and we must ever be alert against their snares. If you come from them, there is no harm in telling you this, since you already know it. But if you seek the Snake Mother and—Suarra—and have happened upon us by chance, it is well for you to know we are outlaws of Yu-Atlanchi, although we are no enemies of those two. Convince us of your honesty, and you shall go from us unharmed, to follow your fortune as you choose; or if you ask our aid, remembering that we are outlaws, we will give you aid to the limit of our means. If you fail to convince us, you shall die as all the baits sent to trap us have died. It will be no pleasant death; we do not delight in suffering, but it is wisdom to discourage others from following you."

"Fair enough," said Graydon.

"You are not of our race," Huon said. "You may be a prisoner sent to betray us, your life and liberty the promised rewards. The bracelet you wear may have been given you to blind us. We do not really know that you passed the Messengers. You may have been guided through the lairs of the Urd, and set down where you met the men who brought you here. That you slew some of the Urd proves nothing. There are many, and their lives are less than nothing to Lantlu and the Dark One whose slaves they are. I tell you all this," he added with a touch of apology, "that you may know the doubts you must dissipate to live."

"And fair enough," said Graydon again. Huon turned to the woman, who had been studying Graydon with a wholly absorbed, puzzled intentness ever since he had named Suarra.

"You will stay with us and help us judge?" he asked.

"As if," drawled Dorina, and stretching herself upon the couch, "as if, Huon, I had the slightest intention of doing anything else!"

Huon spoke to the spider-man; a red arm stretched out and brought a stool to Graydon's feet. Regor lowered his bulk upon another; Huon dropped into his chair. The eyes of that strange quartet upon him, Graydon began his story.

A little he told them of the world from which he had come, and his place in it; as briefly as he could, of his trek into the Forbidden Land with the three adventurers; and of his meeting with Suarra. He heard Regor growl approval as he sketched his battle with Starrett, saw Huon's eyes warm. He told of Suarra's return next morning. And as he spoke of the Lord of Folly, he saw conviction of his truth begin to steal into their faces, and deepen as he told of his glimpse of Lantlu among his hissing pack. But he was amazed to see it turn to such a horror of belief as it did when his story led them into the cavern of the great stone Face.

For as he described that visage of ultimate evil, and the seeming transmutation of the three men into globules of golden sweat, Dorina covered her face with shaking hands, and the blood was drained from Huon's own, and Regor muttered; only Kon, the spider-man, stood unmoved, regarding him with his sorrowful, shining golden eyes.

And this could only mean that none of them had ever seen the Face—and that therefore there were in Yu-Atlanchi secrets hidden even from its dwellers. Some obscure impulse bade him be cautious. So he said nothing of his vision of the Temple, but told them of his awakening, of the Indian he had found beside him as guide, and of his impulsive return. He showed them the scar of the wound that had been its penalty.

"As for what it was that summoned me back," he said, "I cannot tell you—at least not now. It was a summons I might not disobey—" and that was true enough, he thought, as the face of Suarra came before him, and her appeal echoed in his heart.

"It is all I can say," he repeated. "And all I have said is truth. How the summons came to me has no bearing upon the matter, since because of it I am here. Stay—there is something else—"

He took from his pocket the packet that held Suarra's *caraquenque* plume, opened it and held it toward them.

"Suarra's," breathed Dorina, and Huon nodded.

There was no question of their belief now. It might be well to put a spur to their own self-interest.

"And still there is one more thing," he said slowly. "Regor has spoken of some purpose. Of that purpose, it may be I know as little as you. But this happened—"

He told them of the elfin bugles that had led him across the plain of the monoliths, and finally to the cleft in the ramparts. Huon drew a deep breath and stood erect, hope

blazing upon his face, and Regor leaped to his feet, swinging his clubbed arm in a whistling circle.

Huon clasped Graydon's shoulders.

"I believe!" he said, voice shaking; he turned to Dorina;
"And you?"

"Of course it is truth, Huon!" she answered; but some
swift calculation narrowed her lids and clouded her face,
and Graydon thought for an instant she looked menacingly
at him.

"You are our guest," said Huon. "In the morning you
shall meet the Fellowship, and repeat to them what you
have told us. And then you shall decide whether to call
upon us for help, or go on alone. All that is ours is yours
for the asking. And—Graydon—" he hesitated, and then
with abrupt wistfulness—"by the Mother, I hope you
throw your lot with ours! Regor, see to it that the little
beast is cared for. Take this, Graydon," he stooped and
picked up the rifle. "To-morrow you shall show us what
it is. I will take you to your quarters. Wait for me,
Dorina."

He took Graydon by the arm, and led him toward the
wall of the room opposite that which he had entered. He
parted the webs.

"Follow," he bade.

Graydon looked back as he passed after him. Dorina
was standing, watching him with that menacing speculation stronger upon her face.

Graydon passed through the webs, and followed Huon's
broad back into another faintly sparkling, black-walled
corridor.

CHAPTER XI

The Deathless People

"Up, LAD, bathe and break your fast. The Fellowship will soon be gathering, and I am here to take you to them."

Graydon blinked uncomprehendingly at his awakener. Regor stood at the foot of his couch, on his face a broad smile that his scars turned into the grin of a benevolent gargoyle. He had changed the chain armor for the close-fitting garments that seemed to be the fashion of Yu-Atlanchi's men. Black Regor he still was, however, for these were black, and black was the cloak that hung from his immense shoulders.

Graydon looked around that chamber to which Huon had led him, at the thick rugs which were like spun silk of silver, the walls covered by the webs of shadowy silver through which ran strange patterns of a deeper argent, webs which were drawn aside at one end of the room to reveal a wide alcove in which a sunken pool sparkled. He drew together the threads of memory.

Huon had watched and talked while two silent brown men had bathed and massaged away his weariness and the marks of Kon's talons. And then had sat with him whilst he had eaten unfamiliar meats which two Indian girls, with wide wondering eyes, had set before him in dishes of crystal. Huon himself had poured his wine, asking many questions about the people who dwelt outside the Hidden Land. He had not seemed much interested in their arts or sciences or governments; but avidly so upon how death came to them, and what was done with the old, the customs of mating, whether there were many children and their up-bringing. Ever and ever he had returned to the subject of

101

death and the forms in which it came, as though it held for him some overpowering fascination.

And, at last, he had sat silent, thinking; then, sighing, had said:

"So it was in the old days—and which is the better way?"

He had risen, abruptly, and passed out of the chamber; the light had dimmed, and Graydon had thrown himself upon the couch to sink into deep slumber.

Why had Huon dwelt so persistently upon death? There was something about that which vaguely troubled Graydon. Suddenly he recalled that Suarra had said her people had closed the Door of Death. He realized that he had not taken her literally. But might it be truth—

He roused himself from his reverie, shook himself impatiently, and rising, walked over to the pool, splashed about and dried himself upon silken cloths. He returned to his chamber to find a table set with fruits, and with what seemed like wheaten cakes, and milk. He dressed quickly, and sat down to it. Not till then did Regor speak.

"Lad," he said, "I told you that I am a subtle one. Now my subtlety tells me that so are you, and that very subtly you held back much from your story last night. Notably— your command from the Mother."

"Good Lord," exclaimed Graydon, in the Aymara equivalent. "There's nothing subtle in that discovery. I warned you I couldn't tell you how—"

He stopped, afraid that he had hurt the giant's feelings. But Regor smiled broadly.

"I'm not referring to that," he said. "What you were careful not to mention was the reward the Mother promised you if you obeyed her summons—and managed to reach her."

Graydon jumped, in his astonishment, choking on a bite of the wheaten cake.

"Ho! ho!" roared Regor, and gave him a resounding whack upon the back. "Am I not a subtle one, eh?

"Dorina is not here now," he muttered slyly, looking up at the ceiling, "nor am I bound to tell Huon all I hear."

Graydon swung around on his stool and looked at him.

Regor looked back quizzically, yet with such real friendship in his eyes that Graydon felt his resolve waver. There was something about Huon, as there had been about Lantlu, that made him feel lonely; something alien, something unhuman. Whether it was their beauty, so far beyond any dream of classic, antique sculpture, or whether it lay deeper, he did not know. But he felt none of it concerning this man. Regor seemed of his own world. And certainly he had demonstrated his kindliness.

"You can trust me, lad," Regor answered his thought. "You were wise last night, but what was wisdom then may not be so now. Would this help you to decide—that I know Suarra, and love her as my own child?"

It turned the scale in Graydon's mind.

"A bargain, Regor," he said. "Question for question. Answer mine, and I'll answer yours."

"Done!" grunted Regor, "and if we keep them waiting let the Fellowship chew their thumbs."

Graydon went straight to the matter that was troubling him.

"Huon asked me many questions last night. And the most of them were about death in my own land, its shapes, how it came to us; and how long men lived there. One would think he knew nothing of death except that which comes by killing. Why is Huon so curious about—death?"

"Because," said Regor, tranquilly, "Huon is deathless!"

"Deathless!" echoed Graydon, incredulously.

"Deathless," repeated Regor, "unless, of course, some one kills him, or he should choose to exercise a certain—choice which all of us have."

"Which all of you have!" echoed Graydon again. "You, too, Regor?"

"Even I," answered the giant, bowing urbanely.

"But surely not the Indians," cried Graydon.

"No, not they," Regor replied, patiently.

"Then they die," Graydon was struggling desperately to find some flaw in what seemed to him a monstrous condition. "They die, like my people. Then why have they not taught Huon all that death can be? Why ask me?"

"There are two answers to that," said Regor with quite

103

a professional air. "First, you—and therefore your race—
are much closer to us than are the Emer, or as you call
them, the Aymara. Therefore, Huon argues, he might
learn from you what would probably come out of the Door
of Death for us if it should be decided to reopen that door
upon Yu-Atlanchi—all Yu-Atlanchi. It is, by the way, one
of the matters that has made us outlaws. The second answer is, however, all-embracing. It is that, except in the
rarest of cases, the Emer do not live long enough for any
one to find out how they might possibly die except in the
distressingly similar manner in which they do. I mean, they
are killed before they have opportunity to die otherwise!
It is another of the matters that has made us outlaws."

Graydon felt a nightmarish creep.

Was Suarra too—deathless? And if so, then in the name
of God how old was she? The thought was definitely unpleasant. They were unhuman, those hidden people; ab-
normal! Surely Suarra, with all her sweetness, was not one
of these—monsters! He did not dare ask; approached the
question obliquely.

"Dorina too, I suppose?" he asked.

"Naturally," said Regor, placidly.

"She looks very like Suarra," hazarded Graydon. "She
might be her sister."

"Oh, no," said Regor. "Let me see—she was, I believe,
the sister of Suarra's grandmother—yes, or her great-
grandmother. Something like that, at any rate."

Graydon glared at him suspiciously. Was Regor after all
making game of him?

"A sort of an aunt," he observed, sarcastically.

"You might say so," agreed Regor.

"Hell!" shouted Graydon, in utter exasperation, and
brought down his fist on the table with a crash. Regor
looked startled, then chuckled.

"What does it matter?" he asked. "One of your day-old
babes, if it had the brain to think, would probably consider
you an ancient as you do me. But it would accept it as
natural. All these things are comparative. And if our ages
offend you," he added, unctuously, "be thankful that it is

Dorina who is Suarra's great-grandmother's sister, and not the other way about."

Graydon laughed; this was comforting common sense after all. And yet—Suarra centuries old, perhaps! Not Primavera, not the fresh young Springtide maid he had thought her! Well, there was no use crying about it. It was so, or it wasn't. And if it were so—still she was Suarra. He thrust the whole matter aside.

"One more question, and I'm ready for yours. None of you thoroughly believed me until I told you of the Face, and what I told you frightened you. Why?"

Now it was Regor who was troubled; his face darkened, then paled, the scars standing out like livid welts.

"And again you are frightened," Graydon said, curiously. "Why?"

"At a Shadow," answered Regor, and with effort. "At an evil Shadow which you have turned to substance. At an ancient tale—which you have turned to truth. Let be—I say no more."

A shadow...the Serpent-woman had spoken of a shadow...linking it with this enemy they called the Dark One...there had been a name...The Shadow of...ah, yes—he had it now.

"You speak," he said, "in riddles. As though I were a child. Do you fear to name this Shadow? Well, I do not— it is the Shadow of Nimir."

Regor's jaw dropped; closed with a snap. He took a menacing step toward Graydon, face hard, eyes bleak, with suspicion.

"You know too much, I think! And knowing, fear too little—"

"Don't be a fool," said Graydon, sharply. "If I knew why you feared, would I ask? I know the name, and that is all—except that he is foe of the Mother. How I came to know it, I will tell you later—after you have answered my question. And with no more riddles."

For a full minute the great man glared at him, then shrugged his shoulders, and sat facing him.

"You shook me," he said, quietly enough. "Of all the Fellowship, I alone, or so I think, know the name of

Nimir. It has been forgotten. The Lord of Evil—that name all know. But not the name he bore before—"

He leaned over toward Graydon, laid his hand on his shoulder, and his stern mouth quivered.

"By the Power above us all, I want to believe you, lad! I would not have this hope die!"

Graydon reached up, and pressed the clutching hand.

"And by the Power above us all—you can believe, Regor."

Regor nodded, face tranquil once more.

"Thus then it is," he began. "This is the ancient story. That long, long ago Yu-Atlanchi was ruled by the Seven Lords and Adana, the Snake Mother. They were not as other men, these Lords. Masters of knowledge, holders of strange secrets, wielders of strange powers. Both death and life they had conquered, holding back death at will, doing as they willed with life. They came to this land with the Mother and her people, age upon age long gone. Through their wisdom, they had ceased to be entirely human—these Lords. Or at least—we would not think them so; though men like us they must once have been.

"There came a time when one of them plotted secretly against the others, scheming to wrest their power from them. Himself, to rule supreme. And not alone in Yu-Atlanchi, but over all earth, all living things his slaves. Himself enthroned. All powerful. God on earth. Slowly, steadily, he armed himself with dread powers unknown to the others.

"When he felt his strength had ripened—he struck. And almost won. And would have won—had it not been for the guile and wisdom of the Mother.

"That Lord was—Nimir.

"They conquered him—but they could not destroy him. Yet by their arts they could fetter him. And this they did, so the ancient story ran, preparing a certain place, and by their arts prisoning him within the rock there.

"Out of that rock they carved a great Face, in the likeness of Nimir's own. It was not in mockery . . . they had some purpose . . . but what that purpose might have been . . . none knows. And by their arts they set in action within that place forces which would keep him bound fast as long as the land—or Nimir—endured. Of fruit of jewels or flowing gold, such as you described, the tale said nothing.

"All this being done, the Six Lords and Adana, the Mother, returned to Yu-Atlanchi. And for long the old peace reigned.

"Time upon time passed. One by one those whose eyes had beheld the Lord of Evil grew weary, and opened the Door of Death. Or opened the Door of Life, brought babes through it, and then passed through the dark portal, that being the price of children in Yu-Atlanchi! So there came a day when in all this hidden land there was none of its people left who knew the whole truth except a handful among the Dream Makers, and who would believe a Dream Maker?

"That war whose stakes had been a world, faded into a legend, a parable.

"Then, not so long ago as time is measured in Yu-Atlanchi, there came the rumor that this evil Lord had reappeared. A Shadow of him rather; a Darkness that whispered; bodiless but seeking a body; promising all things to those who would obey him; whispering, whispering that he was the Lord of Evil. And that the Urd, the lizard-people, were his slaves.

"When first we heard this rumor of the Shadow and its whisperings, we laughed. A Dream Maker has awakened, we said, and some one has believed him. But as the Shadow's following increased, we laughed not so loudly. For cruelty and wickedness grew swiftly, and we realized that whether Lord of Evil or another, there was poison at the roots of the ancient tree of Yu-Atlanchi.

"Of all the six Lords there remained only one, and the Mother and he had long withdrawn from us. We sought audience with the Mother, and she was indifferent.

"Then Lantlu seized power, and life in the ancient city became intolerable to many of us. Following Huon, we found refuge in these caverns. And ever darker through the years grew the Shadow over Yu-Atlanchi. But still we said—'He is not that ancient Lord of Evil!'

"And then—you come. And you tell us—'I have seen that secret place! I have looked into the eyes of the Face!' "

Regor arose and paced the room; there were little drops of sweat on his forehead.

"And now we *know* that the Shadow has not lied, and that it and the Lord of Evil are one. That he has found means of partial escape, and that once again embodied, as he seeks to be, will have power to break all his bonds, find full release, and rule here and in time over earth, as ages ago he was balked from doing."

Again he took up his restless pacing, and again halted, facing Graydon.

"We fear, but it is not death we fear," he said, and it was like an echo of Suarra. "It is something infinitely worse than any death could ever be. We fear to *live*—in such shapes and ways as this Lord of Evil and Lantlu could devise. And would devise for us, be sure of that."

He covered his face with his cloak. When he uncovered it he had himself in hand once more.

"Well, lad, courage," he rumbled. "Neither Lantlu nor the Dark Master has us yet! Your turn now. What was it the Mother promised you?"

And Graydon, with a dull horror knocking at his own heart, told him fully all that he had heard and seen in that vision of his. Regor listened, silent. But, steadily, hope grew in his eyes; and when Graydon had repeated the Serpent-woman's threat against Lantlu, he leaped to his feet with an oath of joy.

"Win to her you must and shall!" he said. "I am not saying it will be easy. Yet there are ways—yes, there are ways. And you shall bear a message to the Mother from us—that we stand ready to join her and fight as best we can beside her. And that there are perhaps more in Yu-Atlanchi worth the saving than she thinks," he added a little bitterly. "Say to her that we, at least, each and all of us, will gladly lay down our lives if by doing so, we can help her conquer."

From somewhere far away came the mellow golden note of a bell.

"The Fellowship has gathered," said Regor. "It is the

signal. When you come before them say nothing of what you have just told me. Repeat only your story of last night. Dorina will be there. And I have told you nothing. You understand, lad?"

"Right," answered Graydon.

"And if you're a good lad," said Regor, pausing at the curtained door and poking his bar into Graydon's ribs, "if you're a really good lad, I'll tell you something else."

"Yes, what?" said Graydon, intent.

"I'll tell you how old Suarra really is!" answered Regor, and, laughing, marched through the doorway.

CHAPTER XII

The Secret Ancient City

GRAYDON DECIDED that he would have to revise his estimate of Black Regor. He had laughed inwardly at his boasts of subtlety, considering him as transparent as air. He knew now that he had been wrong. The sly reference to Suarra's years showed how accurately Regor had read him. That, however, was only one egg of the omelette. More significant had been his perception that Graydon had held back the most vital part of his story.

There was, besides, his independence of thought, manifest both in word and action; Huon's man he might be, but he was master of his own judgment. His distrust of Dorina was proof of that. And certainly the way in which last night he had infected Huon with that sinister doubt of her had been subtle enough. Also he had a sense of humor, and somehow Graydon was quite sure Huon had none.

The corridor along which they were passing was not long. It ended against a huge door of the black metal, guarded by the yellow-kilted Indians.

"Remember!" warned Regor. The door slid aside, revealing webs of curtains. He parted them, and Graydon followed him through.

He stood at the threshold of an immense chamber from whose high ceiling poured light, golden and dazzling as though from full sun. His vision clearing, he saw curving across the wide floor a double semicircle of seats that appeared cut from rose coral. Occupying them were a hundred or more of Huon's people, the men in yellow, the women dressed in vivid color; and each and all of them, his swift glance told him, possessed of that disturbing beauty which was the heritage of this unknown race.

Graydon, studying them, trembled again at the touch of the strange loneliness.

There was a low dais facing the semicircle, on it a wide and cushioned bench of the rose coral, and in front of it a pedestal, like a speaker's rostrum. Dorina sat there, and rising from her side was Huon. He came swiftly down, greeted Graydon most courteously, and taking him by hand led him up to the dais where Dorina acknowledged his bow by a negligent lifting of black lashes and a careless word. Regor dropped down beside her; then Huon turned him toward the others, raising the wrist that held the bracelet, at sight of which there was another murmuring and hands lifted in salutation.

"This," began Huon, "is the Fellowship, outlaws of Yu-Atlanchi, haters of and hated by Lantlu and the Dark Master, loyal children of the Mother, and ready to serve her if she will so allow. Something I have told them of your story, and that we three believe you. Yet, though they call me leader, still am I only one of them. It is their right to judge you. Speak—they listen."

Graydon mustered his words; then launched his tale. Ever more tensely they listened as that tale progressed, and it came to him that, so far as judgment of him was concerned, this hearing was only a formality; that they had been convinced of his genuineness by Huon before he had entered. With that thought came a greater assurance, and as he sensed their growing sympathy and approval, a greater ease, so that his speech flowed more readily.

And when at last he had led them to the cavern of the Face, all doubt of this was ended, for now they leaned forward in rigid attention, pallid, with whitened lips and in their eyes was horror—they were like seraphs, Graydon thought, hearing suddenly that Satan and his legions had broken through a gate of Heaven. But if there was horror, there was no sign of panic, nor of despair, and no weakening of spirit apparent upon those masks of beauty that stared at him so raptly. When he had ended, a long sigh went up, and a silence fell.

"You have heard," Huon broke that silence. "Now let any who doubts this man rise and question him."

111

A murmuring ran through the Fellowship as one turned to the other; little groups formed and whispered. Then came a voice from among them.

"Huon, we believe. And quickly must he reach the Mother. Remains now to decide how to do it."

"Graydon," Huon turned to him, "last night I promised you that if we believed, you should go your own way, as your own wit might guide you—or you could throw in your lot with us, and call upon our wits to help you. And now you must decide. Stay—" he said, as Graydon was about to speak, "we cozen none with fair promises which we know are doubtful of performance. And it may well be that our help would be more harmful to you than otherwise. Before you decide, see the board upon which the game must be played."

He strode down from the dais and over to the farther end of the chamber. He thrust aside the thick hangings which covered its wall. Behind them was a gleaming black stone. Huon rested his hand upon it, and slowly a circular aperture opened. A little gust of fragrant air came dancing in.

Graydon looked out upon hidden Yu-Atlanchi.

Far beneath him sparkled the blue waters of a long lake. Huon's lair was at one narrowed end of it. Beaches of golden sand and flowering marshes bordered it. Beyond the marshes was thick forest, marching mile upon mile away, to be thrust back at last like a green wave by cliffs, sheer and gray and thousands of feet high. He looked down the lake, following its ever-widening southward course. There was a faint haze over the landscape, but far away he saw a splotch of color, as though a gigantic jewel box had been spilled there. Opposite it, the cliffs marched forward and out into the water, narrowing the lake once more. And set in these cliffs was a row of huge black ovals, like windows opening into darkness. Beside each of them was a gigantic figure.

Of course! That splotch of spilled jewels was the secret ancient city. The oval shadows were those caverns he had glimpsed when summoned by the Serpent-woman; the guarding shapes were the colossi—and there at the left

where a precipice made a mighty buttress, leaning against
its green and ebon breast, was a rod of shining silver. It
was the cataract of his vision.

Huon handed him a mask of crystal, and he set it over
his eyes. The splotch of color leaped forward, swam in
front of him and resolved itself into a towered and tur-
reted city, a city built by Djinns with blocks and scales of
red glowing gold and gleaming silver, and roofed with tiles
of turquoise and sapphire, smoldering ruby and flashing
diamond. He could see the spume of the cataract waving
like signaling veils. He saw that no two of the colossi were
alike, that some were shaped like women, and that some,
like the gods of ancient Egypt, bore the heads of animals
and birds. A hundred feet in height he judged them. His
eyes lingered on one, a naked woman's body, heroically
proportioned, yet exquisite. Her face was that of a grinning
frog.

Behind the city was a long low hill. Crowning it was a
building whose proportions dwarfed even the columned
immensity of ancient Karnak. It was of white marble, and
it brooded over the jeweled city like a white-robed vestal.
Its front was pillared, but the enormous columns were
without ornament. It was of Cyclopean simplicity, aloof;
and, like the colossi, it seemed to watch.

He saw no streets; there were leafy lanes on which was
sparse movement. West, south and east, his gaze was
checked by the sky-reaching ramparts of the mountains.
The hidden land was a vast circular bowl some thirty miles
in diameter, he estimated.

"There," Huon was pointing at the temple, "is your
goal. There dwells the Mother—and Suarra."

The aperture closed; Huon let the curtains drop, and led
Graydon back to the dais.

"You have seen," he said. "What you could not see were
the obstacles that lie between you and that temple, the way
to which seems so near and open. The city is well guarded,
Graydon, and all its guards are Lantlu's men. You could
not get to the Temple without being caught a score of
times. Therefore, dismiss all hope that you can reach the
Mother by stealth, unaided. Inevitably you would be taken

before Lantlu. By the ancient law, your life would be forfeit.

"But it might be that if you went boldly into the city, showing your bracelet as passport, and demanding in its name audience with the Mother—it might be that thus simply you could gain your end. It might be that Lantlu, mazed by the mystery of how you passed the Messengers, of how you were guided to Yu-Atlanchi, would not dare slay you nor hold you back from the Mother."

"The best he would do," growled Regor, "since whatever Lantlu may be he is no fool, would be to greet you fairly, find out all he could from you, put you off on the pretext that the Mother must be prepared for your visit, probably slip some drug into your drink, and while you slept take counsel with the Dark Master as to what was to be done with you. I do not think you would ever reach the Mother by that route."

There was a murmur of assent from the Fellowship, and Huon himself nodded agreement.

"Still, he should weigh the chance," he said. "Now, if you reject that plan, there is the matter of our aid. Frankly, Graydon, it can be none too great. Those of the Old Race who still live are not many. There are in all perhaps two thousand of us. Of these, we account for a scant hundred. Of those within the city, some three hundred more are with us, and serve us better by being there than here. Of those remaining, the Dream Makers number half a thousand. They are not concerned with anything of earth. The others are with Lantlu, one with him in his amusements and aims, followers, more or less, of the Dark Master.

"We are in no position to take issue in the open with Lantlu. He controls the Xinli, both the hunting packs, and those which are ridden—and these latter are as formidable as the hunters. Through the Dark Master he controls the Urd, the lizard-men. Against all these we have for weapons swords and lance, bow and arrow and battle mace. Once we had weapons of a different kind—sounds that went forth like swift sparks, flaming, and slew all upon whom they fell; shadows that flitted where they were willed to go, and turned to ice all upon which they rested; shapes of flame that consumed all living things upon which they rested; and other strange devices of death. But, so our legends run, after a certain war, these were taken and hidden away in one of the caverns, so that never might we use them upon each other. Or it may be they were destroyed. At any rate, we have them not.

"I tell you this, Graydon," added Huon a trifle bitterly, "to show you why it is we do not take you by the hand and go marching up to the white Temple with you. If we had but one of those weapons of the old ones—"

"If we had but one, we would march with you so," roared Regor. "The Mother knows where they are, if they still exist, and, therefore, you must get to her and persuade her to let us have them. By all the Hells, if the Dark Master is the Lord of Evil—then Adana had better be looking for her own safety! Maybe he, too, knows where those weapons are hidden!"

"This we can do, Graydon," went on Huon. "We can arrange to hide you with friends in the city, if we can get you there undiscovered. After that we must plot to get you into the Temple. That done, if Lantlu tries to take you, it will be open war between the Mother and him. And that, frankly, is what interests us. The danger is in your discovery before you can reach her. Yet I do believe you have a better chance to win to her wtih our help than unaided!"

"I too," answered Graydon. "But whether so or not, Huon, something tells me that our fortunes are interwoven. That if I win, there is hope for you, and for all those who would see life changed in Yu-Atlanchi. At any rate, if you will accept me, I throw in my lot with you."

Huon's face lightened, and he caught Graydon's hands, while Regor muttered and struck him on the shoulder, and from the Fellowship arose a hum of relief. And suddenly through it struck the voice of Dorina, sweetly languid.

"But it seems to me that you have missed the simplest solution of all. Clearly, it was Suarra as much as the Mother who brought Graydon here. And clearly Suarra is, to say the least, interested in him. And Suarra is the

Mother's favorite. Well then—let word be sent secretly to Suarra that Graydon has returned, let her say where she will meet him; then, having met, let her tell him how best he can reach Adana."

Graydon saw Regor look at her suspiciously, but Huon hailed the suggestion, and after a little discussion the Fellowship approved it. And so it was decided that a messenger be sent at once to Suarra to tell her of Graydon's presence, and as proof that this was so he wrote at Regor's suggestion one brief line—"by your *caraquenque* feather on my heart this is truth"—that and no more. Also, at Regor's suggestion, the place of meeting was set at the first of the caverns of the colossi which was close to the great cataract and almost at the lake's level.

"There is none to stop her or question her going there," urged Regor. "She can say she is sent by the Mother, for a purpose of her own. None will dare interfere—and why should they? She has visited the caverns before. It should be well after dusk, say the fifth hour. I and a half-dozen of us will be sufficient guard for Graydon. I know a way that has few dangers of discovery."

So it was settled. The message was prepared for Suarra, and its carrier, one of the Indians, departed. Graydon did not have a clear idea how it was to be gotten to her. Vaguely, he gathered that it would be passed along through other Indians not known to be enemies of the rulers, until it reached the Emers who were the servants and bodyguard of the Temple, owing no allegiance to any except the Snake Mother and the Lord of Folly. They would see that Suarra got it.

That day, Graydon spent with Huon and the Fellowship and found them gay, witty, and delightful companions, the women of perilous charm. He dined with them. Dorina, oddly, paid him marked attention, but Huon's jealousy slept. Like Huon, she was curious about death, and that part of his evening he spent at her side Graydon did not find so gay. At last she was silent for many minutes, then said:

"If Huon wins this fight and comes to rule Yu-Atlanchi,

he threatens to open the Door of Death for all of us. Why should we not have the right to choose?"

Without giving him time to answer, she stared at him through narrowed lids, and said with utmost finality:

"Well, *I* for one do not intend to die! You can tell the Mother so—if you ever reach her!"

And abruptly turned away and left him.

Later on, as he was turning in, Regor had come and sat and talked with him.

"Lad," he said, "I have forebodings. It was in my own mind to suggest that meeting with Suarra, nevertheless I like it ill coming from Dorina. So Suarra is to meet us not at the fifth hour, but the third. Also, the place will not be the first cavern, but the cavern of the Frog-woman."

"But the message has gone," said Graydon. "How is Suarra to know?"

"Don't worry about that," retorted the giant. "In my subtle fashion, I sent a message of my own with that other. Even the messenger who bore it did not know what it was. If we get a *caraquenque* feather back from Suarra, it means she understands. If we don't—why, then we'll have to go to the first cavern."

He nodded gloomily.

"I repeat. I don't like that idea coming from Dorina. Oh, well—"

He grumbled a good-night, and stalked out.

CHAPTER XIII

Cavern of the Frog-Woman

THE MORNING of the third day Graydon heard from Regor that Suarra had got his message, and had set that night for their meeting. She had sent a plume of the *caraquenque* bird to show she had understood, and would be at the cavern of the Frog-woman.

"Not even Huon knows it is there we go," said Regor. "If he did, Dorina would wheedle it out of him. And two nights' sleep have not diminished my distrust. In making that suggestion she had something more in mind than making easy your way to Adana, or gratifying your desire to see the young woman whose aunt, in a manner of speaking, she is," he ended with a grin.

Graydon had given considerable thought to that matter himself; and now he repeated to Regor his curious conversation with Dorina.

"She may," he said, "plan a trap to deliver me to Lantlu. She may reason that if I get to the Mother, the issue will be joined at once. Then, if Lantlu is conquered, Huon will rule and open the Door of Death, whatever that may be, which she so greatly dreads. Whereas, if I am put out of the way definitely, things will probably go on much as now, which will give her time to persuade Huon from his resolve. That is the only basis I can think of for your suspicions, if there is any basis for them."

Regor listened thoughtfully.

"It is no secret that Dorina opposes Huon in that matter. There has always been that conflict between them. His desire for children is as strong as hers for deathlessness. Before we came here, he urged her to join him in opening the two Doors. She would not. There are other

118

women who would. But Huon is a one-woman man. He would kill Dorina if he found her in treachery, but he will be the father of no other woman's child."

He paced the room, grumbling.

"You have given words to my thoughts, true enough," he stopped his pacing. "Yet there is another side to the matter which I do not think Dorina would overlook. If you are trapped, so in all probability will be Suarra. She runs great risk in meeting you. Enough to secure her condemnation by the Council, which Lantlu controls—it would mean at best her outlawry. The Council would be within its rights in so dealing with her. But if I know anything of women, and remember the Snake Mother is woman, she would not allow that foster-child of hers to suffer. And then the issue would be joined indeed, and in a way that only the destruction of Lantlu or Adana herself could end. And that, if you are right, is exactly what Dorina does not want."

"Good God, Regor!" exclaimed Graydon, aghast. "Why didn't you let me know that before I told them how Suarra came back to me? Surely that puts her in Lantlu's power if that hell-cat gets the information to him."

"No," answered the giant, "no, it doesn't. You see, lad, then she had the Lord Tyddo with her. She was but obeying his bidding."

"Perhaps he'll come with her to-night," said Graydon, hopefully.

"No," Regor shook his head, "no, I don't believe he will. This is different. Then there were four of you, going to punishment. And if it had not been for the Mother, you would have gone rolling down the abyss, a bit of golden sweat with the others. The Mother interfered there, and I think she would again—for Suarra. But she might not for you. Also, you told me she said you must win to her by your own wit and courage. So, I hardly think that we can count on any protection to-night beyond what we ourselves devise."

Again he grumbled, inarticulately.

"Furthermore," he pointed his bar at Graydon like a

finger, "Adana is woman, and therefore changeable. She might decide that, after all, you are not essential to Suarra's welfare, or she might grow momentarily weary of the whole matter, and that brief abstraction might occur at a most unfortunate time for you—"

"Hell!" cried Graydon, springing up, "you are certainly a cheerful companion, Regor!"

"Well," chuckled Regor, "if it's a cheerful thought you want, here is one. The Mother is woman true enough—but certainly not human woman. Therefore neither of us can possibly know what she may or may not do!"

He left Graydon to wrestle with the depressing conviction that he was completely right.

The balance of the day Graydon spent with Huon and certain members of the Fellowship, as he had the day before, all of them eager to know more of that world which had grown up outside the Hidden Land. Dorina did not appear. They were interested in his rifle and pistols, skeptical as to their effect upon the dinosaurs; like children, they were more interested in the explosions than the work of the bullets. The Xinli, they explained, were vulnerable only in one unprotected place in their necks under the jaw, and an upward thrust from a lance into this spot was about the one way to kill them. There were some two hundred in the hunting packs, and not more than a score of the monsters used for riding. They bred scantily, and their numbers were slowly but steadily lessened by fights among themselves. The greater creatures were tractable as horses, and could be ridden by any one. The packs were ravening devils over which only Lantlu had complete control. There was an amphitheater where races of the great dinosaurs were regularly held; and it was also the arena of combats between selected fighters of the hunting packs and small bands of the lizard-men, raids upon whom were periodically made to keep down their numbers. And now Graydon discovered why none of the Indians died in ways that would have given Huon the enlightenment he sought as to the varied guises of death. When they began to age they were fed to the packs.

Then, too, it appeared, Lantlu had a passion for hunt- ing human game. Offenders against the law, and offenders against him, were often taken—openly in the case of the first and secretly in that of the other—beyond the barriers, given a start and run down. That, he also discovered, was how Regor had gotten his scars and lost his arm. Daring to oppose Lantlu in one of his cruelties, he had been trapped, loosed and hunted. He had managed to evade the pursuers, all except one questing dinosaur; had fought and killed it. Fearfully wounded, he had by some miracle of vitality reached Huon's lair, and had there been nursed back to life. Lantlu's price for his capture was only a little less than that for Huon's.

Rapidly Graydon's understanding of this lost people clarified. Scant remnants of what must have been a race more advanced than any following it on earth—a race that had reached a peak of scientific attainment never afterward touched by man—they were all that was left of a mighty wave of prehistoric civilization, a little pool fast becoming stagnant. Over-sheltered, over-protected, made immune from all attack and necessity for effort, they had retained the beauty of their bodies; but initiative, urge to advance, impulse to regain the lost knowledge of their ancestors had atrophied, or at best was comatose to the point of extinction. Except for that beauty—and the disquieting thought of their age—they seemed normal people, charmingly courteous.

Apparently there had been a sharp line of cleavage among them. Huon and the Fellowship were atavars, throwbacks to a more humane period of the race. Lantlu and his followers had been carried in the opposite direc- tion, toward cruelty, indifference to suffering, pleasure in its infliction, dropping steadily to the black nadir of evil which made them fit tools for the Dark One. Those whom they called the Dream Makers were entirely withdrawn from all that was human, static. And Graydon believed that he could understand why Huon desired to open those mysterious Doors which would, so far as span of years was concerned, rid them of that deathlessness which had been the curse of the race; a vague conviction that by doing this he would get back to the well-springs of the youth of his people, recover from them their olden strength.

For now Graydon accepted that deathlessness as fact. Studying Kon, he could not doubt that the science which had effected that monstrous blend of man and spider was entirely capable of performing the lesser miracle of indefinitely prolonging life. The lizard-folk were other proof of it. And above all was the Serpent-woman, Adana, the Snake Mother, by her indubitable reality saying to him: "When such as I can be, and where such as I am, all things are possible!"

The day wore on, dusk began to fall within the mountain-rimmed bowl of the Hidden Land. A little before the time set to start, Regor brought him a suit of the black chain mail, and he and Huon fastened it upon him. It was oddly light and flexible. Greaves, and the ankle-high, tanned footwear he rejected, preferring his own stout boots. He girdled himself with his own belt, and thrust into it one of his automatics and some extra clips of cartridges. Although he could not get at it, he left the second automatic in its holster under his left armpit—why he did not know, except that the familiar feel of it gave him more confidence. He saw that they had not much confidence in his own weapons, so to satisfy them he let Regor fasten to his belt a scabbard holding a short, stabbing sword of the black metal, and took from him one of the curiously shaped maces. If there was to be any fighting, said Regor, it would be at close quarters; and Graydon reflected that the giant knew what he was talking about, and that the strange weapons might be useful. He told himself that he would put his first trust in the automatic.

His rifle was a problem. Since there was a probability that Suarra might have some plan for his reaching the Snake Mother which would prevent his return to the lair, he did not want to leave it behind. If the possible fighting was to be of the hand-to-hand variety Regor predicted, the rifle would not only be secondary to pistol and mace or sword, but a handicap; he compromised by asking that one of the Indian soldiers be allowed to carry it, and march close behind him or at his side when possible. They agreed to this. Then Huon placed upon his head a cap of mail, padded, close-fitting, covering his ears and falling upon his shoulders.

And when this had all been done, he set his hands on Graydon's shoulders.

"Graydon," he said, "something tells me that with your coming the balances of Yu-Atlanchi's fate, so long motionless, begin to move. You are the new weight that disturbs them, and whether for good or for evil—who knows? Whether, when they come to rest again, Lantlu will have outweighed those who oppose him, or whether he will be outweighed—who knows? But it comes to me that change sweeps swiftly down on Yu-Atlanchi—in one way or another the old order is close to its end. And that you and I, Graydon, will never again meet here—will meet but once more, and briefly ... and part under a crimson sky ... from which shadows drop ... slaying shadows and cold ... cold slaying shadows that clash with shapes of flame ... and then ... meet never again. ...

"Till then—fare you well, Graydon!"

He turned abruptly, and strode out of the room.

"Now I wonder—" muttered Graydon, and shivered, as though two hands of ice had rested fleetingly on his shoulders where Huon's had been.

"I wonder, too," said Regor, brusquely. "But at least you two are to meet again, it seems. Therefore Death does not stalk you to-night."

They passed from that room into a guard chamber where a dozen of the kilted Aymara awaited them. They were sturdy men, armed with maces and spears, in their girdles the short stabbing swords. To one, Regor handed the rifle, and explained what he was to do. The Indian looked at it doubtfully, until Graydon, smiling, snapped the safety lock back and forth a few times, showing him

that the trigger could not move with the catch on. Re-
assured, he threw the thong over his head, and took his
place, the rifle dangling at his side.

Regor led the way. They marched at first along a wide,
well-lighted tunnel from which ran smaller passages. As
they walked along Graydon reflected that the barrier walls
must be honeycombed with these corridors and caverns,
both great and little; wondered whether they had been
shaped by nature or cut out by the ancient Yu-Atlanchan's,
and if by the latter, for what purpose. He had also given
much thought to the luminous properties of the walls, but
without discovering their secret. Either the rock had been
covered with some vitreous substance possessing radio-
active qualities unknown to modern science, or the ancients
had found some way to treat the atomic structure of the
stone so that luminous centers were created at the inter-
section of certain of the crystalline planes. There was no
warmth to the light, which had in it much of the soft brilliancy of the firefly. It cast no shadows.

They had gone well over a mile when the tunnel widened
into a crypt, and ended there against a solid wall.

"And here," said Regor, speaking for the first time, "our
danger begins."

He stood close to the wall, listening; then took from his
belt one of the cone-shaped objects. He pressed it against
a carved symbol at the level of his shoulder. A six-foot
section of the wall began to rise slowly like a curtain.
When it was a few inches from the floor, two of the
Indians dropped upon their bellies and peered through the
opening. The curtain rose a foot higher; they wriggled
under it and disappeared. Regor's hand fell, and the stone's
motion ceased. Perhaps five minutes went by, and then the
pair wriggled back, and nodded to the giant. Again he
pressed the cone to the symbol. The rock rose swiftly,
leaving a squat portal through which the Emers, bending,
streamed, with Regor and Graydon at their heels.

A few yards of this crouching progress, and Graydon
straightened. He looked out into a vast cavern filled with
a faint reddish light so faint indeed that it was barely re-

moved from darkness. He turned to Regor, and saw that he was thrusting the cone back into his girdle. The wall through which they had come was unbroken, with no trace of the passage.

The Indians formed a circle around the two of them, and, noiselessly as ghosts, began a quick march. Graydon, about to speak, caught Regor's warning gesture. The reddish darkness closed about them. Through the dim and strangely oppressive light they sped, over a floor of yellow sand. How the Indians guided themselves he could not tell, but there was no uncertainty in their movements and their swift pace never slackened.

Suddenly they closed around him, touching him, and at that instant they passed out of the murk into absolute blackness. They did not lessen their speed. There came a grunt from Regor, like a long-held breath, and a whispered command. The Indians halted. A ball of the cloudy luminescence flashed out and raced ahead of them. Behind it a pallid light grew, as though it had clothed the particles of air with a misty spray of phosphorescence. They went down a sharply sloping passage which the light had revealed, a thousand feet, two thousand feet, before the glow began to dim.

Five times the luminous ball shot ahead of them, lighting their way through the unbroken tunnel. Four miles and more they must have gone since they had left the lair, and the pace was beginning to tell on Graydon. Again the faint light was dimming, but far ahead was an oval opening behind which there seemed to be a flood of moonbeams. Now they were out of the passage and through that opening. And there Graydon paused, transfixed with amazement and awe.

It was another caverned space whose walls and roof he could not see. It was filled with silvery light like the woven rays of full moons of Spring. Under that light, upon low couches, lay cushioned the bodies of score upon score of women and men, each of their faces stamped with the unearthly beauty of Yu-Atlanchi, and as though asleep. Across the cavern, and back into the mountain as far as his vision could go, they lay. At first he thought that they were sleeping; then he saw that no breath raised their breasts. Staring at silken hair, golden and black and ruddy bronze, at red lips and blossoms of fair bosoms, he thought them exquisitely tinted statues.

Touching the hair, the cheek of one close to him, he realized that they were no effigies, but bodies once instinct with life; transmuted now by some alchemy of this mysterious land not into stone but into imperishable substance retaining both the coloring of the body when it had been living flesh, and its texture.

"Yu-Atlanchi's dead!" said Regor. "The ancient ones who passed before the Gate of Death was closed. And those who since that time opened of their own will that Gate, so new life might stream among us. The dead!"

The Indians were uneasy, eager to be going. Quickly they left that silent place of the dead, and even Regor seemed to be relieved when they had passed into another passage through the rock.

"A few steps more, lad," he rumbled, "and we are out. And here the way is not beset with such dangers. We have passed under five of the great caverns, the place of the dead was the sixth; we skirt the entrances of three more and then we are at the Frog-woman's. And by every scale of the Mother—I will be glad to get once more into the open."

And shortly they passed cautiously out of that passage, and Graydon felt the fresh air upon his face, and looked up into a sky where a half-moon dipped in and out of scurrying clouds.

They dropped down upon a narrow trail. Here the Indians re-formed, part going ahead of them, the others following. At left, the verdure rose high, masking the lake. Looking upward and back, he saw the colossal figure of a woman, in pure white stone, with arms raised to the Heavens—the guardian of that cavern through which they had just passed. Then the vegetation closed round him.

The trail was easy to follow, not dark even when the clouds covered the moon. Louder, and even louder came the roar of the cataract. Through gaps in the trees and bushes, he caught glimpses of the monstrous figure of the Frog-woman, on watch at the entrance of the black oval that was the mouth of her cavern.

The path began to rise. It passed behind a high ledge and became a steep flight of narrow steps. He climbed these. He stood in the shadow close to the opening of the Frog-woman's cavern. He looked up at that colossal figure, a squatting woman, unclothed, and carved of some green stone that glistened beneath the moon as though its rays were falling spray. Her grotesque face grinned at him above the exquisite shoulders and breasts. Beside her gaped the cavern's mouth, inky black.

He was at the inner edge of an immense platform of smooth stone. Directly opposite him, a half-mile across the lake, was the secret city.

More than ever, under the moon, did it seem a city built by Djinns. It was larger, far larger, than he had thought it. Its palaces thrust up their fantastic turrets and domes; their gay colorings as of lacquer of jewels were changed and softened into a tapestry that spread for mile upon mile, an immense rug each of whose irised patterns was surrounded by arabesques of dark green, and black, and white, the foliage and flowers of the trees that circled the dwellings. From minaret and tower and dome sprang tiny arches of light, delicate moon-bows, spanning them like bridges. In the air, above the green and black, and threading them, tiny dancing lights flashed and vanished and flashed out again, fireflies, he thought, playing among the trees. At the right, looking down upon the city, was the Temple, vestal white, majestic, serene.

Somewhere within it might be—Suarra! Perhaps she would not be able to meet him here after all. With half his mind he hoped that she would not, for Huon's farewell still echoed in his heart, and he feared for her. And half his mind willed fiercely that she should come—let the perils be what they may.

There was a rustle close beside him. A little hand caught his. He looked down into soft dark eyes, a tress of cloudy hair kissed his cheek, rocking him with its fragrance.

"Suarra!" he whispered, and again—"Suarra!"

"Graydon!" her sweet voice murmured. "You *did* come back to me—beloved!"

Her arms were around his neck, her lips were close to his, and slowly, slowly, they drew closer. They met, and clung—and for a time there were no such things in all the world as peril or suffering, sorrow or death.

CHAPTER XIV

Shadow of the Lizard Mask

THE SHADOW of the Frog-woman, sharply outlined by the moonlight, lay in fantastic profile from side to side of the great platform. Behind them was the blackness of her cavern, and between them and the city the lake shone like a vast silver mirror, waveless, no sign of life upon it. Below the platform, the Indians watched. The Frog-woman's head seemed to bend lower, listening to their whispering.

"Graydon! Graydon!" Suarra was weeping. "You should not have returned! Oh, but it was wicked of me to call you back!"

"Nonsense!" rumbled Regor. "You love each other, don't you? Well, then, what else was there for him to do? Besides, he has made strong friends—Huon and Black Regor, and one stronger than all of us, or by Riza the Lightning Eater he wouldn't be here! I mean the Mother herself. Child," he said slyly, "has she instructed you how to take him back to her?"

"Ah, Regor," sighed Suarra, "far from it. It is what weighs so upon my heart. For when I received your message I told her straightway of it, and asked her aid, but told her also that with it or without it, still must I go. She only nodded, and said: 'Naturally—since you are woman.' Then after a little silence she spoke again: 'Go, Suarra—no harm shall come to you.' 'I ask protection for him, Mother,' I said, and she did not answer. And I asked: 'Mother Adana, will you not summon him to you through me, so that none will dare harm him?' The Mother shook her head: 'If he loves you he will find his own way to me.'"

"No one saw you? No one followed you?" questioned Regor.

"No," said Suarra, "no, I'm quite sure they did not. We went through the Hall of the Weavers, and into the secret way that leads beneath the cataract, thence out and by the hidden path along the shore."

"You came silently? You heard nothing, saw nothing, as you passed the first cavern?"

"Very silently," she answered. "And as for the cavern, the path dips far below it, so that one can neither see it nor be seen from it. And I heard nothing—nothing but the voice of the torrent."

"Where was Lantlu?" Regor still did not seem satisfied.

"They fed the Xinli to-night!" she said, and shivered.

"Then," said Regor with satisfaction, "we know at least where *he* is."

"Well," Graydon spoke, "the upshot of the matter seems to be that much depends upon my doing obeisance in person to the Mother. And she has put it severely up to me to accomplish that—"

"Graydon," Suarra interrupted softly, "there *is* another way for us. If you wish it—I will go with you to Huon! I love the Mother. But if you wish it—I will not return to her. I will go with you to the Fellowship. This will I do for you, beloved. I would not have you meet any of the deaths of Yu-Atlanchi, and I think they throng thickly about your path to Adana. With Huon, we can live and be happy—for a time at least."

Now Graydon heard Regor gasp at this, and felt that he waited with anxiety for his answer, although he said nothing. He was tempted. After all, there was a way out for them from Huon's lair. And once beyond the barrier, it was probable that the Snake Mother would hold back her hand, not loose the winged Watchers upon them—for Suarra's sake. And if he could get Suarra safely away, what did he care about Yu-Atlanchi or any who dwelt within it?

Swiftly, other thoughts came. The Mother had aided him, not once but twice. She had saved him from the Face! She had bade her Messengers protect and guide him.

She had challenged his loyalty and his courage. And she had shown that in some measure she trusted him.

And then there was—this Dark One! This Shadow of Nimir, Lord of Evil, which menaced her ... Huon and the Fellowship, who also had trusted him ... and Regor ... pinning his hopes upon his meeting with the Serpent-woman to rid the land of evil and to deliver them all from outlawry.

No, he could not run from all this, not even for Suarra!

He told her so. And why.

He felt Regor relax. He had the curious feeling that in some way that weirdly beautiful, unhuman creature named Adana had been following his thoughts, approved his decision, and because of it had come to some final determination of her own which till now had hung in the balance.

Nor did Suarra seem much surprised. So little that he wondered whether that proposal had been her own devising.

"Well," she said, quietly, "then we must make some other plan. And I have thought of one. Listen carefully, Regor. In seven nights the moon is full and on that night is the Ladnophaxi—the Feast of the Dream-Makers. All will be at the amphitheater. There will be few guards in the city. Take Graydon back to Huon. On the fifth night from this, slip out of the lair and around the head of the lake and through the marshes. Let Graydon be dressed as one of the Emer, stain his face and body, make him a black wig cut as the Emer wear their hair. His gray eyes we cannot change, and so must risk.

"You know the palace of Cadok. He is secret foe of Lantlu and friend of Huon, and of you—but that I need not tell you. Get Graydon there. Cadok will hide him until the night of the Ladnophaxi. I will send a guide to be trusted. That guide will lead him to the Temple—and so he shall find his way to the Mother. And it shall be by his courage and wit. For it will take courage. And was it not his wit that rejected my proposal to him. So shall the terms of the Mother be fulfilled."

"It is a good plan!" rumbled Regor. "By the Mother, it is as good a plan as though it came from her! Thus shall it be. And now, Suarra, prepare to go. You have been here long—and at every heart-beat fear creeps closer to me, and I am little used to fear."

"It is a good plan," said Graydon. "And, heart of hearts, go now as Regor bids. For I, too, fear for you."

Her soft arms were round his neck, her lips on his, he felt her cheeks wet with tears.

"Beloved!" she whispered, and again—"Beloved!"

And she was gone.

"Hr-r-r-mp!" Regor drew a great sigh of relief. "Well, the path grows clearer. Now is there nothing for us to do but return and wait the fifth night. And begin to stain you up," he chuckled.

"Wait!" Graydon was listening with all his nerves. "Wait, Regor! There might be danger . . . she might be waylaid. Listen. . . ."

For several minutes they stood quiet, and heard no sound.

"She's safe enough," grumbled Regor at last. "You heard her say the Mother promised her. But we're not, lad. Our path back is just as dangerous as it was coming. Let's start. . . ."

He whistled softly to the watching guards. They came gliding back upon the platform. Graydon, deep in thought, followed abstractedly with his eyes the fantastic profile of the Frog-woman's shadow. The moon had moved higher in the heavens, and cast a sharp shadow of the colossal head upon the smooth face of rock that was the beginning of the cavern's farther wall. He stared at it, awakened from his abstraction, fascinated by its grotesqueness.

And as he watched he saw appear beside it another shadow—the shadow of a gigantic lizard head that crept closer to it. He turned to trace it.

Out from the cliff at the level of the Frog-woman's shoulder peered the head of a lizard-man—an immense head twice at least the size of any he had seen. Its red eyes glared down at him, its great jaws opened.

"Regor!" he cried, and reached to his belt for his automatic. "Regor! Look!"

There was a sickening reek of musk around him. Claws gripped his ankles and threw him to the rock. As he fell, the thing whose head had cast the shadow slid down the face of the stone—and he saw that its body was that of a man! Knew that it was a man, and the head but a mask!

He grappled with the creature that had thrown him. He heard Regor shouting. His fingers clutched and slipped from the leathery skin. Its jaws were so close that the fetid breath sickened him. And while he fought it, he wondered why it did not tear him with its fangs. His hand touched the hilt of the short sword in his belt. He drew it, and thrust the point haphazard upward. The lizard-man screeched, and rolled from him.

As he struggled to his feet, he saw that he had been drawn yards back into the cavern. On the platform was Regor, his deadly bar smiting up and down and around, mowing the hissing pack of the lizard-folk milling about him. Beside the giant were but two of Huon's Indians, fighting as desperately as he.

At the edge of the platform stood the man in the lizard mask. Around him, guarding him, was a ring of Indians dressed in kilts of green. He was laughing and that sound of human laughter coming through the fanged jaws was hideous.

"Caught!" shouted the lizard mask. "Trapped, old fox! Kill—but you'll not be killed! Not here, Regor! Not here!"

"Graydon!" bellowed Regor. "To me, Graydon!"

"Coming!" he cried, and leaped forward.

There was a rain of bodies upon him, leathery bodies. Clawed hands gripped him. He fought desperately to keep his feet—

There was only one Indian now beside Regor, the one who bore his rifle. As Graydon struggled, he saw this soldier's spear wrested from him, saw him throw the rifle thong over his head and raise the gun like a club. And as he did so there came a flash from its barrel and a report that echoed in the cavern mouth like thunder—and another and another in quick succession.

Now Graydon was down and could see no more, smothered under the lizard-men.

And now thongs were all about him, trussing his arms to his sides, binding together his legs. He was carried swiftly back into the dense darkness. One glimpse he had of the cavern mouth before it was blotted from his sight.

It was empty. Regor and the Indian, the man in the lizard mask and his soldiers, lizard-men—all were gone!

The lizard-men carried Graydon along gently enough. There was a considerable body of men; he could hear them hissing and squalling all around him, and the musky saurian stench was almost overpowering. As far as he could tell, he had sustained no wounds of any kind. The armor accounted for part of this, but not for all, since it had not protected his hands and face, and he had lost his cap of mail in the scramble. He recalled that the creatures had made no attempt to use their talons or fangs upon him, that they had overcome him by sheer swarming weight— as though they had been ordered to capture but not to harm him.

Ordered? But that would mean whoever had issued the order had known he would be at the cavern of the Frog-woman that night! And in turn that meant they had been betrayed despite all Regor's precautions.

Dorina!

Her name seemed to leap out of the darkness in letters of fire.

Another thought came to him that rocked him. If his coming had been foreknown by Huon's enemies, then the reason for it must also have been known. Good God—had Suarra been taken after all!

There had been a deliberate attempt to cut him away from Regor, that was certain. It had begun with the first stealthy attack which had drawn him back into the cavern; its second phase had been the rush of the hidden lizard-men upon him, and the wave that had surged up around Regor forming between them a ringed barrier.

Ever and ever as the hissing pack carried him on through the blackness his mind came back to Dorina— Dorina, who would not open the Door of Life with Huon; Dorina, who did not want him to meet the Mother until she had persuaded Huon to keep shut the Door of Death— Dorina, who did not want to die!

He wondered how far they had gone through this blackness within which the lizard people moved as in broad daylight. He could not tell how fast was their pace. Yet it seemed to him that it must have gone several miles. Were they still in the Frog-woman's cavern? What did the colossus guard in this vast lightless space, if hers it was?

He passed out of that blackness, without warning, as though he had been carried through an impalpable curtain.

Red light beat upon his eyes, brighter than the dim, rubrous haze through which he had gone so cautiously with Regor when they had left the lair, but of the same disturbing quality of darkness, shot through with crimson rust of light. All around him were the lizard-men, a hundred or more. He was being borne upon the heads of eight of the creatures, raised upon the pads of their forearms. Under that weird light their leathery skins were dull orange; the cockscombs of scarlet scales cresting their reptilian skulls were turned by it into a poisonous purple. They padded, hissing to each other, over the yellow sand.

He was lying upon his back, and the effort of turning his head was painful. He stared up. He could see no roof above him, nothing but the rusted murk. Steadily the light grew less dim, though never losing its suggestion of inherent darkness. Suddenly the lizard-men set up a louder and prolonged hissing. From somewhere far ahead came an answering sibilation. Their pace grew more rapid.

The red light abruptly lost much of its haziness. His bearers halted and lowered him to his feet. Hooked talons were thrust under his bonds and stripped them from him. Graydon stretched cramped arms and legs, and looked about him.

A hundred feet in front was an immense screen of black stone. It was semicircular in shape, and curved like a shallow shell. Its base was all of another hundred feet between the ends of its arc; its entire surface was pierced and cut with delicate designs through which ran strange patterns, unknown symbols.

Close to its center was a throne of jet, oddly familiar. With a prickling of his scalp he was suddenly aware that it was the exact duplicate of the sapphire throne of the

Lord of Lords in the Temple. Screen and throne were upon a dais raised a few feet above the floor, and up to it ran a broad ramp. Between the throne and the head of the ramp was an immense bowl of the same ebon stone, its base imbedded in the rock. It was, he thought, like an oversized baptismal font, one designed for giants' children. At the end of each wing of the curved screen was what, at that distance, seemed to be a low stone bench.

Empty was the black throne, empty the dais—were they empty? He searched them with his eyes. Of course they were empty! Then whence came his feeling that from every inch of that raised place within the screen something—some one—was regarding him, measuring him, weighing him, reading him with a cold malignant amusement . . . something evil . . . something incredibly evil . . . like the force that had streamed out upon him from . . . from the Face in the abyss. . . .

He turned his back to the dais, with conscious effort. He faced a horde of the lizard-people. There were hundreds of them, grouped in orderly ranks, and at about the same distance away from him as the black throne. They stood silent, red eyes intent upon him. They were so close together that their scarlet crests seemed to form a huge, fantastically tufted carpet. Among them were lizard-women and children. He stared at them, small things like baby demons, little needled yellow fangs glistening between the pointed jaws, small eyes glittering upon him like goblin lanterns.

He looked to right and left. The cavern was distinguishable in a circle perhaps half a mile in diameter. At that distance the clearer light in which he stood ended, bounded by the red rust murk. To his right, the smooth yellow sand stretched to the boundary of that murk.

At his left was a garden! A garden of evil!

There, a narrow stream ran over the floor of the cavern in curves and intricate loops. It was crimson, like a stream of sluggishly running blood. Upon its banks were great red lilies, tainted and splotched with venomous greens; orchid blooms of sullen purple veined with unclean scarlets; debauched roses; obscene thickets of what seemed to be shoots of young bamboo stained with verdigris; crouching trees from whose branches hung heart-shaped fruits of leprous white; patches of fleshy leafed plants from whose mauve centers protruded thick yellowish spikes shaped like hooded adders down whose sides slowly dripped glistening drops of some dreadful nectar.

A little breeze eddied about him. It brought the mingled scents of that strange garden, and these were the very essence of it, distillation of its wickedness. They rocked him with blasphemous imaginings, steeped him with evil longings. The breeze lingered for a breath, seemed to laugh, then fled back to the garden and left him trembling.

He feared that garden! Yes, the fear of it was as strong as the fear of the black throne. Why did he fear it so? Evil, unknown and undreamed evil, was in it. It was living evil— ah, that was it! Vital evil! A flood of evil life pulsed and ran through every bloom, every plant and tree . . . evil vitality . . . they drew it from that stream of blood . . . but, ah, how strong one who fed upon their life might grow. . . .

As that dark thought crept into Graydon's mind, something deep within him seemed to awaken, to repulse it with cold contemptuous strength and to take stern control of his brain. His assurance and all his old courage returned to him. He faced the black throne fearlessly.

He felt its invisible occupant thrust out at him, search for some loophole in his defense, withdraw as though puzzled, drive against him viciously, as if to break him down, and then withdrew again. Immediately, as in obedience to a command, the lizard-people surged forward, driving him toward the ramp. At its foot he hesitated, but a half dozen of the creatures padded from the ranks, closed round him, and pushed him upward. They pressed him to the stone bench at the right of the screen, and down upon it. As he tried to break from those who were holding his arms, he felt the others at his feet. Something circled his ankles; there were two sharp clicks. The lizard-men padded away from him.

Graydon arose from the bench and looked down at his feet. There was a metal ring around each ankle, attached to thin chains running back under the bench. He wondered how long the chains were. He took a step, and another and another, and still the chains did not check him. He reached down and pulled one of them to him until it grew taut. Measuring it, he estimated that it was precisely long enough to enable him to mount to the seat of the black throne. Having thus verified an unpleasant suspicion, Graydon hastily returned to the stone bench.

He heard a subdued hissing, the padding of many feet. The lizard-folk were going. Close-packed, they poured away, a tawny flood of leathery waves crested with leaping tongues of scarlet. None looked back at him. They reached the encircling murk and vanished within it.

Graydon was alone, in the silence—alone with the evil garden and the throne of jet.

Slowly the red radiance that fell upon the dais began to dim and thicken, as though a spray of black light were sifting through it.

Denser it grew about the throne of jet, and upon the throne a deeper shadow formed. Shapeless, wavering at first, slowly it condensed, ceased wavering, took outline—

Within the throne sat the shadow of a man. Faceless, featureless, cloudy hands gripping the arms of the throne, woven of the black atoms within the crepuscular rust—a man's shadow!

The faceless head leaned forward. It had no eyes, yet Graydon felt its eyes upon him. It had no lips, yet its lips began to whisper.

He heard the voice of the Dark One! The whispering of the Shadow of Nimir, Lord of Evil!

CHAPTER XV

"Lend Me Your Body, Graydon!"

THE VOICE of the Shadow was sweet, liquid as a flute heard from a forest at dusk. It lulled his fears, relaxed his guard.

"I know you, Graydon!" ran the whisper. "Know why you came to Yu-Atlanchi. Know how hopeless is your quest —without me. I brought you here, Graydon, commanding no harm to be done you. Else you would have been slain at the cavern. Do not fear me! You do not fear me, Graydon?"

He felt an oddly pleasant lethargy creeping over him as he listened to the melodious whisper.

"No," he said, half-drowsily. "No, I do not fear you, Nimir."

"Ah," the Shadow drew itself up from the throne, something of the lulling sweetness left his voice, something of menace took its place. "So you know me!"

The spell upon Graydon loosened, his mind leaped to alertness. The Shadow saw it, and all the dulcet, soothing lure flowed back into its whisper.

"But that is well! It is very well, Graydon. You have been told many lies about me, without doubt. You have seen these people of Yu-Atlanchi. They are in decadence. They rot. But had they in the olden days followed my council, they now would be a great people—strong, vital, rulers of the world. And the old wisdom would not have perished. It would have shaped a new and better world.

"You have seen these people, Graydon, and I think you have weighed them. Do you believe they have reason to thank those who banished me and so condemned them to this end? I would not have abandoned them as did those other Lords, leaving them to a charlatan and a Snake woman, who, not being human, therefore cannot understand

139

the human need. I would have led them onward and upward to greater strength and greater wisdom. I would have placed them on the heights, Graydon, only the stars above them—not left them in the swamp, there to stagnate and decay. You believe me, Graydon?"

Graydon considered. It was a little difficult to think with this pleasantly lazy feeling holding one; there was a curious exhilaration in it, too. But yes, yes—it was all true. It was clear, cold logic. He had thought the same thing himself, in a way. Certainly it was a damnable thing for those Lords, whoever they might have been, to have gone calmly off as though they had no responsibility for the people. Who was the charlatan? Why, the Lord of Fools, of course. And the Mother? Half a snake! Damned apt descriptions. He quite agreed.

"Right, Nimir—you're right!" he said, nodding solemnly.

A ghost of perfume from the garden stole to him. He drank it greedily. Odd he had thought it evil! It wasn't. He felt damned good, and the scent made him feel even better. What was evil, anyway? Only a point of view. Not a bad sort this Shadow. Quite logical—reasonable. . . .

"You are strong, Graydon," the Shadow's whisper was sweeter still. "Strong! You are stronger than any man of Yu-Atlanchi. Strong of body and strong of mind. You are like those of the Old Race whom I would have raised to the skies had it not been for trickery. It was not strength that defeated me, but the wiles of the Snake-woman who cares nothing for man—remember that, Graydon, the Snake who cares nothing for man! It was not to harm you but to test your strength that I just now wrestled with you. You were strong enough to resist me. I was glad of that, Graydon, for then I knew that at last I had found the man I need!"

So he was the man Nimir needed, eh? Well, he *was* a good man, a hell of a good man. He had gotten this far without help from anybody, hadn't he? No, wait a minute—somebody had helped him. Who was it? No matter—he was a good man. But somebody had helped him . . . somebody. . . .

The whisper of the Shadow broke smoothly into his groping thought.

"I need you, Graydon! It is not yet too late to remake this

world as it ought to be; not yet too late to right the wrong to humanity wreaked by the ancient treachery to me. But I must have a body to do it, Graydon. A strong body to hold me. Lend me your body, Graydon! It will be but for a time. And during that time you shall share it with me; you shall see as I see, enjoy as I shall enjoy, share my power and drink the wine of my victories. And when I have grown to my old strength, then, Graydon, I will leave you in full possession, and I will make it immortal—aye, deathless as long as the sun endures! Let me share your body, Graydon—strong Graydon!"

Now the whispering ceased. Strong wine surged through Graydon's veins, a rich, heady, reckless flood of life. He heard the blast of conquering trumpets! He was Genghis Khan, sweeping over kingdoms with his broom of Tartar horsemen; he was Attila lifted upon the shields of his roaring Huns; Macedonian Alexander trampling the world under his feet; Sennacherib holding all Asia like a goblet! He drank deep of power! He was drunk with power!

Was drunk! Was drunk? Who dared say that he, Nicholas Graydon, Master of the World, could be drunk! Well, all right—he was drunk, then. That was another funny idea—who wanted to be master of the world if all you got out of it was a drunk? Anybody could get drunk—therefore anybody who was drunk was master of the world! That *was* a funny idea . . . logical . . . have to tell that logical Shadow that funny idea. . . .

He found himself wide awake and roaring with laughter. He stared stupidly about him, and no longer felt desire for laughter. For he was halfway to the throne of jet—and the Shadow was bending, bending over it, beckoning him, urging him on, and whispering—whispering—

The spell that had held him, the lure that had played him, as a fish is played, half into the Shadow's creel, dropped from him. Loathing for that cloudy shape on the black throne, loathing for himself, bitter anger, swept him as he staggered back to the stone bench and dropped upon it, face hidden in shaking hands.

What had saved him? Not his consciousness, that thing he called himself. Something deep within his subconsciousness, something unalterably sane which had neutralized by ironic humor the poison his ears had been drinking. And now Graydon was afraid! So afraid that in sheer desperation he forced himself to lift his head and look straight at the Shadow.

It was staring at him, faceless head resting upon one misty hand. He sensed within it that same perplexity as when at first, unseen, it had striven to beat down his defenses—sensed, too, an infernal rage. Abruptly both were cut off; in their place flowed to him a current of calmness, deep peace. He strove to resist it, recognizing it for the trap it was; but it would not be repulsed; it lapped round him like little waves, caressing him, soothing him.

"Graydon!" came the whisper. "I am pleased with you, Graydon! But you are wrong to deny me. You are stronger than I thought, and that is why I am pleased with you. The body I share must be strong, very strong. Share your body with me, Graydon!"

"No! No! By God, no!" groaned Graydon, hating himself for the desire he felt to rush to this shadowy thing and let it merge itself with him.

"You are wrong! I will not harm you, Graydon. I do not want that strong body which is to be my home weakened. What is it you hope? Is it help from Huon? His days are few. Dorina has delivered him to Lantlu, even as she delivered you to me. Before the Feast of the Dream-Makers his lair will be taken, and Huon and all left alive will feed the Xinli, or me—or pray that they had!"

The whisper died, as though the Shadow had paused to watch the effect of this announcement. If it was to test the lethargy that steeped Graydon, it was satisfied; he made no motion, nor did his face change from its fixed, fascinated stare.

"Lend me your body, Graydon! The Snake cannot help you. Whether you lend or not, soon shall I be incarnate. I would have your body rather than a weaker one—only to share, Graydon, only to share—and that but for a little while. Power, immortality, wisdom beyond all others! These shall be yours! Lend me your body, Graydon! You desire one woman? What is one woman to those you can possess! Look, Graydon, look—"

Graydon's dazed eyes followed the pointing cloudy hand. He saw the evil blooms of the garden dipping and nodding to each other as though alive. He heard a witch song, a lilting choral woven with arpeggios of lutes and tinkling sistrums which was the garden-given voice. A gust swept up from it and embraced him. As he breathed its fragrance wild-fire touched his blood. The nodding flowers vanished, blood-red stream vanished; the corroding light of rusted black atoms became lucent. Close to his feet was a rippling, laughing little brook, beyond it a copse of beech and birch. And from the copse women came streaming, women of wondrous beauty, white nymphs and brown; full-breasted Bacchantes; slender, virginal dryads. They held out to him desirous arms, their eyes promised him undreamed delights. They came to the verge of the rill, beckoning him, calling him to them with voices that fanned the fire in his blood to flaming ecstasy of desire.

God—what women! That one with the coronal of bronze tresses might have been High Priestess of Tanith in the secret garden of her temple in old Carthage! And that one with the flood of golden hair might be white Aphrodite herself! Why, any one of them would make the fairest of houris in Mohammed's Paradise look like a kitchen maid! Fiercer grew the fire in his veins—he leaped forward. . . .

Stop! That girl who has stepped out from the others— who is she? She has midnight hair, and it covers her face. She's weeping! Why is she weeping when all her sisters are singing and laughing? He once had known a girl whose hair was that same mist of midnight—who? No matter . . . whoever she had been, none who resembled her must weep! She herself must never weep . . . what was her name. . . .

Suarra!

A wave of pity swept through him, quenching the witch-fires in his blood.

"Suarra!" he cried. "Suarra! You must not weep!"

And with that cry he felt a tingling shock. The wave of beckoning women vanished. The girl of the misty hair vanished. Gone was laughing brook, and copse of birch and beech. The evil garden swayed before him.

He stood more than halfway to the throne of jet. From it,

the Shadow was leaning far out, quivering with eagerness, and whispering—whispering—

"Lend me your body, Graydon! All these you shall have if you will but lend me your body! Lend me your body, Graydon!"

"Christ!" groaned Graydon, and then—"No, you devil! No!"

The Shadow stood erect. The pulse of rage that drove from it struck him like a material blow. He reeled under it, stumbled back to the safety of his bench. The Shadow spoke, and gone was all sweetness from its tone; its whisper was malignant, cold with purpose.

"You fool!" it said. "Now hear me. I shall have your body, Graydon! Deny me as you will, still shall I have it. Sleep, and I who do not sleep will enter it. Fight sleep, and when weariness saps that strength of yours, I will enter it. For a time you shall dwell within it with me, like a slave condemned, so tortured by what you see that again and again you will pray me to blot you out! And, because your body pleases me so, I will be merciful and give you this hope to dwell upon. After I am wearied of you, I will blot you out! Now, for the last time, will you submit to me? Lend me your body, share its tenancy with me, not as a slave but as master of all I have promised you?"

"No!" said Graydon, steadily.

There was a swirling upon the jet throne. It was empty of the Shadow. But still through the light upon the dais sifted the black atoms, and although that throne seemed empty, Graydon knew that it was not. And that the dark power was still there, watching, watching him.

Waiting to strike!

Graydon sat upon his bench, motionless as a man of stone. How many hours had passed since the whispering Shadow had gone, he did not know. His body was numb, but his mind was awake, brilliantly awake. He could not feel his body at all. His mind was like a tireless sentinel upon a sleeping tower. It was like an unquenchable light in a darkened castle. All his being was in that serene concentration of consciousness. He felt neither hunger nor thirst. He did not even think. That which was he, endured; withdrawn wholly into itself; unconquerable in a timeless world.

At first it had not been so. He had been sleepy, and he had fought sleep. He had dozed, and had felt the Shadow reach forth, touching him, testing his resistance. With what had seemed the last of his strength he had fought it back. He had striven to shut his mind from his surroundings, replace them with memory pictures of sane scenes. Sleep had again stolen upon him. He had awakened to find himself away from the bench, creeping toward the black throne. He had fled back in panic, thrown himself down, holding to the sides of the bench like a shipwrecked sailor to a spar.

He realized that the Shadow had its limitations, that it could not possess him unless it could draw him to its throne, or he mounted it of his own volition. As long as he remained upon the bench he was safe. After he had realized that, he did not dare close his eyes.

He wondered if by fixing his mind on her he could get in touch with the Snake Mother. If he could reach the bracelet on his arm, concentrate his gaze upon the purple stones, he might reach her. The sleeve of the coat-of-mail covered it too tightly, he could not get at it. And suppose she should summon him as she had before! Would not the Shadow leap into his unguarded body? The sweat dropped from his cold forehead. Frantically he shut the Serpent-woman from his thoughts.

He remembered the automatic beneath his armpit. If he could only get at that, it would give him a chance. At any rate, he could prevent the Shadow from getting his body to use it in any shape. It wouldn't be much good to Nimir with its brains blown out! But there was no opening in the suit through which he could reach it. He wondered whether by some device he could persuade the lizard-men, if they came back, to strip him. There would be time enough for him to use the gun before they could take it from him.

And then slowly his consciousness had withdrawn to this impregnable fortress. He no longer feared sleep; sleep was of another world. He feared nothing. When that sentinel which was his very essence abandoned its post, it would leave his body dead. Of no value to the Dark One as a habitation. He knew that, and was content that it should be so.

The rusted light about the black throne began to thicken, as it had when first the Shadow appeared to him. Shapeless, wavering at the beginning as then, the thing took form, condensed into sharp outline. He watched, with the detached interest of a casual spectator.

The Shadow took no notice of him, did not even turn its faceless head to him. It sat upon the throne, motionless as Graydon himself, gazing toward the further wall of murk through which the lizard-people had gone. It raised a hand, as though in summons.

There was a far-away thudding of padding feet, scores of them; a faint chorus of hissings that swiftly grew louder. He did not turn his head to look, could not if he had the desire. The padding feet came close and stopped, the hissing ceased, the musky fetor of the lizard-folk crept round him.

Up the ramp strode the man in the lizard mask.

The hideous head rested upon broad shoulders, the body was powerful, graceful, clad in close-fitting green. In his hand was a heavy, thonged whip. He paid no attention to Graydon. He walked to the foot of the jet throne, and bowed low to the Shadow.

"Master! Hail, Dark Master!" the voice that issued from the fanged jaws was melodious and faintly mocking, its arrogance thinly covered. "I have brought you another vessel into which it may please you to pour the wine of your spirit!"

Now it seemed to Graydon that the Shadow looked upon the man in the lizard mask with a malice greatly to be dreaded; but if so, it went unnoticed by him, and the Shadow's whisper held all its sweetness as it answered.

"I thank you, Lantlu—"

Lantlu! Graydon's serenity was shaken. On the instant he regained his poise, and none too soon—for the Shadow had turned its face swiftly toward him, as a fisherman twitches his line when he feels the fish nibble at his bait.

"I thank you, Lantlu," it repeated, "but I have found, I believe, the perfect vessel. It is now being reshaped somewhat upon the wheel, since it thinks itself designed for other purposes."

Lantlu turned the red eyes of his mask at Graydon, and walked over to him.

"Ah, yes," he said, "the hopeful fool from beyond who is to deliver Yu-Atlanchi from you and me, Master! Who conspires with Huon, the weakling, to shake our power. Who slinks through the night to meet his love. His love! You dog —even to look at one upon whom I had set my seal! And Suarra—to give her lips to such as you! Faugh! She would mate with the Urd! Well, after I take her, she shall."

Now at this, Graydon's citadel was shaken indeed; he felt his body again and tensed it to spring at Lantlu's throat. With almost audible clang the opening gates of his mind closed, that aloof consciousness resumed its sway, secure, bulwarked once more from attack. And again it was none too soon, for even as they closed he felt the Shadow thrust upon them. And like a sentence written in one flaming symbol, he read that no matter what he heard, or what he beheld, he must not again heed it. Or the Shadow would reel him in!

Lantlu raised his whip, poised it to bring it slashing down across Graydon's face.

"What?" he sneered. "So even that does not arouse you! Well, this may!"

The whip whistled down—

"Stop!" the whisper from the throne was thick with menace. Lantlu's arm was jerked back as though a stronger hand had gripped his wrist, the whip fell to the stone.

"You shall not touch this man! I, the Shadow of Nimir, tell you so!" the whispering was venom made articulate. "That is *my* body you would have dared to strike! My body you would have dared deface! Sometimes you annoy me, Lantlu. Beware that you do not do it once too often!"

Lantlu stooped, and as he picked up the whip his hand was shaking, but whether with fear or rage Graydon could not tell. He raised his head and spoke, the old arrogance in his voice.

"Every one to his taste, Dark Master," he said boldly. "And since you approve of his body, I suppose there is excuse for Suarra. But it is not one I would choose, with all Yu-Atlanchi to pick from until I found one strong enough."

"There is something more to a body than its shape, Lantlu," whispered the Shadow, sardonically. "Precisely as there is something more to a head than a skull. It is why he beat you just now, although you are free and he is in chains. I had supposed you knew this."

Lantlu quivered with rage, his hand clenched again about the whip. But he mastered himself.

"Well," he said, "he shall see the fruit of his folly. The vessel I bring you, Dark Master, is he who was to shelter this chosen one of yours."

He whistled. Up the ramp, arms held by two of the lizard-men, stumbled a Yu-Atlanchan tall as Lantlu himself. All the beauty of his face was wiped away by the fear that distorted it. His yellow hair dripped with the sweat of terror. He glared at the cloudy shape within the throne with eyes of nightmare. And as he glared, foam puffed from his lips in tiny bubbles.

"Come, Cadok, come!" jeered Lantlu. "You do not appreciate the honor shown you. Why, in a breath you will be no longer Cadok! You will be the Dark One! An apotheosis, Cadok—the only living apotheosis in all Yu-Atlanchi! Smile, man, smile!"

At this sinister jesting Graydon again thought that the Shadow's unseen gaze rested upon the lizard mask darkly, but as before there was nothing of threat in its voice when it spoke.

"I am sure this vessel is too weak to hold me—" the Shadow leaned forward, studying the trembling noble, impersonally. "Indeed, were I not sure, I would not pour myself into him, Lantlu, since there upon the bench is the body I desire. But I will enter him . . . I think that I am a little weary . . . and at the least he will refresh me. . . ."

Lantlu laughed, cruelly. He signaled the lizard-men. They ripped from Cadok his clothing, stripped him mother-naked. The Shadow bent, beckoning him. Lantlu gave him a quick push forward.

"On to your high reward, Cadok!"

And suddenly the face of Cadok was wiped clean of its nightmare terror. It became the face of a child. Like a child's face it wrinkled, and great tears poured down his cheeks.

Eyes fixed upon the beckoning Shadow, he walked to the throne of jet and mounted it.

The Shadow enveloped him!

For an instant Graydon could see nothing but a lurid mist in which Cadok writhed. The mist wrapped him closer, forcing itself within him. The Yu-Atlanchan's great chest swelled, his muscles knotted in agony.

And now his whole body seemed to expand as though rushing out to cover that part of the mist which still clung around him, unable to enter. The outline of his naked body became nebulous, cloudy, as though flesh and mist had merged into something less material than flesh, more material than the avid vapor.

The face of Cadok seemed to melt, the features to run together, then reassemble—

Upon the straining, tortured body was the Face in the abyss!

No longer stone!

Alive!

The pale, sparkling blue eyes looked out over the cavern, at the lizard-folk, now prostrate, groveling upon their bellies, heads hidden; upon Lantlu with Satanic amusement, upon Graydon with a glint of triumph.

Abruptly, what had been the body of Cadok shriveled and collapsed. It twisted and rolled down from the throne to the dais. It lay there, twitching and strangely shrunken to half the size it had been.

Upon the throne sat only the Shadow.

But now the Shadow was less tenuous, closer knit, as though that which had gone from the body of Cadok, leaving it so shrunken, had been absorbed by it. It seemed to breathe. The Luciferean face was still visible within it, the pale blue eyes still glittered.

Again Lantlu laughed and whistled. The two Urd upon the dais hopped to their feet, picked up the shriveled body, carried it to the garden and threw it into the red stream.

Lantlu raised his hand in careless salute to the jet throne, turned on his heel with never a glance at Graydon, and marched away swinging his whip, the Urd pack at his heels.

"Not you, but he is the fool, Graydon!" whispered the

Shadow. "He serves my purpose now, but when I. . . . Better lend me your body, Graydon, than have me take it! I will not treat you as I did Cadok. Lend me your body, Graydon! I will not torture you. I will not blot you out, as I threatened. We shall dwell together, side by side. I will teach you. And soon you will look back upon the man you now are, and wonder why you ever thought to resist me. For never have you lived as you shall live, Graydon! No man on earth has ever lived as you shall live! Lend me your body, Graydon!"

But Graydon was silent.

There came from the Shadow a whispering laugh. It wavered—and was gone!

Graydon waited, like a hare which has heard the fox go from where it hides, but lingers to be sure. After a time he knew definitely that the Shadow had departed. There was nothing of it left; no unseen crouching power awaiting its chance to strike. He relaxed, stood upon numb and uncertain feet, fighting a violent nausea.

And as he stood, he felt a touch upon his ankle, looked down and saw reaching from behind the edge of the carven screen a long and sinewy arm covered with scarlet hair. The needled, pointed fingers felt carefully around the metal link that fettered him, snapped it open, crept to the other and released it while Graydon stood staring stupidly, unbelievingly, at it.

A face peered round the screen's edge, chinless, scarlet elf locks falling over a sloping forehead, golden eyes filled with melancholy staring at him.

The face of Kon, the Spider-man!

CHAPTER XVI

The Painted Chamber

KON'S FACE was distorted by what was undoubtedly intended for a reassuring smile. Graydon, limp with reaction from his ordeal, dropped to his hands and knees. Kon reached over the side of the dais and lifted him up as easily as though he had been a puppy. Grotesque though he was, Graydon saw him then as more beautiful than any of those phantom women who had almost lured him into the Shadow's net. He put his arms around the hairy shoulders and clung tightly to them. The Spiderman patted him on the back with his little upper hands, making odd comforting clicking sounds.

From the garden came a shrill humming as of thousands of bees in swarm. Its flowers and trees were bending and twisting as though blown by a strong wind. Kon's huge eyes scanned it doubtfully, then, with Graydon still held close, he slipped around the edge of the screen. The humming in the garden arose octaves higher in pitch, threatening and—summoning.

As they turned its edge, Graydon saw that the screen was not detached as he had supposed. It was in reality a sculptured alcove, cut from the front of a buttress which thrust into the red cavern like the prow of a ship. A smooth cliff of black rock angled back from it.

Crouching at the base of this cliff, their scarlet hair causing them to be barely discernible in the rubrous haze, were two more Spider-men. They arose as Kon swung toward them. Graydon had a sense of weird duplication as they regarded him with their sorrowful golden eyes—as though not one Kon had come for him, but three. Clutched in the terminations of their four middle arms, or feet, were long metal bars like that which Regor wore, but unlike his, they had

151

handgrips and ended in spiked knobs. Two of these bars they passed to Kon. Mingled now with the insistent humming of the garden was a faint hissing undertone, far away, and rapidly growing closer; the clamor of the Urd.

Graydon wriggled in Kon's arm, and motioned to be set down. The Spider-man shook his head. He clicked to the others, gripped his two bars in the opposite hand, and dropping upon four of his stilts turned sharply from the wall of rock. He scuttled toward the wall of murk half a mile away. His comrades ranged on each side of him. They ran bent almost double, with the speed of a racing horse. They entered the rusty murk. The humming and hissing lessened to a faint drone, were swallowed by the silence.

Ahead, a barrier of reddish rock sprang out of the haze, vanishing in the heights above. At its base were great bowlders, fallen from the cliff, and among them hundreds of smaller ones, smooth and ochreous, and shaped with a queer regularity. The spider-men slowed to a walk, scanning the face of the precipice. Suddenly Graydon smelled the reek of the lizard-folk, knew those oddly similar bowlders for what they were—

"Kon!" he cried, pointing. "The Urd!"

The bowlders moved, sprang up, rushed upon them—a pack of the lizard-men, hissing, slaver dripping from fanged jaws, red eyes glowing.

Before they could turn, the pack was all around them. Kon dropped upon three stilts, out swung two other stilts whirling the great bars. His comrades rose on their hinder legs, a bar gripped in each of their four free hands. They flailed through the first ranks of the encircling pack, mowing them down. They re-formed into a triangle, back to back. Into the center of this triangle Kon set Graydon with an admonitory click. Out swung the bars again, cracking the pointed skulls of the Urd, unable to strike with their stumpy arms under that deadly ring, or to break through it.

The spider-men retreated slowly along the base of the cliff, cutting their way as they went. Graydon could no longer watch the fight, intent upon keeping his feet as he walked over the writhing bodies which paved the way. He heard a sharp clicking from Kon, felt his arm embrace and lift him. There was a quick rush forward. They had waded through the waves of the Urd. Down upon four stilts they dropped, and raced away, clicking triumphantly as they sped along. The hissing of the pack and the pad of their pursuing feet died.

Their pace decreased, they went more and more slowly, Kon studying the scarp. He halted, set Graydon down, and pointed to the cliff. High above the floor of the cavern, set in the red rock face, was an oval black stone. The Spider-man scuttled up to it, raised his long arms, and began feeling delicately around it. He gave a satisfied click, and keeping his talons upon a spot at the side of the stone, beckoned to Graydon.

He took his hand, and placed it against the cliff with the fingers spread wide and the heel of the hand pressing hard against the rock. Thrice he did this, and then, lifting him, carefully placed his fingers where his own claws had rested. Graydon understood. He was showing him where some mechanism was located which Kon's sharp-pointed digits could not motivate. He pressed fingers and heel of hand as directed.

A stone moved slowly upward like a curtain, revealing a dark tunnel. Kon clicked to his comrades. The pair passed warily through the black opening, bars ready. Soon they reappeared and conferred. The Spider-man patted Graydon on the back, and pointing to the tunnel, followed him into it. Here Kon again felt along the inner edge of the opening until he had found what he sought, and again he pressed Graydon's hand upon a spot which seemed to his touch precisely the same as the surrounding surface, as had the outer lock. The curtain of rock dropped, leaving him in utter blackness.

Darkness evidently meant no more to the spider-men than it did to the lizard-folk, for he heard them moving on ahead of him. Momentary panic seized him that they might not be able to understand his limitations and would leave him behind. Before he could cry out, Kon's arm was around him, had lifted him up and carried him away.

On they went, and on, through the darkness. Graydon felt rise around him a fine, impalpable dust, so fine that only by the millstones of incalculable ages could it have been ground to such tenuity. It told him that this passage was one unused by the lizard-folk or any other, and evidently it told the spider-men the same thing, for they went on confidently, with increased speed.

The darkness began to gray; now he could see the walls of the tunnel; and now they passed out of it into an immense chamber cut in the living rock. Dim within it as the light might be, it seemed glaring daylight to Graydon after the rust haze of the Shadow's cavern and the blackness of the passage. It came through fissures in the far side of the place. The impalpable dust was thick upon its floor.

In its center was a huge oval pool in which glimmered water, and around whose raised rim squatted a score of figures like gray gnomes. They were motionless, rigid. The spider-men drew together and clicked busily to each other, looking about them with obvious perplexity. Graydon walked over to the pool and touched one of the squatting gnomes. It was stone. He looked at the figures more closely. They were carven effigies of hairless, tailless, gray ape-men. Their long upper lips dropped to mouths beneath which were well-defined chins. The sinewy hands of their long arms knuckled the stone on which they sat. Their foreheads, though retreating, were semi-human. In the stone sockets of their eyes were gems resembling smoky topazes. With these topaz eyes they stared at the pool with something of that same puzzled melancholy which filled the golden eyes of Kon and his mates.

Walking around them, Graydon saw that they were both male and female, and that each wore a crown. He bent closer. The crowns were miniature sculptures of serpent-people, serpent-men and serpent-women, their coils twisted round the heads of the gray ape-men like the sun-snake upon the Ureus crown of the Pharaohs.

Down into the still pool a flight of yellow marble steps fell, vanishing in its depths.

Wondering, he walked over to a fissure, and as he drew near he saw that this whole face of the chamber had been broken away by the same force, earthquakes or subsidences perhaps, which had opened up the fissures. He peered out. He looked over the plain of the monolithic stones beyond the barrier. The chamber was at the very edge of the sky-reaching wall.

The sun was low—was it rising? If so, the time he had spent with the Shadow had been but a night. He had thought it much longer. He watched for awhile—the sun was setting. His ordeal had lasted a night and a day.

He turned back to Kon, suddenly aware that he was both thirsty and hungry. Under the direct light from the fissures, the wall through which they had come stood out clearly. Looking at it he halted, forgetting both hunger and thirst.

Along all its thousand-foot length it was covered with paintings. Paintings by lost masters, as rich in detail as Michelangelo's Last Judgment, landscapes as mystically beautiful as those of El Greco or Davies, portraiture as true as Holbein's or Sargent's, colorful as Botticelli, fantastic—but only so, he knew, because they pictured an unknown world; nothing in them of the fantasy of the unreal. He ran back to examine them.

Here was a city of rose-coral domes whose streets were bordered by scaled trees red and green, with foliage like immense ferns. Along them the serpent-people were borne in litters upon the heads of the gray ape-men. And here was a night scene with the constellations looking serenely down upon smooth fields covered with rings of pale green radiance through which the serpent-people moved in some strange ritual.

There was something peculiar about those constellations —he studied them. Of course, the outline of the Dipper, the Great Bear, was not the same shape as now. The four stars of its bowl were closer for one thing, a perfect square. And there was Scorpio—its claws not an arc but a straight bar of stars.

Why, if that picture of them were true, it showed the heavens as they must have been hundreds of thousands of years ago. How many ages before those distant orbs could shift to the position they seem to occupy today? It dizzied him.

And there was something peculiar about the pictures of the serpent-people. They lacked that human quality, so marked and so weird, of the Mother. Their heads were longer, flatter, reptilian. Their bodies above their coils were plainly development of the saurian; unmistakably evolved from a reptilian stem. He could accept them as realities—since in varying environments the evolution of almost any kind of intelligent creature is possible. He realized that it was the abrupt transition from serpent to woman that made the Serpent-woman incomprehensible; unreal.

Again he knew the haunting doubt—was she in reality as he had seen her, or, by some unknown power of will, did she create in the minds of those who looked upon her, illusion of childish body and heart-shaped face of exquisite beauty? He went back to the pool and scanned more closely the crowns upon the gray ape-men. They were like the serpent-people upon the wall. He compared them with the bracelet on his wrist. Well, whoever had carved that had seen the Serpent-woman as he had.

Wondering, he went back to his study of the painted wall. He looked long at the painting of a vast swamp in which monstrous bodies floundered; from its mud hideous heads peered, and over it great winged lizards flapped on leathery batlike wings. He stared even longer at the next. It was the same swamp; in the foreground was a group of the serpent-people. They lay coiled behind what appeared to be an immense crystal disk. The disk seemed to be swiftly revolving. And all over the morass, battling with the monsters, were winged shapes of flame. They held a core of brilliant incandescence from which sprang two nebulously radiant wings, like those of the sun's corona seen during some eclipses. These winged shapes appeared to pulse abruptly out of empty air, dart upon the monsters and fold their lambent wings about them.

And there was another city . . . the city across the lake from the cavern of the Frog-woman was a miniature of it, but there were no mountains around it. It came to him that this was the Yu-Atlanchi of the immemorial past, from which the serpent-people and those they had fostered had fled before the flood of ice whose creeping progress all their arts could not check. . . . He saw a fleet of strange ships, one of them fighting off the attack of a group of gigantic sea-saurians whose heads reared high above its masts. . . .

The history of a whole lost world was within that painted cavern. It held the pictured record of a lost era of earth's history.

He saw that at one time the paintings had covered all four walls. They were almost obliterated on two sides, completely so on that of the fissures. Only where the passage had opened were the pictures complete.

What had this chamber been? Why abandoned?

He was again aware of thirst. He walked back to the pool. He heard a warning click from Kon. Graydon pointed to the pool and to his throat. For full measure, he rubbed his belly and made the motions of chewing. The Spider-man nodded, scuttled to the yellow steps and down them. He dipped a hand in the water, smelled of it; cautiously tasted it. He nodded approvingly, bent down and sucked in a huge draft. Graydon knelt and scooped up handfuls. It was cold and sweet.

Kon clicked to his comrades. They went searching about the fissures, and presently returned with large pieces of brown fungi. Kon took a bit, dipped it into water, bit off a corner and handed the balance of it to Graydon. He accepted it doubtfully, but tasting it found that it absorbed the water like a sponge and was somewhat like bread with a pleasant yeasty flavor. He took another piece and dipped it. The three Weavers squatted beside him. All solemnly sopped their fungi in the pool and chewed it.

And suddenly Graydon began to laugh. Surely no man had ever dined as he was dining—squatting there beside the weird pool with the three scarlet grotesques, dipping mushrooms in the water with topaz-eyed, hairless, gray ape-men looking on, and the history of a lost epoch spread out before him for his entertainment. He laughed and laughed, with swiftly growing hysteria.

Kon looked at him, clicking inquiringly. Graydon could not stop his laughing, nor the sobbing hiccoughs that now began to punctuate it. Kon took him up in his long arms, and swung him to and fro like a baby.

Graydon clung to him; the hysteria passed away. And in passing it took with it all the taint of the Shadow's whispers, all the hateful lure of the evil garden. The film of evil which lay upon his mind passed away like scum on water under a strong cleansing wind.

He was sleepy, he had never felt so sleepy! Now he could sleep without fear of the Shadow creeping into him. Kon wouldn't let anything like that happen. The light was dimming fast . . . sun must be almost down . . . he'd sleep for a few minutes . . .

Cradled in the arms of the Spider-man, Graydon dropped into deepest, dreamless sleep.

CHAPTER XVII

Taking of Huon's Lair

DAWN WAS FILTERING into the painted cavern. Graydon sat up and looked uncomprehendingly about him. He was upon a bed of moss. One of the spider-men squatted close to him, studying him with puzzled, sad eyes. There was no sign of the others.

"Where's Kon?" he asked. The Spider-man answered with a string of rapid clicks.

"Kon! Hey, Kon!" called Graydon.

The Weaver sensed his anxiety, and its reason; he sidled to him, patted him with his small upper hands, nodding and softly clicking. Graydon gathered he was being told there was nothing to worry about. He smiled and patted the Weaver upon a shoulder. The Spider-man seemed much pleased. He scuttled over to the crevices, returning with the bread-like fungi. The two went down to the pool and breakfasted; the Weaver keeping up an amiable succession of clicks between bites, and Graydon companionably answering with a totally unrelated monologue. He felt refreshed, ready to cope with anything.

There was a movement in one of the large crevices. Through it came the scarlet body of Kon, and following him the second Weaver. The trio clicked busily. Kon waited until Graydon had finished his last piece of fungi, beckoned him and moved over to the crevice through which he had entered. The other spider-men crawled through it, vanishing. Kon followed, and disappeared. His long red arm stole back into the slit, and looked out. Far below was the plain of the monoliths.

Kon's arm crooked round him, and drew him out. Graydon's head swam, for below him was a sheer half-mile drop.

159

The Spider-man was hanging to the face of the cliff, his supple fingers gripping cracks and projections which only they could have made use of. He tucked Graydon under his arm, and began to crawl along the precipice. Graydon looked down just once more, and was convinced he would feel better if he kept his eyes on the rock. They swung along for about two thousand feet. Another crevice appeared. Kon thrust him through it, and scrambled after him.

They were in a wide passage which had probably once run into the painted cavern. The same destructive agency had been at work. Its end was blocked by a rock fall, and its wall was pierced by scores of holes and fissures. Its floor was littered with fallen stone. Kon looked doubtfully at Graydon and stretched out his arm. Graydon shook his head violently, tired of being carried around like a baby. They set off down the corridor, but his progress was comparatively slow; so slow that Kon shortly picked him up with a conciliatory click. The three Weavers set off at a fast pace over the débris. He resigned himself. After all, as well ride a Spider-man as a camel or an elephant; if one had never seen a camel or an elephant they would seem just as unusual as Kon and his kind.

The passage darkened, blackened and finally curved into a caverned space filled with a dim twilight. There were no fissures. The light was the same as that which streamed from the walls in Huon's lair, but here it seemed to be dying, old and outworn, as though the force which produced it were almost spent. The place was a vast storehouse. Graydon caught glimpses of enigmatic mechanisms of crystal and black metal, among them huge globes of silver; once he saw something which appeared to be the hull of a ship, and once he passed by what was certainly one of the crystal disks painted in the battle in the primeval swamp. They loomed all around him, these vague, shrouded shapes of mystery. The spider-men paid no attention to them, threading their way rapidly.

They entered another black tunnel. They had gone along this for a mile or more when Kon gave a click of warning. He set Graydon down, and the four stood listening. He heard men walking slowly and cautiously, and not far away. A cloudy light abruptly impinged upon the wall of the tunnel, as though a little luminous ball of cloud had been thrown against it. It came from a transverse passage only a few yards ahead. The spider-men gripped their bars, stole softly forward.

Before they could reach the opening, a man's head projected around the side—a head whose hair was silvery-white over a stained bandage, the scars of claws upon its cheek—

"Regor!" shouted Graydon, and rushed by the spidermen.

The giant bounded into the tunnel, embracing him, bellowing amazed joy. The spider-men came forward, clicking like castanets. From the transverse passage emerged five of the Fellowship men, clothing torn, carrying swords and maces and small round shields; all showed the marks of heavy fighting. After them trooped a dozen of the Emers with spears and swords and the same small shields, kilts tattered and none of them without some wound.

One of these grinned at him out of a battered face and held up his rifle.

"How the devil did you know where to look for me?" demanded Graydon when at last Regor had grown coherent.

"I wasn't looking for you, lad," he answered. "I was looking for a way into the Temple to tell Suarra of your capture, hoping she would raise such a storm about it that the Mother could not refuse to aid you—if you were still alive. Also I admit hoping this would involve protection for myself and these with me. And on second thought, I'm not so sure I am glad I did find you. It was our only hope, and now I have no excuse to appeal to Adana." He grinned.

"Protection!" exclaimed Graydon. "I don't understand you, Regor. You must have gotten back to the lair safely."

"The lair is sacked!" said Regor. "Ripped open, gutted. Huon is prisoner of Lantlu. The Fellowship, what's left of it, dispersed, wandering like us about these burrows."

"Good God!" Graydon was aghast. "What happened?"

"Dorina did it," said the giant, and there was a murmur of hatred from the others. "Something told me to kill her, when I managed to get back to the lair after you had disappeared. But I wasn't sure she had betrayed us. Last night,

while we were asleep, she opened a secret door to Lantlu
and a few of his friends. They stole in and killed quietly and
quickly the guards at the great door. Dorina lifted it, and
let in more of Lantlu's supporters and a pack of the Urd.
There was no time for us to gather. Many were slaughtered
in their beds. After that it was group fighting all over the
place. I saw them drag Huon down and truss him. Some of
our Emers managed to escape—how much of the Fellowship, I don't know. Not many, I fear. We were fortunate.
They added a few more scars to my decorations," he touched
the bandage, "but they paid for it."

"Dorina!" whispered Graydon, "Dorina! Then the
Shadow did not lie!"

Regor started, looked at him keenly.

"Lad—you've seen the Shadow! The Dark Master!"

"I'll say I have!" said Graydon, grimly, in his own tongue,
then in the Aymara, "I was his guest for a night and a day.
He was bargaining for my body!"

Regor drew back a step, scrutinizing him. He clicked to
Kon and the Spider-man answered at some length. When he
finished, Regor stationed the Indians at guard at the opening through which they had come, and seated himself on a
block of fallen stone.

"Now tell me everything. And this time—keep nothing
back."

Graydon did, from the first stealthy onslaught of the hidden lizard-man. Regor and the five Yu-Atlanchans listened,
silent, fascinated. When he told the fate of Cadok, Regor
groaned, his face livid, and beat his breast with clenched
fist.

"Good lad! Good lad!" he muttered brokenly, when
Graydon had ended, and sat for a time in thought.

"That cavern where you thought you saw a ship," he
broke his silence. "If you are right—it was a ship. One of
those upon which our ancestors came to the Hidden Land
with the serpent-people, and preserved there with many
other precious things. So long has that cavern been locked
away, unentered, that it was thought to be but another legend, a wonder tale. None but the Snake Mother and the Lord

of Folly remembers the way into it, unless it be Nimir. And if he does, it is plain he has not given the secret to Lantlu.

"The cavern of the Lost Wisdom!" there was awe in Regor's voice. "And it exists! By the Mother, what we have forgotten! How we have fallen from the ancient strength! Once, Graydon, so the story runs, there was a wide entrance to it opening upon the lake. This was blocked with rocks, and the rocks melted, by some device the Old Ones knew, after the war that ended in the prisoning of Nimir. So cunningly was it done that none now can tell that sealed place from the surrounding stone. Yet I have heard a way was left to it from the Temple, through which the Lords and the Snake Mother passed from time to time when desire came to them to look again upon its ancient treasures. Once in, I think we can find its door, and if we do I have that which will open it."

He drew Graydon aside.

"Did you think I had abandoned you, lad?" he whispered, huskily. "The Urd were too thick around me to break through. Although I fought as never before. Then by lucky chance that Emer over there who held your noisy weapon set it going. The Urd scattered squealing and even Lantlu dropped from the platform. But you were nowhere in sight, or hearing. I knew you had been carried off. The Emer and I were away before Lantlu could gather his pack together. When I reached the lair, we took council. It was Huon's idea to send Kon after you. Huon was strange—strange as when he bade you farewell. There was a cavern of red-dust light, he said. There Kon and his Weavers must search. They must start, he said, from the opening through which we passed when we left the lair . . . always have we known that there was danger of meeting the Urd in that place . . . but never dreamed that it was a way to the throne of the Dark One. Back, far back you must go, Huon told Kon. And then . . . his face became drawn and white as when he spoke of the slaying shadows dropping from the red sky . . . and he told of a black precipice ending in a black shrine beside a garden. There they would find you.

"I opened that door and let them out. I watched them merge at once into the murk, and realized how wisely Huon had picked them. Kon says they made their way swiftly far, far back, seeing no Urd, until at last the black cliff sprang up before them. Now which way to follow that wall, he did not know; by chance decided upon the left. On they went and on until he heard the sound of many Urd, and a man's voice, and a voice which Kon says 'spoke without a man to hold it.' They waited until the Urd had gone away and until the bodiless voice had gone—

"And there you were, in the black shrine beside the garden! Strange . . . strange that Huon. . . ."

He paused, shaking his head perplexedly.

"That little beast of yours is done for, I fear," he said. "But just before the raid I took some of your weapon's food."

He called the Indian who held the gun. Graydon took it, rejoicing in the feel of it. The Emer thrust a pouch out to him. Within it were about a hundred cartridges and several clips for his automatics. He looked the rifle over, it was unharmed. He loaded it.

"Put your hand through the slit of this damned armor, Regor," he said. "Reach up under my arm and give me what you find there."

Regor obeyed, drew out the automatic. Graydon thrust it into his belt. He felt much better; swords and maces were all right in their way, but every man knew his own weapons best.

"Let's go," he said.

Regor whistled to the guard, and touched Kon. The Spider-man beside him, he led the way up the black passage, retracing Graydon's journey. The two Weavers fell in behind them, Graydon and the Fellowship men followed, the Indians brought up the rear. Regor did not depend upon Kon's eyes for guidance. Now and again he cast ahead of him the vaporous, light-stimulating ball.

They came to that place Regor had called the Cavern of Lost Wisdom. As he crossed its threshold, he dropped upon his knees and kissed the floor. The Yu-Atlanchans whispered among themselves but did not imitate him.

They threaded their way through it in the crepuscular dusk of the dying atoms; past the dim, vague shapes of the mysterious machines, past immense coffers of metals red and gray that held, Graydon wondered, what relics of the lost world; by the huge silvery globes they went, and he saw that upon them were traced enigmatic symbolings in lacquers of gold and blue; they came to the shadowy hull of the great ship, and here again Regor bent his knee. On and on they went, through the dusk, past the science, the art, the treasures of the serpent-people and the mighty forefathers of the Yu-Atlanchans. They came to their end, and looked out over an empty space whose further side they could not see.

"We must cross there," Regor said, "until we come to the rock that seals the ancient entrance. The corridor of the Lords, so said he who told me of this, is at its edge and in the direction of the cataract, which is at the right. The tunnel runs under the lake and skirts the amphitheater of the Xinli. There we must go softly, for I do not know whether other passages may not open into the one we travel. If so, it seems to me they must be sealed—indeed, must be, since the Old Ones planned to shut this cavern off for all time. Still, we will take no chances. And, somewhere near, there is an entrance into the tunnel which Suarra traveled from the Hall of the Weavers that night she met us."

They set off across the empty space. They came at length to a wall of rock which appeared to be formed of bowlders fused by volcanic heat. Regor grunted complacently. They skirted the wall to the right until Regor saw, set high within the rock, an oval black stone like that Kon had searched for in the red cavern.

Regor clicked to the Spider-man. Kon felt carefully around the stone as he had the other, turned and shook his head. Regor took from his belt the cone he had used to open the door from the lair and gave it to him. Light sprayed from it as the red Weaver pressed it methodically over the face of the barrier. The rock began slowly to open, like the two valves of a sliding door. They peered into a corridor, much more brilliantly lighted, dropping at an easy decline. After they had entered, Kon pressed the cone to the inner sides. The rock portal closed. Look closely as he might, Graydon could see no traces of it; the rock was smooth and unlined.

They went through that passage for a mile or more. Straight at first, it soon began to twist tortuously, as though it had been cut from some soft, meandering vein.

"We have passed beneath the lake, I know that if nothing else," whispered Regor.

Abruptly the corridor terminated in a small crypt. Two of its walls bore a black oval. Regor looked at them, and scratched his head.

"By Durdan the Hairy!" he grumbled. "There were so many turns that I know not which side is toward the Temple and which away from it."

Nor could the others help him.

"Well," he decided, "we go to the right."

Kon manipulated the cone. Almost immediately a stone slid upward. They were in a tunnel brighter still, and running at right angles.

"If this is right, then we go right again," said Regor. They slipped along, cautiously. They stepped out of the tunnel without warning into a guard chamber in which were half a dozen Emer soldiers, not in yellow but in green-kilted kirtles, and an officer, a noble clad also in Lantlu's green.

These stared at the motley intruders, like men of wood. Before they could recover from their amazement, Regor signaled Kon. Instantly the three spider-men sprang upon the Indians and throttled them. Regor's strong fingers went round the officer's throat. And all so quickly that Graydon himself had had no time to move.

Regor loosened his grip, and raised his bar. Kon scuttled over, stood behind the Yu-Atlanchan, pinioned his arms.

"So right was wrong!" muttered Regor. "Speak softly, Ranena. Answer briefly. What place is this?"

Ranena glanced at the bodies of his guards at the feet of the two Weavers, and little beads of sweat stood out on his forehead.

"No need to treat me so, Regor," he said thickly. "I have never been your enemy."

"No?" asked Regor suavely, "and yet I thought I saw you in the lair last night. Perhaps I was mistaken. However —answer quickly, Ranena!"

"It guards a way to the amphitheater," the answer came

sullenly. As though to confirm him, there came a rumbling as of far-away thunder, and the sound of cheering. "They race the Xinli," he added.

"And Lantlu, of course, is there?" asked Regor.

A shade of malice crossed Ranena's fine face.

"And Dorina," he said.

"What have they done with Huon?"

"Listen, Regor," Ranena's clear eyes darkened craftily, "if I tell you where Huon is and how to reach him, will you promise not to kill me, but truss me up and gag me before you go to him?"

"What have they done with Huon?" repeated Regor.

He clicked to the Spider-man. One of Kon's hands covered Ranena's mouth, with the others he began slowly to lift his arms behind him and twist them. Ranena writhed, his face distorted with agony. He nodded.

Kon withdrew his hand, lowered his arms. Little drops of blood ran down the cheek where the needled fingers had pierced it.

"After the next race—he fights the Xinli," he groaned.

"So!" said Regor quietly. "So! And now do I see that though right was wrong, wrong has become right!"

He signaled Kon. The Spider-man bent back Ranena's neck and snapped it.

Regor looked down into the glazing eyes, and turned to his Indians.

"You and you—" he pointed in turn to six of them, "dress yourselves in their clothes. Notalu," he spoke to one of the Yu-Atlanchans, "strip Ranena, and change your yellow for his green. Then watch. Probably none will come, but if they do—slay them swiftly before they have a chance to cry out. I will leave you two of the Weavers—you know how to command them. Kon goes with me. But first we must get rid of this carrion."

He clicked to Kon. The Spider-man picked up the bodies, and carried them into the corridor which Ranena had said led to the amphitheater. They laid the stiffening figures along its walls, out of sight of the guard room. They returned and two of them dropped behind the stone benches, hidden.

"Now let us see what can be done for Huon," said Regor.

They stole down the corridor, past Ranena, glaring at them with dead eyes.

There was a blaze of sunlight, dazzling Graydon. Squares of black danced in it. He heard the thunder of monstrous feet.

His vision cleared. He stood before a door grated with heavy metal bars. He looked through it into the arena of the dinosaurs.

CHAPTER XVIII

The Arena of the Dinosaurs

THE FLOOR of the arena was an immense oval about five hundred feet across, a half-mile in length, and covered with smooth yellow sand. Around this oval ran a wall of polished, jade-green stone four times the height of a tall man. There were grated openings in it here and there, a few much larger than that through which he peered. Beyond the wall, tier upon tier of stone seats stretched back to the amphitheater's rim a hundred and fifty feet on high. Here banners streamed. Within the greater oval was a smaller one, made of a thick, four-foot wall; the two made a track about fifty feet wide.

Almost directly opposite Graydon was a wide section thronged with the Yu-Atlanchans. Slender, green lacquered pillars arose from its supporting silken awnings. It was like a gigantic flower garden with the gay and vivid hues of the women's garments blossoming out of the dominant green which evidently was Lantlu's chosen color.

Bordering this enclosure of the nobles was a double file of the green-kirtled Emers bearing javelins and bows; then came a wide and empty area of the seats, another double file of the soldiers, and beyond them thousands of the Indians in holiday dress. And beyond them stretched untenanted tier upon tier—proof of the dwindling numbers of the ancient people.

In the curiously clear air, distances were foreshortened. At the very front he saw Lantlu, surrounded by a group of laughing nobles. Who was the woman beside him?

Dorina!

He heard Regor cursing, knew he, too, had seen her.

But Dorina was not laughing with the others. She sat, chin on clenched hands, looking somberly across the arena, staring straight at where they hid, as though—as though she watched them. Graydon drew hastily back.

"Will that weapon of yours reach her?" Regor's face was black with hate.

"Easily—but I'd rather try it on Lantlu," answered Graydon.

"No—on neither of them. Not now—" he shook his head, recovering his control. "It would bring us no closer to Huon. But that rotting daughter of a carrion eater, that *buala*—to come to watch him die!"

"Well, she doesn't seem very happy about it," said Graydon.

Regor groaned, and began searching around the sides of the grating.

"We must get this open," he grumbled. "Get Huon to us when they let him out . . . where's the cursed lock . . . then we can run back to the tunnel and get away by that other door . . . better send Kon to carry him back . . . no, Kon can run faster than any of us, but not faster than the arrows . . . they'll fill him with them before he is halfway there . . . no, we'll have to wait . . . by the Seven . . . ah, there it is!"

There was the sound of bolts slipping. He tried the door. It was open. Twice they locked and unlocked it, and to make certain no time would be wasted on it when the moment came, Graydon marked the pressure spots with the end of a cartridge.

There was a fanfare of trumpets. A grating below Lantlu swung open. Out of it leaped six of the riding Xinli. Tyrannosaurs, thunder-lizards dwarfed like those of the hunting packs, but not so greatly. Monstrous black shapes shining as though covered with armor of finely cut jet. Their thick tails, twice as long as their bodies, tapered to a point; the tails curved up, twitching restlessly. Their small reptilian heads turned nervously upon long, slender, snake-like necks. They bent forward upon hind legs heavy and cylindrical as those of an elephant. They held their small forelegs close to their breasts, like kangaroos—whose attitude when at rest, in fact, almost precisely simulated that of these dinosaurs.

Where the slender necks ran into the sloping shoulders a rider sat, each clad in different color, like jockeys. They were of the nobles, and despite their height they were monkey-small against the bulk of their steeds. They squatted upon little saddles, stirruped, holding reins which manipulated a massive bit. The dinosaurs champed at these bits, hissing and grumbling, striking at each other with their absurdly small heads like spirited racers at the starting post, chafing to be gone.

There was another fanfare of the trumpets, and immediately upon it the thundering of the huge feet. The Xinli did not hop, they ran as a man runs, legs pumping up and down like pistons. Necks stretched rigidly ahead of them, they swept round the oval course. They passed Graydon in a bunch and with the speed of an express train. The wind from their passing rushed through the grating like a whirlwind. He shuddered, visualizing what would happen to a file of men trying to oppose those projectiles of sinew and bone.

They passed the enclosure of the nobles like a rushing black cloud. From Yu-Atlanchans and Indians came a storm of cheering. And now, as they neared him again, Graydon saw that there was another phase to this racing of the dinosaurs. They were no longer grouped. Two were in the lead, a rider in green and one in red. The green rider was trying to force the red over against the inner wall of the course. The four thundering close behind seemed to be in *mêlée,* each jockeying to force the other against the same low buttresses. The boa-like necks of the Xinli writhed and twisted, the small heads darting at each other like striking snakes.

The rider in green suddenly lurched his mount against that of the red. The red rider made a desperate effort to lift his monster over the barricade. It stumbled, went crashing down into the island. The rider went flying from it like a red ball from a tennis racket, struck the sand, rolled over and over and lay still. The green rider drew ahead of the ruck; a rider in purple drew out of it and came thundering down upon him, striving to keep the other between himself and the low rail. A burst of cheering drowned the thunder of the Xinli's flying feet.

Again they rushed past, the green rider now two lengths ahead of the purple, the three remaining riders spread out in line close behind them. They charged by the stand of the nobles and, sliding in a cloud of the yellow sand, came to halt. There was a wilder burst of cheering. They padded back, and Graydon saw a glittering circlet tossed down to the green rider.

The dinosaurs filed through the opening and out of sight. Soldiers came through it when they had disappeared, picked up the limp body of the red rider, and carried him away. One of them took the reins of the dinosaur he had ridden and which had stood stupidly, head lowered, since its fall. He led it off like a horse through the gate. The gratings clanged.

There was another loud fanfare of the trumpets. A silence fell upon the arena. Another grating opened, close by the other—

. Out of it walked Huon.

He carried a short sword and a javelin, upon his left arm was one of the little round shields. He stood for a moment, blinking in the dazzling sun. His eyes rested upon Dorina. She shrank and hid her face in her hands—then lifted her head and met Huon's gaze defiantly.

He began to raise his javelin, slowly, slowly. Whatever was his thought, he had no chance to carry it into action. A grating not a hundred feet from him swung softly open. Out upon the yellow sand sprang one of the dwarfed dinosaurs of the hunting packs. While it halted there, motionless, glaring around, Graydon learned how much can pass through the mind in the time it takes to draw a single breath. He saw Lantlu lean forward with ironic salute to the man Dorina had betrayed. He saw the fighting Xinli in every detail—the burnished scales of sapphire blue and emerald green that covered it gleaming like jewels, its forelegs, short and powerfully thewed, its talons like long curved chisels protruding from the flat hands, the vicious flailing tail, the white-fanged jaws, the eyes of flaming red set wide apart like a bird's on each side of the visored head.

His rifle was at his shoulder, the sights upon Lantlu. He hesitated—should he drop Lantlu or try for the dinosaur? In only one place was it vulnerable to a bullet, through one of those little red eyes. Wavering, he turned the sights upon it, drawing finest bead . . . no, better not risk that tiny target . . . back again to Lantlu . . . but he was leaning, half-hidden behind Dorina, talking to some one beside her . . . steady, steady till he swings back . . . ah, that was it. . . . Hell, Regor's moved the grating, spoiled the aim. . . .

All in a breath this went racing through Graydon's mind. And then the dinosaur was rushing upon Huon. Regor was shaking his arm, pointing at the charging monster, beseeching him to shoot. Hell . . . there was no use in a wild shot . . . the bullet would ricochet off those scales like armor plate . . . better try Lantlu . . . what use would that be now . . . better wait . . . better wait for a chance at the devilish brute. . . .

Huon leaped backward, out of the path of the dinosaur's rush. It whirled within its own length, sprang back at him with talons upraised to smite. It leaped. Huon dropped upon one knee, thrust upward with the javelin at the unprotected spot in its throat. The javelin struck, but not deeply enough to kill. The shaft snapped close to the hilt. The dinosaur hissed, pivoted in mid-leap, and dropped to its feet a few yards away. It felt of its throat with oddly human gesture, then began to circle Huon warily, flexing the muscles of its arms like a shadow-boxer. Huon kept pacing it, broken javelin shifted to his left hand, sword in the other, shield on left arm and close to his breast.

"Huon! I'm coming! Hold fast!"

Shouting, Regor rushed by Graydon, and out over the sand. His cry shattered the silence that, except for the hissing of the wounded dinosaur, had hung over the arena. A deeper silence, one of sheer stupefaction, followed. Huon stared at the running figure. The dinosaur turned its head. The sun fell straight upon one of the crimson eyes. It stood out against the skull like a small bull's-eye of fire. Graydon drew quick sight on that red target and fired.

The crack of the rifle echoed over the arena. The dinosaur sprang high, somersaulted, and hopped staggering over the sand, clawing at its head. From the crowded tiers arose a great sigh like the first sough of a tempest, a surging of bodies. Past Graydon, clicking violently, raced Kon in Regor's wake. He raised the rifle upon Lantlu, and saw him drop behind the protecting wall as though something had whispered warning.

Dorina sat motionless, looking down at Huon. She was like one who knew her weird was upon her.

Regor was half across the arena, Kon scuttling beside him. Huon, looking not once again behind him, eyes fixed on the woman, stepped a pace nearer the wall.

He hurled his broken javelin. There was a flash of light as it sped. The light was quenched in Dorina's breast.

Silence again for another long moment. And then the whole amphitheater roared. A shower of arrows fell round the outlaw of the lair. Kon sped past Regor, caught Huon in an arm, and came racing back. Graydon emptied his rifle into the line of archers; the storm of arrows abruptly ceased.

The trumpets sounded, peremptorily. Through opened gratings and down over the wall streamed the green-kirtled Emers. Closer to them, from each side ran others emerging from the nearer openings. Kon was close, Regor drawing near. Graydon, with burning desire for just one machine-gun, emptied his rifle into those who menaced them from the sides. They halted. The frenzied dinosaur raised its head and came charging with great leaps down upon the line of soldiers pursuing Regor. They scattered out of its path. The giant swung shut the heavy doors and set the bars. The dinosaur hurled himself against them, tearing at them with its steel-like claws, dripping yellowish blood from a skull partly shattered by Graydon's bullet.

"You're damned hard to kill!" he muttered, and raised the rifle for another close, certain shot at the unhurt eye.

"No!" panted Regor, and caught his arm. "It will hold that door for us."

Huon, dropped upon his feet by the Spider-man, stood like an automaton, head bent. And suddenly deep sobs shook him.

"It's all right now, lad—it's all right now!" comforted the giant.

An arrow flew past the dinosaur, through the grating, barely missing Graydon, then another and another. He heard the blaring of many trumpets, angry, summoning.

"Best move quickly!" grunted Regor. Arm around Huon, he ran back through the corridor, Graydon at his heels, the little hands of Kon patting him approvingly, affectionately, as they went. The others pressed close behind. They came to the guard chamber. They opened the secret door through which they had entered that place, and closed it with the clatter of pursuing feet already near. And in the little crypt, Kon sought and found the means of unlocking the passage beneath the left-hand oval stone.

They closed that last portal. They set off in silence down the corridor into which it had opened, to the haven of the Temple.

CHAPTER XIX

The Snake Mother

THEY WENT SILENTLY, Regor's arm around Huon's shoulders. The five Fellowship men had passed the Weavers; they marched with drawn swords behind their chief. The Indians followed Graydon. Whenever he turned he found their eyes upon him—as though they now regarded him as their leader. The one who carried his rifle had plainly become a personage, stepping proudly ahead of his fellows almost on Graydon's heels. They came to the end of the passage, and opened without difficulty its entrance.

They stepped out of it into the columned hall of Graydon's dream!

The beams of dimly azure light played down from its soaring, vaulted roof like the lanced rays of the aurora. Mistily radiant, they curtained a spacious alcove raised high above the tesselated, opaline pave. Behind their veil Graydon saw a sapphire throne, and lesser thrones of red, golden and black at its base of milky crystal—the seats of the Seven Lords.

A girl stood there, just beyond the top of a broad flight of steps dropping from the alcove, a girl with white hands clasped tightly to her breast, red lips parted in wonder, soft black eyes staring at him incredulously—

"Graydon!" she cried, and took a swift step toward him.

"Suarra!" the warning voice was lisping, tinglingly pure, in it the trilling of birds. A pillar of shimmering mother-of-pearl shot up behind the girl; over her shoulder peered a face, heart-shaped, coifed with hair like spun silver, purple-eyed—

The Snake Mother!

"Let us see who are these visitors who come so unceremoniously in the train of your man," she lisped, "and by a way I thought surely none now in Yu-Atlanchi knew."

She raised a little hand, in it a sistrum within whose loop, instead of bars, a glistening globule danced like quicksilver.

Regor stifled an exclamation and dropped upon his knees, the others hastily following suit with the exception of the spider-men, who stood quietly watching. Graydon hesitated, then also knelt.

"Ah, so you have remembered your manners!" there was faint mockery in the tinkling voice. "Come nearer. By my ancestors—it is Regor—and Huon . . . and since when did you don Lantlu's green, Notalu? It is long since you bent the knee to me, Regor."

"That is not my fault, Mother!" began Regor, indignantly. "Now that is not just—"

A trilling of laughter silenced him.

"Hot tempered as ever, Regor. Well, for a time at least, you shall have much practice in that neglected duty. You too, Huon, and the others of you—"

Graydon heard the giant groan with relief, saw his scarred face light up; his bellow interrupted her.

"Homage to Adana! We are her men now!" He bent until his bandaged brow touched the floor.

"Yes!" said the Mother, softly, "but for how long—ah, that even I cannot tell. . . ." She dropped the hand that held the quivering globe, bent further over Suarra's shoulder, beckoned to Graydon—"Come up to me. And do you shut that door behind you, Regor."

Graydon walked to the alcove, mounted the steps, his fascinated eyes upon the purple ones fixed upon him so searchingly. As he drew close, the Serpent-woman moved from behind the girl, the shimmering pillar from which sprang her childish body between him and Suarra. And he felt again that curious, deep-seated throb of love for this strange being— like a harp string in his heart which none but she could pluck. He knelt again, and kissed the tiny hand she held out to him. He looked up into her face, and it was

177

tender, all age-old weariness gone, her eyes soft—and he had not even memory of those doubts which had risen in the Painted Cavern; so strong her witchery—if witchery it was.

"You have been well brought up, child," she murmured. "Nay, daughter—" she glanced at Suarra, mischievously, "be not disturbed. It is only to my years that he does reverence."

"Mother Adana—" began Suarra, face burning—

"Oh, go over there and talk, you babes," the scarlet, heart-shaped lips were smiling. "You have much to say to each other. Sit on the golden thrones, if you like. What were you thinking then, Suarra's man? That a golden throne was symbol to you of journey's end? Surely, you were. Why it should be, I do not know—but that was your thought. Well then, take one."

Graydon, beginning to rise, dropped back on his knee. When she had spoken of the golden thrones lines of an old negro spiritual had cropped up in his head—

> When I'm through with this weary wanderin',
> When I'm through, Lawd!
> I'll sit on a golden throne—

The Snake Mother was laughing. She beckoned Suarra. She took the girl's hand and put it in Graydon's. She gave them a little push away.

"Regor," she called. "Come to me. Tell me what has happened."

Swinging his bar, marching jauntily, Regor approached. Suarra drew Graydon back to a nest of curtains at the rear of the alcove. He watched Regor mount beside the Serpent-woman, saw her bend her head to him, prepare to listen. Then he forgot them entirely, absorbed in Suarra, overflowing with concern for him, and curiosity.

"What did happen, Graydon?" her arm slipped round his neck. "We had gone quickly, and were close to the cataract. It was very noisy, but I thought I heard your weapon. I hesitated, thinking to return. But there was no further sound, so I went on. And Regor and the others—how did they get their wounds?"

"Lantlu sacked the lair. Huon was betrayed by Dorina. Lantlu took Huon and matched him against one of his cursed Xinli. We rescued him. Huon killed Dorina," he told her, staccato.

"Dorina betrayed him! He killed her!" Her eyes widened.

"She was an aunt of yours, in some way, wasn't she?" he asked.

"Oh, I suppose so—in a way—long, long ago," she answered.

And suddenly he determined to settle once for all that question which had been tormenting him—he'd find out if she was one of these "deathless ones" or just the normal girl she seemed . . . if she was like the rest of them, then he'd have to accept the fact he loved a girl old enough to be his great-grandmother, maybe—if she wasn't, then he didn't give a damn about all the rest of the puzzles—

"See here, Suarra," he demanded, "how old are you?"

"Why, Graydon, I'm twenty," she answered, wonderingly.

"I know," he said, "but do you mean you're twenty, or that you were twenty, the Mother alone knows how many years ago, when you closed those infernal Gates, whatever they may be, on yourself?"

"But, beloved," said Suarra, "why are you so disturbed? I've never gone into the Chamber of the Gates! I'm really twenty—I mean not staying twenty, but getting older every year."

"Thank God!" exclaimed Graydon, fervently, a load rolling from his mind. "Now after the good news, comes the bad. Lantlu, and most of Yu-Atlanchi, I gather, are out hunting for us at this very moment."

"Oh, but that doesn't matter," said Suarra, "now that the Mother has accepted you."

Graydon had his doubts about the accuracy of that, but he did not trouble her with them. He began the tale of his adventures. In the middle of his first sentence he heard a hissing exclamation from the Serpent-woman; heard Regor rumble—

"It is truth. Kon found him there."

He looked toward them. The Snake Mother's eyes were upon him. She beckoned him; and when he stood beside her she raised herself, swayed forward until her face was almost touching his.

"The Shadow, Graydon—tell me of it. From the moment you saw it appear upon the black throne. Nay wait—I would see while you tell me—" she placed a hand upon his forehead—"now speak."

He obeyed, going step by step over his ordeal. He lived it again; so vivid were the pictures of it that it was as though his brain were a silver screen upon which a camera unreeled them. At his recital of the death of Cadok he felt the hand upon his forehead tremble; he spoke of Kon, and the hand dropped away.

"Enough!"

She drew back; she regarded him, thoughtfully; there was something of surprise in her gaze, something of wonder—something, the odd idea came to him, of the emotion a mathematician might feel if in a mass of well studied formulæ he should suddenly come across an entirely new equation.

"You are more than I thought, Graydon," she echoed that odd ideation. "Now I wonder . . . up from the gray apemen you came . . . yet all I know of men is from those who dwell here . . . what else have you developed, you who have grown up beyond our barrier . . . I wonder. . . ."

Silent again, she studied him; then—

"You thought the Shadow real—I mean, no shadow, no shade, not—immaterial—"

"Material enough, substantial enough to pour itself into Cadok," he interrupted. "Substantial enough to destroy him. It poured into Cadok like water in a jar. It sucked from him —life. And for—ten heartbeats—the Shadow was no Shadow, Mother. If indeed you saw into my mind you know whose face it wore."

'I saw," she nodded. "Yet still I cannot believe. How can I believe when I do not know—"

She stopped; she seemed to be listening. She raised herself upon her coils until her head was a full foot above tall Regor. Her eyes were intent, as though she looked beyond the walls of that great chamber. She dropped back upon her coils, the rosy pearl of her body slowly deepening.

"To me, Huon!" she called. "Your men with you. Kon—" she clicked some command, pointed to the opposite side of the alcove.

Again she listened.

"Suarra," she pointed toward the girl, "Suarra, go you to your rooms."

Then, as Suarra faltered, "Nay, stand behind me, daughter. If he has dared this—best for you to be near me!"

Once more the Serpent-woman was quiet; gaze withdrawn. Huon and his men climbed the steps; ranked themselves where she had bade: Suarra stepped by Graydon.

"She is angry! She is very angry!" she whispered. She passed behind the Serpent-woman's coils.

And now Graydon heard a faint, a far-away clamor; shouts and ring of metal on metal. The tumult drew close. At a distant end of the columned place was a broad entrance over which the webbed curtains fell. Abruptly, these were torn apart, ripped away, and through the opening poured blue-kirtled Emer soldiers, fighting to check some inexorable pressure slowly forcing them back.

Then over them he saw the head of Lantlu, and behind and around him a hundred or more of his nobles.

They made their way through the portal. The Emer fought desperately, but gave way, step by step, before the push of long javelins in the hands of those who drove them. None fell, and Graydon realized that their assailants were deliberately holding back from killing, striving only to break through.

"Stop!" the cry of the Snake Mother had in it something of the elfin buglings of her winged Messengers, the flying, feathered serpents. It halted the struggling ranks.

"Dura!" an officer of the blue-kirtled Emer faced her, saluting. "Let them through! Escort them to me!"

The guards drew aside, formed into two lines; between them Lantlu and his followers marched to the foot of the steps. He smiled as he beheld Graydon, his eyes glinted as they roved from Regor to Huon and his band.

"All here, Bural!" he spoke to a noble beside him whose face was as beautiful and cruel as his. "I had not hoped for such luck!"

He made an ironic obeisance to the Serpent-woman.

"Hail, Mother!" Rank insolence steeped the greeting. "We ask your pardon for our rough entrance, but your guards have evidently forgotten the right of the Old Race to do you homage. We knew that you would punish them for their forgetfulness, so we did them no harm. And it seems we have come barely in time to save you, Mother, since we find you beset by dangerous men. Outlaws whom we have been seeking. Also an outlander whose life was forfeit when he entered Yu-Atlanchi. Evil men, Mother! We will lift their menace from you!"

He whispered to Bural, and took a swaggering step up the stairway. Up came the javelins of the nobles, ready to hurl, as they followed him. Graydon threw his rifle to his shoulder, finger itching on the trigger. Under stress, he reverted unconsciously to his English.

"Stop! Or I'll blow your rotten heart out of you! Tell them to drop those javelins!"

"Silence!" the Mother touched his arm with the sistrum, a numbing shock ran through it; the gun fell at his feet.

"He said you would be safer where you are, Lantlu. Safer still with javelins lowered. He is right, Lantlu—I, Adana, tell you so!" lisped the Snake Mother.

She raised the sistrum high. Lantlu stared at the quivering globe, a shade of doubt on his face. He halted, spoke softly to Bural; and the javelins were lowered.

The Serpent-woman swayed slightly, rhythmically, to and fro, upon the upper pillar of her coils.

"By what right do you demand these men, Lantlu?"

"By what right! By what right?" he looked at her with malicious, assumed incredulity. "Mother Adana! Do you grow old—or forgetful like your guards? We demand them because they have broken the law of Yu-Atlanchi, because they are outlaws, wolf-heads, to be taken where and how it

182

may be. By right of the old law, Mother, with which, by virtue of a certain pact between your ancestors and mine, you may not interfere. Or if you do—then, Mother, we must save your honor for you, and take them nevertheless. Bural —if the outlander stoops to pick up his weapon, skewer him. If one of those outlaws moves toward his, let the javelins loose. Are you answered, Mother?"

"You shall not have them," said the Serpent-woman, serenely. But the pillar of her body swayed in slowly widening arcs, her neck began to arch, thrusting her head forward —like a serpent poising to strike.

Suarra slipped from behind her, thrust her arm through Graydon's. Lantlu's face darkened.

"So!" he said, "Suarra! With your lover! Your people howl for you, you wench of the Urd! Well—soon they shall have you—"

Red light flashed before Graydon's eyes, there was a singing in his ears. Hot hatred, dammed up since Lantlu had taunted him in the shrine of the Shadow, swept him. Before the Serpent-woman could stay him, he leaped down the steps, and shot a hard fist squarely into the sneering face. He felt the nose crunch under the blow. Lantlu tottered, staggered back. He recovered his poise with cat-like quickness; he rushed at Graydon, arms flexed to grip him.

Graydon ducked under his clutching arms, drove two blows upward into his face, the second squarely upon his snarling mouth. And again he felt bone give. Lantlu reeled back into the arms of Bural.

"Graydon! Come to me!" the Snake Mother's cry was peremptory, not to be disobeyed.

He walked slowly back up the steps, head turned on the watching nobles. They made no move to stop him. Halfway up, he saw Lantlu open his eyes, break away from Bural's hold, and glare uncomprehendingly about him. Graydon halted, fierce elation filling him, and again, unknowing, he spoke in his own language.

"That'll spoil some of your beauty!"

Lantlu glared up at him, vacantly; he wiped a hand over his mouth, stared at its scarlet wetness stupidly.

"He says your women will find it difficult to admire you hereafter," trilled the Serpent-woman. "Again he is right!"

Graydon looked at her. The little hand holding the sistrum was clenched so tightly that the knuckles shone white, her red forked tongue flickered upon her lips, her eyes were very bright. . . . The Mother, he thought, might be angry with him, but she appeared to be uncommonly enjoying the sight of Lantlu's battered countenance . . . he had seen women at the prize ring watch with exactly that expression the successful mauling progress of their favorite. He drew up beside her, nursing his bruised knuckles.

And now Lantlu was trying to break from the hands of his men who were holding him . . . Graydon rather admired him at that moment . . . certainly the brute had courage . . . quite a hog for punishment. . . .

"Lantlu!" the Snake Mother raised herself until her head swayed a man's full height over them, her eyes were cold purple gems, her face like stone—"Lantlu—look at me!"

She lifted the sistrum. The globe stopped its quick-silver quivering, and out of it sprang a ray of silvery light that flashed on Lantlu's forehead. Instantly he ceased his struggling, grew rigid, raised his face to her. The silvery ray flashed across the faces of his followers, and they too stiffened into men of wood, silent.

"Lantlu! Carrion carrier for Nimir! Listen to me! You have defiled the Temple, the only one of all the Old Race to do that. By violence you have forced your way to me, Adana, of the Older Race who fed your forefathers with the fruit of our wisdom. Who made you into men. You have mocked me! You have dared to raise armed hands against me! Now do I declare the ancient pact between my people and yours broken—broken by you, Lantlu. Now do I, Adana, declare you outlaw, and outlaws all those with you. And outlaw shall be all who hereafter throw their lot with yours. I cast you out! Go to your whispering Shadow, tell it what has befallen you. Go to your Dark Master, Lantlu, and beg him to make you whole again, restore your beauty. He cannot—not he, whose craft has grown so weak that he cannot find himself a body. Let this comfort you. Tempted as he may have been, he will not now try to hide behind that face of yours. Tell him that I, who worsted him long time ago, I, Adana, who prisoned him in the stone, am awake, and on guard, and will meet him once again when the hour has struck—aye, and worst him again. Aye, utterly destroy him! Go, you beast lower than the Urd—Go!"

She pointed with the sistrum to the tattered curtains. And Lantlu, head swaying in weird mimicry of hers, turned stiffly, and paced away. Behind him, heads swaying, went his nobles. The blue-kirtled soldiers herding them, they passed from sight.

The Serpent-woman's body ceased its movement, her pillared coil dropped, she rested her little pointed chin on Suarra's shoulder. Her purple eyes, no longer cold or glittering, weighed Graydon quizzically.

"As the brutes fight!" she mused. "I think there must be something human in me after all—so to enjoy those blows and the sight of Lantlu's face. Graydon, for the first time in ages, you have lifted all boredom from me."

She paused, smiling at him.

"I should have slain him," she said. "It would have saved much trouble. And many lives—maybe. But then he would have had no time to mourn his vanished beauty—nor to eat his vain heart out over it. No, oh no—I could not relinquish that, not even for many lives. Augh-h!—" she yawned, "and for the first time in ages, I am sleepy."

Suarra leaned against the side of the alcove. A golden bell sounded. A door opened and through it came four comely Indian women, carrying a cushioned litter. They set it beside the Serpent-woman, stood waiting, arms crossed on brown breasts, heads bowed. She swayed toward it, stopped—

"Suarra," she said, "see that Regor and Huon and the others are shown to their quarters, and that they are properly cared for. Graydon, wait here with me."

They knelt to her once more, then followed Suarra through the opened portal.

Graydon stood with the Mother. She did not speak, was deep in thought. At last she looked at him.

"That was a boasting message I sent to Nimir," she said.

"I am not so sure of the outcome, my Graydon, as I seemed to be. You have given me several new things to think about. Still—it will also give that creeping Evil something to think on besides his deviltries—perhaps."

She was silent until Suarra returned. Then she slipped out of her nest, thrust her body into the litter and slowly drew her shimmering coils after her. She lay for a moment, chin cupped in her tiny hands, looking at them.

"Kiss him good-night, daughter," she said. "He shall rest well, and safely."

Suarra raised her lips to his.

"Come, Graydon," laughed the Serpent-woman, and when he was close, she put her hands on each side of his face, and kissed him, too.

"What abysses between us!" She shook her head, "and bridged by three blows to a man I hate—yes, daughter, I am woman, after all!"

The women picked up the litter, Suarra beside her, they moved away. From the entrance came two blue-kilted Emers, who with low bows, invited him to follow them. The Mother waved a hand toward him, Suarra blew a kiss. They were gone.

Graydon followed the Indians. As he passed the red throne he saw a figure within it—a shrunken figure all in tasseled robe of red and yellow.

The Lord of Folly! He had not seen him enter. How long had he been there? He paused. The Lord of Folly looked at him with twinkling, youthful eyes. He reached out a long white hand and touched him on the forehead. At the touch, Graydon felt all perplexities leave him; in their place was a careless gayety, a comfortable feeling that, despite appearances, things were perfectly all right in a world that seemed perfectly all wrong. He laughed back into the twinkling eyes.

"Welcome—son!" chuckled the Lord of Folly.

One of the Indians touched him upon the arm. When he looked back at the red throne, it was empty.

He followed the Indians through the portal. They led him to a room, dimly lighted, cob-web curtained, a wide couch in its center. There was a small ivory table on which were bread and fruit and a pale mild wine. As he ate, the Indians took from him his suit-of-mail, and stripped him to the skin. They brought in a basin of crystal, bathed him, and massaged him and rubbed him with oil. They drew a silken robe around him, and put him to bed.

" 'Welcome—son!' " muttered Graydon, sleepily. "Son? Now what did he mean by that?"

Still wondering, he went sound asleep.

CHAPTER XX

Wisdom of the Serpent Mother

IT WAS MID-MORNING of the next day when an Emer came to Graydon with a summons from the Snake Mother. He had awakened to find Regor and Huon watching him from the doorway. Regor still wore his black, but Huon had traded the yellow of the Fellowship for the Serpent-woman's blue. As he arose, he found on a settle beside his bed a similar costume. He put on the long, loose blouse, the hose and the heelless, half-length boots of soft leather. They fitted him so well that he wondered whether some one had come in during the night and had measured him.

There was a circlet of gold upon the settle, but he let it be. After a moment's hesitation he thrust his automatic into the inner fold of his wide girdle. A blue silken cloak, fastened at the shoulders with loops of gold, completed his dress. He felt rather self-conscious in it, as though he were going to a costume party—something he had always loathed; but there was nothing else to wear, his suit-of-mail had vanished, and his other clothing was in the ravished lair.

He breakfasted with the pair. Huon, he saw, was taking matters badly, his beauty grown haggard, his eyes unhappy. Also, much of Regor's buoyancy had fled, whether through sympathy for Huon or for some other reason he did not know. Neither of them made slightest reference to his fight with Lantlu, and that aroused in him a piqued curiosity. Once he had led the talk close to it; Huon had glanced at him with a flash of irritated distaste; Regor had given him an admonitory kick under the table.

He did not find it a pleasant meal, but he had been enlightened as to Huon's manner. Regor and Huon had started to go out. Graydon would have accompanied them, but the giant told him gruffly that he would better stay where he was, that the Mother was sure to send for him, that she had turned over all her soldiery to Huon and himself and that they would be busy drilling them. In a few moments he returned, alone.

"You did well, lad," he grumbled, slapping Graydon's shoulder. "Don't mind Huon. You see, we don't fight each other in just the way you did. It's the way of the Urd. I tell Huon that you're not supposed to know our customs but—well, he didn't like it. Besides, he's heartbroken about the Fellowship and Dorina."

"You can tell Huon to go to hell with his customs," Graydon was hurt and angry. "When it comes to a brute like Lantlu, I fight tooth and nail, and no hold barred. But I see why Lantlu beat him. He was on the job while Huon, probably, was considering how to say it to him with flowers!"

"Much of that was in your own tongue," grinned Regor, "but I get your meaning. You may be right—but Huon is Huon. Don't worry. He'll be over it when you meet him again."

"I don't give a damn whether he is or not—" began Graydon, furiously. Regor gave him another friendly slap, and walked out.

Still hotly indignant, Graydon dropped upon a settle and prepared to await the expected summons. The walls of the room were covered with the filmy curtains, dropping from ceiling to floor. He got up and walked around them, feeling through the webs. At one spot, his hand encountered no resistance. He parted them and stepped into another room, flooded with clear daylight from a balconied window. He walked out on the balcony. Beneath him lay Yu-Atlanchi.

The Temple was high above the city, the ground falling away from it in a gentle slope. Between it and the lake the slope was like a meadow, free of all trees, and blue as though carpeted with harebells. And the opposite side of the lake was nearer then he had judged, less than a mile away.

He could see the spume of the cataract, torn into tattered banners by the wind. The caverns of the colossi were like immense eyes in the brown face of the precipice. The figure of the Frog-woman was plain, the green stone of which she was carved standing out in relief against the ochreous rock.

And there was the white, exquisite shape which guarded the cavern of the dead.

There was another colossus, cut, it seemed, from rose-quartz, shrouded to the feet, its face hidden behind an uplifted arm; and there was a Cyclopean statue of one of the gray and hairless ape-men. These stood out clearly, the outlines of the other he could not distinguish for their color merged into that of the cliffs.

At his left, the meadow changed to a level plain, sparsely wooded, running for miles into the first wave of the forest, and checkered by the little farms of the Indians. At his right was the ancient city and, now seen so closely, less like a city than a park.

Where the city halted at the edge of the Temple's flowering mead, and halfway to the lake, was a singular structure. It was shaped like an enormous shell whose base had been buried to hold it upright; its sides curved gracefully, drawing closer in two broad, descending arcs, then flaring out to form an entrance. It faced the Temple, and from where he stood Graydon could see practically all of the interior.

This shell-like building was made of some opaline stone. Here and there within it glowed patches of peacock fires of the Mexican opal's matrix, and here and there were starry points of blue like those which shine from the black opal. The reflected rays from them appeared to meet in the center of the structure, stretching across it like a nebulous curtain. And, like a shell, its surface was fluted. The grooves were cut across, two-thirds from the top, by tier upon tier of stone seats. Its top was all of three hundred feet high, is length perhaps thrice that. He wondered what could be its use.

He looked again over the city. If Lantlu were preparing attack, there was no evidence of it. Along the broad avenues skirting the lake was tranquil movement, Indians going about their businesses, the glint of jeweled litters borne on the shoulders of others; a small fleet of boats with gayly colored sails and resembling feluccas skimmed over the water. There was no marching of armed men, no sign of excitement. He watched laden llamas swinging along, and smaller deer-like animals, grazing. The flowering trees and shrubs hid the lanes threading the grounds of the palaces.

Then he had been summoned to the Serpent-woman.

Graydon followed the messenger. They paused before a curtained recess; the Indian touched a golden bell set in the wall. The hangings parted.

He was on the threshold of a roomy chamber through whose high, oval windows the sunlight streamed. Tapestries covered its walls, woven with scenes from the life of the serpent-people. Upon a low dais, her coils curled within a nest of cushions, was the Snake Mother. Behind her was Suarra, brushing her hair. The sun made round it a halo of silver. At her side squatted the Lord of Folly in his cloak of red and yellow. Suarra's eyes brightened as he entered, dwelling upon him tenderly. He made obeisance to Adana, bowed low to the Lord in motley.

"You look well in my blue, Graydon," lisped the Serpent-woman. "You haven't the beauty of the Old Race, naturally. But Suarra doesn't mind that," she glanced slyly at the girl.

"I think him very beautiful," said Suarra, quite shamelessly.

"Well, I myself find him interesting," trilled Adana, "after all these centuries, the men of Yu-Atlanchi have become a bit monotonous. Come and sit beside me, child," she motioned toward a long, low coffer close to her. "Take a pillow or two and be comfortable. Now tell me about your world. Don't bother about your wars or gods—they've been the same for a hundred thousand years. Tell me how you live, how you amuse yourselves, what your cities are like, how you get about, what you have learned."

Graydon felt this to be a rather large order, but he did his best. He ended almost an hour later, feeling that he had made a frightful jumble of skyscrapers and motion pictures, railroads and steamships, hospitals, radios, electricity and airplanes, newspapers and television, astronomy, art and telephones, germs, high-explosives and arc lights, he tripped on the electronic theory, bogged hopelessly on relativity, gulped and wiped a wet forehead. Also he had been unable to find Aymara words to describe many things, and had been forced to use the English terms.

But Adana had seemed to follow him easily, interrupting him seldom, and then only with extremely pointed questions.

Suarra, he was sure, had been left hopelessly behind; he was equally sure that the Lord of Folly had kept pace with him. The Serpent-woman had seemed a little startled by the airplanes and television, much interested in skyscrapers, telephones, high-explosives and electric lighting.

"A very clear picture," she said. "And truly amazing progress for—a hundred years, I think you said, Graydon. Soon, I should think, you would do away with some of your crudities—learn to produce light from the stone, as we did, and by releasing it from air. I am truly concerned about your flying machines, much concerned. If Nimir wins, they may soar over Yu-Atlanchi and welcome! If he does not— then I shall have to devise means to discourage any such visits. Truly! I am not so enamored with your civilization, as you describe it, to wish it extended here. For one thing, I think you are building too rapidly outside yourselves, and too slowly inside. Thought, my child, is quite as powerful a force as any you have named, and better controlled, since you generate it within yourself. You seem never to have considered it objectively. Some day you will find yourselves so far buried within your machines that you will not be able to find a way out—or discover yourself being carried helplessly away by them. But then I suppose you believe you have within you an immortal something which, when the time comes, can float out of anything into a perfect other world?"

"Many do," he answered. "I did not. But I find my disbelief shaken—once by something I saw in the Cavern of the Face, once by a certain dream while I slept beside a stream, and later found was no dream—and again by a whispering Shadow. If there is not something to man beside body—then what were they?"

"Did you think it was that immortal part of me which you saw in the Cavern? Did you think that, really?" she leaned forward, smiling. "But that is too childish, Graydon. Surely my ethereal essence, if I have it, is not a mere shadowy duplication! Such a wonderful thing should be at least twice as beautiful! And different—oh, surely different! I am a woman, Graydon, and would dearly like to try a few new fashions in appearance."

It was not until after he had left her that he recalled how

intently the Serpent-woman had looked at him when she said this. If she thought something was within his mind—some reservation, some doubt—she was satisfied with what she found, or did not find. She laughed; then grew grave.

"Nor did anything of you rush forth from your body at my call. It was my thought that touched you beside the brook; my thought that narrowed the space between us—precisely as your harnessed force penetrates all obstacles and carries to you a distant picture. I saw you there, but it pleased me to let you see me as well. So it was that I watched Lantlu march into the Temple. Once we of the Older Race could send the seeing thought around the world, even as you are on the verge of doing with your machines. But I have used the power so little, for so long and long and long again, that now I can barely send it to the frontiers of Yu-Atlanchi.

"And as for Nimir—" she hesitated. "Well, he was master of strange arts. A pioneer, in a fashion. What this Shadow is —I do not know. But I do not believe it is any immortal—what do you name it, Graydon—ah, yes, soul. Not his soul! And yet—there must be a beginning in everything . . . perhaps Nimir is pioneer in soul making . . . who knows! But if so—why is it so weak? For compared to that which was Nimir in body this Shadow is weak. No, no! It is some product of thought; an emanation from what once was Nimir whom we fettered in the Face . . . a disembodied intelligence, able to manipulate the particles that formed the body of Cadok—that far I will go . . . but an immortal soul? No!"

She dropped into one of her silences; withdrawn—then—

"But the seeing thought, I do know. I will show you, Graydon—will send my sight into that place where you saw the ship, and yours shall accompany it."

She pressed her palm against his forehead, held it there. He had the sensation of whirling across the lake and through the cliffs, the same vertiginous feeling he had experienced when he had thought he stood, bodiless, within the Temple. And now he seemed to halt beside the hull of the ship in the dim cavern. He looked over its shrouded, enigmatic shapes. And as swiftly he was back in Adana's chamber.

"You see!" she said, "nothing of you went forth. Your sight was lengthened—that was all."

She picked up a silver mirror, gazed at herself complacently.

"That is fine, daughter," she said. "Now coif it for me."

She preened herself before the mirror, set it down.

"Graydon, you have aroused old thoughts. Often I have asked, 'What is it that is I, Adana'—and never found the answer. None of my ancestors has ever returned to tell me. Nor any of the Old Race. Now is it not strange, if there be another life beyond this one, that not love nor sorrow, wit nor strength nor compassion has ever bridged the gap between them? Think of the countless millions who have died since man became man, among them seekers of far horizons who had challenged unknown perils to bring back tidings of distant shores, great adventurers, ingenious in artifice; and men of wisdom who had sought truth not selfishly but to spread it among their kind; men and women who had loved so greatly that surely it seems they could break through any barrier, return and say—'Behold, I am! Now grieve no more!' Fervent priests whose fires of faith had shone like beacons to their flocks—have they come back to say—'See! It was truth I told you! Doubt no more!' Compassionate men, lighteners of burdens, prelates of pity—why have they not reappeared crying, 'There is no death!' There has come no word from them. Why are they silent?

"Yet that proves nothing. Would that it did—for then we would be rid of sometimes troublesome thoughts. But it does not, for look you, Graydon, we march beside our sun among an army of other stars, some it must be with their own circling worlds. Beyond this universe are other armies of suns, marching like ours through space. Earth cannot be the only place in all these universes upon which is life. And if time be—then it must stretch backward as well as forward into infinitude. Well, in all illimitable time, no ship from any other world has cast anchor upon ours, no argosy has sailed between the stars bearing tidings that life is elsewhere.

"Have we any more evidence that life exists among these visible universes than that it persists in some mysterious, invisible land whose only gateway is death? But your men of wisdom who deny the one because none has returned from it, will not deny the other though none has come to us from the star strands. They will say that they do not know—well, neither do they know the other!

"And yet—if there be what you name the soul, whence does it come, and when, how planted in these bodies of ours? Did the ape-like creatures from which you grew have them? Did the first of your ancestors who crawled on four pads out of the waters have them? When did the soul first appear? Is it man's alone? Is it in the egg of the woman? Or in the seed of the man? Or incomplete in both? If not, when does it enter its shell within the mother's womb? Is it summoned by the new-born child's first cry? From whence?"

"Time streams like a mighty river, placid, unhurried," said the Lord of Fools. "Across it is a rift where bubbles rise. It is life. Some bubbles float a little longer than the others. Some are large and some small. The bubbles rise and burst, rise and burst. Bursting, do they release some immortal essence? Who knows—who knows?"

The Serpent-woman looked at herself again in the silver mirror.

"I do not, for one," she said, practically. "Suarra, child, you've done my hair splendidly. And enough of speculation. I am a practical person. What we are chiefly concerned about, Tyddo, is to keep Nimir and Lantlu from bursting those bubbles which are ourselves.

"There is one thing I fear—that Nimir will fasten his mind upon those things of power which are within that cavern of the ship; find some way of getting them. Therefore, Graydon and Suarra, you shall go there tonight, taking with you fifty of the Emer to carry back to me what I want from it. After that, there is another thing you must do there, and then return speedily. Graydon, arise from that coffer."

He obeyed. She opened the coffer and drew out a thick, yard-long crystal bar, apparently hollow, its core filled with a slender pillar of pulsing violet fire.

"This, Graydon, I will give you when you start," she said. "Carry it carefully, for the lives of all of us may rest upon it. After the Emers are laden and in the passage, you must do with it what I shall shortly show you. Suarra, within the ship is a small chest—I will show you where it lies—you must bring me that. And before you set this bar in place, take

195

whatsoever pleases you from the ancient treasures. But do not loiter—" she frowned at the throbbing flame—"I am sorry. Truly! But now must great loss come, that far greater loss does not follow. Suarra, child—follow my sight!"

The girl came forward, stood waiting with a tranquility which indicated it was not the first time she had made such journey. The Serpent-woman pressed her palm upon her forehead as she had on Graydon's. She kept it there for long minutes. She took away her hand; Suarra smiled at her and nodded.

"You have seen! You know precisely what I want! You will remember!" They were not questions, they were commands.

"I have seen, I know and I will remember," answered Suarra.

"Now, Graydon, you too—so there may be no mistake, and that you work quickly together."

She touched his forehead. With the speed of thought he was once more within the cavern. One by one those things she wanted flashed out of the vagueness—he knew precisely where each was, how to go to it. And unforgettably. Now he was in the ship, within a richly furnished cabin, and saw there the little chest Suarra was to take. And now he was beside a curious contrivance built of crystal and silver metal, the bulk of it shaped like an immense thick-bottomed bowl around whose rim were globes like that of the sistrum, ten times larger, and with none of its quicksilver quivering; quiescent. Within the crystal which formed the bulk of the bowl was a pool of the violet flame, quiescent too, not pulsing like that within the rod. Looking more closely, he saw that the top of the bowl was covered with some transparent substance, clear as air, and that the pool was prisoned within it. Set at the exact center, and vanishing in the flame, was a hollow cylinder of metal. Before him there appeared the misty shape of the rod. He saw it thrust sharply into the cylinder. He heard the voice of the Serpent-woman, whispering—"This must you do."

He thought that even at the spectral touch, the globes began to quiver, the violet flame to pulse. The rod vanished.

He began the whirling flight back toward the Temple—

was halted in mid-flight! He felt the horror he had known when bound to the bench before the jet throne!

Red light beat upon him, rusted black atoms drifted round him—he was in the cavern of the Shadow, and on its throne, featureless face intent upon him, sat the Shadow!

The dreadful gaze sifted him. He felt the grip relax; heard a whispering laugh—

He was back in the room of the Snake Mother, trembling, breathing like a man spent from running. Suarra was beside him, his hands clutched in hers, staring at him with frightened eyes. The Serpent-woman was erect, upon her face the first amazement he had ever seen. The Lord of Folly was on his feet, red staff stretched out to him.

"God!" sobbed Graydon, and caught at Suarra for support. "The Shadow! It caught me!"

And suddenly he realized what had happened—that in the brief instant the Shadow had gripped him, it had read his mind like an open page, knew exactly what it was that he had looked upon in the Cavern of the Lost Wisdom, knew precisely what the Mother wanted, knew what she planned to do there—and was now making swift preparation to checkmate her! He told the Serpent-woman this.

She listened to him, eyes glittering, head flattening like a snake's; she hissed!

"If Nimir read his mind, as he thinks, then he must also have read that it was to-night he was to go," said the Lord of Folly, quietly. "Therefore, they must go now, Adana."

"You are right, Tyddo. Nimir cannot enter—at least not as he is. What he will do, I do not know. But he has some plan—he laughed, you say, Graydon? Well, whatever it is, it will take him time to put it into action. He must summon others to help him. We have good chance to outrace him. Suarra, Graydon—you go at once. You with them, Tyddo."

The Lord of Folly nodded, eyes sparkling.

"I would like to test Nimir's strength once again, Adana," he said.

"And Kon—Kon must go with you. Suarra, child—summon Regor. Let him pick the soldiers."

And when Suarra had gone for Regor, the Snake Mother handed the crystal bar to the Lord of Folly.

"Nimir is stronger than I had believed," she said, gravely. "That whispering Shadow left its mark upon you, Graydon. You are too sensitive to it to risk the carrying of this key. Tyddo will use it. And take my bracelet from beneath your sleeve. Wear it openly, and should you feel the Shadow reach out to you—look quickly into the purple stones, and think of me. Give it to me—"

She took the bracelet from him, breathed upon its gems, pressed them to her forehead, and returned it to him.

In half an hour they were off. Regor had begged to go with them, argued and blustered and almost wept; but the Serpent-woman had forbade him. The Lord of Folly leading and bearing both crystal staff and his red rod, Suarra and Kon on each side of Graydon, half a hundred picked Emers of the Temple guard behind him, they were on their way to the Cavern of the Lost Wisdom.

CHAPTER XXI

The Cavern of the Lost Wisdom

THEY WENT by another passage than that by which they had entered the Temple, high-roofed and wider. The Lord of Folly, for once, did not flitter. He walked purposefully, as though eager for some rendezvous. They entered the Cavern of the Lost Wisdom by a door which opened to the touch of Tyddo's red rod. The new corridor had cut off all that empty space they had traversed before, and the sealed treasures of the Serpent-people and most ancient Yu-Atlanchi lay before them.

There was no sign of the Dark Master, nor of any of his followers, man nor lizard-people. The cavern seemed untouched, crystal shimmering palely, metals gleaming and jewels glinting fugitively, the puzzling shapes designed for uses unguessable, shadowy in the dim light.

They first took two of the crystal disks. At close range, Graydon saw details not perceptible in the painting of the primeval swamp. They were twenty feet high, lens-shaped, a yard in thickness at their centers. They were hollow. Within the center was a foot-wide disk milky as curdled moonlight. From its edges ran countless filaments, each fine as a hair on the Serpent-woman's head, and as silvery. They were crossed by other filaments, making them resemble immense, finely spun cob-webs. Spaced regularly around the rim of the larger disk were a dozen little lenses of the moon-ray material. Where the radiating strands passed from the last encircling one, they were gathered into these lenses, like minute reins. The disks rested upon bases of gray metal fitted with runners, like a sled. Their bottom edges dropped into deep grooves. Whatever held them upright was hidden in their bases.

The Indians produced long thongs, tied them to the runners, the Lord of Folly directing; then still under his eye they drew them away and into the passage. When they were safely there, he drew what seemed to Graydon a breath of relief, clicked to Kon, and the Spider-man followed on the trail of the Emers.

"Best to make sure of those," said the Lord of Folly. "They are our strongest weapons. I bade Kon see they are taken straight to Adana. Now do you two gather those other things she wants. I go to mount guard."

He walked away into the obscurity of the cavern.

They went quickly about their business, dividing the remaining Indians between them. Mainly the objects were coffers, some so small that one man could carry them, others under whose weight four strained. There were seven of the symboled silver globes in the Serpent-woman's inventory, and he was amazed to find them light as bubbles, rolling over the floor before the push of a hand. They came at last to the end, and with the last of their men, remained only to get the chest from the ship.

The ship rested upon a metal cradle. A ladder dropped from its side, and as Graydon clambered up it Suarra at his heels, he wondered how the ancient people had managed to get this Ark of theirs over land and through the barrier of mountains into this place; remembered that Suarra had told him the mountains had not then arisen, and that in those far-gone days the ocean had been close.

Still—to carry this ship, and it was all of three hundred feet long, into the cavern implied engines of amazing power. And how had it been preserved during the ages preceding the upthrust of the barrier? It was hard wood, almost metallic; schooner rigged, its masts thick and squat, and, curiously enough, yardless. He caught at its stern a gleam of blue, saw there one of the great disks, deep cerulean, not transparent like the others. Wondered whether it had furnished the propulsive power for the craft, and if so, then why the masts? Except for disk and squat masks the deck was clear. He remembered now that the ships upon the wall of the Painted Cavern had shown tall masts, he had not seen among them any boat such as this. Well, it might have been among the pictures of the ruined walls. He looked out over the cavern. The Lord of Folly, a patch of red and yellow, was beside that strange contrivance in whose bowl lay the pool of violet flame. He stood, motionless, listening, the crystal rod poised over the hollow cylinder.

"Graydon!" called Suarra, beckoning from an open hatchway. "Make haste!"

A cleated ramp dropped down into dark depths, and Suarra was tripping down it with the sure feet of a fawn; he followed her. From a light-cone in her hand spurted one of the luminous clouds. Under his feet was a silken carpet, deep and lush as a June meadow; in front of him a row of low oval doors, tightly shut. Suarra counted them, sped to one and thrust it open. The sparkling light streamed through after them.

It was a wide cabin, tapestry-hung, and clearly a woman's. What princess of most ancient Yu-Atlanchi, flying uncounted centuries ago through racked seas from the ice flood, had preened herself before that silver mirror? He glimpsed a nest of silken cushions, and knew. Suarra was beside it, lifting the little chest. He saw another coffer nearby, and opened it. Within was a long strand of gems blue as deepest sapphire, unknown radiant jewels gleaming with their own imprisoned light. He drew it out, wound it within Suarra's midnight hair; it glittered there like captured stars. There was a book! A book whose pages of metal, thin and pliable as papyrus, were like those of some ancient missal, rich in pictures and margined with unknown symbols, letterings of the Serpent-people. He thrust it into his tunic, drew his girdle tighter to hold it.

The purple gems of the bracelet caught his gaze. They were shining—warning him! Suarra, admiring herself in the silver mirror, saw them.

"Quick!" she cried. "The deck, Graydon!"

They ran up the ramp. They were just in time to see the Lord of Folly thrust the crystal rod down into the pool of violet flame.

Instantly, a pillar of amethyst fire shot up from it, reaching toward the roof of the cavern. It was smoothly round as though carved by sculptor's chisel, and as it drove up there came from it a sustained sighing like the first breath of a tempest. It lighted the cavern with a radiance stronger than sunlight; it destroyed all perspective, so that every object seemed to press forward, standing out in its own proportions as though rid of spacial trammels, freed from the diminishing effects of distance.

The Lord of Folly, far away as they knew him to be, seemed in that strange light to be close enough to touch. The quicksilver globes around the rim of the great bowl beside which he stood had begun to quiver like that in the sistrum of the Serpent-woman.

He looked at them, lifted his rod and pointed to the passage. They could not move, staring at that radiant column, fascinated.

A pulse shook the pillar; a ring of violet incandescence throbbed out of it, like the first ring in a still pool into which a stone has been thrown. It passed through the Lord of Folly, obscuring him in a mist of lavender. It swelled outward a score of feet—and vanished. Of all it had touched, except that figure, there remained—nothing! And from the Lord of Folly, the motley had vanished. He stood there, a withered old man, naked!

Around the pillar for a circle twice twenty feet wide was emptiness!

The sighing pillar pulsed again. A thicker ring widened slowly from it. Ahead of it hopped the Lord of Folly, shaking his staff at them, gesticulating, calling to them to go. They leaped for the ladder—

High over the sighing of the pillar sounded a hideous hissing. From the rear of the cavern poured the lizard-men. They vomited forth by hundreds, leaping down upon the withered figure standing there so quietly. And now the second ring of lambent violet touched the Lord of Folly, passed through him as had the other and went widening outward. It reached the first ranks of the onrushing Urd, lapped them up, and died away. And now within a circle twice twenty feet the cavern floor stood empty.

Into that circle swept more lizard-men, pressed onward by those behind them. The Lord of Folly stepped back, back into a third flaming ripple from the pillar. It widened on, tranquilly. And, like the others, it left behind it—nothing!

"Suarra! Down the ladder! Get to the passage!" gasped Graydon. "The rings are coming faster. They'll reach us. Tyddo knows what he's about. God—if that hell spawn sees you—"

He stopped, both speech and motion frozen. Above the hissing of the horde, the louder sighing of the pillar, arose a screaming like that of a maddened horse. The lizard-men scuttled back. Out through them, halting at the edge of emptiness left by the last ring of flame, came—Nimir!

And dreadful as he had been as the Shadow, dreadful when as Shadow he had poured himself into Cadok, they had been pleasant pictures to what he was now.

For the Dark Master had gotten himself a body! It had been a Yu-Atlanchan, one, no doubt of Lantlu's enemies, provided hastily for his Dark Master's needs. It was swollen. Its outlines wavered, as though the Shadow found it difficult to remain within, was holding its cloak of flesh together by sheer force of will. Its head lolled forward, and suddenly up from behind it shot the face of the Lord of Evil, pale eyes glaring. And Graydon's heart beat chokingly in a throat as dry as dust as he looked upon that bloated, cloudy body, its corpse-face and the face of living evil over it.

Another ring of flame came circling. Whatever the Lord of Folly's immunity from that noose of flame, it was clearly not shared. For Nimir retreated from it, stumbling back on dead feet.

And as he went, the Lord of Folly pointed his rod toward him and laughed.

"Fie upon you, Nimir!" he jeered, "to greet me after all these years in such ill-fitting garments! Draw your tattered cloak more tightly round you, Great One—or better still, go naked to the flame like me! But, I forgot, Master of the World, you cannot!"

Now it seemed to Graydon, mind swimming up through the wave of horror that had covered it, that the Lord of Folly was deliberately baiting Nimir, playing for time or for some other purpose. But the Dark Master took the bait, and rushed at him—and barely saw the hook in time; barely could stagger beyond the reach of the next obliterating ring before it had died, all that had been in its path eaten.

He stumbled back, into the halted horde. At once there was motion among it. Graydon, dropping down the ladder behind Suarra, saw the lizard-men scurrying beyond the widening circle of emptiness, tugging, pulling, hauling away at this and that while the Shadow, holding tight around him its borrowed body, urged them on.

Louder and ever louder grew the sussuration of the flaming pillar, faster and faster its pulse, and swifter and wider the flaming rings flung from it.

He ran, Suarra gripping his hand, head turned, unable to take his eyes from that incredible scene. A ring enveloped the ship—and the ship was gone! Another caught a line of the lizard-men laden with coffers, and they were gone! He heard the howling of Nimir—

Suarra drew him, the Lord of Folly pushed him, into the passage. Its opening dropped. He went with them, unseeing, unhearing, as powerless to tear his mind away from what he had just beheld as he had been to tear his gaze from it.

They found the Snake Mother in a room so cluttered with her salvaged treasures that there was little room to move. She had been opening the coffers, rummaging through them. Her hair was threaded with sparkling jewels, there was a wide belt of gems around her waist, and others fell between her little breasts. She was admiring herself in her mirror.

"I am rather beautiful in my way," she said, airily. "At least I have this satisfaction—that there is no one more beautiful *in* my way! Suarra, child, I'm so glad you found those jewels. I always meant to get them for you. Tyddo"— she raised her hands in mock astonishment—"where are your clothes! To go thus—and at your age!"

"By your ancestors, Adana, I had quite forgotten!" the Lord of Folly hastily snatched up a piece of silk, wrapped it round his withered frame.

"Is it done?" the Serpent-woman's face lost all laughter, was sorrowful.

"It is done, Adana," answered the Lord of Folly. "And none too soon!"

She listened, with no lightening of sorrow, as he told her what had happened in the cavern.

"So much lost!" she whispered. "So much that never can be replaced, never—though the world last forever. My people—oh, my people! And the ship—Well," she brightened, "we got the better of Nimir! But again I say it, he is stronger than I believed. Dearly would I like to know what he saved. I hope he found something that will give him a permanent costume! I wonder whose body he was wearing? Now go away, children—Tyddo and I have work to do."

She dismissed them with a wave of her hand. But as Graydon turned to go, he saw the sorrow creep again over her face, her eyes fill with tears.

CHAPTER XXII

The Feast of the Dream Makers

FOR THE NEXT two days, Graydon saw nothing of the Snake Mother; little of Regor and Huon. He spent most of his time with Suarra, and glad enough were both to be left alone. He wandered with her through the vast place at will, beholding strange and often disquieting things, experiments of the serpent-people and the ancient Yu-Atlanchans in the re-shaping of life, experiments of which the spider-folk and the lizard-folk had been results; grotesque and terrifying shapes; androgynous monstrosities; hybrid prodigies—some of them of bizarre beauty. There was a great library, filled with the metallic paged and pictured books; their glyphs understandable now only by Adana and the Lord of Folly.

He had looked into the Hall of the Weavers with Suarra, and had lingered long, fascinated by the scarlet people clicking at their immense looms along whose sides they ran, weaving patterns which through the ages had become as instinctive to them as the pattern of the spider-webs to their makers. They were not more than a hundred of them left, and in their immense workshop most of the looms swung empty.

Beneath the Temple, Suarra told him, were other chambers and crypts, and she herself did not know what was in them. There was that mysterious place whose two doors, one of Life and one of Death, were opened for those who desired children and were willing to pay the price—the canceling of their deathlessness.

Neither Nimir nor Lantlu had as yet made any open move. From Graydon's eyrie the city seemed quiet, untroubled. But Regor said his spies had reported unrest and uneasiness; the story of Lantlu's humiliation had been whispered about. It had shaken the confidence of some of his followers.

Regor's emissaries had been at work among the Indians; they could count, he thought, upon about half of them. Graydon had asked how many that was, and had been told that those with soldierly training numbered some four thousand. Of the remainder, he thought that many would take to the forest and await the outcome of the conflict; in fact, were already filtering away. He did not believe those who remained with Lantlu would be formidable—for one thing, they were held to him mainly by fear; for another, they hated the lizard-men and would not relish fighting with them. Far more than the hordes of the Urd, Graydon dreaded the dinosaur pack and the charge of the riding monsters; felt that against them the whole four thousand of the Emer could put up feeble defense, would go down before them like stubble before fire. Regor seemed not to think so, hinted of other resources.

He had other news—some twenty of the Fellowship had survived the raid and probably a hundred of their Emer, all of them soldiers of the first class.

This night was the Feast of the Dream Makers, the Lad-nophaxi. It would drain the city of the nobles. The Emers were rigidly excluded, forbidden even to watch from vantage points outside the shell-like structure which Graydon had learned was dedicated to this yearly fête; they held their own moon festival far away at the verge of the forest. Of all the nights, therefore, it was the best to smuggle in the remnants from the lair, since the city would be deserted, its guard negligible. Huon and Regor were to lead a little force which would meet his men at a certain point on the lake, and guide them to sanctuary.

Graydon's curiosity about this Feast of the Dream Makers was avid. He was on fire to witness it. He determined that by hook or crook he would do so. He could say nothing to Suarra about it, fearing that she would either put her little foot inflexibly down, or that she would insist upon going with him—something clearly not to be thought of since Lantlu's threats and the Snake Mother's declaration of war. He wondered whether he could cajole Adana into devising a means of getting into the place, came to the speedy conclusion that Adana would even more speedily devise some means of keeping him under lock and key. The Lord of Folly? It was a foolhardy enough idea to appeal to him. But since the affair in the Cavern of the Lost Wisdom, Graydon had realized that whatever the kind of folly of which that able person was Lord, it was not this kind. Nevertheless, he was not going to miss the Ladnophaxi.

While he was turning the matter over, the Mother sent for him. He found her alone in her tapestried room. The great disks were gone, as were most of the other things they had brought her. Her eyes were bright, her neck undulated, her gleaming coils stirred restlessly.

"You are so different from any one I have seen for so long," she said, "that you take my mind out of its old ruts, freshen it. I know how unutterably strange Yu-Atlanchi must seem to you—myself, perhaps, strangest of all. Yet this which seems so strange to you is all too familiar to me. And what is everyday matter to you would be to these people quite as fantastic—yes, much of it even to me. I would draw away from my closeness which is both a strength and a weakness; look through your eyes a little, Graydon; think as you, the outlander, think. How do you sum up this situation into which you have been thrust? Speak freely, child, without thought of offending me."

As freely as she had bade him, he spoke; of the stagnation of the Old Race, of its decline into cruelty and inhuman indifference, and what he believed the cause; of what he felt to be the monstrous wickedness in the creation of such creatures as the lizard-people, and the cynical perversion of scientific knowledge that had gone into the making of the spider-men; and that although the Urd, at least, should be exterminated, still the fault lay not with them; nor even with Lantlu and his kind, but with those who at the beginning had set working the relentless processes of evolution whose fruits they were. At last, of his fear of the fighting dinosaurs, and of the smashing comber of the Xinli steeds and in their wake the fanged and tearing waves of the Urd.

"But you have said nothing of Nimir—why?" she asked, when he had ended.

"Neither have I said anything of you, Mother," he answered. "I have spoken only of the things I know—and I know nothing of what weapons or powers you two may command. But I think that in the end it will be only you and Nimir—that all other things, the Urd and the Xinli, Lantlu and Regor and Huon, and myself are pawns, negligible. The issue lies between you two."

"That is true," nodded the Serpent-woman. "And I do wish I knew what Nimir managed to take away with him from the cavern! There was one thing there I hope he found," her eyes glinted maliciously, "and hope still more that, finding, he will use. It would give him that body he desires, Graydon. Yet he might not like the result. As for the others —do not fear too much the Xinli and the Urd. My winged Messengers will cope with them. Nor are the rest of you as negligible as you think. I may rest upon that quick eye and steady hand of yours at the last. But in essence you are right. It does lie between me and Nimir!"

She dropped into one of her silences, regarding him; then—

"As for the rest—does not Nature herself constantly experiment with the coverings of life? How many models has she made, more monstrous than anything you have seen here, and, as cynically, as you charge against us, stamped them out. What shapes, loathsome, ravening, has not Nature turned out of her laboratory? Why should not we, who are a part of her, have followed the example she set us? As for the Old Race and what they have become—if you save another man's life, nurse him through sickness, are you thereafter responsible for what he does? If he slays, tortures —are you the slayer, the torturer? My ancestors released this people from Death, under certain necessary conditions. If we had not, at the rate men breed there would soon have been no place to stand on all the crowded globe. We ridded them not alone of death but of sickness. We placed in their hands great knowledge. Is it our fault that they have proved not worthy of it?"

"And built a barrier around them so they could not use their knowledge!" said Graydon. "Men develop through overcoming obstacles, not by being hot-housed."

"Ah, but was not that an obstacle?" asked the Mother shrewdly. "If they had been worthy would they not have surmounted the barrier?"

He had no answer for that.

"But one matter you have clarified," she said. "If I win from Nimir, I will destroy the Urd. And I will leave only a few of the Old Race. Those errors shall be wiped out—as Nature at times wipes out hers. The swamp shall be cleansed—"

She picked up her mirror, caressed her hair; put the mirror down.

"The crisis is close. Perhaps it comes to-night. Lantlu appeared in the city a few hours ago, swaggering, strangely confident, more arrogant than ever, boasting. Is it bravado? I do not think so. He knows something of a broth that Nimir is cooking. Well, let him! Yet I do wish I knew what Nimir took away—I have tried to see, but I cannot—he blocks me ... he has found something ... I wonder if I dare ..."

She leaned forward, put her hand upon his forehead. He felt the swift vertigo, was swirled across the lake. He was in the red cavern of the Shadow! But what was the matter with it? The rusted light was thick, impenetrable. Go where he would, it closed around him like a mist of iron. He could not see—

He was back beside the Snake Mother. He shook his head.

"I know," she said. "I sent your sight with mine on the chance that sensitivity to the Shadow would let your gaze penetrate where mine cannot. But you saw no more than I. Well—" she smiled at him with one of her abrupt changes of mood, "I'm sorry you can't go to the Feast of the Dream Makers, child. I could send your sight there, with mine. But not long enough to let you see anything. It would be too great a strain for you. A little—and it does no harm; but for any length of time—no."

Not long after that she dismissed him. He went from her with a bad conscience, but with his determination unchanged.

He was back in his own quarters when an idea came to him.

Kon!

210

There might be the solution. Since his fight with Lantlu, the Spider-man had apparently tucked him under his heart as tightly as he had under his arm during the scramble across the precipice; never passed him without clicking affectionately and giving him a pat or two with his little paws. Could he persuade Kon to scale the walls of the great shell with him, find a place where he could see but not be seen? How the devil could he cajole Kon when he didn't know how to talk to him? He turned the matter over and over, then laughed. Well, his idea might work. He could only try it.

The full moon arose over the barrier of peaks three hours after the sunset. That meant sunset in Yu-Atlanchi, which by reason of those same peaks was dark when it was still twilight outside. The Feast of the Dream Makers would not begin until the moon shone full upon the amphitheater. That much he had gathered from Suarra. And even now dusk was thickening in the bowl of the Hidden Land. He would have to work quickly.

He dined with Suarra, and the others. She told him that the Mother wanted her attendance that night, gathered that the Serpent-woman intended to miss nothing of what went on at the Feast, and that Suarra had certain duties of her own in that surveillance. To his relief, he found that he was not asked to accompany her. He told her he was tired, would take some of the pictured books to his room, read awhile and sleep. Her solicitude made him feel guiltier, but did not shake his determination. Casually, he asked her where Kon kept himself. She said he had taken a fancy to the chamber of the thrones, was usually there when not scuttling around after Huon.

After she had gone, he stole away to the throne chamber. There, sure enough, was Kon, and sitting, of all places, in the throne of the Lord of Folly. Graydon, taking it as a happy augury, grinned widely. He seated himself beside him, drew out a stick of red pigment and a piece of white silken stuff. Kon clicked, interestedly. Graydon drew on the silk the outline of the amphitheater. Kon nodded. Graydon pointed to the entrance and to himself. The Spider-man shook his head, vigorously. Graydon drew a picture of the back of the shell as he thought it might be, and an outline of himself climbing up it. Kon looked at the picture scornfully, took the stick from him, and drew an excellent picture of what, clearly, was the actuality. He made it curved outward, instead of flat as in Graydon's drawing, covered its face with scrolls which apparently were carvings upon it, and then with that extraordinary facial contortion meant for a grin, sketched on it an outline of himself with Graydon under his arm. He patted Graydon on the back, and broke into a weird burst of sounds plainly intended for a laugh.

Kon had told him as clearly as by words—"The only way you can get up there is to have me carry you, and I know damned well you won't want that."

Didn't he? It was exactly what he did want!

He patted the Spider-man on the shoulder approvingly, pointed to the sketch and nodded. The grin faded from Kon's face. He seemed surprised; disconcerted. He clicked warningly, even angrily. Kon, reflected Graydon, was undoubtedly giving him hell—but he kept his finger on the drawing, nodding stubbornly. Kon seemed to have an idea; he caught up the stick and drew a recognizable picture of Lantlu, mainly so because it showed a face with a fist planted on its nose. Then he drew Graydon again with his rifle pointing at the face. Graydon shook his head. The Spider-man looked puzzled.

His next picture showed him crawling down the Temple wall with Graydon apparently held by a foot, headfirst, in Kon's hand. Graydon nodded cheerfully. If clicks could swear, Kon was swearing. He drew another picture of himself swinging through the branches of the trees with Graydon hanging on behind—still by his foot. Graydon clapped him on the shoulder, nodding complete acquiescence. Kon swore again, stood for a moment in thought, then rapidly sketched himself bringing down four bars on Lantlu's head. Graydon shrugged, indifferently. Kon emitted one despairing click, and surrendered.

He stalked out of the throne chamber with a gesture to Graydon to follow. He led him to a balcony at the end of a corridor. He scuttled away. Graydon looked out. The bowl of Yu-Atlanchi was filled with darkness, the sun had set behind the barrier. He saw lights, like trains of fireflies, making their way to the amphitheater of the shell. There was a touch on his arm. Kon was beside him, carrying two of the mace-headed bars. Without a single click, the Spider-man took him under his arm, swung over the edge of the balcony and seemed to scuttle down the sheer face of the Temple. Graydon noted with amusement that Kon did not hold him upside down as he had threatened.

They stood close to the edge of the great flight of steps leading down to the meadow. They passed cautiously along them, and reached the bordering fringe of trees. There Kon again lifted him, but not to swing him behind him through the branches. The Spider-man kept to their cover, flitting from trunk to trunk.

There was a murmur of voices, rapidly growing louder. The fireflies became flambeaux—pale, motionless lights like frozen moonbeams. Faintly by them he saw Yu-Atlanchi's nobles, men and women, streaming through the narrow entrance to the enormous shell. Here and there among them were the jeweled litters. The flambeaux were pallid ghost-lights, gave out no glow, intensified the darkness beyond them.

Kon detoured, and scurried silently through the trees to the back of the amphitheater. He passed the two bars to Graydon, took a firmer grip on him, and began to climb it, making a ladder of those carvings he had sketched, but which Graydon could not see in the blackness. They were at the top.

Here was a broad parapet. Kon straddled it, set Graydon upon it with a bump, and disappeared. Soon he was back, picked him up and slid with him into the dark void beneath. Graydon gasped, then their flight was ended so abruptly that his teeth shook. Around him was the faintest of light, starshine reflected from the opaline wall towering behind and above him. Kon had slid down one of the furrows. He wondered how in the devil the Spider-man was going to slide back up it with him under his arm.

He looked around him. They were in the topmost tier of the stone seats. In front of the seats was a three-foot parapet, protecting it. Not far below him he heard rustlings, whisperings, soft laughter.

Kon took his shoulder, slid him off the seat, forced him down behind the parapet; crouched there beside him, peeping over it.

Above the western mountains a faint glow of silver appeared. It grew brighter. The whispering below him ceased. Between two of the towering peaks a shimmering argent point sprang out. It became a rill of silver fire.

A man's voice, a vibrant baritone, began a chant. He was answered with strophe and anti-strophe by the unseen throng below.

Steadily as that chant arose, so arose the moon.

Behind him, at first in fugitive sparklings, then in steadily rising rhythms of opal radiance, the great shell began to glow —brighter and ever brighter, as steadily the moon swung out of the stone fingers of the peaks.

The feast of the Dream Makers had begun.

The chanting ended. The light of the risen moon fell within the amphitheater and full upon the conchoidal walls. Their radiance quickened, the shell became a luminous opal. Rays streamed from the starry points of blue and peacock patches. They met and crossed at the center of the amphitheater, weaving a web that stretched from side to side. Steadily this ray-woven web grew denser; against it were silhouetted the heads of the nobles, many empty tiers below.

Another chant began. A point of silver light appeared within the opposite wall, high up and close to the opening of the shell-like valves which formed the structure's entrance. It expanded into a little moon, a replica of the orb swimming across the sky. Three more shone softly into sight beside it. Their rays crept out, touched the luminous web, spread over it. The web held now the quality of a curtain, transparent but material.

And suddenly, through that curtain, high up on the other side of the shell, a larger moon swelled out of the semi-darkness, since there the moonlight did not fall full upon the walls. Within the glowing disk was a woman's head. She was one of the Old Race, and aureoled by that silver nimbus, her face was transformed into truly unearthly beauty. Her eyes were closed, she seemed asleep—

A Maker of Dreams!

She was, he thought, within a wide niche or alcove, but whether she sat or stood he could not tell. Her body was indistinguishable. The orb behind that exquisite head throbbed, swelled, became still. The Dream-Maker seemed to merge with its luminescence, become only a mist against it. The chant soared into a shouting chord, and died.

Something sped from the orb, something without shape or form, realized by another sense than sight. It struck the web. Under its impact the curtain trembled. And suddenly—there was no web, no ray woven curtain! Graydon looked out into space, into the void beyond this universe. He saw the shapeless thing racing through it with a speed thousands of times that of light. Knew it for a thought from the Maker of Dreams. Following it, he felt probing into his brain something like a numbing finger, cold with the cold of outer space through which the thought moved. On and on, into unfathomable infinitude it went.

It stopped. It became a vast nebula, spiraling like Andromeda's starry whirl. The nebula came rushing back at the same prodigious speed, a cosmic pinwheel of suns, threatening annihilation.

It resolved itself into its component stars, huge spinning spheres of incandescence, of every color. One sun came rolling out from its fellows, an immense orb of candent sapphire. Beside it appeared a world, fit child of that luminary in size. The sun drew away, the world drew nearer—

It was a world of flame. He looked into jungles of flame through which moved monstrous shapes of fire; at forests built of flames over which flew other shapes whose plumage was fire of emeralds, of rubies and of diamonds; at oceans which were seas of molten jewels and through whose iridescent spray swam leviathans of fire.

Back whirled fire world and sapphire sun among their fellows.

Striding through the void came gigantic men, god-like, laughing. They stooped and plucked the whirling suns. They tossed them to each other. They hurled them into the outer void, streaming like comets. They sent them crashing into

215

each other with storms of coruscant meteors, cascades of sparkling star dust.

The laughing gods strode off, over where had lain the garden of Suns they had uprooted. For an instant the void hung, empty.

Graydon, gasping, looked again upon the curtain of woven rays.

Had it been illusion? Had it been real? What he had seen had seemed no two-dimensional picture thrown upon that strange screen. No, it had been in three dimensions—and as actual as anything he had ever beheld. Had the thought of the Dream Maker created that wrecked universe? And the playful gods—were they, too, born of her thought? Or had they been other realities, happening upon that galaxy, stopping to destroy it, then carelessly passing on?

There was a murmuring among the nobles, a faint applause. The orb behind the head of the Dream Maker dimmed. When it pulsed out, it held within it the head of a man, eyes closed as had been the woman's.

Again the thought of the Dream Maker sped. The ray curtain quivered under its impact. Graydon looked upon a desert. Its sands began to sparkle, to stir and grow. Up from the waste a city built itself—but no such city as Earth had ever borne. Vast structures of an architecture alien and unknown to man! And peopled with *chimerœ*. Their hideousness struck his eyes like a blow. He closed them. When he opened them, the city was crumbling. In its place grew a broad landscape illumined by two suns, one saffron and one green, which swiftly circled each round the other. Under their mingled light were trees, shaped like hydras, like polyps, with fleshy, writhing reptilian limbs to which clung great pulpy flowers of a loathsome beauty. The flowers opened, and out of them sprang amorphous things which fought among the dreadful growths like obscene demons, torturing, mating—

He closed his eyes, sickened. A wave of applause told him the Dream Maker was finished. He felt a deeper hate for these people who could find delectable such horrors as he had beheld.

And now Dream Maker after Dream Maker followed one

another, and dream upon dream unfolded in the web of rays. Some, Graydon watched fascinated, unable to draw his eyes from them; others sent him shuddering into the shelter of the Spider-man's arms, sick of soul. A few were of surpassing beauty, Djinn worlds straight out of the Arabian Nights. There was a world of pure colors, unpeopled, colors that built of themselves gigantic symphonies, vast vistas of harmonies. Such drew little applause from these men and women whose chant was interlude between the dreams. It was carnage and cruelty, *diablerie,* defiled, monstrous matings, Sabbats; hideous fantasies to which Dante's blackest hell was Paradise itself which stirred them.

He heard a louder whispering, over it the voice of Lantlu; arrogant; vibrant with gloating anticipation.

Within the silver orb was a woman's head. The beauty of her face was tainted, subtly debased, as though through her veins ran sweet corruption. As her head merged into misty outline on the disk, he thought he saw the closed lids open for an instant, disclose deep violet eyes that were wells of evil, and which sent some swift message toward where Lantlu boasted; they closed. For the first time, an absolute silence fell over the amphitheater; a waiting silence; a silence of suspense—of expectation.

The curtain shook with the speeding thought of the woman. But the web did not vanish as heretofore. Instead, a film crept over it; a crawling film of shifting hues, like oil spreading over the surface of a clear pool. Rapidly the film became more dense, the motion of its shifting colors swifter.

Dark shadows began to flit through the film, one on the skirts of the other, converging toward, settling at, the edge of the ray web. Faster they flitted, one by one, from all parts of it, gathering there, growing steadily denser—assuming shape.

Not only taking shape—taking substance!

Graydon clutched the stone balustrade with stiff fingers. There upon the web was the shape of a man, a giant all of ten feet tall, tenebrous, framed by the crawling colors—and no shadow. No—something material—

Over the rim of the amphitheater shot a wide and vivid ray of red. It came from the direction of the caverns. It struck the sombrous shape, spread fanwise over it, changing it to a rusty black.

The red ray began to feed it, to build it up. Through the beam streamed a storm of black atoms, the shape sucked them in, took substance from them—it was no longer tenebrous.

It was a body, featureless but still a body, caught high in the web, held there by the force of the red ray.

Borne in the wake of the black atoms came the Shadow!

It did not come swiftly. It floated through the beam cautiously, as though none too sure of its progress. It crept, its faceless head outstretched, its unseen eyes intent upon its goal. It covered the last few yards between it and the hanging shape with a lightning leap. There was a cloudy swirling where the black body had hung, a churning mist shot through with darting crimson corpuscles.

Something like a spark of dazzling white incandescence touched the churning mist, was swallowed by it. To Graydon it had seemed to come from outside, opposite the source of the red ray—from the Temple.

The mist condensed, vanished. The body hung for a breath, then slithered through the web down to the ground.

No longer the body of a man. A crouching thing, misshapen, deformed—

Something like a great frog—and on its shoulders—

The head of Nimir!

Graydon thought he heard the laughter of the Serpentwoman!

But Nimir's pale blue eyes were alive with triumph. The imperious, Luciferean face was radiant with triumph. He shouted his triumph while a frozen silence held those who looked upon him. He capered, grotesquely, upon his sprawling legs, roaring in the lost tongue of the Lords his triumph and defiance!

The red ray blinked out. A flare of crimson light shot up into the skies from beyond the lake.

The hideous hopping figure became rigid; its face of a fallen angel staring at that flare. Its gaze dropped from it to its body. Graydon, every nerve at breaking point, watched incredulity change to truly demonic rage—the eyes glared like blue hell flames, the mouth became an open square from which slaver dripped, the face writhed into a Gorgon mask.

Slowly Nimir turned his gaze to that evil Maker of Dreams who had been his tool and Lantlu's. She was standing, awake enough now, in the niche of the silver orb.

The monstrous arms of Nimir swung wide, he made a squattering leap toward her. The woman screamed, swayed, and fell forward from the niche. On the floor of the amphitheater, far below where she had stood, a white heap stirred feebly for an instant and was still.

Slowly the eyes of Nimir drew from her, searched the empty tiers, drew closer—closer—to Graydon!

CHAPTER XXIII

The Taking of Suarra

GRAYDON DROPPED flat behind the parapet; covered there, hiding his face, fear such as he had never known—no, not even in the red cavern—numbing him. He waited with dying heart for the sound of hopping pads . . . coming for him . . . coming to take him . . .

He raised his hand, fixed his eyes upon the purple stones of the Serpent-woman's bracelet. Their glitter steadied him. Desperately he thrust from his mind everything but the image of the Mother—clung to that image as a falling climber clings to a projecting root that has stayed his drop into some abyss; filled his mind with that image; closed his ears, closed his mind to all but that.

How long he crouched there he never knew. He was aroused by the patting of Kon's little hands. Trembling, sick, he raised his head, stared around him. He was in semi-darkness. The moon had traveled past its zenith, was descending. Its rays no longer shone upon the shell behind him. The opaline glow was dim, the web of rays gone.

The amphitheater was empty.

After a little time, Graydon mastered his weakness, crept with the Spider-man, hugging the shadow, down the wide aisle that led to the pave; slipped without challenge through the valves of the entrance and into the shelter of the trees.

He reached the Temple. He was lifted by Kon up to that balcony from which they had set forth. He stared from it down upon the city.

The city was ablaze with lights; it was astir and roaring!

He hesitated, uncertain what to do; and while he hesitated, the curtains parted. Into the chamber marched Regor at the head of a score of Emers armed with bows and spears.

His face was haggard. Without a word to Graydon, he stationed the Indians at the opening. He clicked to Kon, and for a minute or two a rapid conversation went on between them. Regor gave some command; with more than his usual melancholy, the Spider-man looked at Graydon, and sidled out.

"Come," Regor touched him on the shoulder, "the Mother wants you."

A chill of apprehension shot through Graydon. If his conscience had not been so troubled, he would have burst into immediate questions. As it was, he followed Regor without speaking. The outer corridor was filled with Indians, among them a sprinkling of the nobles. A few he recognized as of the Fellowship—some of Huon's rescued remnant. These saluted him, with, he thought, pity in their gaze.

"Regor," he said, "something's wrong. What is it?"

Regor mumbled inarticulately, shook his head, and hurried on. Graydon, fighting an increasing dread, kept step with him. They were mounting toward the top of the Temple, not going to the room where always heretofore he had been summoned to the Mother.

And everywhere were companies of the Emers, threaded by the nobles. A number of the latter were clothed in Lantlu's green . . . the defection from the dinosaur master must have been more considerable than Regor had reckoned . . . plenty of women among them, too—and armed like the men with the short swords and javelins and small round shields. Plenty here for defense . . . and all of them seemed to know exactly what they were doing . . . under perfect discipline. . . .

He realized that in reality he didn't care whether they were or not; that he was deliberately marking time, desperately taking note of exterior things to check a fear he had not dared put into words. He could do it no longer. He had to know.

"Regor," he said, "is it—Suarra?"

The big man's arm went round his shoulders.

"They've taken her! Lantlu has her!"

Graydon stopped short, the blood draining from his heart.

"Taken her? But she was with the Mother! How could they take her?"

"It happened in the confusion when the Ladnophaxi ended." Regor hurried him onward. "Huon and I had gotten back an hour before that. The Indians were filtering in. There was much to do. And fivescore and more of the Old Race upon whom we had not counted had come, swearing allegiance to the Mother, demanding entrance by their ancient right. Some say Suarra went seeking you. And, not finding you, sought Kon. And that while she was seeking, a message came to her—from you!"

Graydon halted abruptly.

"From me! Good God—no!" he cried. "How could I have sent her a message? I was at that cursed Feast—forced Kon to take me. I'd only gotten back when you appeared—"

"Ah, yes, lad," Regor shrugged his broad shoulders, helplessly. "But it is now the hour after midnight. The Feast ended an hour before midnight. What of the two hours between?"

Now Graydon felt his head whirl. Could it be that he had crouched behind the parapet for two whole hours? Impossible! But even so—

He thrust out his hand, struck the giant such a blow on his breast that he reeled back.

"Damn you, Regor!" he cried, furiously. "Do you hint I had anything to do with it—"

"Don't be foolish, lad," Regor showed no resentment. "Of course I know you sent no message. But this much is certain —had you been here, Suarra would have fallen into no such trap. And it seems just as certain that those who decoyed her must have known you were not here. How did they know it? Why did they not try to intercept you on your return? Maybe the Mother knows all that by now . . . she was raging . . . the one she loved best snatched from under her eyes. . . ."

He stopped where the corridor ended in a rounded buttress of wall. He touched it, and a door slid open, revealing a small circular vault or well, its sides sheathed with polished amber metal. Regor stepped into it, drawing Graydon beside him. As the door closed, he had the sensation of swift upward flight. The floor came to rest. He stood upon the roof of the Temple, under the stars; he caught the shimmer of the Serpent-woman's coils, heard her voice, vibrant with anxiety but without reproach or anger.

"Come to me, Graydon. Go you back, Regor, and get for him the clothing of one of those who abandoned Lantlu. A green cloak with it—and an emerald fillet. Do not tarry!"

"You will not be hard on the lad, Mother?" muttered Regor.

"Nonsense! What blame may be, is mine! On with you, and return quickly," she answered; and when he had gone she beckoned Graydon to her side, cupped his face with her little hands, and kissed him.

"If I had it in my heart to scold you, child, I could not—seeing into your heart with its load of self-reproach and misery. The fault is mine! Had I not yielded to impulse, had let Nimir take the shape woven upon the web instead of malforming it, he would not have struck back at me through Suarra. I wanted to shake his will, weaken him at the outset —oh, why justify myself? It was my woman's vanity—I wanted to show him my power. I invited reprisal in kind—and it was not long coming. The fault is mine—and so enough of that."

A thought which had been knocking at Graydon's mind, a thought so terrible that he had fought its shaping, found utterance.

"Mother," he said, "you know that, disobeying you, I slipped away to the Feast. When the change came upon Nimir, and after the evil Maker of Dreams had fallen to her death, his gaze began searching the tiers as though for some one. And I think he suspected I was there. I set my thought on you, hiding from him in you. But Regor tells me almost two hours passed while time went by me, unknown. During that time, even though Kon was with me and knows I did not move, could Nimir have stolen my thought, used my mind by some infernal art, to lure Suarra from the Temple? A week ago, Mother, I would have held such a thought sheer madness. But now—after what I beheld at the Feast—it no longer seems madness."

"No," she shook her head, but her eyes narrowed and she studied him. "No, I do not believe he knew you were there.

I did not—but then it never occurred to me to look for you—"

"He did know I was there!" Conviction came to Graydon, and with it full vision of his dreadful thought. "Again he snared me, and he left me there, like a bird on a limed twig, until he had carried out his purpose. He did not molest me on my way back. And that was after Suarra had been taken. This is what I believe is in Nimir's mind, Mother—that he will exchange Suarra for—me. He wanted my body. He knows I would not surrender to him to save myself from torment or death. But to save Suarra—ah, he believes I would. So he binds me helpless, takes her and will offer to return her—for what he wants from me."

"And if he makes that offer—will you accept?" the Serpent-woman leaned forward, purple eyes deep in his.

"Yes," he answered, and although the old horror of the Shadow rocked him, he knew that he spoke truth.

"But why did he let you return?" she asked. "Why, if you are right, did he not take you after Suarra had been trapped and while you were on your way back to the Temple?"

"That answer is easy," Graydon smiled wryly. "He knew that I would fight, feared that this body he covets might be injured, marred, perhaps, even be destroyed. I heard Nimir express himself very clearly on that point. Why should he run that risk—if he could make me come to him of my own volition, entirely intact?"

One of the Mother's childish arms went round his neck, drew his head to her shoulder.

"How far you have marched, you children of the gray apemen!" she whispered. "And I can offer you little comfort, Graydon, if the truth be that. But this is also true—Nimir will think long before he shakes off the body he now has. The mechanism which sent the feeding ray is destroyed. I sent back on the ray the force which annihilated it. So not again may Nimir weave clothing for himself in that manner, even though he may be able to shed what he wears. It may be that he can become Shadow once more, an intelligence disembodied—and enter you. If you throw open your gates to him. But would he dare take the chance at this moment?

Not now, when I am ready to strike. If he could but be sure he could enter you—ah, yes. But he cannot be sure. If such bargain is in his mind, he would hold you beside him until the issue between us is settled. And then, if he won, put on your strong clean body—if he could."

"There's a large flaw in his reasoning, if that's his idea," said Graydon, grimly. "If he destroys you, Mother, it is not likely Suarra would survive. And then I would very speedily put this body of mine in such condition he could not occupy it—as once before, when captive to him, I had planned to do."

"But I don't want to be destroyed, nor Suarra, nor you, child," replied the Mother, practically. "And I don't intend we shall be. Nevertheless, whether you are right or wrong as to Nimir's motives, it amounts to the same thing. You are the only one who can save Suarra—if she can be saved. It may be that I play directly into Nimir's hands by what I have decided. I cannot see, though, how we are any worse off by taking the aggressive. If you fail, you only anticipate by a few hours what you fear—"

She rose high upon her coils, all bird-trills gone from the lisping voice.

"Alone, as soon as may be, you must go to the house of Lantlu, face that spawn of evil and his Dark Master, take Suarra from them. If you fail, then this I promise you—you shall not become the habitation of Nimir. For I, Adana, will blast Yu-Atlanchi and every living thing within it from earth's face—though in doing this I, too, must pass with them!"

She sank down, red tongue flickering.

"You would have it so, Graydon?"

"I would, Mother," he answered, steadily, "if in that annihilation Nimir is surely included."

"Ease your mind of any doubt on that score," she answered, dryly.

"Then the sooner I go the better," he said. "God—what's keeping Regor!"

"He comes," she answered. "Look around you, Graydon."

For the first time, he took conscious note of the place. He was upon a circular platform raised high upon the roof of

the Temple. Above him were the stars and in the west the
sinking moon. At the right and far below was the city, its
agitated lights like a panic among fire-flies. Its clamor came
faintly to him. Across the lake, the caverns of the colossi
were black mouths in the moon-glow on the cliffs. At his left
was the shadowy plain.

And now he saw that this platform was a circle some two
hundred feet wide, rimmed with a high curb of the amber
metal. At its edge, facing the caverns, was one of the great
crystal disks; a second disk looked down upon the city. The
metal bases in which they rested were open; within them
were oblong coffers of crystal filled with the quicksilver of
the Mother's sistrum. From these coffers protruded rods of
crystal filled with the purple flame of the destroying pillar
in the Cavern of the Lost Wisdom.

Close by where the Serpent-woman lay was a curious contrivance resembling somewhat the bowl from which the pillar of violet light had ascended, but much smaller, and tipped
as though it were a searchlight which could be swung upward or around in any direction. This, too, bristled with the
crystal rods. There were other things whose uses he could
not guess, the contents he supposed of those mysterious
chests they had carried to her. And set here and there within
the circle of the platform were the seven huge silver globes.

"Adana in her arsenal," she smiled for the first time. "And
if you only knew, my Graydon, what weapons these are! I
wish that we could have destroyed all in the Cavern before
Nimir came to it. Yes, and especially that feeding ray by
which in ancient times my ancestors built up many strange
beings for use—and for amusement—but always destroyed
when their uses were done. Aye, much do I wish it now—
who a little time ago hoped as earnestly that Nimir had found
it. Ah, well—go to the curb and pass your hand over it."

Wonderingly, he obeyed, stretched out his hand over the
amber curb—felt nothing but air.

"And now—" she leaned over, touched a rod in the bowl
beside her. From the curb flashed a ring of atomically tiny
sparks of violet light. It rushed up, a hundred feet into the
air, contracted there into a globe of violet fire, and vanished.

"Now stretch your hand—" she said. He reached out.

His fingers touched substance. He pressed his palm against it; it seemed slightly warm, glasslike and subtly conveyed a sense of impenetrability. The noise of the city was stilled—there was absolute silence about him. He pressed against the obstacle, beat his closed fist on it—he could see nothing, yet there was a wall. The Serpent-woman touched the lever again. His hand went out into air so abruptly that he almost fell.

"Not even the strongest of your weapons could break that, Graydon," she said. "Nor has Nimir anything that can penetrate it. If I could extend that wall around the Temple, as I can round myself here, there would be no need for guards. Yet there is no magic in it. Your wise men believe that what you call matter is nothing but force, energy, in another form. They are right. All this is energy somewhat more abruptly made matter—of a sort—and a most stubborn matter, child. Oh, most stubborn—Regor, you took your time!"

The opening in the platform through which they had risen had disgorged the giant, with a little pile of clothing over his arm.

"Not the easiest thing to find anything to fit him," he rumbled.

"Take off your clothes," the Mother nodded to Graydon, "put those on. Nay, child, don't be disconcerted. Remember—I am a very old, old woman!" Her eyes had danced at his involuntary movement of embarrassment. "And while you dress, listen to me."

He began to strip.

"Now this it is," she said. "I could loose destruction upon the city, or loose it upon the palace of Lantlu alone. But such weapons as I handle make no distinction between friend or foe. Suarra would be slain with the others. Therefore, that is barred—at least—" she looked at Graydon, a message in her eyes—"at least for the moment. Nor can we send out any force to rescue her, since that would mean open fighting, and before they could reach her, she would be spirited away where we could not find her. It is a matter for stealth and cunning, courage and ready resource—and one man. One man can pass unnoticed where many could not. It cannot be you, Regor, for you bear too many distinctive marks for successful disguise. Nor Huon, since his strength is not in cunning nor resourcefulness. Nor would I trust any other Yu-Atlanchan.

"It must be you, Graydon—and you must be alone. Also it will be the last thing they will expect—or at least, I hope so. You shall carry your own weapons."

Graydon, half-dressed, nodded approvingly at that.

"She is in the house of Lantlu. Whether Nimir is there or not I do not know. As he obscured my sight when I tried to find him in his den, so has he there. Where Suarra is, in what plight, I cannot see—always the veiling murk balks me. Ah—I told you Nimir is more cunning than I had thought —But I can send your sight as far as that place, Graydon, so that you will know how to go to it. And another thing I can do to help you—but that later. Bend to me—"

She pressed her hand against his forehead as when she sent his sight to the cavern that time Nimir had noosed him. He seemed to float from the roof, pass as fast as a man could run away from the Temple, along this lane and that, pausing now here and now there to note a landmark, until he came to a palace of turquoise and opal set around with trees from which drooped long panicles of flowers all red and silver. There were immense windows, casemented, latticed with fretted metal delicate as lace-work, set in walls and turrets, and behind them light and the movement of many people. Light and movement he sensed, rather than saw, for ever as he strove to look within, his sight was met by what seemed a fine dark mist through which it could not penetrate.

Back he returned, at the same pace, pausing again at the landmarks that were his clews in this labyrinth of lanes. He stood, swaying a little, beside the Serpent-woman.

"You know the way! You will remember!" As before, they were less questions than commands. And, as before, he answered:

"I know. I will remember." And realized that every foot between the Temple and the palace of Lantlu was etched into his memory as though he had traversed the way ten thousand times.

She took the fillet of emerald and pressed it down upon his forehead; threw the cloak of green over his shoulders, drew a fold of it up over his mouth. She pushed him away—regarded him, doubtfully.

"For the first time, child, I'm sorry you haven't the beauty of which I am so weary. You look somewhat like some one half between the Emers and the Old Race. By my ancestors, why weren't you born with blue eyes instead of gray, and with your hair yellow? Well—it can't be helped! The tide of things is with you—there is great confusion, and they will not expect attack; certainly, not attack from you, single-handed. And if you fail—I will avenge you as I have promised."

He bowed over her hand, turned to go.

"Wait!" She drew up her body, sent out a soft call like a faint echo of the elfin bugles. And now he realized that if those winged serpents she called her Messengers were invisible to him, they were not so to her. Forth from the shadows came a beating of strong pinions. The air about him eddied with the sweep of unseen wings. She reached out her arms, seemed to gather something within each, drew them close, looking, with eyes that plainly saw, into eyes none else could see. She began a low, sweet trilling. Weird enough it was to hear those birdlike notes answered by others out of empty air close beside her lips. She dropped her arms.

Graydon heard the wings close over his own head. Something touched his shoulder, wrapped itself gently about his upper arm and sent a coil around his waist; something pressed his cheek, caressingly. Involuntarily, he thrust up a hand and gripped it. It was a serpent shape, yet contact with it brought no shrinking, nor repugnance. It was cool, but not cold; he drew tentative fingers around it. The coil, he thought, must be all of eight inches through. It puzzled him that the creature had so little weight. There was a rapid pulsation above him like the whirring of an enormous humming-bird; he knew that it was holding its weight off him—that it meant its embrace to be reassuring.

He patted it, as he would have a dog. The coils slipped away. The whirring continued. Listening, he thought that there were two there.

"Go now, Graydon," said the Mother. "Go quickly. These two shall attend you. You cannot talk to them. Point to those you would have slain—and they will slay them. Trust them. They have intelligence, Graydon. You cannot understand, but they have it. Trust them—go—"

She pushed him away from her. Regor wheeled him round; marched him to the edge of the Temple's roof. There he stooped and drew forth a stout rope at whose end was a grappling hook. He fastened the hook to the cornice, threw the rope over.

"There's your path, lad," he said, huskily. "The Mother wants none to see you leave. Over with you! And take this—"

He thrust his long poniard into Graydon's girdle. Rifle slung over his shoulders, he caught the rope, slipped over the parapet. He slid down, the whirring of the winged serpents accompanying him. He reached the end of the rope, stood for an instant in the darkness, wondering which way to go.

He felt the touch of one of the Messengers, urging him on. And suddenly, in his brain, he saw the way to Lantlu's palace sharply outlined as a map.

Graydon began to run along these lanes his sight had followed when the Serpent-woman had touched him. Over him, matching his pace, beat the unseen wings.

CHAPTER XXIV

Bride of the Lizard-Man

It was a luminously clear night. He found his way easily, as though his feet had been long trained to every turn and curve. After a little he stopped running; for one thing, to conserve his strength for what was to come, for another, lest it draw attention to him from those who might also be traveling his path.

He was close to the palace of Lantlu when he had his first encounter. It proved to him the deadly mettle of those animate rapier blades the Mother had assigned to him for servants. From a shrubbery-concealed lane emerged a couple of Emers carrying javelins and flambeaux in which, instead of flames, were globes gleaming with a golden light. Behind them came a litter carried by four Indians. In it was a noble clad in green. He was followed by another pair of guards.

Graydon had no chance to retreat, nor to slip into the shadow. The occupant of the litter waved his hand, greeted him. Graydon, holding his cloak to hide his face as much as possible, returned the greeting briefly, tried to pass on. Such brusque behavior was apparently not the custom, for the noble raised himself, gave a sharp command to his men, then leaped out and advanced toward him with drawn sword.

There was but one thing to do, and Graydon did it. He pointed at the Emers, and hurled himself upon the Yu-Atlanchan. He ducked beneath a vicious thrust of the sword, and the next instant had caught the noble's right wrist in one hand while the other throttled him. It was no time for niceties. Up came his knee, and caught his opponent in the groin. Under the agony of that blow, the Yu-Atlanchan relaxed, his sword dropped. Graydon pinned him through the heart with Regor's dagger.

He did not dare use his rifle, so bent swiftly, picked up the dead man's sword, turned to face the Emers.

They, too, were dead.

They lay, the eight of them, pierced by the rapier bills of the winged serpents before they could make out-cry or lift a single javelin, slain in that brief moment it had taken him to kill one man.

He looked down at their bodies. It semed incredible that those eight lives could have been wiped out in such little time. He heard the wings of the creatures whirring close over his head, and stared up toward the sound. Above him, as though an unseen finger had traced them in the air, were two slender crimson lines. They shook, and a little shower of crimson drops fell from them—

The winged serpents cleansing their beaks!

He went on with a ruthless elation in his heart. All sense of aloneness had fled; he felt as though he had an army at his back. He sped on, boldly. The lane entered a dense coppice of flowering trees. He crept softly along through the copse. He halted in the deepest shadow. Not a hundred yards away was the palace of Lantlu. The structure covered, he estimated, a little more than an acre. It seemed to be octagonal, not lofty, the bulk of it composed of two high-vaulted floors. From its center arose a dome, shimmering sapphire and opal; and shaped like that which Tamerlane the Conqueror brought back from ravished Damascus to grace his beloved Samarkand. Up to its swelling base pushed clusters of small jeweled turrets, like little bowers built by gnomes for their women.

The octagonal walls were sheathed with tiles glimmering as though lacquered with molten pale rubies, sun-yellow topazes, water-green emeralds. They contained windows, both rectangular and oval, casemented and latticed by fretwork of stone and metal delicate as lace. Out from their base extended a tessellated pave, thirty feet wide, of black and white polished stone. Slender pillars of gold were ranged at its edge, bearing silken canopies. Soft light streamed from every window through webbed curtainings. There was no door.

Graydon crept forward to the edge of the copse. Between him and the pave was a smooth stretch of sward, open, and impossible to cross without being detected by any one on watch. He saw no one, but from the whole palace came a confused murmur. A hundred feet or more to his right the flowering trees pressed closer to the walls. He flitted along the rim of the boskage until he reached this verdant tongue. Working cautious way to its tip, he found he was now within fifty feet of the pillars.

He faced another side of the palace. On the ground floor were a trio of wide oval windows, almost touching, through which came a brighter glow than from the others. And now voices came to him plainly, voices of the nobles, both men and women. They came from this chamber wherein shone the brighter lights. Here beside the pillars was a guard of a dozen Indians armed with javelins and bows.

As he stood hesitating, wondering what was best to do, he heard from the room a tumult of shouts and laughter, and the sound of pipes playing a curious jigging tune. Then above all, stilling both clamor and music, the jeering voice of Lantlu:

"Welcome Suarra! Welcome to the bride! Ho, there—bring forth the bridegroom!"

And then the beginning of another tumult of applause and laughter.

Graydon leaped out of the protecting shadow of the trees, and pointed to the Emer guard. He heard the swish of pinions. He ran toward the palace, unslinging his rifle as he went. Before he could take his second step he saw two of the Indians go down, then another pair, while the others stood frozen, paralyzed by this invisible death striking among them. And here was swordplay swifter than he had ever beheld in any salon of French or Italian master of fencing. He had not covered half the fifty-foot strip before all that guard lay stretched at the edge of the pave, hearts pierced, throats torn. Precise, unerring, with the speed of a spray of machine-gun bullets, the rapier beaks had reached their marks. Silently they had struck—and silently those Emers had died.

He strode over a body, and to the curtained windows. Whether there were other guards close by, he neither knew nor cared, gave indeed no thought to it. The oval windows were grilled like those he had first noted. He tried the first, but it was immovable. The second swung quietly under his hands. He snapped open the safety lock of his rifle, gripped the gun in his left hand, softly parted the curtain webs with his right, and looked into the chamber.

His gaze flew straight to Suarra—took her in, and for the moment nothing else.

She stood on a dais in the center of the great room beside a flower-decked couch. She was clad in a robe of green through which her white body gleamed. Around her head was a wreath of crimson flowers. Her feet were bare. Her hands were crossed over her breasts, and around their wrists he saw the glitter of golden manacles.

Her mouth had been painted, her cheeks rouged, and these spots of color stood out against the waxen pallor of her face like those upon a doll's. Like a waxen doll she seemed, lifeless, eyes closed, scarcely breathing. And even as he gazed, she shuddered, swayed, and dropped upon the edge of the couch.

"The bride is becomingly disturbed at the approach of the bridegroom," spoke Lantlu, suavely, sonorously, like a mocking showman. "It is fitting. It is the traditional attitude. Her virginity is alarmed. Shyness overcomes her. But soon—ah, soon—Ho, ho, ho!" laughed Lantlu. From all the room a chorus of malicious laughter answered him. Suarra's head drooped lower.

There were red lights dancing before Graydon's eyes. Rage so great it half strangled him beat through him. He mastered himself, vision clearing. He saw now that all around the dais was a circle of low couches, and upon these were a score of the Yu-Atlanchans. So far as their beauty went, they might have been angels, but through those masks of perfection peered devils of cruelty and cold lusts. There was no pity in the eyes that sparkled upon Suarra.

At the far end of the room, half-risen, one knee upon the couch, a hand caressing the hair of a woman lying there, was Lantlu. With a satisfaction that for a moment overrode his red wrath, Graydon noted the flattening of the once perfect nose, the still disfigured mouth, the signatures of his fist. He looked away from him quickly examining the chamber for its entrances and guards.

There was only one doorway, draped like the windows; and no guards, at least not within the room. Well, that was good . . . Lantlu was an easy target . . . the best plan would be to step in, put a bullet through his head, shoot a few more, get Suarra and escape with her before the others could recover from the surprise of the attack. He hated to let that mocking devil off as easily as that . . . what he would prefer was the use of a fully equipped medieval torture chamber for a day or two . . . however—one couldn't have everything. After all, he was playing in luck that the Dark Master was absent. Yes—that was the best way. Hell! He was forgetting his best cards of all! The Mother's two Messengers! With them and his rifle he could clean up this whole devil's outfit! Where were they?

As though in answer to his thought, he felt the pressure of a coil on each side of him; knew that the two creatures were poised, waiting to enter the window with him.

He gave a swift glance at Suarra before he tensed himself for the leap within. He saw then what he had not noticed before—that between her and the doorway the circle of couches was broken, leaving a wide passage straight from it to the dais.

And as he looked, the webs were drawn aside, and through the opening walked two Emer women, naked, carrying great baskets filled with flowers from which, as they marched, they drew handfuls of blooms strewing them on the floor.

Close behind them came four Emers, armed with maces.

"Behold!" chanted Lantlu. "The bridegroom!"

Through the portal shambled a lizard-man!

He was clothed, like Suarra, in a robe of filmy green through which his leathery yellow skin glistened, as though it had been oiled. His red eyes darted right and left, viciously, challenging. Around his scaly head was a wreath of white blossoms out of which his red comb protruded, hideously.

From some hidden place the jigging music sounded again, loudly. The crimson eyes of the lizard-man fell upon the crouching figure of the girl upon the dais. His lips drew back along his snout, showing the yellow fangs. He leaped forward.

"Christ!" groaned Graydon—and shot through the curtains.

The leap of the lizard-man was checked as though by a sledge blow. He spun in mid-air. He dropped with the top of his head blown off.

Graydon vaulted over the low sill of the oval window. He fired again, with half-raised rifle, at Lantlu. As the shot rang out, the master of the dinosaurs dropped behind the couch, but Graydon knew that he had missed him. All right, he'd get him later! Now for the Emers. He raised his gun— the Emers were down!

The winged serpents! Again he had forgotten them. This time they had not waited for his orders. The guards lay slain.

"Suarra!" he called. "Come to me!"

She stood, gazing at him incredulously. She took one tottering step.

Without a twinge of compunction he sent bullets through the heads of two nobles upon couches between them, breaking the circle. That would teach them a lesson . . . but better not kill any more now . . . better not turn the Messengers upon them until Suarra was under his arm . . . keep 'em quiet till then . . . then send 'em all to hell where they belonged. . . .

If he only knew how to talk to the Messengers! He'd send them after Lantlu. But you couldn't just say, "Go get him, Towser," to things like those.

"Suarra!" he called again. She had slipped over the edge of the dais, was running to him . . . better watch that doorway . . . those shots must have been heard . . . how about that open window at his back . . . well, you couldn't look two ways at once. . . .

Suarra was beside him!

"Beloved! Oh, my beloved!" he heard her broken whisper, felt her lips press his shoulder.

"Buck up, darling! We're going to get out all right!" he said. He kept eyes and rifle ready on the ring of silent nobles and the doorway.

He wondered whether they were going to get out. He'd

better keep to that idea he had a moment ago . . . launch the winged serpents, get out the window and away with Suarra while the two Messengers were slaughtering, leave them to follow, catch up and cover their retreat . . .

Too late.

In the open doorway, appearing abruptly as though he had stepped out of the air, was Nimir!

Too late now. No use to loose the winged deaths, or try to flee. Graydon had clear conviction of that. He had walked into Nimir's trap, and must make his bargain. He lowered his gun, drew Suarra close to him.

A doubt assailed him. Had it been Nimir's trap? The Lord of Evil had moved a step into the great room, and was staring at him and Suarra, astonishment in his pale blue eyes. Up from beside him rose Lantlu, laughing—pointing derisively, gloating upon them.

Graydon threw up the rifle, covered him. Before he could press the trigger, one of Nimir's long, misshapen arms had circled Lantlu, had thrust him behind the shelter of his own body. The rifle spat. It seemed to Graydon that the bullet went through Nimir's breast.

Silent, unheeding, the Lord of Evil's puzzled gaze traveled from man and girl to the body of the Urd, the wreath of white blooms yellowed with its blood, mockery of green wedding garment torn in its death agony. His eyes passed along the path of flowers, over the dead Emers, to the blossom-strewn couch on the dais, and rested again upon green-robed Suarra.

Then Graydon saw comprehension come to him.

The crouching, frog-like body seemed to expand; it drew erect. The beautiful, Luciferean face above it became white and hard as stone, the pale eyes like ice. He wheeled, gripped Lantlu, lifted him and held him high over his head as though he meant to dash him to the floor. The master of the dinosaurs writhed and fought vainly against that grip.

For an instant the Lord of Evil held him thus, then mastered his passion, lowered him, and thrust him down prone at his feet.

"You fool!" he said, and there was a dreadful tonelessness in his voice, "to set your lusts and your hatreds against my will! Did I not tell you that this girl was to be held safe, inviolate? And did I not tell you why? How did you dare to do this thing? Answer me, fool!"

"I promised her I would mate her with the Urd. I keep my promises. What difference would it have made? The outlander would have come at your summons. Nor never have known—until too late. And no harm has been done, since you have him now. And even somewhat sooner than you had planned, Dark Master!"

There was no fear in Lantlu's voice, and there was more than a trace of his mocking arrogance in his salutation. The Lord of Evil did not reply, looking down upon him inscrutably. Stubborn lad, Lantlu, thought Graydon. Thoroughly rotten—but hard to break.

He studied the monstrous body, with its face of a fallen angel, the noble head, the imperial power and beauty of it— he felt a pang of pity for the Lord of Evil! After all, why not have let him have a body which would have gone with that head . . . damned if he could see what was gained by saddling Nimir with that monstrosity . . . Nimir had worked long enough for proper clothes . . . a woman's trick . . . it wasn't decent fighting. . . .

Suddenly he was aware that Nimir's eyes were upon him, that he had read his thoughts.

"You and I are not so far apart after all, Graydon!" said the Lord of Evil, with all that alluring sweetness which he had fought when battling against him as the Shadow on the jet throne.

It brought Graydon back with a jolt. After all, what business had he pitying Nimir! It was his business to get Suarra out of peril—save himself if he could!

The cold eyes of the Lord of Evil were bluer, there was friendliness in them—real or assumed.

"I must talk with you, Graydon."

"I know it," said Graydon, grimly. "And it will be right here, Nimir. And now."

The Lord of Evil smiled, and the smile lightened the dark power throned upon his face, gave it something of that dangerous attraction which lived in the sweetness of his voice. Graydon felt the spell, and braced himself against it.

"Get up, Lantlu. Do not go from here until I permit you. See that you do nothing to interrupt us. I warn you—and for the last time!"

Lantlu arose leisurely, gave Graydon and Suarra an indifferent glance, sauntered over to his couch, dropped beside the woman there and drew her arm around his neck. It was rather well done, Graydon thought, grudgingly.

The Lord of Evil shambled toward him. He felt Suarra's uncontrollable shudder. And when he was within a half-dozen paces, Graydon drew Regor's poniard, set its point on the girl's breast, over her heart.

"Stop there, Nimir," he said. "That is close enough. And hear me first. I know what you want. I am willing to discuss it. If we cannot agree, and if I am convinced we cannot escape, I will kill Suarra. She would have it so. Is that not true, Suarra?"

"It is true, beloved," she answered, tranquilly.

"I will then," continued Graydon, "do my best against you with this—" he touched the rifle—"If I find I can't stop you, I'll use my last bullet to blow my own head off. And that, I think, you won't like. But I'll do it. I mean it, Nimir."

The Lord of Evil smiled again.

"I believe you. And that is, as you surmise, the last thing I would like to see happen. Nor will it be necessary—if you are reasonable."

"My mind is wide open," said Graydon, "but only to your words. You understand me?"

The Lord of Evil bowed, then looked at him for a time without speaking. A feeling of unreality stole over Graydon. He felt as though he were in some play, a dream play in which he ran no real risks; that he could pick his own lines, mold his situations. He lost entirely the sense of grimmest reality that had held every nerve and muscle taut as drawn bow strings. And, oddly, that feeling of the unreal buoyed him, filled him with a heady recklessness—nor did it occur to him—then—that the Lord of Evil might be responsible for all that.

"Neither of you can escape—unless I let you," said Nimir. "You cannot harm me, nor can those servants of Adana whom I see hovering. That is truth, Graydon. This shape of mine, built as it was, is not in any manner like yours. Material, yes—in a way. Send your missiles through it, plunge your poniard into it—they cannot harm me. If you do not believe me—try it, Graydon."

He plucked open his cloak, revealing the distorted barrel of his chest, and stood waiting. Graydon raised the rifle, minded for the moment to accept the challenge. He dropped it—useless to waste the cartridge, Nimir spoke truth—

"But you," the Lord of Evil covered his monstrous torso, "you and Suarra I can destroy. Oh, very easily. Yet here once more we are at stalemate—since I want you, Graydon—let us say, intact."

"You made that quite clear once before," said Graydon curtly. "Well—then what?"

"A better bargain for you than if that wilful fool had not spoiled my plan," answered Nimir. "And not alone because by doing so he has put it in your immediate power to make yourself—uninhabitable. No—quite as much because of a certain thought you had of me and the Snake-woman not so long ago. It has been so long since any one has thought kindly of me," said Nimir, and laughed—"I find it oddly pleasant."

"The bargain?" said Graydon, impatiently.

"Quite so," went on the Lord of Evil, gently. "I never intended this shape of mine to be—permanent. Even if it had not been marred, it would still have been but—temporary. No, Graydon, I much prefer good human flesh and blood, which, adequately treated, can be made to last forever. And, as I have told you, as you remind me, rather often, I much prefer yours. Therefore, I will send Suarra and you safely back to the Temple—yes, even with a guard of honor—if—"

"I was waiting for the—if," said Graydon.

"If you will promise me, should I win the coming battle, that you will come to me of your own free will and, after I have cast aside these present coverings, let me enter as permanent tenant of that body of yours—I mean, of course, as co-tenant, I renew, in short, my offer of sharing your habitation with you without crowding or other molestation," smiled the Lord of Evil.

"Fair enough," said Graydon, unhesitatingly. "I agree."

"No, beloved, no!" cried Suarra, and clung to him. "Better death for both——"

"I don't think he will win, darling," said Graydon; the heady recklessness was stronger within him . . . it was a damned sight better dicker than he had expected . . . rather a sporting proposition . . . he didn't believe Nimir could win . . . even if he did—well, he, Graydon, was strong . . . he could fight this companion once he was seated in his brain beside him . . . control him . . . make him sick of his bargain . . . and, at the worst, life would be interesting—to put it mildly . . . hell, where were those ideas coming from? . . . why was he thinking like that? . . . weakening . . . no matter, he had to save Suarra . . . he *had* to save Suarra . . . it was the only way!

"I know I will win," said the Lord of Evil, softly. "You know it, too, don't you, Graydon!"

"No!" said Graydon, and slipped away from that spell of helpless acquiescence which had stolen over him. He drew a deep breath, all recklessness and sense of the unreal gone, bitter anger and a fierce determination taking their place. "No, I don't know it, Nimir. And don't cast any more of that sorcery of yours around me—or I may decide to end things right here and now. Let it stand! I agree! Now let us go!"

"Good!" the Lord of Evil laughed, the sweetness that had laden the whisperings of the Shadow strong in that laughter, "now would you make me even more determined to win, Graydon, did I not know that my victory is certain. There is only one more detail. I will not demand that you remain within the Temple during my little debate with the Snakewoman. Indeed—I do not think you would be able to," he looked at Graydon with a sparkle of amusement in the pale eyes—"But now that I have such a personal interest in you, it is surely within my rights to insist that every precaution be taken to keep—well, to employ a polite phrase—to keep my stake in the contract in usable condition! Therefore, you shall wear—this——"

He took from his girdle a broad collar of faintly gleaming red metal, stepped forward with it in his hand.

"What is it?" asked Graydon, suspiciously.

"Something that will keep certain powerful servants of

241

mine from killing you," answered the Lord of Evil, "if and when you are shaken out of the Temple. I don't mind your telling Adana that. She will be fully aware of what I mean when she sees it. Really, it gives you quite an advantage. I waive that, however—for broader considerations. Come," into his voice crept implacable command—"it is necessary. It gives me no power over you, if that is what you fear. But until you wear it—the girl cannot go."

Graydon bent his head, felt the touch of the misshapen fingers on his throat, heard the click as they fastened the collar around his neck—heard Suarra sobbing.

"And now," said the Lord of Evil, "for your escort back to Adana—so anxiously trying to see what is happening to you! So furious because she cannot! Follow me."

He shambled to the doorway. Hand in hand, they followed him, through the broken ring of the silent, staring nobles, past the hideous body of the lizard-man and the Emers whom the winged-serpents had slain. As Graydon passed, he heard the pinions of those unseen guardians above their heads. He stifled an impulse to send them darting at Lantlu.

The Lord of Evil leading, they passed out of that chamber into a great hall filled with the Emer soldiers and with nobles who shrank back as Nimir squattered by—shrank back and let them pass and kept lips closed and faces expressionless. Only, he noted, they looked furtively at the dully gleaming collar that fettered his throat—and over some of their faces quick pallor spread.

They came at last to the entrance to the palace. The Lord of Evil beckoned a captain, and gave swift orders. A double litter was brought, borne by eight strong green-kilted bearers. Into it, courteously, Nimir waved them.

The bearers raised the litter, a score of the soldiers led by another Indian officer, surrounded it. The doors swung open, and through them marched their escort.

"Until we meet again," smiled the Lord of Evil.

"May it be never!" answered Graydon, whole-heartedly.

"I look forward to many pleasant centuries together!" said the Lord of Evil—and laughed.

That laughter, still ringing in his ears, they entered the shadows of the trees. In the hands of the guards shone out flambeaux of clear white light. And suddenly Suarra thrust arms round his neck, drew his head down upon her soft breast.

"Graydon—Graydon, beloved—I am afraid! I am greatly afraid! It was too great a price, beloved! Better, far better, had I slain myself before you came! But I did not know . . . I hoped . . . until it was too late, and they fettered me . . . and then I could not kill myself. . . ."

Well—so was he afraid! Bitterly afraid! He comforted her as best he could.

They came at last to the Temple. They halted while the officer and a squad of his men mounted the broad steps, signaling with their flambeaux as they went. Graydon heard a challenge, the rumbling of Regor's voice. Then down the great stairway leaped the giant, to the side of their litter; lifted them out; embraced them as though they had been children returned from the dead.

The green-kilted guard saluted, stood at attention until they had come to the massive doors. Graydon heard the pinions of the winged serpents, darting upward to where the Mother waited; turning, saw the escort beginning their return.

He felt an immense weariness; he swayed, was caught by Regor's strong arm, carried forward.

The doors of the Temple clanged shut behind him.

CHAPTER XXV

The Collar of Nimir

SUARRA'S SOFT HANDS caressed him, she was murmuring broken words of pity, of endearment. He mastered his weakness, and broke away from Regor. The immense vestibule was filled with Indian soldiers in the Mother's blue, and some score of the nobles. Now these latter strode toward them, eagerly, their customary poise banished by devouring curiosity. But Regor waved them aside.

"To the Mother—and at once. Suarra, you are not harmed?"

She shook her head, and he hurried them onward. His eyes fell upon the metal collar around Graydon's neck, and he paused, staring at it perplexedly.

"The badge of Nimir!" laughed Graydon, mirthlessly. The giant reached out his hand, as though to tear it from him.

"No," Graydon pushed him away, "it's not so easy as all that, Regor."

The giant glared at the collar, uneasily, his brows knitted.

"It is a matter for the Mother," said Suarra. "Quickly, for the night wanes."

She took Graydon's hand, sped on with him, leaving Regor to follow. On they went through wide corridors filled with the Emers and little knots of the Old Race, stopping not even for greeting, until they came to that curving buttress up through which ran the shaft to the Serpent-woman's sanctuary. They stepped from it out onto the roof of the Temple.

"Mother!" cried Suarra.

There was a gleam of rosy-pearl, flashing to her, the coils of Adana undulating over the platform. Her body arose beside the girl, her childish arms went round her neck, drawing her head down to her little tilted breasts. For the first time, Graydon heard something suspiciously like a human sob in the Serpent-woman's voice.

"My daughter! Suarra! My daughter!"

And Suarra clung to her, weeping, while the Mother's heart-shaped mouth caressed her misty hair.

The Mother raised her head, thrust out a hand to Graydon. Her gaze fell upon the collar of the Lord of Evil. She grew rigid, her eyes dilated, her neck thrust forward, her pointed red tongue flicked out—once, twice—like a snake's.

She dipped from Suarra, reached out and touched Graydon upon the heart, the forehead; then cupped his face in her tiny hands and stared deep into his eyes. And gradually into the purple pools came pity, regret—and a certain apprehension, or so it seemed to him.

"So!" she whispered, and dropped her hands. "So—that is what he plans!" Her gaze drew inward, it was as though she were talking to herself, unseeing, unaware of them— "But he will be loath to use that weapon—until the last. I can meet it, yes. But I, too, am loath to use that power—as reluctant as he. By my ancestors—had I but one of my own people to stand beside me! Yes, had I but another of the Lords to stand with Tyddo—I would not fear. Well—there is no choice. And if between us Nimir and I unloose that which we cannot again leash, will not destruction spread like a swift pestilence over all this spinning globe . . . make of earth a desert indeed . . . bare of life? Ah—but then Nimir himself cannot escape destruction. . . ."

Her gaze came back to Graydon.

"There, child," she said, softly. "Don't despair. So you pitied Nimir, did you? And made his bargain! While he dropped his poison into your mind so cunningly—oh, so cunningly! Well, it was written, I suppose—and had to be. Nor was it your fault. It was I who baited that trap, though unknowingly, when I gave way to my woman's vanity and altered his clothing to my whim there at the Ladnophaxi. What has happened is but the pattern *I* made. You could have done nothing else—and it might be worse. We will let the dice lie as they have fallen. Oh, do not stare at me. It is no sorcery. I have read your thought, that is all. But I would hear the tale in words. Suarra—"

She turned to the girl. She saw, apparently for the first time, the bridal robe of green, the painted cheeks and lips. And at the sight, all her wrath against Nimir, all her hours of anxiety for Suarra, came to a focus and exploded. She threw out her hands, ripped the robe from the girl, leaving her revealed in all her white loveliness.

"Go over there and wash your face!" hissed the Snake Mother, as angrily as any old-fashioned woman might to a daughter she had caught surreptitiously dipping into the rouge pot.

The girl gasped, then fled, an ivory shadow, into the dimness around Adana's cushioned nest. And Graydon, despite all his weariness and trouble, chuckled; it was one of the flashes of purely human character that took away from this entirely unhuman being any mind-clogging awe or sense of terrifying strangeness; that made him doubt the doubts which, significantly enough, never crossed his mind when he was with her.

The Mother looked at him angrily, raised her hand as though half inclined to slap him; then glided to Suarra. He heard her talking gently, even remorsefully, to the girl. Then she called him.

A globe of dim luminescence pulsed out beside her. By its light he saw that Suarra had thrown round herself a covering cloak, and that she had cleansed her face of paint. She glanced at him, and dropped her head. The Serpent-woman laughed, brought their faces together, cheek by cheek.

"Don't mind, child," she said. "He knows women have bodies, I'm sure. Or should, by this time. And Regor is old enough to be your great-grandfather, at least. Come over, Regor. Now tell us, daughter, just what happened. Here, drink this."

She reached down into her coffer, took from it a small phial, filled a crystal goblet with water, and into it a drop from the phial. Suarra sipped, and handed it to Graydon. He drank, a tingling went through him, all weariness vanished; tenseness relaxed, his mind cleared, and he sank back beside Regor, listening to Suarra.

There was little of what she told, save how she had been trapped, that he did not know. An Emer officer had come to her after she had left the Mother and was watching the arrival of Huon's refugees from the lair. He bore a message from the Lord Graydon, he told her, who was on the lower terrace of the Temple. The Lord Graydon had discovered something there he wanted her to see before they went to the Mother with news of it. The Lord Graydon had commanded the speaker to find her and guide her to where he waited.

The very boldness and simplicity of the ruse had snared her. She knew that the Temple terraces were guarded, and it never occurred to her to doubt the genuineness of the summons. She had gone along the lower terrace, passing several squads of guards and answering their challenges. She had just gone by one of these squads when a cloak was thrown over her head, and she was lifted up and borne away.

"They were Lantlu's men," said Regor. "They had killed our guards, and taken their places. They were clad in the Mother's colors. We found the bodies of our men where they had been hurled over the terrace."

When they had gotten into the shelter of the trees, Suarra continued, her wrists and ankles had been bound and she had been placed in a litter. She had been taken straight to Lantlu's palace. There, Indian women had rouged and wreathed her and before she could suspect what was intended, had stripped her, clothed her in the green robe and snapped the golden manacles. Then she had been led to the room where Graydon had found her—to learn from Lantlu's jeering lips what he had in store for her.

The Serpent-woman listened, head swaying back and forth menacingly, eyes glittering; she asked no questions, did not interrupt.

"Regor," she said quietly, when Suarra was done, "go you

now, and make sure there has been no chink left through which any other rat of Nimir can creep. Take what sleep you can—for at dawn all within the Temple must be awake and at their posts. By another dawn, either I or Nimir will have conquered. Suarra, Graydon—you two sleep here beside me for what remains of this night."

And when Regor had gone, she took a hand of his in both of hers.

"Child," she said, softly, "do not fear. You shall sleep deep, and without dream or fear of Nimir. There are still four hours before dawn. I will awaken you—and then we shall talk of what is to be done. About this, I mean—" she touched the sullenly glowing collar—"and other things. Now drink this—you, too, Suarra."

She dipped again into her coffer, drew forth another phial, dropped one colorless globule into the goblet. They drank of it. Suarra yawned, sank down upon the cushions, smiled at him sleepily; her eyes closed. He felt a delicious lethargy stealing over him, let his head fall upon his cushions. He looked again at the Serpent-woman. She had drawn forth her sistrum, was holding it on high. From it streamed a slender pencil of milky light. She pointed it to the zenith, began to trace within its depths an ever-widening spiral.

She was signaling. Signaling, he wondered drowsily, to whom—to what? He fell asleep.

The Mother's touch awakened him; he looked up into her face bending over him. Her purple eyes were dilated, phosphorescent, enormous in the heart of her childish face. He sprang to his feet. At the edge of the platform was the Lord of Folly, peering over toward the lake; the scarlet figure of Kon, the Spider-man, and the black bulk of Regor beside him. Suarra was still asleep, her cheek nestled in the crook of one white arm stretched from under a heap of silken coverings.

Graydon shivered, feeling suddenly chill. For the first time since he had entered the Hidden Land, the sky was obscured. The clouds hung low, not more than three hundred feet above the Temple. They were less like clouds than a solid steel-gray ceiling, motionless.

Above him, and all around him, was a continuous soughing and whispering like the circling flight of countless and immense birds. Rhythmically they pulsed, this beating of unseen pinions—

The winged serpents! The Messengers of the Snake Mother! It was they she had been summoning from beyond the barrier with her slender beam of light!

She took his hand, glided with him over to the platform's edge, gave him a lens similar to that he had used in Huon's lair, pointed a finger to the nearer shore of the lake. He looked through it.

The shore was encrusted with the lizard-men! They surged there by the hundreds, by the thousands, it seemed to him; their ranks moving slowly forward as others joined them, wading up from the waters. And now he saw that the Urd horde was streaming across the lake from the caverns, that the surface was streaked from side to side with the swimming horde. And that along the front of those who had landed rode a half dozen of Lantlu's nobles upon the black dinosaurs, whipping them into order with huge lashes shaped like sjamboks. One of them leaned over the side of his monstrous steed. Graydon caught the dull glimmer of red metal around his throat, looked more closely.

It was a collar such as that which the Lord of Evil had snapped around his own neck.

Another of the dinosaur riders bore this badge of Nimir —and another. He dropped the lens, turned to the Serpent-woman. She nodded, answering his unspoken question.

"Yes," she said, "Nimir has linked you to him. Part of what he told you was truth, Graydon—but part of it was lies. When he said that it would protect you, he spoke truth. But when he said it gave him no power over you—there he lied, indeed."

She was silent, while he stared at her, miserably.

"And that is why you may not stay here with me to help us as I had hoped. For Nimir is cunning and desperate—and

I hope will soon be much more desperate—and it might be that in one unguarded moment of yours he could wreck through you all that I plan."

"Not through me!" groaned Graydon. "No, no!"

"We cannot afford to run the risk," answered the Mother. "Now I could rid you of his mark—but something whispers to me to let it be. That in doing this to you, Nimir has made a mistake. That if he had been wise he would have let the cards fall as I had disposed them for him. That he should have bent his mind solely upon this issue, but that his eagerness to possess you may react upon him, even as my vanity has reacted upon me. How this advantage may come, I do not know—but it is there—"

"The last Urd has reached the shore, Adana," muttered Regor. "We should go."

"Go you then with Regor and Huon," said the Mother. "They have use for you. And of this be sure—Nimir shall not have you. This I have promised you. And I, Adana, tell you that thus it shall be."

And suddenly she leaned forward and set her lips to his forehead.

"Awaken Suarra," she said. "Bid her good-by—then go swiftly. If we meet never again—I loved you, child."

Again she kissed him, then pushed him away. He bent over the sleeping girl. She opened drowsy eyes, looked up at him, dropped an arm around his neck and drew his lips down to hers.

"Oh, but I have slept," she murmured, but half-awake. "And is it already dawn?"

"It is well beyond dawn, heart of mine," he told her. "And I must go with Regor and Huon down into the Temple—"

"Into the Temple!" she sat up, all awake. "But I thought you were to be here. With me. Mother—"

"Have no fear, darling," he laughed, and only Adana knew what that laughter cost him, "I have the habit of coming back to you."

Regor tapped his shoulder. Graydon gently withdrew the clinging arms, kissed her once more, strode swiftly away between the giant and Huon. His last glimpse of her as the three dropped down the shining shaft was her head against the breast of the Serpent-woman, her hand raised to her lips to throw him a parting kiss—and doubt beginning to darken her clear eyes.

CHAPTER XXVI

Ragnarok in Yu-Atlanchi

NOW OF THE FREIGHT of those dread hours following his parting with Suarra, Graydon saw with his own eyes only a part. The complete picture he had to arrange from the stories of others.

They passed on quickly, the three of them, stopping only to get his pouch of cartridges. They came to the entrance of the chamber of the thrones. Here Regor halted.

"We have destroyed the opening mechanism of every tunnel entrance to the Temple except one," he began, abruptly. "That one cannot be forced. This was at command of the Mother. Unless she has miscalculated, we cannot therefore be taken by surprise from without. It will be Nimir's and Lantlu's object to get us out of the Temple, where they can overwhelm us with the Xinli and the Urd. Ours to prevent it.

"We threw up during the night strong barricades across the great stairs. We have stationed regiments upon the three terraces all around the Temple. If the attack becomes too hot, they can swarm back into the Temple by means of scaling ladders from the windows and through the great doors. Every window and opening is manned by archers and javelins and mace-men. Huon commands the barricade. You, Graydon, are to fight beside him. If they charge with the riding Xinli, try to kill their riders with that weapon of yours. If you can sting the Xinli into turning back upon those who follow—it will be very good. At the worst, a Xinli with none to guide it is not of much use to Lantlu. We must beat them off—that is all. What Nimir has hidden in his girdle we don't know. Above us all fights the Mother—who probably does know. And who has weapons as deadly as any possessed by the Lord of Evil, be sure of that! I do not

252

think this is farewell, lad," the giant's voice grew husky—
"but if farewell it be—" he threw his sound arm around
Graydon, hugged him mightily, gripped the hand of Huon,
and strode away.

"You and I, Graydon." Huon's voice was grim. "You remember what I told you that night you set out for the cavern
of the Frog-woman. You and I together—under a red sky
from which icy shadows dropped and battled with shapes of
flame. It is the hour—and I am glad. Look."

He pointed to a high window out of which a dozen bow-
men peered. Through it could be seen a little square of sky.
The ceiling of cloud was no longer steely gray. It was becoming lurid, tinged with a sinister red which slowly deep-
ened as he looked.

"Come!" said Huon. Silently, they passed on into the vast
vestibule into which the portals of the Temple opened. It
was crowded with Emers armed with bows and the crushing clubs, swords and javelins. Captaining them were some
twenty of the Old Race, armed only with swords and maces.
They had been waiting for Huon, for as he approached the
massive metal valves of the doors swung back. The soldiers
marching behind them, they passed out upon the broad platform which met the colossal flight of stone steps.

The parapets of the three terraces were lined with soldiers,
like the walls of some beleagured city. A double barricade
of stone blocks had been raised across the stairway. These
barricades were about six feet high, the first beginning at
the lowest terrace, the second some fifty feet behind it. At
the base of each were blocks upon which the defenders could
stand. He thought what an excellent trap that fifty-foot enclosure could be made into, wished heartily for just half a
dozen machine guns to station on the top of the hither barricade. What a shambles they could make of it!

He checked himself—no use of thinking in terms of modern warfare in this game, where the opposing generals held
powers of which neither their officers nor rank and file knew
anything. He reached the further wall, unslung his rifle, drew
the little bag of cartridges in front of him, and felt through
its contents. Not more than a couple of hundred, he reflected
ruefully. Well, with careful shooting, that many could do a

lot of damage. He charged his magazine, while Huon disposed of his force.

Graydon peered down toward the lake edge. It was a damned nasty color—that reddish light from the cloud canopy made it mighty hard to see anything at any distance. Nimir was doing it, of course. Where was Nimir? Would he fight with his followers, or was he, like the Serpentwoman, in some secret place directing his mysterious forces?

Nimir had seemed very certain of winning. He might have lied to him about some things—but he hadn't been lying about that. He meant it. Wouldn't it be better after all to vault the barricade, get to the Lord of Evil, and—give himself to him? Force immediate trial of that infernal experiment? It would hold Nimir back, cause an armistice until the Dark Master was within him. After that, he could fight it out with Nimir. By God—why not? That would be worth the trying! If he won—he'd have saved Suarra—and the Mother—and Regor—fine old boy, Regor. Why have all this slaughter when he could stop it?

The thought was like a whisper in his mind.

A whisper!

Graydon pulled himself up, gasping. A whisper? Like the whisper of the Shadow!

The Serpent-woman had been right! It was Nimir—whispering to his mind, luring him, tempting him, lying to him. Playing him! Thank God she hadn't let him stay up there on the roof! His hands flew up to the collar, tore at it —he seemed to hear the laughter of the Lord of Evil!

Huon gripped his arm. Graydon turned to him, trembling, the cold sweat pouring down his face.

"Huon," he said, breathlessly, "if I start to run to the enemy, if I do one single thing that seems to you to be—not myself—knock me on the head with your sword. Or put the sword through me, if it seems necessary."

"Do not fear," Huon nodded, gravely. "I am watching, and you shall not be betrayed."

From the Temple came the blare of warning bugles. Far away, on the fringe of the meadow, there was movement, the glinting of black scales, and the dull gleaming of yellow leathery skins.

"They come!" said Huon, and shouted to his men. The shout was echoed along the terraces. There was a whistling of bowstrings being tested. Then silence as the defenders watched the approach.

The attackers came slowly at first. In the van were the great dinosaurs spread out some fifty feet apart. With chagrin, Graydon saw that these riders were clad in coats-of-mail, their faces visored. He had never tried a bullet against that armor; wondered how pierceable it might be; took comfort in the thought that, at worst, the impact would probably knock them from their saddles.

Behind the dinosaurs padded the horde of the lizard-men. And it was a real horde six deep and shoulder to shoulder over a thousand foot line. If the Urd had leaders, then they were of their own kind and not to be distinguished from the mass. On they padded in the wake of the black saurians, their red eyes glittering, their heads thrust forward, talons outstretched.

A hundred yards behind the Urd marched ordered companies of green-kilted Indians led by Lantlu's nobles.

Graydon thought he recognized the plan of attack. It was to be a sledge blow—no subtle strategy. The great dinosaurs, impervious to arrows and, except for a skilful and lucky thrust, to swords and javelins, were to crush like battering rams through the defense. Into the gaps would stream the Urd, hard to kill, fighting with poisonous fang and claw. . . . The Emer would mop up after them, penetrating the Temple with Lantlu's nobles. . . . But where was Lantlu and his scaled pack?

There was a tumult of trumpets in the oncoming ranks. The black dinosaurs stamped thunderously and broke into a run. Like a long yellow hissing comber the lizard-men rolled forward. They swept down upon the Temple.

A ray of milk light flashed up from the roof. Instantly all the air was filled with the buglings of the winged serpents!

And instantly the rush of the dinosaurs and the lizard-men was checked. From the saddles of a full third of the Xinli their riders were flung, as though torn off by lariats. Caught in the invisible coils of the winged serpents and dragged to earth.

Among the lizard-men began a maelstrom milling. Squalling and hissing they leaped and hopped, striking with their chisel-edged talons; bringing some of the Messengers down, tearing at them with fang and claw, as movements here and there plainly showed. But the Urd themselves were falling by the hundred, pierced through heart and brain by the rapier beaks.

From the backs of the dinosaurs half the riders were gone. And the monsters were faring badly. Graydon saw them whirling frantically upon their heavy hind legs, hissing in rage, hitting out with their absurdly small forelegs, striking viciously with their snake-like necks.

One pivoted, then another and another. They went crashing back through the lizard-men. The Indians had halted, and now as the saurians tore through the Urd they wavered, broke formation, fled out of their paths. Into those paths ran nobles who sprang up and snatched at dangling reins, struggled to bring the monsters into subjection. Many of them they did, but a score or more of the Yu-Atlanchans were trampled into the grass before it was done.

From the Temple came a summoning blare of the bugles. It was answered from the left by others. Over the meadow charged regiments of blue-kilted Emer led by mailed nobles from whose shoulders streamed blue cloaks, the livery of the Mother. They had lain hidden until now, and Graydon's blood sang victory as he watched them charge. Their front line dropped upon their knees. A cloud of arrows whistled into the broken ranks of Lantlu's soldiery. They arose, rushed on again, and struck against the green-clad Indians like a wave.

And now there were two battles upon the mead—winged serpents against Xinli and Urd, and behind them the locked lines of nobles and Emer.

From all the Temple rang out a wild shout of triumph.

Out of the distance, from the direction of the caverns, came a vast humming, a drone rising to a shrieking wail which tortured the ears; then, falling below the range of hearing, became an unheard sound that shook the brain and every nerve to the verge of madness. Closer drew that droning, traveling with projectile speed. It paused overhead and came to rest directly above the Temple. Up rose the maddening note, then down—and up and down—

And suddenly all the space between earth and the lurid sky was shot through with rays of dull red light. They seemed rigid, those rays—striated. They tore at the eyes as the drone tore at the brain.

But not then did Graydon know that. He felt nothing; the drone of madness was to him only a humming as of some gigantic top, nothing more; the red rays spared him.

Uncomprehending, he watched Huon's sword drop from his hands, saw him reel, hands clasped over eyes—

And saw appear in that inexplicable, rigid light—the winged serpents. The Messengers of the Mother—no longer protected by their cloak of invisibility!

They were black shapes, caught in the rays. And they, too, were blinded. Whirling and tumbling, striking against each other, they fell. Little and great, the winged serpents dropped, coils lashing, into the talons of the Urd, the lizard-men, immune like Graydon himself to that intolerable vibration of linked light and sound.

Within the Temple sound and light brought full madness, as though they were intensified. In tortured brains of one and all was but one thought—to get into the open; to run and run—away from drone and searing ray. The huge doors flung open. Out of them poured Emer and noble, men and women alike. They came dropping from the windows—

Shaken out of the Temple even as the Lord of Evil had promised!

Through the droning came a hideous sussuration, a hellish hissing. He knew it for what it was before his eyes told him. The hunting packs of the dinosaurs. Emerald and sapphire scales glittering in the crimson light, crimson eyes flaming, they burst from the shelter of the trees that stretched between the Temple meadow and the city. Ahead of them rode Lantlu, alone, mounted upon his Xinli. Shouting, he raced to the stairway.

Graydon broke the bonds of his paralysis, raised his rifle; cursing, he sent bullet after bullet at the master of the pack. Untouched, unharmed, Lantlu drove on, the Xinli leaping at his heel.

Out from the Serpent-woman's sanctuary upon the Temple roof shot one of the immense silver globes; swiftly in its wake soared the others. They halted, hovering in a thousand-foot circle high above the plain. They began to pulse with a brilliant white radiance; and as they pulsed they expanded, became a coronet of little incandescent suns which sprayed their rays of white incandescence through the striating rays of sullen red.

Abruptly the drone ceased. The turmoil of the winged serpents ended. They faded back into invisibility. And the torment of brains and nerves and eyes was lifted.

Now it was Graydon's turn to feel agony. The white radiance seared his eyes, sent needles of torment through them into his brain. And in this torture again was he one with Urd and saurian and those of the Old Race who wore the collar of Nimir. From drone and red ray that collar had protected him——but to this weapon of the Serpent-woman it had betrayed him.

Before the agony mastered him, sent him writhing, face to ground, hands clasped tight over eyes, he saw Lantlu's monstrous mount rear, twitch its head from reins, tear its jaws from cruel bit and stagger blindly back, screeching. Saw Lantlu pitch from its saddle, regain his feet with his panther quickness and stagger, face covered by his arms. Saw the lizard-men running this way and that, and falling under the thrusts of the winged serpents.

Down upon Xinli and Urd the soldiery of the Temple surged, striking the lizard-men to earth with their maces, hamstringing the monsters with their swords, thrusting up with their javelins at the vulnerable spot in their throats, slaughtering Lantlu's crazed pack.

Intent upon his enemy, Huon had forgotten Graydon. He had leaped upon the barricade, was half over it, when he turned to look for him. Only for a breath did he hesitate between concern for him and hatred for Lantlu. He sprang back, lifted him in his arms, started to carry him up into the Temple——

A wind whose breath bore the cold of outer space sighed round them. And at its touch Graydon's agony ended. He writhed from Huon's grip. They stood, staring at the radiant globes. Their brilliancy had dimmed. A film of darkness was gathering round them. Steadily that film grew denser.

The globes went out!

Together the two leaped the barricade. Close to the base of the stairway, sword dripping blood, the body of a blue-cloaked noble at his feet, was Lantlu, glaring up at them, freed like Graydon from the torture.

And over all the meadow noble and Emer and Urd were locked together in death struggle. Of the hunting pack not one was left. And the giant Xinli had vanished.

Graydon raised his rifle, took deliberate aim. Before he could press the trigger, Huon struck the gun from his hands.

"Mine to kill! Not yours!" he cried, and ran down the steps sword in hand to where the master of the dinosaurs waited him, lips drawn back over his teeth, his own red sword ready.

The crimson sky pulsed—once, twice, thrice—as though it were a giant heart. Down from it like enormous bats dropped black shadows. And bitter and ever more bitter grew the cold.

For a moment Graydon watched that dread rain. The shadows appeared to form directly beneath the canopy of crimson mist. They were shapeless, formless, yet densely black as though torn from the cloak of deepest night. They swirled down, spinning as they dropped. They fell with the swift dart of the swallow. They were falling over all the plain, on lizard-men and Emer and noble alike.

He heard the clash of sword on sword, saw Huon and Lantlu thrusting, beating at each other with their blades.

Between him and the pair swirled a knot of fighting Urd and Indians. A shadow dropped upon them, enveloped them, hid them, swirled upward again. He looked upon the little group it had covered. They were no longer fighting. They stood there, motionless, immobile. They swayed. They fell. He ran down the steps, stopped beside them. The grass was black as though burned. He touched them. They were stiff and icy cold. He touched the ground. It, too, was frozen.

He looked toward Huon. His sword was sweeping down upon Lantlu's right wrist. It struck and half severed it. The master of the dinosaurs howled, sprang back, catching his weapon in his left hand before it could fall. Heedless of his wound, he rushed upon Huon.

And Huon avoided the rush, stepped aside, and as Lantlu twisted toward him thrust him through the belly and with swift upward lift ripped him to the breast.

The master of the dinosaurs dropped his sword, glared at his killer, his hands at his navel, the blood spurting through his fingers. He sank to his knees. Fell forward—

A shadow came silently spinning down. It enveloped both quick and dead.

Graydon heard the shrieking of a voice he did not know; realized it was his own! raced forward.

The shadow lifted, recoiled from him as though he had thrust it away, swirled skyward. Huon stood rigid, glaring down upon his enemy.

"Huon!" cried Graydon, and touched him upon the shoulder. It was icy cold.

And at the touch, Huon toppled, fell prone over the body of Lantlu.

He stood up, staring around him stupidly.

What were those lights? Winged shapes of greenish flame with cores of incandescence . . . flitting out of the air, pulsing from it . . . grappling with the shadows. Shapes of flame that battled with slaying shadows . . . and Huon dead there at his feet beneath a crimson sky.

As Huon had foretold—when was it? Ages upon ages ago.

His brain was numb. And despair . . . black despair that slowed his heart and set him gasping for breath was overwhelming him. Whence came that black tide . . . he'd never felt anything like that before? Hatred, too . . . cold hatred, cold and implacable as those slaying shadows . . . it was woven with the despair. Who was it he hated so . . . and, why? . . . if he could shake that creeping numbness from his brain.

Those damned shapes of flame! They were everywhere. And look at them running. . . . Emer and Urd and spawn of the Old Race. My men . . . running . . . conquered! My men . . . what did he mean . . . my men? What a hell of a light . . . what a hell of a night! Good rhyme that . . . it seemed to stop the spread of that cursed numbness. Try another—

ashes to ashes and dust to dust, if the shadows don't get you the winged flames must. No . . . that didn't help any. What the hell was the matter with his head? Poor Huon . . . wonder if Suarra knew he was down here . . . wonder where Nimir was . . . ah, now he knew whom he hated so . . . the Snake-woman . . . damned monster . . . *Yes, Dark Master, I am coming!*

Hell—what had made him say that? Brace up Nick Graydon . . . Nick Graydon of Philadelphia, Harvard School of Mines, U.S.A. . . . brace up! . . . *Yes, yes, Dark Master . . . I . . . am coming!*

An arm encircled him. He drew back, snarling. Why—it was Regor.

Regor! Something of the creeping deadness lifted from his brain.

"Head—Regor! Something wrong!"

"Yes, lad. It's all right. Come now—with Regor. To the —to Suarra."

Suarra? Yes, sure he'd go with Regor to Suarra. Not to that Snake woman though! No, no! Not to her . . . she wasn't human . . . *No, not to her, Dark Master.* . . .

Why, here he was back in the Temple! How the devil had he gotten there? Something was pulling at that collar. Pulling him by it. He wouldn't go! That's where that numbness came from—up from the collar. Ah—but he would have to go! But not before he had told Suarra about it all. Ah, there she was! Not the Snake woman though . . . *No, Dark Master, I'll not* . . . it was good to have Suarra's arms around you . . . your head on her breast. . . .

"Hold him tight, Suarra," said the Mother, quietly. "Kiss him. Talk to him. Do anything—but keep him aware of you. Kon!"

The Spider-man drew from the shadows, looked down upon the muttering Graydon sorrowfully.

"Watch him closely, Regor. Kon may have to help you hold him. When the full call comes to him, his strength will be out of all bounds. If you must—bind him. But I would rather not—for my own reasons. Yet Nimir shall not have him. Ah—I feared it! Stand ready, Tyddo!"

A green glare, bright as daylight, flooded all the Hidden

Land. The slaying shadows had vanished, the crimson light had gone from the clouds. Up from the plain midway between Temple and lake arose an immense pillar of coruscant green flame. As it arose it roared. It pulsated with a slow, regular rhythm. Around its girth and above it and at its feet, lightnings flashed, and thunder crackled like torrents of shattering glass.

Beneath that terrifying glare the battling figures upon mead and plain stood motionless, then in shrieking panic raced for cover.

From every quarter the winged shapes of flame throbbed into being. They swept toward the pillar, merged with it, fed it.

"His last play, Tyddo," whispered the Serpent-woman. "Yet it may be his best."

The Lord of Folly nodded, and took his station at the mechanism of crystal rods. The two great disks of moonlight radiance and cobweb strands were whirling. The Serpent-woman glided first to one, then the other, manipulating levers at their bases. Slowly their speed decreased.

"Now my ancestors aid me!" murmured the Snake Mother.

More slowly spun the disks. Fewer and fewer became the shapes of flame that fed the column. And now no more appeared.

The pulsing column quivered, swayed, and with a bellowing of thunders leaped a hundred feet from the ground. It dropped upon the amphitheater of the Dream Makers. Bellowing, it leaped again—from where the amphitheater of the Dream Makers had been.

Higher it drove this time. It came down among the trees of the city. Again the thunderous bellow—

The disks were still. The pillar of flame came rushing toward the Temple.

"Now!" cried the Serpent-woman to the Lord of Folly. From the mechanism he was manipulating spread out a gigantic fan of violet radiance—straight toward the racing column. It met and held it. It mingled with it. The pillar bent, twisted, struggled like a living thing to escape.

There was a vast screaming, a crash like mountains falling.

Then darkness and an appalling silence.

"That was well done," breathed the Mother. "And thanks be to all my ancestors that done it is!"

Graydon raised his head from Suarra's breast. His face was white and drawn, the eyes turned upward so that the pupils were almost covered by the upper lids. He seemed to be listening.

The Serpent-woman drew to him, watched him closely. His lips moved.

"Yes, Dark Master—I hear!"

"It is close. Take him, Regor. No—let Kon hold him." She glided to her coffer, took from it the sistrum of the quicksilver globe, and another larger one threaded with many beads of the same gleaming substance; took from it also a blunt crystal tube in which glowed an imprisoned purple flame like that of the rod the Lord of Folly had used in the Cavern of the Lost Wisdom. She handed the second sistrum to him.

The Spider-man lifted Graydon in his arms. He lay there, inert, apparently still listening. The Mother undulated to him.

"Regor," she whispered rapidly, "stay you here with Suarra. No, child, no use to plead nor weep. You cannot come. Be still!" she said sternly, as the girl lifted beseeching hands, "I go to save your lover. And to end Nimir. Regor—I take Kon with me. Quickly now—"

She clicked to the Spider-man. Carrying Graydon, he stepped upon the movable platform which masked the shining shaft. She glided beside him, coiled herself, made room for the Lord of Folly. The platform dropped. They passed out into the corridor of the shaft.

Graydon's body bent into a bow.

"I hear! I come, Dark Master!" he cried, and tore at the Spider-man's arms.

"Yes," hissed the Serpent-woman. "But by my way—not Nimir's. Set him down, Kon. Let him go."

Graydon, eyes still strained sightlessly upward, was turning his head like a dog seeking scent. He began to run down the corridor, straight to the portals of the Temple.

Behind him, sistrum raised, in her other hand the tube of violet fire, swept the Serpent-woman, matching effortlessly his pace, and behind her, as effortlessly, the Lord of Folly with Kon. They came to the corridor that led to the chamber of the thrones. From the sistrum shot a tiny ray. It touched Graydon's head. He swerved, turned. Again the ray flashed, over his head, striking against a wall. Up rolled one of the curtains of stone, unmasking the passage. Again the ray touched Graydon. He ran into that passage.

"Good!" breathed the Mother.

Twice more the ray of the sistrum opened a passage. Graydon sped on. He never turned his head, never looked back, seemingly was unaware of the three who followed. And weird enough must have been that sight—the running man, and behind him the gleaming undulating rosy-pearl length of the Serpent-woman bearing high her exquisite face and body, the scarlet, many-armed shape of the Spider-man, the ancient wise face of the Lord of Folly with its sparkling youthful eyes.

On and on went Graydon, like a straw drawn to a whirlpool, a grain of iron to a lodestone.

"But, Adana, will not Nimir know we follow?" the Lord of Folly spoke with unhurried breath.

"No," the Mother answered as tranquilly. "When Nimir hid himself from my seeing thought, he hid me from his as well. He can no more look through that veil at me than I can at him. He draws this man to him—but he does not know how he comes. Only that he *is* coming."

"He goes more swiftly," said the Lord of Folly.

"He nears Nimir," said the Serpent-woman. "I do not guide this man, Tyddo, he guides me. All that I do is to open the shortest way for him to that which summons him—Ah, I thought so!"

Graydon had been running, blindly, straight toward a blank wall. At the touch of the sistrum ray, a stone had drawn up. Through the aperture streamed red rust of light.

They passed into the lair of the Shadow.

Faster sped Graydon, a racing shadow in the murk. Up

loomed the black cliff. Along it he ran. It ended. He turned the edge. There was the carven screen, the dais, the throne of jet.

Stretched out on the cavern's floor, prone upon their bellies, lay hundreds of the lizard-people, the females and young of the Urd, and those who, surviving the Ragnarok of the Temple, had scuttered back to the red cavern. Mingled with the reek of their bodies was the obscene fragrance of the Shadow's garden.

And crouching upon the jet throne was Nimir!

"Dark Master—I am here!" Graydon's voice was toneless; he halted as though awaiting command.

Nimir's pale eyes lifted from the groveling remnants of the horde. His monstrous body expanded, lifted itself from the throne; his long, misshapen arms thrust out hungrily, his face was filled with triumph.

"Come!" he whispered, and as though his muscles had been taut steel strings, Graydon bounded up the side of the dais.

"No!" the cry of the Serpent-woman was shrill. From the sistrum in her hand the thin ray shot, touched Graydon's head. He spun and dropped, almost at Nimir's feet.

The gaze of the Lord of Evil fell upon the Serpent-woman, abruptly became aware of her—as though some veil between them had been rent apart, revealing her. His eyes flashed from her to the Lord of Folly and the Spider-man, and then blazed out with the fires of hell itself.

His hands darted to his girdle, darted out with something that glittered like frozen green flame. Before he could raise the object, the Serpent-woman had leveled the crystal tube in her left hand. A ray of intense violet darted from it. It struck the hand of Nimir and that which was clenched within it. There was a tinkling explosion, and a cloud of sparkling purple atoms swirled round him, hiding both the Lord of Evil and his throne.

The Serpent-woman snatched the larger sistrum from the Lord of Folly. Out of its innumerable tiny globes shot moonlight radiance, and condensed into a three-inch sphere of dazzling brilliance. It darted into the swirling purple mist at the level of Nimir's head—and passed on. It struck the carven screen of rock, and sprayed over its surface. From side to side and from top to bottom, the screen cracked and split, came crumbling down.

Where screen had been yawned the black opening of a tunnel.

At the touch of the sphere the purple mist had dissolved. Head bent low, squatting close to the floor of the dais, was Nimir, untouched by the Mother's missile. Before she could hurl another, he had snatched up Graydon's body, thrown it over his back like a cloak, arms over his shoulders, and had leaped into the darkness of the tunnel.

The Serpent-woman hissed, furiously. High reared the coil that held her body. Her gleaming length flowed over the edge of the dais and through the black opening. And in her wake sped the Lord of Folly, and Kon.

They needed no light to guide them, that three to whose eyes, like those of Nimir's, darkness and light were as one. And suddenly against the end of the passage was silhouetted the monstrous shape of Nimir. It blackened into outline, and vanished—

The passage had opened into the Cavern of the Face. It ended close to the top of that Cyclopean stairway which was the pathway to the Face. Despairing, hunted, Nimir had doubled back to his dungeon.

The Serpent-woman halted there. Half down the steps Nimir was plunging, holding tight to his shield of living flesh and blood. Through the storms of luminous atoms streaming from the cavern's walls the great Face brooded upon her. From the circlet around its brow the golden sweat still dropped; still from its eyes ran the tears of gold, and from the drooping corners of the mouth the golden slaver dribbled.

The Face's eyes of wan blue gems were lifeless. They glittered—but they were empty. No prisoned thing peered through them. Gone was all imperious summonings, all subtle promises of domination. The Face stared indifferently, unseeingly, over the head of Nimir—Nimir who for so long —so long—had dwelt within it.

From the throat of the Serpent-woman came a bugle note. It was answered from beyond, where the cavern's floor edged the immeasurable depths. Out of the space that overhung the abyss arrowed a pair of the winged serpents.

One dropped upon the shoulders of the Lord of Evil, buffeting him with its pinions. The second twisted its coils around his legs.

The Lord of Evil staggered, dropped Graydon, struck out at the beating wings.

The coils about his legs drew closer. The Lord of Evil toppled.

He went rolling down the steps. Graydon's body lay, motionless, where it had fallen.

The Serpent-woman clicked. The Spider-man scuttered down the steps, grasped Graydon, rushed back with him, and dropped him beside her.

Buffeting wings and clinging coil of the winged serpents withdrew from Nimir. He stumbled to his feet. He hopped to the Face.

He reached its chin. He turned, facing the Mother. Two faces of the Lord of Evil were there. The great face of stone, lifeless, indifferent—and its miniature of dream stuff and rusted atoms interwoven, instinct with life.

Against the cliffed chin pressed the Lord of Evil, arms outstretched, facing the Serpent-woman. In living eyes that matched the glittering ones far above them was neither fear nor appeal for mercy.

Only hate—and merciless threat. He spoke no word, nor did she.

The Lord of Evil turned. Like a great frog, he swarmed up the stone.

The Serpent-woman raised her sistrum. Out shot a radiant sphere. After it another—and another. The first struck the Face squarely upon the brow, the other two, almost simultaneously, upon eyes and mouth.

They burst and sprayed. Tongues of white lightning licked out. The Face seemed to grimace; contorted. Its stony mouth writhed.

Out sped a fourth sphere. It struck the climbing body of the Lord of Evil, and climbing figure and Face were hidden by the tongues of the white lightning.

They vanished—those tongues.

There was no Face in the abyss! Only a smooth smoking surface of black stone.

There was no Lord of Evil! Only a smear of rusted atoms against the blasted rock. The smear quivered. It seemed to be feebly trying to cling.

Another of the brilliant spheres struck it. The white tongues licked it—

The rock was clean!

And now shining sphere upon sphere shot from the sistrum. They struck the walls of the cavern, and the tempests of shining atoms died. The gemmed flowers and fruits upon those walls dulled, and dropped.

Darker grew the cavern where the Face in the abyss had been—darker and darker.

Densest darkness filled it.

The Serpent-woman's voice lifted into one long, wild, shrilling, clarion note of triumph.

She beckoned the Spider-man and pointed to Graydon. She turned her back on the black tomb of the Lord of Evil. She glided into the portal of the passage.

Behind her followed the Lord of Folly, and Kon . . . holding Graydon's body to his scarlet breast like a child—nuzzling him with his lips—crooning to his unhearing ears.

CHAPTER XXVII

Farewell of the Snake Mother

IT WAS FIVE DAYS before Graydon opened his eyes to consciousness. During all that time he had lain in the bower of the Snake Mother, Suarra attending him. Nor would the Mother take the collar of Nimir from his neck.

"I am not yet sure," she told the girl and Regor when they begged her to open it, rid Graydon of it. "It will not hurt him. Or should it threaten him, then will I take it off quickly enough—I promise you. But it was a link, and a strong link, between him and Nimir, and may still be so. I am not yet sure that which we knew as Nimir has been wholly absorbed in what sent him forth. I do not yet know what was that Shadow. But if something of it still survives, it will be drawn by that symbol, try to enter him through it. Then I will see what measure of strength that something possesses. If nothing of Nimir survives, the collar can do no harm. But until I know—he wears it."

That ended the matter. The first day Graydon was restless, muttering of the Dark Master, listening as though to spoken words, speaking now and then to one unseen. Whether to some beseeching wisp of Nimir or to some phantom of his sick mind only the Serpent-woman knew. His unease increased until the second night, and so did his mutterings. The Mother came now and then and coiled herself beside him, lifting his lids, examining closely his eyes. On that night when his restlessness reached its peak, she had Regor lay his naked body on her own nest of cushions. She took the smaller sistrum and held it over his head. A soft radiance began to stream from it. She moved the sistrum around him, bathing him from head to feet in its light. On the third day he was much quieter. That night she examined him intently, nodded as though satisfied, and sent a strong ray from the sistrum upon the collar. Graydon groaned feebly, began to raise trembling hands as though to protect it.

"Hold his hands, Regor," said the Mother, impassively. A stronger ray sprang from the sistrum. The collar of the Lord of Evil lost its sullen gleaming; changed to a lifeless brown. She took it between her hands and broke it. It crumbled to a pinch of dust in her fingers. Immediately Graydon relaxed and passed into deep normal sleep.

On the morning of the fifth day he awakened. Suarra and Regor were beside him. He tried to rise, but his weakness was too great. He was drained of all strength. His mind, however, was crystal clear.

"I know everything you're going to say against it," he told them, grinning faintly and holding tight to Suarra. "But it's no good. I feel as though I've been shot through a dozen windmills. In fact, I feel like hell. Nevertheless, I'm not going to close my eyes again until I'm brought up to date. First —what happened to Nimir?"

They told him of the pursuit of the Lord of Evil, and of his end in the cavern of the Face, as they themselves had been told it by the Mother.

"And then," said Regor, "she blasted the tunnel through which Nimir had gone so that it is sealed forever. She blasted Nimir's throne and the dais. The strange garden she destroyed utterly. It screamed and shrilled its agony as the tongues of the white lightnings licked it up."

"Evil was that garden," said Suarra. "Evil beyond all imaginings, the Mother told me. And that for its creation Nimir alone deserved annihilation. But what sorcery he wrought there, to what uses he had put it or what uses he intended it—she will not tell me."

"The Urd had fled from the red cavern," Regor took up the tale. "Ran, what was left of them, to hide in their deepest dens. And so the three came back to the Temple, bearing you. The next day the Mother took stock of what remained in ancient Yu-Atlanchi. Of the Old Race who defended the

Temple, there was a scant hundred left. Of those who had fought for Lantlu, some four-score sent an ambassador to the Mother asking truce and pardon. She ordered them before her, slew a dozen of them, and forgave the others. There are, I suppose, as many more who, knowing they can expect no mercy, have taken to the caves and forest—become outlaws, as we were before you came, Graydon.

"She had the Dream Makers, over whom the battle had passed unheeded, awakened and brought to the chamber of the thrones. Or the most of them—for there were some she commanded slain out of hand. She gave them the choice of abandoning their dreams and opening upon themselves the Doors of Life and Death, or—well, just death. Some fifty preferred to live. The others could find no attraction in it. They were allowed to go back to their homes, enter their favorite world of phantoms—and shortly thereafter they and their worlds ceased altogether to be.

"Of the winged serpents, the Messengers of the Mother, not more than a quarter survived. Of the Emer there are about a thousand left—I mean men. Mostly, they are those who took no part in the battle. Our soldiers and those of Lantlu were rather thoroughly wiped out. Nimir's shadows and the Mother's flames made no distinction between friend and enemy. Two days ago, at the command of Adana, the bulk of these Emers were sent to the caverns to exterminate the remnants of the Urd. Oh, yes—about a half dozen of the hunting Xinli escaped, and an equal number of the riding Xinli. The first are being tracked down and killed; the others we will keep.

"That seems to be about all. We start life in Yu-Atlanchi afresh with some three hundred of the Old Race, of whom considerably more than half are women. Each and all have, perforce, put off our deathlessness. The Mother herself saw that the Two Doors were flung wide open. Having more than half of us women is better, however," said Regor, thoughtfully, "than having more than half of us men."

Graydon closed his eyes; lay thinking over what he had heard. The Serpent-woman was certainly efficient once she started! Ruthless! He visioned the Dream Makers blotted

out in the midst of their mirages which were so real—so
real. He hoped that the one who had created on the web
of dream the miraculous world of color had chosen life.
Drone and light of madness—how had Nimir created them?
Some manipulation of the infrared rays, he supposed. Light
waves of the lower spectrum linked in some way, transmuted
somewhere in their range, to sound vibration. That the two
had been so linked, were parts of the same phenomenon, he
felt sure. And the Mother's little diadem of suns? Manipulation of other radiant waves which had cancelled Nimir's.
Why had the collar saved him from one—delivered him over
to the other? Some sort of receiver, probably . . . tuned up
to Nimir's stuff . . . well, it was off him. . . .

He sank into deep sleep.

He saw nothing of the Serpent-woman for several days.
She had gone off to the caverns, Suarra said, with the Lord
of Folly and Kon, borne by the Indian women in her litter,
only her Messengers guarding her. His strength returned
slowly. He was carried out in Suarra's own litter one day,
the girl beside him. The once flowering plain between the
Temple and the lake was blackened and desolate, blasted by
the icy shadows and the leaping pillar of flame. A thin covering of impalpable dust marked where the amphitheater of
the Dream Makers had stood. Many trees along the mead
were dead or dying. And where the pillar had leaped upon
the city there was a roughly circular place two thousand feet
in width from which habitations and vegetation had been
turned into the same thin ash.

He asked Suarra what had been done with the dead. The
Emer had gathered them together in great heaps, she told
him; then they, too, had been blasted into dust by contriv-
ances the Mother had ordered set up. Huon lay with his ancestors in the Cavern of the Dead.

He told her to turn the bearers of the litter back to the
Temple; recovered in the silence of the chamber of the
thrones his peace.

The next day the Mother returned; and thereafter for a
week Graydon was with her many hours each day; answering
her countless questions, telling her in detail of the life of

men beyond the barrier, their habits and aspirations, and this time, too, of their wars and gods, and all the long history of the race since the fires of the Cro-Magnons were quenched in their caves twenty-five thousand years ago. Of the aims and conditions of the races, white and yellow, black and brown, he spoke; and of Russia's drab experiment in communism, and the great unrest in Asia among the Chinese and Indians.

Then for another time she ceased her questionings, told him in turn of that forgotten civilization of which her strange race was the head, and of how it had come into being; of other lost civilizations and races, buried beyond trace under the dust of time; gave him blinding glimpses of attainments in science as advanced over those he knew as Einstein's geometry over the Euclidean; conceptions of mind and matter and energy that dazed him.

"In nothing," she told him, "that you have seen was there touch of sorcery or magic. All that you have beheld, each manifestation, was nothing but conscious manipulation of purely natural forces, my Graydon. The slaying shadows?— a definite energy made obedient by purely mechanical means to Nimir's will. In words of your own to make it understandable—etheric vortices, power condensed from that universal ocean of energy about us from which all energy and mind and what you term matter comes. The shapes of flame I summoned to meet them? Another harnessed force which neutralized the shadows—and more. The pillar of flame? Nimir's last play and one I truly feared. For by his swift shutting off of that which brought the shadows into being, he disturbed abruptly the interaction of the two forces, overbalanced me; hoped that before I could gain control of it, the tremendous freed energy which shaped itself into that pillar would overwhelm me. And he came within a hair of being right!"

She sat silently for a time; then seemed to have come to some decision; roused herself.

"Go you with Suarra, child," she said. "Amuse yourselves. Get strong quickly. For two days I shall have no need for either of you."

And when those days had passed, summons from the Snake Mother came to him by way of Regor. He found her coiled upon her cushions in her bower, complacently gazing at herself in her mirror while Suarra coifed her hair. The bower seemed oddly empty; stripped. And Suarra's eyes were misty with unshed tears. With her was the Lord of Folly. She laid down her mirror, gave Graydon her hand to kiss.

"I am going to leave you, child," she began without preamble. "I am tired. I am going to sleep—oh, for a long, long time. Nay—do not look so startled and unhappy. I don't intend to die. I know of no other world to which to go. But I don't intend to grow old—" her eyes sparkled at Graydon's uncontrollable expression of surprise at this remarkable statement, considering her thousands of years. "I mean I do not intend to let myself look old. Therefore, I shall sleep and renew myself—and my looks. It was the custom of my people.

"Now thus have I decided. There are not many of you left in Yu-Atlanchi, it is true. But shortly there will be more. Trust your race for that—if for nothing else. Let you and Regor govern here—with Tyddo to aid you. Nimir is gone forever. Those of his who still lurk, outlaw—destroy as speedily as you can. Let nothing of him nor of Lantlu remain. If any of the Makers of Dream—relapse—kill them. Danger lurks in that—Suarra! Stop your crying! You're pulling my hair!"

She frowned for a moment into the mirror.

"I have told you," went on the Mother, briskly, "that I do not intend to die. And certainly I do not intend to be made uncomfortable while I sleep. I do not think so highly of those people you've told me so much about, Graydon. Oh, I have no doubt that they include any number of persons as estimable as yourself. But collectively, they irritate me, to put it mildly. I don't propose to have them digging around where I am sleeping, nor blowing up things with their explosives, nor building—what is your quaint word—skyscrapers over me. Nor ransacking the caverns for their treasure, nor poking around trying to find out things they're much better off not knowing—and wouldn't know what to do with if they did find them. I will have no invasion of the Hidden Land.

"Therefore, during the last two days I have seen to it that there cannot be. I have destroyed much of what Nimir recovered from the Cavern of the Lost Wisdom, including that which evoked the shadows. I have destroyed my two disks which summoned the shapes of flame. You will not need them—nor shall I, again.

"And, Graydon, I have sent my Messengers on guard beyond the barrier, and especially against those flying boats of yours which have done so much to make barriers negligible. They will bring them down without mercy. They will as mercilessly destroy those who may survive the fall. No eyes shall peer down on Yu-Atlanchi to bring back strong companies who would—destroy my slumber. I put it that way, child, not to hurt your feelings.

"That is definite. That is irrevocable. And thus shall it be," said the Serpent-woman, and Graydon had no doubt at all that quite as ruthlessly as she promised it, so would it be carried out. "And if by any newly discovered wisdom they overcome my Messengers, Tyddo will awaken me. And me, Graydon, they will not overcome. That, too, is certain."

She glanced again at her hair—

"Suarra—that is really fine. Ah-h—but I am tired!" she she yawned, her little pointed tongue flickering in the scarlet, heart-shaped mouth. "It has all been enjoyable—but rather fatiguing. And I think—" she looked again into the mirror—"yes, I am certain I have acquired a few wrinkles. Ah-h—it is time I slept!"

Her eyes dwelt lovingly upon the weeping girl, and they were misted, too. Whatever the urgency that prompted the Serpent-woman to go, Graydon had swift perception that in her heart she did not feel the lightness she affected.

"Children," she twined her arm around Suarra's neck. "Come with me. On my way I must seal that chamber on which open the Doors of Life and Death. You shall see it."

She nodded to Suarra. Under the girl's touch the wall opposite the doorway swung open. The scarlet body of Kon swayed through, behind him four of his kind, carrying the

Mother's litter. She gave one last look in her mirror, then drew her coils into the litter's cushions. Kon leading, Graydon and Regor on each side, Suarra lying beside her with head hidden in the Mother's breast, the Lord of Folly following, they passed into a great empty chamber, out through its farther wall, and down a wide ramp.

Down went the ramp, and down—far below the foundations of the Temple. They came to an alcove that curved shallowly into the wall of the passage. Here the Mother signaled her bearers. They halted close beside it. She stretched out a hand, within it the smaller sistrum. A faint ray touched the wall. An oval opening appeared, as though the ray had melted the stone away. She beckoned Graydon, drew Suarra over her body so the girl could look within.

They peered down into a place that was like the half of a gigantic pearl. Its circled floor was some twenty yards in diameter. It was filled with a limpid rosy light as though a sun were shining behind its curved walls. The floor was like black obsidian, and set within it were two pools, oval, some twenty feet in length and half that in width. Between them was a couch of the same black glassy substance and hollowed with the outlines of a human body—as though, indeed, some perfect body of woman or man had been pressed there while the material was still plastic and, hardening, had retained the stamp.

In one pool the water, if it was water, was like pale rose wine, shot through with sparklings and eddies of deeper rose. The liquid in the second pool was utterly colorless, translucent, still—awesome in its tranquility.

While they watched, this tranquility was disturbed. Something came floating up from its depths. And as it approached the surface, the liquid in the rosy pool too became disturbed, its sparklings and its eddies dancing jubilantly.

Out of each pool a bubble arose, slowly expanding until they had domed them from edge to edge.

Rosy bubble and crystal clear bubble broke. A rainbow mist filled the chamber, hiding pools and couch. It was shot through with tiny darting particles of irised light. It pulsed for no more than three heartbeats. It vanished.

The Serpent-woman raised the sistrum. She sent from it a ray straight into the still pool. The pool quivered as though it had been a living heart. Its translucency clouded. A cloud of little bubbles rushed up through it as if trying to escape the ray. They burst with a faint, mournful sighing. The pool again was still—but all awesome tranquillity had gone.

The sistrum's ray plunged into the rosy pool. There was a moment of frantic swirling in its depths. Again the bursting cloud of sighing bubbles. And it too lay still—and dead.

"It is done!" said the Serpent-woman, tonelessly. Her face was drawn, her lips pale, her eyes like stone.

She passed the sistrum over the aperture. The wall reappeared, seeming to form out of air as it came. She signaled the Spider-men. They resumed their journey, in silence.

They came at last to another shallow niche. Here, under the sistrum, the wall drew away into a low and rounded portal. They entered. It was circular like that of the two pools but not more than half its size. A faint blue radiance streamed from its walls, centering upon a huge nest of cushions. Around its walls were several coffers. Save for these, it was empty. Graydon was aware of a slightly pungent, curiously fresh, fragrance.

The Serpent-woman flowed out of her litter, coiled herself upon the cushions. She looked at them, tears now frankly in the purple eyes and rolling down her cheeks. She gave the sistrum to the Lord of Folly, strained Suarra to her bosom. She beckoned Graydon, and gently brought the girl's lips and his together.

And suddenly she held them a little away from her, bent and kissed each upon the mouth, twinkled on them mischievously, wholly tenderly, and laughed her bird-like trill.

"Waken me to see your first-born!" said the Snake Mother.

She thrust them from her, settled down on her cushions, and yawned. Her eyes closed, her head nodded once or twice; sleepily moved to find a better place.

But as Graydon turned to go, he thought that a change had begun to creep over her face—that its unearthly beauty was beginning to fade . . . like a veil dropping . . .

Resolutely, he turned his head, forbade himself to look

... let that doubt remain unresolved ... as she had willed him to see her, so he would remember her. ...

They passed out of the low doorway, Suarra clasped close to Graydon, weeping. The Lord of Folly raised the sistrum. The stone of the portal thickened into place.

The hidden chamber where the Snake Mother slept was sealed.

AVON ◆ MEANS THE BEST IN FANTASY AND SCIENCE FICTION

URSULA K. LE GUIN

The Lathe of Heaven	38299	1.50
The Dispossessed	38067	1.95

ISAAC ASIMOV

Foundation	38075	1.75
Foundation and Empire	30627	1.50
Second Foundation	38125	1.75
The Foundation Trilogy (Large Format)	26930	4.95

ROGER ZELAZNY

Doorways in the Sand	32086	1.50
Creatures of Light and Darkness	35956	1.50
Lord of Light	33985	1.75
The Doors of His Face, The Lamps of His Mouth	38182	1.50
The Guns of Avalon	31112	1.50
Nine Princes in Amber	36756	1.50
Sign of the Unicorn	30973	1.50
The Hand of Oberon	33324	1.50

Include 25¢ per copy for postage and handling,
allow 4-6 weeks for delivery.

Avon Books, Mail Order Dept.
250 W. 55th St., N.Y., N.Y. 10019

SUPERIOR
FANTASY AND SCIENCE FICTION
FROM AVON BOOKS